New York Times bestselling author **Christine Feehan** has over 30 novels published and has thrilled legions of fans with her seductive and sensual 'Dark' Carpathian tales. She has received numerous honours throughout her career including being a nominee for the Romance Writers of America RITA, and receiving a Career Achievement Award from *Romantic Times*, and has been published in multiple languages and in many formats, including audio book, e-book, and large print.

For more information about Christine Feehan visit her website: www.christinefeehan.com

Night Game

Christine Feehan

piatkus

PIATKUS

First published in the US in 2004 by The Berkley Publishing Group,
A division of Penguin Group (USA) Inc., New York
First published in Great Britain in 2008 by Piatkus Books
This paperback edition published in 2008 by Piatkus Books
Reprinted 2009, 2010

A CIP catalogue record for this book
is available from the British Library.

ISBN 978-0-7499-3890-1

Typeset in Times by Action Publishing Technology Ltd, Gloucester
Printed and bound in Great Britain by
Clays Ltd, St Ives plc

Papers used by Piatkus are natural, renewable and
recyclable products sourced from well-managed forests and certified
in accordance with the rules of the Forest Stewardship Council.

Mixed Sources
Product group from well-managed
forests and other controlled sources
www.fsc.org   Cert no. SGS-COC-004081
© 1996 Forest Stewardship Council

Piatkus
An imprint of
Little, Brown Book Group
100 Victoria Embankment
London EC4Y 0DY

An Hachette UK Company
www.hachette.co.uk

www.piatkus.co.uk

For one of my dearest friends,
Cheryl Lynn Wilson,
because Gator has her name tattooed
on a certain portion of his anatomy
and it very clearly says property of

Acknowledgments

There are several people I have to thank. First and foremost, Jennifer Lasseter and Brian Feehan for their unfailing help with so many aspects of this book. Special thanks to Wilson and Rose Maeux for their help with the Cajun language. And especially Paula and Mike Hardin who so graciously time and time again found books and information and even made a couple of trips to the bayou for me. Thank you to Damon Weed of the Friendly City Tattoo Shop for bringing my GhostWalker crest to vivid life.

The GhostWalker Symbol Details

SIGNIFIES
shadow

SIGNIFIES
protection against
evil forces

SIGNIFIES
the Greek letter Psi, which
is used by parapsychology
researchers to signify ESP or
other psychic abilities

SIGNIFIES
qualities of a knight—
loyalty, generosity,
courage, and honor

SIGNIFIES
shadow knights protect
against evil forces using
psychic powers, courage,
and honor

nox noctis est nostri

The GhostWalker Creed

We are the GhostWalkers, we live in the shadows
The sea, the earth, and the air are our domain
No fallen comrade will be left behind
We are loyalty and honor bound
We are invisible to our enemies
and we destroy them where we find them
We believe in justice and we protect our country
and those unable to protect themselves
What goes unseen, unheard, and unknown
are GhostWalkers
There is honor in the shadows and it is us
We move in complete silence whether in jungle or desert
We walk among our enemy unseen and unheard
Striking without sound and scatter to the winds
before they have knowledge of our existence
We gather information and wait with endless patience
for that perfect moment to deliver swift justice
We are both merciful and merciless
We are relentless and implacable in our resolve
We are the GhostWalkers and the night is ours

Chapter One

Raoul 'Gator' Fontenot paused in the act of stuffing his shirt into his duffel bag when someone knocked on his door. The men in his Special Forces paranormal squad weren't all that polite and tended to just barge right in, no matter what time, day or night. In all the time he'd known them, no one had ever actually knocked on his door and definitely not with such a timid tap.

Holding a pair of faded jeans under his chin, he haphazardly attempted to fold them as he jerked open the door. Dr. Lily Whitney-Miller was the last person he expected to find. His squad, the GhostWalkers, as their psychic unit was often referred, owed Lily their lives. She'd rescued them from their laboratory cages and saved them from being murdered. Lily owned the eighty-room mansion where the men often stayed, but she never ventured into their wing. She preferred to address them together as a unit in the more formal conference rooms.

'Lily! What a surprise.' He glanced over his shoulder at the disarray in his bedroom. 'Did I miss a meeting?'

She shook her head. She looked calm and cool. Reserved. The usual Lily, but she held herself tight, too tight. Something was wrong. Worse, her gaze avoided his, and Lily always looked a man straight in the eye.

'Gator, I need to speak to you privately.'

Raoul was trained to hear the slightest nuance in a voice, and there was hesitation in Lily's. He'd never heard it before. He looked past her, expecting to see her husband, Captain Ryland Miller. His dark brow shot up when he saw she was alone. 'Where's Rye?'

Dr. Peter Whitney, Lily's father, had talked the men, all from various branches of Special Forces, into volunteering to be psychically enhanced. The doctor had removed their natural filters, which had left them extremely vulnerable to the assault of the emotions, sounds, and thoughts of the world around them. It was Lily who had helped them build shields to better function in the real world when they were without their anchors. In all those months, Gator had never seen her without Ryland. He knew Lily felt guilt over the things her father had done and was uneasy in their presence, but she was as much a victim as they were – and she hadn't volunteered.

He reluctantly stepped back to allow her entry into his room. 'Sorry about the mess, *ma soeur.*' He left the door wide open.

Lily faced him in the middle of the room, her hands tightly linked. 'I see you're nearly ready to go.'

'I told *Grand-mere* I would come as soon as possible.'

'So your friend is still missing? How awful.'

'Yes, Ian's agreed to come with me to help search. I don't know how much use we'll be, but we'll do whatever we can.'

'Do you honestly believe this girl isn't a runaway? That's what the police believe,' Lily reminded him. She'd been the one to use her contacts to get all the information for Gator. 'I personally looked into every

2

report they had on her. Joy Chiasson, twenty-two, nice-looking girl, sang in the local blues clubs. The police believe she wanted out of Louisiana and took off. Maybe with a new man.'

He shook his head. 'I know this family, Lily. So does *Grand-mere*. I don't believe for a moment she ran away. Two years ago another woman disappeared. Different parish, no known connection, and the police thought she'd left of her own volition as well.'

'But you don't?'

'No. I think there is a connection. Their voices. They both sang. One in clubs, one in church and theater, but I think the connection is their voices.'

Lily frowned. 'If you need anything, we can help from this end. Just call and anything we have is at your disposal.'

She was still avoiding his eyes, and her knuckles were white from twisting her fingers so tightly. Gator waited in silence, forcing her to speak first. Whatever she had to say, he had a feeling he wasn't going to like much.

Lily cleared her throat. 'While you're there in the bayou, would you mind keeping an eye out for one of the girls my father experimented on? I've been running computer probabilities, and the likelihood of Iris "Flame" Johnson being in that area right now is very high. This might be one of the few chances we have of locating her.'

'The bayou is a big place, Lily. I can't imagine just running into her. Why would you think she'd turn up in my backyard?'

'Well, it might not be that big, not if you're searching the clubs for clues to Joy's disappearance. Oddly enough, Flame sings too. She works the clubs in the cities she passes through.'

'And why would she be in New Orleans?'

3

'The burning down of the sanitarium in the bayou was well publicized, and I think it will draw her to your hometown. I think she's looking for the other girls my father experimented on, the same as we are.'

Gator took his time answering, studying her face as he did so. Mostly he replayed the sound of her voice in his head, the tiny vibrations only he could hear, the ones that told him she was nervous and giving him only pieces of information – or that she was lying. Lily had no reason to lie to him. 'What makes you think she would be looking for the other girls?'

There was a small silence. Lily let her breath out slowly. 'My father wrote a computer program and input what he knew of her personality and decision-making traits. The program calculated that there was an eighty-three percent chance that she would hunt for the girls. And when I fed the news article into the program it also gave an extremely high probability that she would suspect the fire had something to do with Dahlia and the Whitney Trust.'

'I read several of the accounts,' he admitted. 'They did report the murders, and they obviously knew it was a hit of some kind, an assassination squad, so yeah, she might come looking for more information.'

'I'm sure of it.'

'Which of the missing girls is Iris?' Raoul already knew the answer. Long before Dr. Whitney had experimented on the adult men, he had acquired girls from foreign orphanages and experimented on them, psychically enhancing them. When things had begun to go wrong, he had abandoned all of them except Lily, whom he'd kept and raised as his own daughter. Iris had been a small redhead with defiant eyes and an attitude the size of Texas. The nurses had nicknamed her "Flame," and from the moment she learned

4

Whitney forbade the name, Iris used it to make him angry. She'd been four years old.

Raoul had studied the tapes of the little girl far more than any of the others. She had a few abilities the others knew nothing about – but he did – he shared those same abilities. Even as a child she'd been smart enough – or angry enough – to hide her talents from Whitney. Her nickname was appropriate: Flame, a little matchstick that could flare up and be as destructive as hell under the right circumstances. Whitney didn't know how very lucky he was.

'Iris had deep red hair, almost the color of wine, and she has acute hearing. She's able to manipulate sound in extraordinary ways.'

'And she's an anchor.' That would mean she wasn't as vulnerable as some of the other girls. She could exist in the world without a shield.

Lily nodded. 'I believe she is. I know it would be like looking for a needle in a haystack trying to find her, but you never know. She'd be somewhere between twenty-two and twenty-five now. My father kept meticulous records, yet he didn't bother to record our birth dates, which makes no sense to me. I did an age simulation on the computer. Here's what she'd look like now.' She handed him the photograph.

His heart nearly stopped beating, then accelerated wildly. Flame was beautiful. Not just striking, but truly exquisitely beautiful, unlike any woman he'd ever seen. Even in the photograph her skin looked so soft he found himself running the pad of his thumb over her face. He kept his expression relaxed, charming, unworried – the usual mask he wore. 'You know, Lily, the chances of finding her are almost nil.'

She nodded her head and her gaze skittered away from his. It wasn't the real reason she'd come. Gator

5

waited. She shuffled her feet but didn't speak.

'Spit it out, Lily. I've never been much for games. Say what you came to say.'

She slid past him to catch the edge of the door, peering out into the hallway before shutting it carefully. 'This is confidential.'

'You know we're a unit. I don't keep things from Ryland or my men, not if it impacts them and what we do.'

'That's just it, Gator, I don't know if it does. I've discovered a couple of things, and I'm checking them out. You have to understand these experiments have spanned more than twenty years. There are dozens of computers and hard drives, storage disks and zip drives I haven't even gotten to yet, and that doesn't include handwritten notes. I started with the girls because we wanted to find them, but my father's observations are mostly on paper and old archived disks. He references nearly everything with numbers. I have to figure out what the number refers to before I can keep going in my research to see what he did. It's very time-consuming work, and it isn't easy.'

Lily didn't make excuses. This was so far out of character for her. Had she discovered the truth about him? He had watched the video of Iris "Flame" Johnson so many times maybe she'd become curious. Maybe she'd seen him stop the tape and study the picture – the one that showed the walls expand and contract slightly. The one where the floor shifted minutely when Flame's little gaze had narrowed on the doctor. She'd detested Dr. Whitney and her temper had barely been controlled.

'What have you discovered, Lily?'

'I think my father also did gene enhancing on the girls – as well as on some of you men.' The words left her in a

6

little rush. This time her gaze met his squarely as if trying to read his reaction.

He counted to ten in silence before he spoke. 'Why would you think that?'

'The referencing numbers have two letters beside them, and I couldn't figure it out. *G.E.* I went through a million possibilities until I found a small hidden cabinet in the laboratory. It was locked and coded. There were several notebooks on Iris. She was definitely genetically enhanced. *G.E.* Those letters were throughout the files, and I've seen them on several other files. Most of the files. I think the letters reference back to genetic enhancement.'

'The girls. You used the phrase *the girls* rather than *on us*. As in including yourself.'

Lily shook her head. 'There are no *G.E.* notations in my files anywhere. Believe me, I looked.'

'Why do you think that would be, Lily?' He kept his voice flat, even, ultra-calm.

'He used viruses to introduce the therapy to the cells.' Her voice faltered for the briefest of moments, but she carried on, her chin up. 'I don't think he wanted to take any chances with me, and he could use me as the control subject.'

'What was in the file that I should know about?'

'Flame had cancer. The symptoms presented nearly the same as leukemia. Bruising, fatigue, abnormal bleeding, bone and joint pain. All of it. He put it into remission, but . . .' She trailed off.

'But he didn't stop. He continued to enhance her cells.'

Lily looked miserable as she nodded. 'Yes. He continued to experiment on her. One of the problems when using a virus to infect the cells is the body produces antibodies to fight it off. By the second or third round,

7

it does no good to use that virus.'

'So he made up another one.'

'Several of them. He obviously wanted to perfect his technique for later use. I think all of us girls were his first tries—'

'You mean his expendable rats,' Gator interrupted harshly. He curled his fingers into tight fists. 'You were all expendable. No one wanted you. And he didn't like her, did he? She was a lot of trouble because she was so strong-willed, just as Dahlia was – Dahlia, who was raised in a sanitarium, not a home.'

'That's true, Gator, but thankfully, although Dahlia is enhanced, she has never had cancer. Nor could I find references to cancer in the files of any of the other girls he experimented on.'

Lily pressed her fingertips just above her eyes. 'I haven't gone through everything in Flame's file but the cancer returned several times and each time he adjusted the virus and continued doping her after he put the cancer in remission. She's very enhanced.'

'And you suspect I am as well.'

She bit her lip, but nodded again. 'Are you, Gator? Can you run faster, jump higher? None of you have ever mentioned it to me – not even Ryland.'

He avoided the question. 'Are you warning us that anyone who might be enhanced is susceptible to cancer?'

'I have no idea,' she said truthfully. 'I believe he was working on a way to prevent the doping from stimulating the wrong cells. I think he used Flame to perfect his technique so he could make certain you and the others had fewer problems.'

'Charmin' son of bitch, wasn't he?' Gator stuffed the jeans into the duffel bag with a short violent stabbing motion. 'He used her like a damn lab rat.'

'It's worse than that, Gator. I hope to God I'm

wrong. I can barely conceive of the idea that the man I knew as my father could have been such a monster, but I don't think he wanted to cure Flame. I think he knew she'd get sick, and he figured her adopted parents would bring her back to him.'

'But they didn't.'

'Not that I can see. But the chances of the cancer recurring seem likely. Regular treatment for leukemia would help, but it wouldn't cure her. The cancer is caused by one particular wild cell.'

'And he knew that.'

Lily nodded reluctantly. 'Without a doubt he knew it. The first time he experimented with putting the cancer into remission, he used a virus to insert DNA that caused the cancer cells to self-destruct by producing a protein that was deadly to itself. The second time he used a method of actually forcing the cancer cells to produce a protein that identified itself to her immune system, thereby causing her immune system to attack in a concentrated force, successfully destroying the cancer. It was brilliant really, far ahead of his time.' There was a trace of admiration in Lily's voice she couldn't hide from him.

Fury swept through him. Ugly. Dangerous. A snarling demon triggering an aggressive response. Gator turned his back and dragged air into his lungs. He noted the way the walls expanded and contracted, the movement nearly imperceptible. 'If he was so damned brilliant and successful at destroying cancer, Lily, why didn't he report his findings to the world? Why did he secret away his data in a hidden laboratory?'

'Any hospital, university, or private facilities involved in human experiments such as the Whitney Trust are required to have Institutional Review Boards to ensure

9

the research complies with Department of Health and Human Services regulations for the protection of human subjects. And any experiment involving gene insertion must be approved in advance by an Institutional Biosafety Committee.'

He turned to lock his gaze with hers. 'So bringing unwanted orphans into the country, virtually buying them and using them as human lab rats to experiment with genetic enhancement, psychic enhancement, and cancer doesn't fall into the accepted regulations? He would have been labeled the monster he was and he would have been jailed. He *tortured* that child. And now she's out there somewhere, isn't she, Lily? She's out there and you want her found because you and I both know she's very, very dangerous and she's got a hell of a mad on for the Whitney Trust, doesn't she?'

'I want her found because she needs help and she's one of us,' Lily corrected, her chin up. When he continued to look her steadily in the eyes her gaze shifted down to her hands.

'Spit it out, Lily.'

'He also found a way to stimulate the growth of tumors with genetic therapy and then he caused the cancer cells to cut off their own blood supply so the tumor withered and died. That kind of research is invaluable.'

'On *her*? Flame? He *gave* her cancer, deliberately? He was a son of bitch, wasn't he, Lily? A pathetic monster who had to find some kind of kick in torturing children. How old was she when he did this to her? How long did he have her? Why didn't you tell us all this?'

'You aren't helping me by talking this way, Gator. This happened a long time ago. I'm finding all this out about my father. *My father.* A man I loved and respected. I can't

10

help but see his brilliance. And yes, it was monstrous to perform such experiments on children, on any human, but he did and that doesn't change the fact that he was able to perform medical miracles. He was light-years ahead of anyone else in his field. I want her found, Gator, because she needs us. And she needs medical help. Her body is a ticking bomb and will turn on her sooner or later. She must come back here and let me help her.'

Suspicion flickered for a moment in his eyes but he quickly masked it. 'She makes a hell of an experiment, doesn't she? She must be a walking medical miracle.'

'That's not why, Gator. She needs to be where we can help her.'

'Has it occurred to you that she'll think you want her back here for more experiments? I hate to be the one to point this out to you, Lily, but you have that same love of science. You put it before morality, and you admire a monster who tortured children. If I can see that in you, so will she.'

'You can say whatever you like about me, Gator. I believe we need research and yes, I admire his brilliance, even while I condemn the things he did. I do *not* put it before morality, but do you have any idea how far ahead of his time he was?'

'So you've said, more than once. Who are you trying to convince, Lily?'

'DNA was first sequenced in 1977. It wasn't until 1997 the first genome was sequenced. Don't you see what that means? He had to have been years ahead of the game. With the things he did, we should be able to figure out better gene therapy and possibly which viruses to use as vectors without the possibility of triggering cancer in unstable cells.'

'Lily . . .' Gator raked a hand through his hair in agitation. 'You aren't going to get me to see him as some

11

kind of a world savior. He deliberately caused a child to get cancer, not once but repeatedly.'

'You aren't listening to me, Gator. Don't you see how the research he did, monstrous or not, could be beneficial? It all happened years ago. We can't change what he did, but we can acknowledge his brilliance and use what he found out. It's the only way to bring some good out of the horror he inflicted on us all.'

He breathed deeply to calm the temper pushing so close to the surface. Lily didn't know what he was capable of doing. No one did. Not even Whitney. And he suspected Flame was just as capable of the same mass destruction as he was. 'Damn him to hell, Lily, for what he did to her. For what he did to all of you. All of us. I'll do my best to find her, but I doubt she'll be very cooperative. I wouldn't be under the circumstances. I guess you'd better explain exactly what genetic enhancement and gene doping is to me. And do your best to explain in terms I can understand.'

He couldn't look at her. Didn't dare look at her. He didn't want to have to kill Flame Johnson. He didn't want to have to look at her face, knowing what a monster had done to her and put a gun to her head, but he might have no choice. Lily was giving him no choice, and right at that moment, he was nearly as angry with her as he was with her father. She had no right to ask this of him. They both knew it wasn't going to be simple bringing Flame back into the fold. Damn both Whitneys to hell for this.

'Basically, gene therapy uses genes to treat or prevent disease. A gene can be inserted into a damaged cell to repair it. At this time, researchers are testing different approaches to gene therapy. They can replace a damaged gene that causes disease with a healthy one. They can knock out a mutated gene that is malfunctioning and they can introduce a new gene into the body to fight a disease.'

Gator stuffed two more shirts into his duffel bag. 'In theory, gene therapy is a good thing.'

'In any experiment, Gator, there's going to be failures; it's how scientists learn.'

'Tell that to Flame.'

'I don't have to. Do you think I don't know what she went through? I'm the one reading her files firsthand. You're getting the watered-down version.' For the first time, Lily looked angry, her eyes dark with temper. 'I thought you'd be the best person to approach about this. You're always calm and you think things through. Throwing stones at me isn't going to help Flame.'

'Is that what you think I'm doing? I'm hearing this for the first time. I'm struggling to understand not only what he did to Flame, but how it impacts all of our lives. How did you react, Lily, the first time you realized what he'd done? Did you immediately think to yourself what a brilliant scientist he was, or did you wonder how it would affect you and Ryland and your kids, because it damn well made me think about it. Did you picture Flame as a child so sick and miserable she couldn't walk, with no one to comfort her? Because I did. I'm sorry I'm not handling this to your liking, but someone needed to kill the son of a bitch.'

Lily winced. 'Someone did, Gator.'

He rubbed his forehead and the sudden headache pounding at his temples. 'I'm sorry, Lily, that was completely uncalled for. Tell me a little more about enhancement and why gene therapy is such a great thing. I swear, I'll try to listen with an open mind.' He flashed a small grin at her. 'And try to speak English. I have to actually understand what you're telling me.'

Grateful that he was at least willing to try, Lily sent

him a small smile in return. 'I'll do my best. Gene therapy research has expanded to include the ability to not only correct faulty genes, but also enhance normal ones. This is where it gets a little complicated.'

'I'm following you,' Gator said.

'A carrier molecule or vector is used to introduce the desired gene – or genes – into a patient's target cells. A virus is used as the vector because viruses have evolved a way of encapsulating and delivering their genes to human cells in a pathogenic manner. Are you following me?'

'So far. I think being around you so much, I'm beginning to pick up all your scientific jargon.'

'Besides viral-mediated gene delivery systems, there are several nonviral options for gene delivery. The simplest method is the direct introduction of therapeutic DNA into target cells. But that approach is limited in its application because it can only be used with certain tissues and it requires large amounts of DNA.

'Another nonviral approach involves the creation of an artificial lipid sphere with an aqueous core. This liposome, which carries the therapeutic DNA, is capable of passing the DNA through the target cell's membrane.'

'Hell, Lily, you just went into the ozone with that explanation.'

'Sorry. It wouldn't enhance, let's say, your legs. You'd need to reach a tremendous number of cells to do that. But . . .' Lily frowned and something in the way her face stilled and her voice lowered made Gator pay closer attention. 'There are forty-six chromosomes in the human body. My father appears to have been working on a forty-seventh chromosome. One that would exist autonomously alongside the standard forty-six – not affecting their working or causing mutations. It appears to be a large vector capable of carrying

14

substantial numbers of genetic codes. If he succeeded, the body's immune system wouldn't attack it. The difficulty, of course, is how to deliver such a large molecule to the nucleus of a target cell. If he managed to do that, it would solve a lot of the problems with gene therapy, but create other, much more frightening hazards.' One hand fluttered protectively over her stomach. 'In the data we have so far, gene enhancement doesn't appear to affect the next generation, but if he inserted a new chromosome, all bets would be off.'

'You have to discuss this with Ryland.' Gator couldn't help but notice that her hands were shaking.

'I don't know anything for certain, I wouldn't have come forward yet, but you were leaving for New Orleans and this is probably our best opportunity to find Iris Johnson.' She tilted her head and stared up at his face, her gaze meeting his squarely. 'When I realized Flame might be in New Orleans, I really paid attention to the data we have on her. Most of it was on her health and genetic enhancements, not on her psychic abilities. She could do extraordinary things from the enhancement, but little was said about her potential as a weapon. She can manipulate sound, Gator. She can use her voice for a wide range of sounds including the lower frequencies that we now have learned make excellent weapons. Given the fact that I've found years of research on her and she could be both ill and dangerous, not to mention she's invaluable to medical research, she has to be found.'

Gator kept every expression from his face. He was beginning to feel like a lab rat all over again. He felt very sorry for Flame. She had to have had a miserable life, used solely as a caged experiment. Mostly he detested that Lily sounded so much like her adoptive father. Disconnected. Impersonal. More scientist than human. 'How do you know she can manipulate sound?'

'I pay attention to detail, the same as you do. Don't play dumb with me.' She pressed her fingertips harder just above both eyes, obviously trying to ease a bad headache. 'I'm angry. You're angry. I can accept that, but we're in this together. Why are you being so difficult?'

'Why aren't you talking to everyone about this?' Gator asked. 'We've always done things a certain way, Lily. We've always been a team. You're deliberately dividing that team. Why?'

'Because I just had a very fast lesson in how sound can be used as a weapon and, quite frankly, it scared the hell out of me. Dahlia is a very frightening person with the powers she wields, and if what I suspect about Flame is true, with her personality she's even more so. Flame could be a major threat to all of us.'

Gator studied Lily's expression. 'You know she's royally pissed, don't you? You know more than you're letting on to me. I don't like games. I never have. You can either tell me what you know and let me decide for myself whether or not I want in, or you can forget about receiving any help from me.'

'I don't *know* anything for certain, Gator, I only *suspect*. There's a huge difference between the two. If you asked me straight-up what I believe about Flame, I'd have to tell you I don't think there was any home or any adopted parents. Not ever. I think the story in the computer is a complete fabrication.' She sank down onto his bed as if her legs wouldn't support her anymore. 'I think she was held somewhere and the experiments continued long after her childhood, maybe even until she was in her late teens. I think she escaped.'

Gator took an aggressive step forward, looming over Lily. 'And you're still defending that bastard? What the hell is the matter with you?'

'I've never defended him. *Never.*' She lifted her face to his, tears swimming in her eyes. 'I don't trust what I'm reading anymore. I can't even tell you exactly what's making me suspicious, but I have this horrible feeling the stories about the girls are planted. Or at least about Flame.'

Gator forced his temper under control. Lily suddenly looked fragile enough to shatter. 'Why haven't you gone to Ryland with this?'

'We've been trying to have a baby.' Lily burst into tears and covered her face with her hands, her slender shoulders shaking as she wept. 'We've been trying for months. I was so excited, and now I'm terrified. I'm not enhanced, but he is. I know he is. And how much more can he take before he looks at me the way you just did a few minutes ago?'

'Lily . . .'

'I'm like him, like my father. I have the same mind, the same drive to get answers. The same need to push everything to the limit. Eventually, if all I suspect is the truth, if it all comes out, Ryland will leave me. He won't be able to look at me.'

'That isn't true.'

'Yes it is. I loathe my father. Every time I look in the mirror, I feel like I'm looking at him. When I'm reading about the things he did, instead of thinking what a monster he was, I can't help my first reaction, the awe that his mind was capable of visualizing so far in advance of our most gifted researchers. What does that say about me, Gator? How can I look Ryland in the eye knowing I have that kind of reaction? I just stood here arguing with you about what a brilliant man my father was after admitting he deliberately gave a child cancer. If he's a monster, what does that make me?'

'Are you pregnant, Lily?' Gator guessed shrewdly, watching the way Lily pressed her hands to her stomach.

A fresh flood of tears answered him. His stomach twisted in sympathy and sudden understanding. In fear for her and his friend. 'You need to talk to Ryland.' His voice was much gentler.

She shook her head adamantly. 'I don't have all the facts yet, Gator. There's just so much data to sift through. When I finally realized what I'd stumbled onto, I started working as many hours as possible to compile information to get a clearer picture.' She wiped at her eyes again. 'The picture just keeps getting worse and worse. I don't know if anything is true. I'm tired and discouraged and overwhelmed. How can I tell any of you what my father did when I don't know for certain myself?'

'You need to tell all of this to Ryland,' he repeated, sitting beside her and taking her hand. 'He'll understand.'

She sighed. 'I don't understand. How can I expect him to understand? If the stories and the letter from my father asking me to find the girls and help them is all a sham, what's going on? Why would he bother to write me such a letter? I'm spending a fortune trying to find the other girls he experimented on.' She leaned toward Gator, visibly trying to get a handle on her emotions and become the scientist she was much more comfortable with. 'Do you know that the computer is programmed to send a flag each time someone with the screen name of "babyblues" logs on to one particular blues site? Why would that be, Gator?'

'You have an idea.'

'I don't much like the idea I have. I think babyblues is really Flame. I think she loves blues music and someone was smart enough, after she escaped, to figure out her screen name. They attempt to find her location whenever she goes online and happens to get an update of what is happening in the blues community. And that scares the hell out of me. Who programmed the computer to do that? If it was my father, why did he write the letter to me stating the girls were all given away for adoption and he wanted me to find them? How come, with all my resources, I haven't been able to track them?'

'Where do you think they are? He can't have sanitariums scattered all over the United States housing these women, can he?'

'I'm beginning to think he could do anything. And I'm beginning to think some of this was government sanctioned. Not outright of course, but he had to have had help. He had money, Gator, more money than even I can conceive of. And he had top security clearance. How much they knew, I have no idea, but they had to have wanted the weapons he could provide. If Flame can do the things I think she can, she would be invaluable. Even as an experiment. It's possible they allowed her to escape with the idea she'd get sick and have to come back.'

'Like Dahlia and the sanitarium. She had to return because she couldn't make it on the outside. It was her only refuge.' Gator was beginning to feel very protective toward the absent Flame. 'So Flame goes out into the world and does whatever it is she does, and they know she has to come home sooner or later because her body is going to betray her.'

Lily nodded. 'That's my guess. And to be strictly honest, Gator, I'm a scientist and I don't do guesses. I prefer to deal in hard facts, something I can prove. At this point, I don't have enough information to prove anything. It's a gut feeling. Sometimes I know things.

And I know she's out there, she's in trouble, and she's going to come after us if she hasn't already, especially if she thinks she's going to die.'

'That bad?'

'Worse. The things she can do with her voice are incredible. And if she were down the street, she might, under the right circumstances, be able to hear our conversation. The key would be to filter out multiple sounds and not get inundated by all the sounds surrounding her.'

Gator didn't even flinch, not even when her shrewd gaze rested on his face.

'Well,' she continued, ignoring the fact that he hadn't responded, 'maybe not in this house. The walls are sound-proofed. And maybe that's why my father had it built this way. For his protection, not mine.' She wiped the tears from her face and stood up, pacing restlessly across his room. 'Have you kept up with the latest research on sound as a weapon?'

He had, but he wasn't going to admit it. GhostWalkers rarely volunteered information, especially when it concerned their own talents. He remained silent.

Lily cast him a small glance, clearly waiting for him to speak. When he didn't she sighed. 'Flame can use sound as sonar. She can literally "see" in the dark like a bat or a dolphin. As a weapon, infrasound can debilitate by causing nausea, bowel spasms, change of heart rhythm, interference with lung capacity, vertigo, etc.'

'In other words, she can kill a human being.' He said it without looking at her. He knew firsthand what low-frequency sound could do and it sickened him.

'Absolutely she could kill a human being. Also, infrasound is nondirectional in its propagation, there-fore it envelops without any discernible localized source. She could produce the "weapon" without her

20

direction being detected.' Lily squarely met his gaze again. 'Another thing that is interesting about what she can do, Gator, is aside from "talking" to animals, she could conceivably create a mass exodus of, say, bats from a cave or rats from an abandoned complex using a high frequency. She could even draw or repel insects such as mosquitoes.'

Lily was well aware she was talking about things he could do, and she was looking for a reaction. He remained absolutely without expression. She lifted her chin at him. 'Can you use ultrasound to detect problems in people, Gator? Can you "see" organs by using a high frequency?'

'I believe the idea was to be able to help should anyone in my unit be injured. We'd have a walking ultrasound machine.'

'Which is no answer at all. If you find her, Flame could be very ill. She might not let a doctor get near her, but she might let you. Would you be able to detect cancer?'

'I've never tried.'

'If she tried to kill you, Gator, would you be able to defend yourself against her, or would you allow sentiment to get in your way?' She asked it bluntly.

'Don't you think it's a little late to be asking me that?'

She had the grace to blush. 'I'm sorry. I didn't know where else to turn. You're heading back to the bayou and I think there's a very good chance she'll be in the same vicinity. Look in the blues clubs. She won't be able to resist them. She has to have a dynamite singing voice – like you. And you'll be there looking for information on Joy anyway.'

'You've never heard me sing.'

'I don't have to hear it. I know you have the ability.

21

I have no idea what Flame's going to be like, and I'm sorry I'm dumping this in your lap, but I have all I can do trying to sort out the mess we're all in. Something's wrong, but I can't figure it out.'

'Talk to Ryland, Lily. That's your first mistake, not trusting him to help you.'

She hung her head. 'I hate the way you all look at me.'

'The guilt is in your own mind, Lily. I don't blame you for what Whitney did. We volunteered. You didn't.'

'Please know I wouldn't have asked you to do this, but I honestly believe it's imperative to find Flame. She may be very sick.'

'I'll look for her, Lily.'

'Thank you and please, Gator, be careful.'

Chapter Two

Four weeks later

Gator shoved the gas hose into the tank of the Jeep and stretched his tired muscles while he waited for the tank to fill. Another long night and, if one considered listening to great blues music all night a failure, he'd had another unsuccessful search. He'd asked more questions and received absolutely no answers in his hunting for Joy Chiasson. No one seemed to know anything. Everyone remembered her beautiful voice, but no one knew anything about her disappearance. Joy had completely disappeared and not a single person seemed to know anything about it.

As for sighting Iris Johnson, he hadn't even come close to seeing anyone who looked like her. He must have hit every club within five square miles while hunting for information on Joy's disappearance and he'd still come up empty on both women. He'd taken personal leave and so had Ian. They'd been in the bayou nearly four weeks and they couldn't stay there forever. If he didn't find something on Joy soon, he would have to leave, and his grandmother's heart would be broken. She was so certain he would solve the mystery of Joy's disappearance and bring her home safely. He was beginning to believe that wasn't going to happen.

His restless gaze shifted in a continual sweep of the area. Recon. Always recon. He would never be free of the need to be on his guard. He'd picked the gas pump in the deepest shadow with the easiest exit back onto the street, and he'd done it without conscious thought. With a small sigh, he glanced up at the stars. He loved the night. It was the only time he felt truly comfortable, and tonight he needed a little comfort.

He hadn't thought all that much about a woman of his own, or a family. He wasn't the kind of man to settle down, but Lily's disclosure of genetic enhancement had hit him unexpectedly hard. For some reason he couldn't get it out of his mind. In the beginning when he realized he could leap up onto a roof with little or no effort, he thought it was cool, an extraordinary side benefit of his psychic experiment. The word *virus* had never come into his mind, and neither had cancer. He'd never really questioned the physical things he could do and, other than the uses as weapons, he hadn't discussed the enhanced physical abilities with the GhostWalkers. Maybe none of them really wanted to know, but now it seemed all-important.

He hadn't signed on for genetic enhancement. Psychic yes. As a child growing up, he had noticed he had some small psychic talent. Animals responded to him. Sometimes he caught impressions of what they were feeling. He had an extraordinary memory and his mind would figure out patterns the moment he saw them. He had exceptional hearing as well. Little things, nothing big, but he knew he could do things others couldn't. Not wanting to be different, he'd kept it hidden, much like the rest of the GhostWalkers had done.

He'd trained in the military, was gifted with explosives, building bombs fast and efficiently as well as dismantling with equal speed and care. He'd been recruited by special operations, and the moment he'd heard of Dr. Whitney's psychic experiment and the special psych unit he'd jumped at that as well.

The idea of a unique group of soldiers, able to use psychic skills, to slip in and out of enemy territory using hit-and-run tactics, really appealed to him. He'd seen too many people – good friends – die and he thought it would be a way to stop so many unnecessary deaths.

What did genetic enhancement mean for the GhostWalkers' already uncertain futures? Would they be able to have families and, if so, would they pass the traits on to their children? What in the world had he been thinking to do such a stupid thing? He groaned aloud. It should have occurred to him that Whitney would use them as human lab rats. Gator hadn't known of Whitney's earlier experiments with the little girls when he'd signed on, but still, that was no excuse. He should have been smarter. He might have thrown away his entire future.

Gator leaned against the Jeep and pushed a hand through his thick black hair. Growing up in the bayou had been an experience that taught him different wasn't always good. His parents had died during a flood, a freak accident, and his grandmother had taken on the task of raising the four boys. Wild, fiercely loyal, and proud, Raoul was the oldest and took care of the others. That responsibility had transferred over into his military life. And now, here he was, looking for a woman who was probably dead and another who didn't want to be found.

He caught a flicker of movement out of the corner of his eye and immediately went on alert. A woman slipped out of the shadows. She must have been in the store. More than anything else, it was the way she moved that caught his attention. She flowed in silence, her black, tight-fitting pants molding to her hips and legs. She wore gloves and a leather jacket. Her hair was thick and dead straight, ending just about her shoulders. She glided to her motorcycle, a crotch rocket, a lightning bolt if his guess was correct, built for nothing but speed and handling.

Like the woman. The thought came unbidden, but lodged somewhere in the vicinity of his groin.

As she leaned over the bike a car swept into the gas station, headlights catching her momentarily in the glare. She kept her head down, fiddling with something he couldn't see on the other side of the motorcycle, her jacket and shirt riding up, exposing her narrow waist, lower, the sweep of her hip – the tattoo there.

Raoul's breath caught in his throat. It was an arc of flames, which rode just above the bone of her hip and emerged from either side of her low-riding pants. His heart accelerated. Could it be that simple? Could he have spent nights visiting club after club on the off chance that she might be singing in one, only to spot her at a gas station? How bizarre would that be? He almost didn't believe it, but something in the way she moved, a stealth, an ease, a predatory silence gave him the impression of a GhostWalker. And the way she had emerged from the shadows . . .

Raoul raked his fingers through his hair in agitation. He was letting his imagination get away from him. Women had all sorts of tattoos. Just because she had a crescent of flames over her hip didn't mean a thing. He was really losing it, but he couldn't take his eyes from her. Her pants had compartments built into them everywhere, perfect for tools. So, okay, that was a style some people wore, but they fit so perfectly, as if the tight-fitting cargo pants had been specially made, just for her.

She straightened slowly and pulled on goggles and a helmet. She turned, a small, casual movement that was barely discernable in the shadow she was in, but he felt the sweep of her gaze and he stopped the gas from flowing, taking great interest in putting the nozzle back on the pump. He *felt* her probing gaze. The back of his neck itched. He held his breath until she started the motorcycle.

His turn was every bit as casual as hers had been. As she moved forward, light from the streetlamp spilled momentarily across her face. Strands of wine-red hair peeked out from beneath the helmet. Raoul let his breath out slowly. He was certain he was looking at Iris 'Flame' Johnson.

The taillight of the motorcycle galvanized him into action. He slapped on the gas cap before throwing himself into the driver's seat. The motorcycle had already made a turn, but he noted the street.

He kept a good distance from her, running a couple of streets parallel to her at times to keep her from catching a glimpse of the Jeep. He ran without headlights, relying on sound and sonar to keep from an accident. It was obvious he had the advantage of knowing the terrain. She knew where she was going, but didn't know the alleyways and shortcuts he did. If she slowed down at all, he turned onto a side street immediately. He followed her through the business district and through the residential areas until they were in the very high-end estates, many with high fences and electrical gates.

The woman parked her motorcycle deep in the shadows of a park, the bushes and trees concealing her from his vision. He nearly missed her. There was nothing, no whisper of movement, no barking of dogs, not a single footstep. Gator didn't spot her, but he *felt* her. He allowed his GhostWalker instincts to take over, trusting his highly developed senses to guide him when he had absolutely nothing but a gut feeling to go on.

He moved in silence past the first brick-walled estate with its wrought-iron front gate. Two large mastiffs stood near the fence staring down the street. He whispered to them without conscious thought, calming them so they wouldn't alert anyone to his presence. He'd taken two steps before it sunk in that she must have done the same. The dogs were obviously on guard, yet neither had raised an alarm and both whined softly, looking eagerly in the direction she had taken.

He knew where in the shadows to look for a GhostWalker, but even with that knowledge, it took several long minutes of trying to pierce the darkness to spot her. She moved with stealth, flitting from shadow to shadow, bush to tree, avoiding the spill of light pouring from the overhead lamps. She stayed small, arms and hands in close to the body, clothes tight to avoid the whisper of sound. She wore a skullcap to keep any hair from being left behind at the scene. She knew what she was doing as she surveyed the tall wall surrounding the estate.

As she moved along the base of the north-facing wall, a dog roared a challenge. She froze, turning her head toward the sound. Abruptly the barking turned to a soft, eager whine. Raoul smiled. Definitely a GhostWalker. He stayed back, careful not to stare at her, not wanting her instincts to detect his presence. He found himself utterly fascinated by her.

The woman stared up at the wall, glanced left and right and moved back a few feet. To be safe he sank low, his movements slow so he wouldn't draw her gaze. His breath exploded out of his lungs as she leapt over the wall. There was no doubt left in his mind. She had to be a GhostWalker. Dr. Whitney had used genetic enhancement on her. It was impossible to clear the height of the wall with a straight-up jump. His physical capabilities were enhanced and he hadn't been positive he could take the wall, yet she had gone over it with ease.

Gator hurried across the street and waited in the darkness, 'feeling' with his mind. She was leery, probably sensing him, but unable to determine just what was tripping her alarms. He waited patiently, frozen in place. He was highly trained, and there were times he'd been locked into position for hours waiting for a target. He could outwait her if necessary. Whatever she was up to had to be time sensitive. The longer she was inside the estate walls, the more danger she was in. Hit, scatter, and run. Even as a child it would have been drilled into her.

The moment he sensed she was on the move, he cleared the fence in the exact same spot she had. He hadn't cased the place so it was the only safe spot to go over when he was landing blind on the other side. He landed in a crouch, just in the shadows of the hedges on the other side, automatically calming the guard dog with his mind. He took a cautious look around.

The rolling lawns were well manicured, and flowers and plants were grouped in a small area complete with fountains and statues, giving the appearance of a small private park. The house was enormous, two stories with numerous balconies and lots of brick and fancy, scrolled wrought iron. The house even boasted a jutting tower.

'Flame, what are you up to?' He whispered the words to himself, thinking of her as Flame rather than Iris. It didn't look like a rendezvous with a wealthy

29

businessman. He ignored the out of character posses-sive feeling that churned in his gut as his gaze pierced the night to find her.

He caught a glimpse of her near the thick vines growing up the side of the house. She moved with stealth, knees bent, carefully placing each foot as she skirted the huge windows. She turned her head sud-denly and looked right at him.

Someone was following her and he was damned good at it. Flame hadn't spotted him, but her heightened awareness told her she wasn't alone. And that meant he was a professional. She waited, flattened against the wall, her breath slow and even, her body perfectly still. He was there, close, somewhere inside the estate walls. *And the dog hadn't given a warning.*

Her heart lurched. She had cased the area many times and if anyone went near the brick wall, the dog roared a challenge. It was always on the alert, well-trained and eager to ferret out any intruder. She should leave, wait for another night, but she had run out of time. She had to pull off the job tonight in order to meet the deadline. Who else could control a dog that ferocious? She was keeping it from giving away her presence with little effort, but if someone else was also manipulating the dog, that meant they could take control of it.

She swore under her breath. Whitney had found her. It had to be that. She knew she couldn't run forever. The story in the newspaper about a sanitarium out in the bayou burning to the ground had drawn her. It was exactly the type of situation she knew better than to pursue. If Peter Whitney or some covert branch of the government he was connected to was looking for her, they would know she wouldn't be able to resist hunting information. The moment she realized the trail led back to the Whitney estate, she should have gotten out. She'd gotten involved with some of the locals, the way she always did, and she'd stayed much too long.

Had they sent an assassin? The fire in the sanitarium had been a hit, plain and simple. The Whitney Trust had wanted to cover up the fact that genetic and psychic experiments had been done on babies. Damn Whitney and his government contacts. It wasn't all that hard to create accidents and make people disappear, especially girls who were considered unbalanced or different.

Anger smoldered and that was bad. The ground shifted slightly, a minor seismic anomaly. Flame took a deep breath and let it out slowly to calm herself. That wouldn't help matters. The dog whined off to her left, sensing the small shift beneath the ground. She quieted the animal with a touch of her mind as she weighed her chances. They would send someone well trained after her, someone with at least equal the skills they would assume she possessed. Chances were better than good that they would underestimate her. And chances were better than good Whitney would want her alive.

She'd hacked into Whitney's secret files and destroyed what she'd found on her training and had even managed to destroy some of the files on the other girls after first copying them. Whitney had an impressive empire and his contacts within the government ran deep. There was no doubt in her mind he would eventually send an assassination squad to get rid of the evidence if he couldn't bring her in – and she wasn't going back alive. The fire in the sanitarium was proof she was right. She'd read about Whitney's death, a murder with no body and she doubted the truth of it. He was a monster, pure and simple, and he would do anything to cover up his crimes.

Flame tapped her finger against her thigh while she worked out her next move. She could play cat and mouse with the hunter, but she couldn't afford one screwup. Using every sense she had, she once again attempted to locate the shadow. Absolute stillness came back to her. Not even a scent. She wanted to doubt the shrieking alarm bells in her head, but she knew, *knew*, someone was on to her. Then it hit her – the dog. She reached for the animal, trying to connect enough to get the impression of where the other intruder was. The dog would know and if she could get it out of the animal's mind, she'd be in a much better position.

The moment she touched the dog she knew it was completely under the control of the other intruder. Her heart accelerated abruptly and she had to breathe deeply to counteract the sudden flood of adrenaline. 'Rat bastard,' she whispered to herself. 'You only think you have the edge.'

She slid farther into the darkness behind the hedges and vines crawling up the side of the massive house. She knew exactly where the safe was and how to get to it. She was fast and strong and could be in and out in minutes. Whitney's hunter had no idea what she was doing or where she would go in. She went up the side of the house, clinging like a spider, moving with stealth and speed to gain the second-story balcony. She went up and over the wrought-iron railing, dropping into a crouch and remaining still while she listened.

Flame glanced at her watch. The guard would be patrolling on this side of the house. She'd timed his movements several times and the idiot always took the same route. He was as reliable as a Swiss clock. She stayed very still, waiting until he had gone around the corner before unzipping her pack and pulling out her crossbow and hook. This balcony was the only real access to the tower roof and the skylight above the office where Saunders kept his safe. Smug jerk that he was, he thought he had it covered with his narrow staircase, the only exit in and out with two guards situated in the house at the bottom of the stairs. The tower had no balcony and no other access, only sheer walls and wrought-iron stakes below should one fall in an attempt at climbing it.

'Amateur,' she sniffed. Saunders was as dirty and as greedy as they came. She had no compunction whatsoever about proving him an amateur in the area of crime.

The angle to reach the roof was tricky, and there was only one small target she could hook, but she was sure of her aim and took the shot without hesitation. She controlled the sound, keeping the noise of metal grinding on the roof from reverberating through the night. Crouching, she waited for a reaction, hoping the darkness would cover the line pulled taut from balcony to roof. Saunders had some very good guards, but he also had a few lazy ones. She didn't imagine that he would have many intruders and the guards had to be bored. Still, Saunders had the reputation of being as mean as a cottonmouth. He'd probably put a few dead bodies in the swamp over the years. She didn't plan on being one of them.

The guards wouldn't hear the hook, but she had to believe there was a possibility that the man hunting her might if Whitney had sent him. The smart thing for him to do would be to kill her while she was breaking into Saunders's tower, but it would be nearly impossible for him to collect her body and Whitney would definitely want it. Flame weighed the odds. More than likely, her stalker was sure of himself, certain he could take her when she came out, but much more likely, he was sent to bring her back. Whitney wouldn't want his multimillion-dollar experiment axed if he could still find a way to use her.

She shrugged, shouldered her pack and hooked her legs around the line, sliding hand over hand out above the grounds toward the tower. She couldn't help the little twinge of fear rushing through her at the expectation of a bullet, but she held on to the fact that she was worth more alive than dead to Whitney.

Whitney was a man who liked answers and his adopted daughter was very much like him. Flame had hacked into Lily's computer a couple of times and had recognized the quick mind and the same driving love of science. *Traitor.* That was how Flame saw Lily. There had been so much favoritism on Whitney's part, Lily had done what he wanted, become his willing puppet, his accomplice, his doting daughter so he could continue his vile experiments.

What did Lily think happened to the rest of them? Did she believe the bullshit stories in the computers? How could she when Dahlia had been locked in a sanitarium and a hit squad had destroyed everything she held dear? Lily would pay for that too. Flame would find a way. The Whitney money was an easy and obvious target, but Lily had too much, and hitting a few accounts here or there wasn't going to make much difference.

As Flame began her hand-over-hand climb to the roof, she focused on finding the man stalking her. She was positive he was the same man she'd noticed at the gas station. He had been putting gas in the Jeep, but he had been back in the shadows, almost impossible to see, and something about him had had her warning radar shrieking. Several times on the way to Saunders's estate, she'd had the eerie feeling she was being followed, but there was no sound and no headlights. He *had* to be one of Whitney's experiments. She knew she wasn't wrong.

She gained the roof without incident and stored her supplies in the pack just to the left of the skylight. Now, the biggest danger was that the hunter might follow her to the tower roof as well. She rigged the line to slip should he attempt to use it. He had to think she was going down the same way she'd come up. Flame made her way to the skylight, gliding with care so her footsteps couldn't possibly betray her presence to anyone inside.

Saunders was hunched over his desk, glass of whiskey in hand. He looked pleased with himself. 'Slimy little weasel sitting in your ivory tower thinking no one can get to you, but I'm going to take you down.' Flame sank down beside the skylight and lifted her face to the stars. She had to concentrate on the small things, the things she could do, the people to whom she could bring a little justice, not her past.

She couldn't think about the rigorous training, the long days and nights locked in a cage like an animal, feeling deprived of all dignity, of company, of anything that mattered. In the end, she had triumphed because she'd learned to be what they'd wanted her to be and she was far better than any of them had ever discovered. She'd escaped. She smiled, thinking of the bogus trust fund in the computer all set up in her name. She'd made it real and the money came in handy on the run. She'd stolen it from the monster, just as she'd stolen the money for the others, and had it locked up in off-shore accounts where the bastard couldn't touch it. If she succeeded in finding the girls they would at least have money to start some kind of a life. Computer skills came in handy.

She should have left New Orleans the moment she realized she wasn't going to find Dahlia, but she'd heard about a missing girl. Joy Chiasson. For some terrible reason she identified with the girl, was afraid someone like Whitney had her. It made no sense, but she thought she'd poke around a little and just make certain.

Her throat was sore from singing so much in the last couple of weeks. She'd done three sets in a small club just a half-mile from the station where she'd gassed up her motorcycle, and her vocal cords were feeling the strain. The idea had been to see if anyone was abnormally interested in her because of her voice, but that idea had been sheer idiocy. Too many people followed her from club to club to know if someone was fixated on her the way they might have fixated on Joy.

Practically everything dirty in New Orleans led back to this place, this man. Kurt Saunders. He sold property and stole it back. He was behind most of the gambling, whores, and drug trafficking. His house was in the most elite part of the Garden District and he rubbed shoulders with politicians and celebrities. Men like Saunders didn't come down easily, but it was just possible that while she was helping out a friend tonight, she might also stumble across something to do with Joy's disappearance. It wouldn't surprise her in the least.

Flame focused back on the stalker. She felt him. Knew he was somewhere close to her, but couldn't pinpoint his location. He couldn't have a scope on her; she wasn't visible from the ground. He *had* to be the man from the gas station. He hadn't shown any interest in her at all. She tapped her thigh with her index finger, replaying the small moment over and over in her mind. She hadn't gotten a good look at him; he'd seemed to blend into the night. What made him memorable to her? *Nothing. Absolutely nothing.* She sighed and rubbed at her temple. She was getting a killer headache, something that often happened when she used psychic talents for long periods of time.

The splash of lights and a sudden flurry of activity at the gate, accompanied by the ferocious barking of the dog, had her crawling across the tower roof to peer over the edge. The guards had arrived, guns in plain sight, as the gate swung open allowing a black town car to sweep onto the circular drive.

Flame narrowed her vision, studying the car. She'd seen it before. A photographic memory helped keep small details filed away until she needed them. She'd seen the car several times on the frontage road out by the houseboat where she was staying. She'd also seen it around several of the clubs where she sang. The car always had the same driver. He stayed out of sight except to open and close the door for his passenger, Emanuel Parsons. Parsons was an older man, whom Flame guessed to be somewhere in his sixties. He carried a silver-handled cane, but she doubted he really needed it. He seemed to like the distinguished look and the deference everyone gave him.

She made a face as the driver opened the door and Parsons emerged wearing a long coat, his silver hair gleaming in the lights flooding the entryway. It didn't surprise her in the least that the man knew Saunders. Emanuel Parsons was the head investigator for the DEA and more than likely investigating Saunders for laundering money while playing friends with him. In the clubs he held himself aloof from everyone else, insisting on extra attention. He brought his grown son with him a couple of times, but most of the time he surrounded himself with other businessmen hardly deigning to notice most of the locals. He and his son had sent her a drink twice. *And his son had dated Joy Chiasson*. That alone put them on her radar screen.

She watched Parsons until he disappeared under the roof of the giant columned porch. With a little sigh she crawled back to the skylight. Why was it that in every town there were men who believed themselves above the law, men who had such a sense of entitlement? She didn't get it, probably never would get it. Dr. Whitney, just as these men, was a respected professional. He had the ear of people in high places. He had trust and even high security clearance, yet he was a predator, ruthlessly destroying the lives of others to further his own cause. Saunders was also such a man, and she had no doubt, just by observing Parsons in the clubs, that he was the same, even though they were on different sides of the law.

'It's like a damned secret society,' she whispered under her breath. 'To get in you just have to screw everybody.' And why did people believe that sharks like Whitney and Saunders would eventually be brought to justice? In her experience they were *never* brought to justice. They schemed and muscled and killed and grew fat on their profits and everyone turned a blind eye. More than likely Parsons would end up dead someday, alligator bait in the bayou while Saunders got fatter off of his illegal profits. Her headache was getting worse and if she didn't tamp down her anger, the house was in for an unexpected shaking. Did Louisiana get earthquakes? She hadn't bothered to check.

The light in the room below went off suddenly, alerting her to the fact that Saunders was heading downstairs to greet his guest. The door to the office closed and she could hear the distinct click of a lock. Immediately she moved to the skylight and peered down. Sure enough, the tower room was empty.

Flame smiled – securing a little justice went a long way in curing headaches. Staying low to prevent skylining her body, she examined the skylight, looking for evidence of magnetic switches or motion detectors inside the frame. It didn't seem possible that Saunders could be so arrogant as to not install security on the skylight itself. Surely he wasn't that stupid? She'd come prepared for a difficult task, but she found nothing to do but use her laser cutter to open the glass dome. Before lifting the glass free with the attached suction cup she once more checked for security, this time using all senses, not just visual.

The sound was much too high for the human ear to detect. Flame froze without pulling away the glass. Saunders was using an old-fashioned ultrasonic motion detector. It was placed inside the skylight where little would disturb it. She rarely encountered them anymore because they were just too sensitive and often produced far too many false alarms. And that meant when she lifted the glass away the slight rush of air into the room would trigger the alarm.

It was a simple enough device. A transmitter sent out a frequency too high for the human ear and the receiver picked up the sound waves reflected in the area under protection. Motion would cause a shift in the frequency of sound. The larger the object the greater the shift in frequency. Most detectors were configured to ignore the small shifts that might be caused by insects, but a larger shift would trip the circuit and set off the alarm.

'You have the old Doppler effect going, don't you, Saunders?' Flame murmured aloud, under her breath. 'Well, sound just happens to be my specialty, you cheap slimeball. Your little old detector is simply comparing the frequency emitted by the transmitter when no motion is detected to the frequency of sound that results when motion occurs. And that, my lovely little mark, is easy enough for someone like me to work around.'

She cocked her head to one side, pressing close to the dome to listen, determining the pattern in the high-frequency sound. With no motion present, the sound bouncing back was an even, steady configuration. She simply had to find that exact frequency and pattern and make certain that nothing interrupted it when she removed the glass and dropped down into the room.

Flame nearly laughed. Here she was with all the latest high-tech equipment a cat burglar could possibly need, and she had to run into someone with an old-fashioned setup. 'Cuz you're just too cheap where it counts, Saunders. You think because you rip off a lot of really nice people that makes you smart. It only makes you a mark, just like the ones you steal from.'

It was gratifying how all those government-given talents came in handy when she went to work. Dr. Whitney and his little team of scientists would be so pleased to know their work had gone to a good cause.

She maintained the high-frequency pattern even as she pulled the circle of glass away and set it aside so that the sudden air shift wouldn't trigger the alarm. She dropped a line slowly, careful of the pattern, as she lowered her body into what Saunders believed was his impenetrable fortress. Landing lightly, she began a thorough search of the room all the while making certain the high-frequency signal remained a nice steady pattern. Saunders had money in the bank, but everything he stole was going to be in the tower room, in cash, hidden away.

She found the safe behind a section of wall panel looking just as smooth as the rest of the walls, but as she tapped lightly with the pad of her index finger along the textured surface, she could hear the slight differences in sound. It took only seconds to locate the hidden mechanism to slide the panel aside.

The safe gleamed at her, outrageously shiny in order to provide as many great fingerprints as possible should it be broken into. Flame smiled at it. 'Hello, baby.

40

Mama's come to free your soul.' She peered closer. 'You're a primo model, aren't you, hon? I'll just bet you've got a few layers of hard plate behind the door, don't you? I'll also bet you have a few ball bearings in the hard plate to chew up the drill bits too. That's just not nice, but then I'm not going to drill into you. That would hurt, wouldn't it, gorgeous?'

The safe also had a remote relocking device. If she punched out the combination, the remote relocker would engage, but she had no intention of cutting out the lock. She did everything by sound. She closed her eyes as she spun the tumbler, listening for the drop in sound. The first number was six and dropped easily into place. Flame spun the lock and heard the drop at nine. The third number was six. Scowling, she wasn't surprised when nine came up again. Four more times the numbers repeated.

'Idiot. You're such a freakin' cheesy sleazebag,' she said as she swung open the safe's door. Four briefcases fit snugly into the safe. All four had combination locks. She didn't bother to ascertain they contained cash. It stood to reason they did. Scooping out all four, she secured them to her belt and carefully, without haste, put everything back exactly as it had been.

The climb hand-over-hand up the rope back to the roof was easy enough, and she kept the high-frequency pattern going in a nice steady beat the whole while. Back outside, she restored the skylight glass, using a high-end glue to replace the cutout, holding it in place until it sealed. They would find out, but it was always fun to make them work a little to figure it out.

Stashing the four briefcases in her bag, she crawled quickly to the hook, retrieved the anchor, and shoved it in her bag with the other tools. She left the line, to provide the illusion of an expected escape route to whomever the Whitney Trust had sent against her. Let him wait for her. If she was really lucky, when the break-in was discovered, he might even get caught.

She slipped the pack on her back and slithered over the roof to the front edge. It was a long drop to the ground, but she had no intention of going down that way. She'd already calculated the jump between the tower roof and the small guesthouse at the back of the property Saunders used for his playtime. During surveillance she'd seen his men bring several different women there. Saunders liked to play rough. The women always came out looking battered and bruised rather than happy with whatever he paid them.

The distance between the tower and the guesthouse was far too great for anyone to believe she could use it as an exit. A sweeping lawn and several flower beds separated the two buildings. Flame straightened up, a momentary risk as she took a running start across the tower roof to leap for the roof of the guesthouse. She landed in a crouch, gaze already probing the darkness for danger.

Best scenario, the theft wouldn't be discovered until morning and she could leisurely get away, mask the sound of her motorcycle and hope one of Saunders's really alert guards didn't spot her. If so, well, that was one of the reasons for having the motorcycle in the first place.

Flame ran along the side of the guesthouse to the back of the property. The guards occasionally gathered to play a game of cards where Saunders never bothered to look for them. She made out two large men sitting in the gazebo housing a hot tub. Saunders went for the intimidation factor in his men, wanting them pumped-up in order to bully people with appearance alone. She could hear the murmur of conversation as they discussed a club in the French Quarter both were particularly fond of.

She moved past them easily, creeping along the hedge until she found the small rock, which she had painted white to make it easy to spot in the dark. Pocketing it, she looked left and right, listened for a minute, and leapt over the fence, landing blind on the other side. She'd dropped the rock hours earlier to mark the only place along the back fence she could go over and land in a clear spot inside the thick foliage surrounding the brick wall. She remained crouched, her heart beginning to accelerate again. Whitney's man would know she was up to something. She would never stay inside the estate grounds so long. He was probably stalking her.

She sent every psychic and natural sense she had out into the night, searching for information, listening for the sound of footsteps, the whisper of clothing sliding through vegetation. Even the sudden silence of insects would tip her off to the other's location, but she heard only the regular sounds of the night.

Flame didn't wait for the alarm to be raised behind her. Staying low in the shadows along the brick wall she moved quickly, keeping to the foliage as much as possible, all the while scanning the area for sound or movement. She shushed several guard dogs as she passed more houses. When she was three blocks from the Saunders's estate, she halted. She had to cross the street to get to the park where she'd left her motorcycle and the lamps were spilling light brightly across the paved road.

She waited there in the darkness. The feeling that she wasn't alone crept in. The weight of the four briefcases was heavy on her shoulder, but she could use it as a weapon if necessary – if she got that close.

Soft male laughter reached her from deep within the

trees of the park. 'You may as well come on over, *cher*. Aren't 'cha getting all hot and bothered standin' there wonderin' whether or not I've got me a gun?'

Chapter Three

The low Cajun drawl was as smooth as molasses and set Flame's heart pounding. Could he see her? Or, like her, did he just sense her presence?

'You've been a very bad girl tonight. I don' know what was so important to you, *cher*, but someone should have told you stealin', it be a bad, bad thing.'

She remained stubbornly silent, trying to get a fix on his voice. Was he throwing it? Projecting it from a false direction in order to trick her? She was fast, incredibly fast. She could streak across the lighted street and make a run for her bike, but he'd know exactly where she was. Damn Whitney and his experiments. She had no choice but to work her way down several more blocks. She could feel the minutes ticking by. Saunders wouldn't stay too long out of his ivory tower and the theft would be discovered.

When she had gone several blocks down and around the corner from her motorcycle, Flame burst out from the foliage, sprinted across the lighted street, and up three blocks until she gained the relative safety of the park. She slowed immediately, not wanting to give away her exact location by stepping on crisp leaves or dried twigs. She crouched low in the shadows and controlled her breathing. Sounds carried at night, even harsh breathing and more than once she'd slid past guards, knowing exactly where they were only by their ragged breath coming in short gasps after exertion. Flame used her psychic ability to keep any sound she might make from traveling.

She stayed low, moving with slow caution, taking care not to allow movement to draw the eye as she worked her way across the park. Nearing her motorcycle, she was dismayed to see a man sitting on it, casually swinging one leg back and forth while he waited. He didn't have a gun in his hands; in fact, when she looked closer she noticed he'd been busy trying to steal her bike. There was a small piece of metal attached to her ignition.

Her motorcycle was her baby, one of the few items she bought wholly for herself and she'd made certain it wouldn't be all that easy to steal, locking up the ignition and housing for the wires with a secondary lock needing a password. He'd evidently managed to either bypass the lock or found her password.

Anger swept through her and she stepped forward. 'Get the hell off my bike.'

He whistled softly. 'Woman, you have a foul temper.'

The way he drawled out 'woman' did something funny to the pit of her stomach. His dark hair curled every which way and his generous mouth curved with amusement. His shoulders were broad and she could see the strength in his arms and upper chest. The man was built and he looked like he'd be good in a fight – or in bed. The unbidden thought pushed her temper up a notch.

'Get. Off. My. Bike.'

'And you're stubborn too. I like that in a woman. Never have gone for the submissive type.' He winked at her. 'I like a tigress in my bed.'

'Oh shut up.' This wasn't going anything like she'd

thought it would and he was throwing her off-kilter with obvious flirtation. 'I certainly don't care about your sexual preferences. Who are you anyway?'

He put a hand over his heart. 'You wound me, *cher*. I thought we were going to get along so well.'

Flame put one hand on her hip and studied his face. It was a strong face with a very intriguing mouth that laughed often – if one could believe it, which she didn't. She believed in the eyes, and his eyes didn't laugh at all. They were focused and hard and moved ceaselessly, taking in every detail about her and the surrounding area. 'Who are you?'

'My friends call me Gator.'

Her eyebrow shot up. 'I'll just bet they do. I'll just bet you got that name from wrestling alligators when you were a kid like every other boy in the bayou.'

'Ouch. That one struck home. Don' be like that, *cher*. I'm *famille,* a GhostWalker, same as you.'

'You're not my family. And you're wasting your charm on me. Get off my bike.' She took an aggressive step forward, hoping he would meet her advance with one of his own.

He grinned at her, just sitting there, swinging his leg as if he didn't have a care in the world. 'So you noticed right away how truly charmin' I am.'

'I noticed you have an ego the size of Texas. And you're still sitting on my bike.' She lowered her pack to the lawn. He was a solid man, heavy muscle, but she had the feeling he'd be fast – maybe even as fast as she was.

'I'm comfortable, thank you.'

'You're not going to be comfortable in another minute. What is that thing on my motorcycle?' She indicated the small piece of metal attached to the ignition.

'You stole whatever you've got in that bag of yours.

47

Maybe we have something in common. I like vehicles.'

She shifted position slightly, giving less targets, making herself more mobile. 'You're such a liar. Whitney sent you after me, didn't he?'

Raoul shook his head. 'Not he, *she*. Lily. The old man is dead.'

Her eyes flashed fire. 'For all your nonsense, I didn't take you for a complete fool, but if you believe Dr. Whitney is dead, you deserve anything that happens to you.'

She moved again, a slight, nearly imperceptible gliding of her feet. Without warning, she launched herself, leaping into the air, shooting both feet at his broad chest. She went at him in an angle, determined to knock him off the bike, but at the last possible second, he deflected the double kick, driving her legs away from him with a powerful block of his forearm that sent her tumbling to the ground.

Flame leapt to her feet, landing in a fighter's crouch, fists up and ready.

Raoul smirked at her. 'You don' play well with others, do you, *cher*?'

'I don't play at all, especially with Whitney's little puppets.'

The lazy swinging of the foot halted abruptly and the smile faded. 'Now you done gone and insulted me, *ma petite enflamme*. That's not a good thing to do when I'm holding your motorcycle hostage.'

She circled the bike, studying him from every angle. He could call her his fiery little one all he wanted, but he was the one about to be burned. He was far too sure of himself and, as most of her opponents did, he underestimated her. 'Why are you here?'

'To bring you home, *cher*, where you belong.'

'Like hell you'll take me back. I'd rather be dead.'

She leapt into the air a second time, going over him and the motorcycle, one boot aiming for his face.

Gator whipped his head to one side. Her boot barely skimmed his jaw, burning a line across his five o'clock shadow. He caught her leg in a scissor lock and shoved, sending her sprawling toward the ground. Flame rolled with the scissor lock, tucking into a somersault, doing an aikido roll, and coming right back up into fighting position.

The man just sat on the motorcycle, a small irritating smirk on his face. Nothing seemed to ruffle him and Flame felt the small shift under her feet that indicated *she* was definitely ruffled. She'd been taking it easy on him, mainly to see what he'd do, but the more he sat there looking all puffed up and satisfied, the madder she was getting. Flame couldn't afford to lose her temper.

Before she could launch another attack she saw his gaze shift toward the street. The small smile hovering around his mouth faded and he held up his hand in a silent signal of danger. His hand moved across his throat before showing four fingers. He had gone from amused male to commander in a split second. He looked lethal, dangerous, and every bit the predator.

Flame backed away from him, shaking her head. She wasn't his ally. Anyone sent by Whitney was her enemy.

She crouched lower and studied the street. Not only were four guards spreading out, armed to the teeth with automatic weapons and heading straight into the park, but several black SUVs had pulled out of the Saunders estate and onto the street to patrol the area. She was certain they were looking for whatever she had taken from the safe. Anyone caught was going to be interrogated and searched.

Gator gestured imperiously toward the bike, clearly ordering her to get on it.

Flame ran to her bag, staying low as she swooped it up and secured it on her shoulder. She wasn't about to get caught between a rock and a hard place. She'd take her chances with civilian guards rather than a genetically and psychically enhanced soldier. She wasn't about to kid herself. No matter how charming the Cajun might be, he was a weapon, the same as she was.

She ran for the center of the park where the shadows were the darkest. She heard Gator swear and her motorcycle start up, the engine loud in the silence of the night. He revved it up, deliberately drawing attention to his presence. Flame skidded to a halt and watched as he did several doughnuts with the bike, luring the guards in closer to him. They talked frantically into their radios and the SUVs circling the park changed directions to home in on the site.

Gator stopped his sweeping circles and signaled Flame to run. She heard the pulsing notes in her head, and realized he commanded sound in the same way she did. He could disrupt communications between the guards anytime he wanted. Flame found a tree with high branches and heavy foliage and leapt up to conceal herself in its limbs.

The motorcycle roared off. The SUVs fell in behind him and, at the end of the street, the bike's headlight went out. Once he got away from the streetlights, she knew Gator could maneuver by sound. The motorcycle was fast enough to outrun the SUVs. She sat there motionless, trying to puzzle out Gator's motives. Nothing he did made sense, and she never went into battle without clear lines between friend and foe. He said he'd been sent to bring her back, but he hadn't tried to force her. He hadn't even asked her what she'd stolen or why.

The problem was – she liked him. She made up her mind fast about people. She was adept at reading them, and despite knowing she shouldn't fall for his Cajun charm, and in spite of the bleak and dark and lethal shadows in his eyes – she liked him. She was honest enough to admit she probably was a little drawn to him because he was enhanced and he felt the same rush of power and same terror of making mistakes that she did. He had to suffer the same physical drawbacks and feel the same isolation.

It both amused and annoyed her that she couldn't quite shake the pack mentality. She was solitary, yet she still wanted friendships and family and people around her, even though her particular brand of genetically engineered talent made it impossible for her. She was too sensitive to sounds. Filtering noises all the time was a difficult and wearing process. Flame required a lot of downtime when she could retreat into the haven of silence. She imagined Gator did as well. When she became intrigued by something she had a tendency to become obsessive-compulsive about it until she'd satisfied her curiosity – another one of her many failings. She was definitely intrigued by Gator.

The guards had fanned out and were covering the park, paying particular attention to the area where she'd parked her motorcycle. None of them thought to look up, but all of them were nervous. And it had nothing to do with being afraid of finding the thief. They talked in low voices when they came together and all of them were afraid of their boss. He wanted his briefcases back and he wanted them immediately.

Flame smirked. Let Saunders know how it felt. How many people in the bayou had he robbed? She listened carefully to the whispers, hoping to hear something about Joy Chiasson's disappearance, but no one mentioned her. The smirk disappeared to be replaced by a frown. The authorities refused to believe that something

51

had happened to the girl, but Flame was certain they didn't want to know. Just as anyone in authority over Whitney hadn't wanted to know how his valuable research had been done. As long as they got results, that was all that mattered.

She had hacked into Whitney's files and learned about gene doping and genetic enhancement. He had used a virus to deliver the genes into her cells, and her immune system had tolerated it. She could run twice as fast for twice as long as most humans as well as do a host of other things, enough to know he had delivered the genes throughout her entire body.

She had a quick mind and she'd read everything she could find on gene therapy and knew Whitney was ahead of the game with his experiments. Of course, he'd used humans – not rats. She didn't think he wanted the perfect soldier, or even the perfect child; he wanted his own creation. It was the end product that mattered, the idea that his brain had conceived and developed something superior. And if there were problems, it was the fault of the defective human – not his work.

As a child she had developed a very rare type of cancer, a blood disorder that Whitney had treated successfully enough to put in remission, not cure. And now, when bruises didn't heal or she felt exhausted, she knew it was there, lying in wait to destroy her. The knowledge didn't stop her from living her life or finding scumbags like Saunders to bring a little justice to. She might never have a chance at Whitney, but she could even the odds with others like him.

Saunders sold property to the older people in the bayou, the ones who didn't believe in banks. He took their payments and when it came time for a balloon payment, just before they handed the money over, they were mysteriously robbed. Tonight, maybe a little justice was done.

The guards' voices were beginning to fade and Flame immediately bounced sound waves through the park, using echolocation to pinpoint the position of each guard. Two patrolled on the side nearest the Saunders estate, while three others roamed through the interior of the park. Flame took the opportunity to leap from the tree, dropping close to the base, gloved hands up for defense, but close to her body so she presented the smallest possible target.

Where had Gator parked his Jeep? He wouldn't park it on the street to be noticed by one of the guards, and he couldn't have left it in the park. Where? She moved toward a cross street, down from Saunders's estate but parallel to the park, keeping to the heavier foliage. She relied on sound to keep her informed, concentrating on echolocation, but keeping a visual as well.

The Jeep was parked in a driveway a block up and over from Saunders and just down from the park. The vehicle had the top up, but no doors on. Flame wrinkled her nose. She knew they were in for a shower and she was bound to get wet. On her motorcycle, it was perfectly fine, part of the entire experience, but in Gator's Jeep, when she was already annoyed, the rain was going to be one more reason for revenge.

She waited until the guards were concentrated at the far end of the park before hot-wiring the Jeep and taking off. She didn't use the headlights until she turned the corner and was out of harm's way. She didn't have the kind of patience needed for an encounter with Saunders's men when she was angry and damn it, she was definitely angry that Whitney's hunter had taken her beloved motorcycle.

She drove through New Orleans until she found a quiet street where she could pull over and, using a penlight, search the glove compartment for an address. The necessary insurance document and vehicle registration was neatly stuck in a plastic case. 'Thank you, Mr. Fontenot,' she said aloud.

He lived along the river, just north of the canal, in the same parish she was staying in, although she often used a boat to get to her current residence and Wyatt Fontenot had a much more convenient drive. *On her motorcycle.* The bastard. *Rat* bastard.

Flame pulled back on the street and drove with care, not wanting to bring attention to herself as she located the address. The last thing she needed was for a cop to stop her. In any case, she wanted Gator to feel very pleased with himself. She wanted him lured into a false sense of security and settled nice and comfortably into his own bed. If her motorcycle had been looked after properly, she might just be a nice girl and not drive his Jeep into the Mississippi, which is what he deserved.

All the while she drove, she thought of each item in her saddlebags. Had she left anything that might be a trail leading back to her? The address on her insurance and registration was from long ago. What else did she have? She often traveled with emergency belongings in the off chance she had to run. She had money stashed in the bike, but most likely, Gator would never find it, not unless he took the bike apart, and nothing would help him if he did that. *Nothing. No one.*

Flame crossed the bridge and worked her way through a ribbon of narrow streets surrounded by water until she found the long drive that circled back toward the river and the Fontenot home. When she was certain she had the right property, she parked the Jeep beneath a canopy of trees and curled up on the seat to go to sleep.

All the girls in Whitney's school of torture had been trained to set and use internal clocks. She slept for two hours, giving Gator Fontenot plenty of time to feel safe and secure. Stretching to get the kinks out, Flame left the Jeep at the end of the road and took off on foot, not chancing alerting him to her presence. She walked slowly, taking her time, orienting herself to the place. She wanted the quickest escape routes possible. The property had iron gates and few people in the parish had them. These were high and closed to seal the property off from the road.

She could jump over the gates, of course, but why would Fontenot have his home fenced in? She noted an old flatbed with the wheels off one side and a broken-down pickup, just inside the fence, but nothing else. Certainly nothing to warrant a fence. Unless . . . She reached out with her mind and found the dogs. Hunting dogs if she wasn't mistaken, already becoming aware of her presence. Before they could send out a chorus of warnings, she stopped them.

Of course he'd have dogs. Careless mistake. 'And all because I lost my temper. See, Flame. That's what happens when you get all bent out of shape. It's not personal. Don't take it personally.' Like hell it wasn't personal. It didn't get any more personal than someone stealing her motorcycle. Her fingers itched to wring his neck. She went over the fence, landing lightly, waiting to make certain the dogs stayed quiet and no sound gave her presence away.

There were two large buildings. The main house was dark and silent. The dogs moved restlessly in a nearby kennel. The second building, obviously the garage, was set slightly back from the house and had locks on the pull-down double door and the smaller, single entrance. Flame circled closer, wary of the entire setup.

She knew better than to get in a hurry. She cased the place first, checking on the enemy, determining how much room she'd have for escape, how long it would take her and mentally mapping out several routes if she ran into trouble.

Flame knew she could be walking into a trap, but she wasn't leaving her bike behind. *First rule: Never treasure anything so much you can't leave it behind on a moment's notice.* 'Damn you to hell, Whitney. I won't live like that. You can't rule my life.' But he did. He would always rule her life until he had her killed. He played her like a puppet. She knew not to go into the garage. Whitney had taught her that. And he knew her inside and out, knew she detested his authority. Refused his authority.

The ground beneath her feet shifted and the trees swayed ominously. The dogs in the kennel whined. Flame leaned against the broad base of a tree and forced air through her lungs. Her head was killing her. She'd used too much psychic energy tonight and she was already paying for it. That was a bad sign. And she absolutely had to stay under control.

Gritting her teeth, she approached the garage. It wasn't all that difficult to dispense with the locks and there wasn't an alarm anywhere, so she gained entrance quickly. No motorcycle. Her precious baby was being held prisoner somewhere else.

Without hesitation, Flame made for the house. The stairs creaked under her weight and she moved off of them immediately, circling the deep porch to find a way to the roof. She was always more comfortable in high places. She went up the side of the house, using the porch railing and roof to gain the second story with ease. She crept onto the small balcony and found the French doors unlocked.

Easing the door open just enough to slide inside, Flame went in low, close to the wall, shutting the door without a sound. She stayed motionless, waiting for her eyes to adjust to the difference in lighting. The room smelled of gardenias and lavender. A rose-colored sheet covered a gray-haired woman sleeping in the four-poster bed. She looked especially fragile and Flame frowned, wondering why Whitney's hunter had led her to civilians – unless he'd stolen the Jeep.

Flame moved with care, not wanting the floorboards to creak as she moved across the room to the door. There was a vanity with an old-fashioned brush and mirror set and several pictures just to the left of the door. Flame glanced at the pictures, trying to make out the faces in the dark. This was a home. It had the bayou trappings, but smacked of money. Somewhere along the line the family had come into money. She wondered if the money had come from Whitney, a bribe for Gator to hunt her down and bring her back.

Had Gator gone after Dahlia? Poor Dahlia. Flame remembered all of the other girls, every single one of them. Whitney hadn't been any fonder of Dahlia than he had been of Flame. He'd locked Dahlia up in a sanitarium and kept her from the world, kept her from a home and family – just as he'd done with most of the others one way or the other. Dr. Whitney had experimented on infants, continued the experiments on them as toddlers, teens, and even into their adult lives. He was never going to let them go and he sure as hell wasn't going to let the world discover what he'd done.

She looked around her, shocked that Whitney could get anyone to leave such a beautiful home to work for him. The structure had probably started out as a more traditional frame house, one and a half stories, with a covered porch or *galerie* raised on pillars to keep the sill from the soggy ground. The Fontenot farm had a frontage on the bayou to ensure travel on the waterways as well as harvesting the waters. They had plenty of woods for hunting and harvesting trees as well as fields for growing what they needed to survive. From the looks of the house, they'd done well.

She crept down the hall to the long staircase, studying the layout below her as she went. How had Whitney lured someone like Gator Fontenot into his world of deceit and treachery? This was a home filled with love. She could tell by the pictures of laughing faces. Someone, most likely the woman asleep in the upstairs bedroom, quilted and wove cotton for material. There were beautiful home-crafted items throughout the house, items fashioned with care to detail. Something none of the girls Whitney had experimented on had ever known.

No wonder they were all so dysfunctional – they hadn't grown up in a nice family environment with a sweet old lady to cook them breakfast every morning like this one. What had gone wrong with Gator? What would make him trade all that to work for Whitney? A flash of anger curled through her and she felt the house shift ever so slightly. Forcing air through her lungs, she continued moving, trying to think of other things.

She flashed the small penlight on the pictures above the stairs. Little boys smiled out at her, surrounding an older woman who looked both proud and stern. As Flame moved down the stairs, the boys became older, barefoot teens with alligators and fish, the same silly grins of their faces. She recognized Gator. He seemed the oldest of the brothers with their mops of black, curly hair and bright eyes.

At the bottom of the stairs was a chest with a marriage quilt thrown over the top of it. Three more chests stood in a row, each covered with a marriage quilt. In spite of the gravity of the situation, Flame found herself smiling. Someone was trying to not so subtly tell the boys something. It was amazing to think that families like this really did exist and Gator had been lucky enough to grow up in one. The knowledge made her angrier at him. It seemed a betrayal, taunting her with the very thing she had craved all her life. She fought back her rising temper. Maybe whoever raised him should have given him a swift kick. It wasn't too late to administer one and she was the woman to do it.

She found him in the second bedroom, sound asleep, his hand on the seat of her motorcycle where it was parked only inches from his bed. Sliding a knife from the scabbard hidden in her boot, she positioned herself above his head, crouched against the wall so that her breath stirred the waves in his hair as she placed the blade against his throat with exquisite gentleness.

He woke instantly, completely alert, danger flooding the room, expanding the walls. Even the floorboards creaked as if disturbed, but he never moved a muscle.

'*Cher*. How nice to see you again.'

'You stole my bike.'

'I saved your pretty little ass is what I did.'

She felt the ripple of his muscles, actually *felt* it, tension was so strong in the room, yet she wasn't actually touching his skin. He was far more dangerous than she'd given him credit for and her senses went on heightened alert. 'Don't move, *Wyatt*. I wouldn't want to accidentally cut your throat and this blade is sharp.'

'Don' go makin' a mistake, *cher*, I'm *Raoul,* not Wyatt and I wouldn't take kindly to you messin' with my lil brother.'

His tone was light, cheerful even, but she caught the edge of something lethal buried deep. Raoul Fontenot wanted people to think he was Mr. Charm, but his easy laughter hid something deadly, something only waiting for the right trigger. Her heart kicked into high gear, pounding hard with the knowledge she had a tiger by the tail.

'All I want is what belongs to me, *Raoul*. I couldn't care less about you or your brother or the Whitneys. Just remove your hand from my bike and sit up very carefully and won't have a problem.'

'We already have a problem, *cher*. You stuck a knife in my throat and I don' take kindly to that.'

Flame snapped her teeth together. 'Stop being unreasonable. It isn't *in* your throat, it's *against* your throat. I'm not buying the good old boy routine either, you snake. You tell your boss to back off and leave me alone. I'll never go back there.'

His eyebrow shot up. 'Who do you think is my boss?'

'I'm not playing games with you. I know you're dangerous. You know I am. Let's not be dumb. I just want my bike and I want to get out of here. I won't even push your Jeep into the Mississippi. And I'll leave you the keys. I think that's a fair trade.'

'The Jeep belongs to Wyatt and he wouldn't like losing it, but on the other hand, he's a sucker for a beautiful face.' A slow, melting grin crept over his dark features. 'And *cher*, you have a damned beautiful face.'

Her breath left her lungs in an unexpected rush and wings seemed to flutter lightly against the inside of her belly. The man was lethal. 'I also have a very sharp blade and you're irritating the hell out of me.'

His white teeth flashed at her. 'I can hardly believe that. Most women find me charmin'. I think you're lyin' to us both, Flame.'

His voice was pitched so low, so sultry, drawling with enough molasses that her insides melted. The reaction to him scared her. She didn't have those kinds of connections with people – especially not traitors. She *despised* men like Gator, throwing away everything she would have given her right arm for, just for money or power. Flame sucked in her breath sharply, trying to see him as the enemy when, for some strange reason, her body wanted to see him in a completely different light.

'You're enhanced.' She made it an accusation. Maybe Whitney had figured out how to heighten sexual magnetism and Gator was the ultimate weapon against women. She gritted her teeth and inwardly vowed resistance.

'So are you.' He shifted enough, careful of the sharp blade against his skin, that he could rest his gaze on her face. 'You look tired, *cher.*'

There was concern in his voice, in the depths of his eyes. Knowledge. Her heart thumped hard again and something close to fear curled in the pit of her stomach. 'Don't you worry about me, Gator. I'm not so tired I can't slit your throat. Let's get this done. Sit up slowly.'

'I don' know if you want me to do that.' Amusement was plain in his drawling voice. 'I'm in my altogether so to speak. I don' like many clothes when I sleep.'

She couldn't stop the color stealing into her cheeks. Damn him, he seemed to be so in control, so calm and sure of himself in spite of the fact that she had a knife to his throat. *Was he really that good?* For the first time doubt crept in.

The door to the bedroom burst open so hard it bounced against the wall with a hard crash and nearly swung shut. A hard foot smashed it back open, splintering the wood, and a younger copy of Gator stood framed in the doorway, his narrowed gaze fixed on the knife at his brother's throat.

'You look like you're havin' woman trouble, Gator,'

he greeted, confirming Gator's belief that he wasn't the only one in the family with natural psychic talents.

Flame tightened her grip on Raoul. 'Tell him to back the hell off,' she snapped.

The tension in the room stretched to a screaming point. Without warning, Gator caught her wrist in a gripping vise, thumb digging hard into her pressure point so that her fingers involuntarily opened and dropped the knife. At the same time, he jerked down, relieving the pressure on his throat, his other hand whipping up to catch her around the neck in a throw.

Flame went sailing over his head to land at the bottom of the bed. He was already on top of her, pinning her to the mattress. He looked up at his brother with a huge grin on his face. 'I don' never have trouble with the ladies, Wyatt.' He lowered his head until he could nuzzle Flame's neck. 'Ah *cher*, you smell so good.'

Fury burst through her, a bright bubble of anger so that the room narrowed, her vision tunneled, and she saw red as she glared up at his smirking face. The house shook, the walls vibrating, and Wyatt clutched his stomach, doubling over.

The smile was gone in an instant, Gator's black eyes glittered dangerously as his fingers closed like a vise over Flame's trachea. 'Stop now.'

'Kill me then,' she dared, her voice hoarse, eyes defiant.

'Wyatt, get out of here,' Gator directed.

'That won't save him.' She gasped for breath, but refused to panic. If she panicked the entire house and all its occupants would go down with her.

'He's an innocent. You keep this between us.' He bit out each word distinctly between his white teeth, his black gaze narrowed and hard.

'I don't know if I can.' Flame tried to be honest. Her gaze met his squarely, wanting him to see the truth there.

He let his breath out slowly, easing the pressure on her trachea. 'Breathe, *cher*. Breathe it away. You do it every day of your life. I know. I'm the same.' He glanced toward the door, toward his brother, but both of them heard the soft footsteps hurrying toward them.

Her gaze clung to his and she reached with desperation for his breath, for the air moving in and out of his lungs, regulating her own breathing, pushing the anger away enough to regain control.

'That's it *ma petite enflamme*. You're fine.'

Her eyes softened for just a moment, a hint of gratitude there and then she glared at him. 'I won't be fine until you give me back my bike, you thief.'

'That's the pot calling the kettle black,' he retaliated.

'Raoul Fontenot!' A woman's voice cut through the tension. 'What are you doing with a woman in your bed and you nekkid as the day you were born?'

Shocked, Flame looked at the little old lady wrapped in a robe and holding a shotgun nearly as big as she was in her hands. Her silver-white hair was braided and looped in a neat bun at the back of her head. Her skin was paper thin and white, but her eyes were clear and steady, her lips compressed tightly in disapproval.

Gator scrambled to drag up a sheet, half standing as he did so. '*Grand-mere Nonny—*'

His grandmother cut him off without a word, sending him a glare. The older woman was magnificent. Flame would have given anything to be related to her. She sat up slowly, ignoring Gator's hasty scramble to cover himself. She did sneak a peek though. 'I'm so sorry, ma'am. I shouldn't have come.' She lowered her gaze looking young and vulnerable, allowing her voice to tremble. 'I sing in a club and he came in sweet-talkin' and smiling at me and I know I was wrong. I'm really a good girl. And now there's a baby on the way and I . . .' She pressed a hand to her stomach as she stood up shakily. 'I thought if I came, he'd do the right thing, but . . .' she trailed off pathetically.

Nonny lowered the barrel of the shotgun to the floor, not appearing to notice as Wyatt took it out of her hand. He had a huge grin on his face.

'*Grand-mere,*' Gator protested. 'Don' be listenin' to—'

Her hand came up sharply, palm flat and she waved him to silence with an imperious gesture, effectively cutting him off from explaining that he couldn't possibly have been there long enough to do what Flame accused him of.

His grandmother stepped forward and put her arm around Flame. 'You poor child. You look very pale. Let me get you a cup of tea.'

'*Bien merci!* You're so kind.' Flame cast a small triumphant glance over her shoulder at Gator behind his grandmother's back before putting her head down as she walked off. 'My family is going to disown me. I don't know what to do, but I'm so sorry for coming here, I shouldn't have. It was a mistake. Now he hates me more than ever.'

'He don' hate you, child. He's just shocked. Men never think their chickens is goin' to come home to roost. Don' you worry, *cher*, I'll help you. We'll get this straightened out fast. Gator, he lives up to his responsibilities. He's been brought up right.'

'I need to leave. I can't face him right now,' Flame said, flicking a glance toward the door. She'd have to leave without her bike, but she could make it to the Jeep before he could get dressed, pacify his grandmother and come after her.

'You look ill, child. Let me help you.'

Flame patted her arm, swallowed the sudden, unexpected lump forming in her throat. Gator's grandmother's concern was genuine and there was no doubt in Flame's mind that she would have done her best to help out a pregnant, unwed mother. Damn Gator for his selfish choices. This woman was to be treasured, his family valued. He had no right to sell himself as a Whitney puppet.

'Merci. Bien merci.' She stammered it several times as she bolted toward the door and out into the heat and rain of the night. There were tears in her eyes and she didn't know why, refused to ask herself why. She dashed them away and ran for the Jeep.

Chapter Four

The sun sank deep in the bayou, raining fire and pouring gold into the dark waters. Several great blue herons silhouetted against the horizon appeared like enormous stick figures cut from black paper as they crept slowly through the shallower edges of the canal. Long ropes of moss dangled from cypress trees and swept the water creating a red and gold jungle of feathery arms dipping into the shimmering surface. With humidity so high, even the night creatures moved slowly and easily. Snakes plopped into the water from the low-slung branches and snapping turtles slid much more silently into the murky depths.

The cloying perfume of gardenia and jasmine hung heavy in the air adding to the oppressive heat. A small expanse of grass and several stumps of trees covered a small area between a large cabin and the rickety pier. One alligator stretched along the pier, much like a guard dog, eyes half closed, mouth wide open exposing sharp teeth, watching the boats chugging toward the cabin with lazy disinterest. Two other alligators snoozed on the grass in between the stumps and flowers quite close to the stairs leading to the porch. Neither looked up as several noisy people tied off pirogues and small fishing boats and clambered along the pier. The crowd made wide berths around the guard alligator with small salutes. Friday nights brought the boisterous throng and the loud, upbeat music.

'*Laissez le bon temps rouler!*' Wyatt grinned at his oldest brother, and pointed to the ice chest in their boat as he shoved the long pole along the bottom of the canal, driving the pirogue toward the pier. 'Of course, *Grand-mere* may never forgive you if you don' marry that girl and raise a family with her.'

'*Oui, tais toi,* Wyatt,' Gator groused. 'Although the idea of taking her to bed does make my heart sing.'

Wyatt toed at him good-naturedly. 'And other body parts as well. She was damned fine-looking, even when she had the knife to your throat.'

'I've seen him in action,' Ian MacGillicuddy announced, shoving at the lid of the ice chest. 'I believe her. He's been frequenting the clubs and I'd be willing to bet he charmed her into his bed.'

Gator threw a beer cap at Ian. 'You know I haven't been here long enough to be makin' babies, much as the idea of trying with her may be appealin'.'

'I don' know, bro, they have these tests now that can tell practically overnight. *Grand-mere* has a royal bee in her bonnet now. She wants a marriage and it ain't gonna be me.' Wyatt grinned at his brother. 'And that woman, she held that knife like she knew how to use it. She's a wildcat, that one.'

Gator's teeth flashed. 'Yeah, she's that, all right. Made me sit up and take notice.' He hadn't stopped thinking about her. When he'd thrown his body over hers, her skin had been the softest thing he'd ever touched. He'd wanted her with every cell in his body. The blood had surged hot and greedy through his veins, pouring into his groin so that he still ached just thinking about her. He liked women, loved women, but he didn't lust after any particular one – not like this. He forced his smile wider. '*Laissez le bon temps rouler!*'

'What the hell does that mean exactly?' Ian demanded. 'That and your *tuto* comment to your brother. I had the feeling that wasn't very nice.'

'He told me to shut up.'

'Let the good times roll,' Gator interpreted for the big Irishman, ignoring Wyatt. 'The Huracan Club is owned by Delmar Thibodeaux. And his place is always hoppin'.'

'It's good to have you home, Gator,' Wyatt said. 'You made *Grand-mere* happy. I haven't seen her smile like that in a couple of years. Well, until you got that woman pregnant, but I think if you marry her, *Grand-mere* will forgive all.'

Unfortunately, his grandmother wouldn't listen to him even when he pointed out he'd only been home four weeks. Technically four weeks was plenty of time for a Fontenot to get a woman pregnant. Nonny wanted her grandsons married and settled down, not wild and running free. She wanted another woman close and little babies to hold in her arms. He turned his head away from his brother and Ian, afraid his expression might give him away. He had a sudden longing for those very things – now that they might be out of his reach. Funny how he'd taken it all for granted. The home. The family. A wife and children.

'*Grand-mere* says twins run in the family, Gator. She's hoping for two from you right away. You best be finding that woman and ropin' her in fast, bro.'

'Keep talking and I'm going to pin your ears back for you,' Gator said, forcing a soft laugh as he turned back toward his brother. The sound carried in the stillness of the swamp, but the smile didn't reach his restless eyes.

He searched the bayou, noting every canal, the lay of the land, the birds in flight. Even here at home with his friend and family, he made sure nothing got by him.

Wyatt leaned on his pole a moment, studying the harsh planes and angles of his brother's face. 'You haven't changed much. You still act as easygoing as ever, but there was no one tougher in the bayou.' He grinned at Ian. 'The boys want to fight every night, but not Gator. They never wanted to get him stirred up.'

Gator grinned but kept his gaze on the people on the pier and in the boats. It was good to be home in spite of the reason for his homecoming. His last trip had been so fast, a hit-and-run through the bayou with trouble on his tail. This time, he could savor being home. The way his grandmother's face lit up when she saw him had been worth the trip alone.

Well . . . until she got it in her head he needed to take responsibility for his actions. Flame had made quite the impression with her poor-innocent-woman-seduced-by-the-charming-playboy act. It didn't help that he had a certain reputation with the ladies and his grandmother knew it. She'd always been sharp; the boys had been certain when they were growing up she had eyes in the back of her head catching their misdeeds. And now she wanted Flame brought into the family fold. He'd stopped denying he'd slept with her. And he'd even stopped denying she might be carrying his child. What was the use? His grandmother wanted it to be true and nothing he said was going to change that fact.

'I'm about to die of thirst,' Ian said. He pressed the icy bottle of beer Wyatt snagged for him to his brow. 'I'm just replacing what I been sweating out.'

Wyatt laughed at him. 'You're soft, *mon ami*, can't take the heat with all that fine living you been doing.'

'Fine living?' A slow grin spread over Ian's face. He shook back his shock of red wavy hair. 'Oh, I like that, Gator. We been living fine up there in Miss Lily's big house.' He tipped half a bottle of beer down his throat. 'You're a good man, Wyatt, but you don't know the half of it.'

Gator snorted derisively. 'Don' let the boy fool you, Ian. Wyatt's been up to no good. He's been doin' nothing but partying, fighting, and getting into trouble with the ladies. *Grand-mere* wrote me 'bout the hell-raising you been up to, Wyatt, and me, I've come home to straighten you out.'

Wyatt winked at Ian. 'Oh, I don' think I have much to worry about anymore, big brother. I think *Grand-mere* has a new bee under her bonnet and it isn't me in trouble this time! I phoned the boys and let them know you were about to tie the knot with some high-stepping voodoo queen. They were pleased for you.'

'You're enjoying the hell out of this, aren't you, Wyatt?' Gator asked.

'Absolutely I am.' He leaned on the pole again, pushing the pirogue closer to the pier. 'For once in my life, I'm not the one *Grand-mere Nonny* is going to slap upside the head and it feels damned good.'

'I'm sure your grandmother will understand when you get around to telling her the truth,' Ian soothed.

Both Wyatt and Gator shook their heads simultaneously. 'Once *Grand-mere* gets a notion, she never lets up,' Wyatt explained. 'Gator's gonna have to find himself a bride, willin' or not.'

Gator replayed the feel of Flame's soft body against his. She was so damned soft. And her eyes . . . Vivid. Green. A man could drown in her eyes. Maybe he might be more willing than he thought he was. He shook his head as if that might dislodge such an idiotic thought.

She'd looked at him almost desperately there at the end, when she was under his body, his fingers squeezing her trachea, the two of them head to head, dangerous and angry with each other. '*I don't know if I can.*' He listened to the words replay in his head. There had been fear and honesty mixed together. She'd sounded so damned vulnerable he ached inside. Everything protective in him had risen up and reached out to her. She had been afraid of hurting his family. She hadn't wanted to, but she'd been afraid she might.

Damn Whitney. Damn both Whitneys. He was home looking for a lost friend. Poor little Joy. Her parents weren't rich and it was easier for the police to believe she'd taken off to the big city rather than to launch a full-scale investigation that might cost the taxpayers money. *She* was his priority, not Iris 'Flame' Johnson. He didn't give a damn what Lily said. He didn't have to bring Flame back to a place that must have been hell for her. A place that would only have bad memories and . . .

'What the hell!' Wyatt crouched low and gripped the sides of the pirogue as it rocked unexpectedly.

Gator glanced up quickly, saw the churning water and met Ian's gaze over the top of his brother's head. He drew in a long, slow breath and let it out to calm his mounting temper. Ian raised an eyebrow at him and Gator shrugged it off. He needed to find his balance and maintain it at all times. He reached out and snagged another cold bottle of beer from the ice chest and downed a third of it, the liquid giving him a measure of coolness in the heat.

'Any news on Joy, Wyatt?' he asked, suddenly.

Wyatt sighed. 'Nothing. No one seems to have heard or seen a damn thing.'

Gator glanced up sharply at his tone, noting the

shadows in Wyatt's eyes, the somber face.

'You said you were putting out feelers about the boy she was seein', talking to some of your friends.'

'James Parsons. About twenty-four, good-looking, at least all the girls say so. His daddy hobnobs with the politicians and knows just about anyone who is anyone. Rumor is, James brought Joy home for dinner and Daddy and Mommy objected. Said she wasn't quite good enough for their circle of friends and he could sow his wild oats, but forget about anything permanent. From what her sister told me, it was said right in front of her and James didn't put up a word of protest.'

'What an ass,' Ian said as he exchanged a quick glance with Gator. They both knew of the elder Parsons. He was head investigator in the DEA and was presently scrutinizing a local businessman for money laundering. They also knew he had a reputation for being a first-class snob.

'Joy's brothers expressed their opinion in much harsher terms,' Wyatt said.

'After that kind of humiliation, maybe she did want to leave,' Gator ventured. 'I'll bet she didn't date Parsons again.'

'No, but he kept comin' 'round,' Wyatt said. 'Her oldest brother, Rene, beat the hell out of him, but it did no good.'

'Lily said the police questioned him and he appeared to be genuinely upset over Joy's disappearance.'

'Her brothers and uncles think he had something to do with her disappearance. I don't. I think he's just afraid to stand up to his daddy. I think he was working up the courage to run off with her. Joy wasn't the runaway kind. She wasn't ashamed of her family and she wasn't ashamed of the bayou. She's smart and talented and when James Parsons didn't stick up for her she told

72

him to go to hell.' The edge to Wyatt's voice became sharper.

'You know her long?' Ian asked Wyatt.

'I went to school with her. She was way out of my league.' Wyatt cast a sly glance at his brother. 'Kinda like the little she-devil you played jump the broom with. A real looker and sassy as hell.'

'I didn't think any girl was outa your league, Wyatt.' Gator paused in the act of taking another pull on his beer to eye his younger brother. 'You like this girl?'

Wyatt shrugged. 'She was nice. Always had a friendly smile in school. I hadn't seen her in a couple of years other than at a distance, but, yeah, I liked her.'

'Did you ask *Grand-mere Nonny* to have me come home?' Gator asked shrewdly.

Wyatt shrugged a second time and busied himself tying up the pirogue to the dock, absently waving to several people as he did so. 'I might have mentioned you could help. You always were like a bloodhound. You know things other people don't. And you have connections, people who might get involved. There was a better chance that she could be found if you came home.'

'You pick up any information at the clubs?'

'Not really. Not of any use. I thought you might hear things I can't.' It was the first time Wyatt had ever acknowledged he knew his older brother was different. When Gator continued to stare at him he finally nodded. 'I watch you. I'm not nearly as dumb as I look.'

Gator unfolded his legs and stretched, toeing Ian's cowboy boots. 'You're really going to stand out there, Irishman.'

'I stand out everywhere,' Ian replied with pride. He chugged another beer. 'Hotter than hell here. Kind of makes me wish for the cool of Ireland. All emerald carpets and rain.'

73

'We have emerald.' Wyatt pointed his pole toward several plants. 'And it rains every other hour. Just wait and we'll get a shower soon enough.'

'Aw, laddie, that's not what I mean by the cool of Ireland,' Ian protested.

'Don't let him fool you, Wyatt,' Gator said. 'He's never been to Ireland in his life. He thinks the ladies will like him with that brogue he affects.'

'Pathetic,' Wyatt stated. 'Everyone knows ladies love Cajuns. It's in our blood, and our language is the language of romance.'

'Your language is the language of bullshit,' Ian corrected. 'You're a couple of good ole boys with pretty faces. Women just ought to know better. They should be looking for a real man.'

'You have red hair, Ian,' Wyatt said with feigned sadness, his hand over his heart. 'It's never going to happen for you.'

'There's always dye,' Gator pointed out, eyeing Ian's wild hair judiciously. 'We could dye it black and help him learn to speak without that funny little accent.'

Ian reached for him, shockingly fast for a big man, whipping his arm around Gator's throat and rubbing the top of his head with his knuckles. 'I'll show you a funny accent,' he threatened. 'It's a *brogue*. And a good Irish brogue at that.'

The pirogue tilted dangerously and the ice chest skittered toward Wyatt, who dropped the pole in the bottom of the boat and made a grab for the all-important beer. 'Save the fightin' for inside, you'll need it,' he cautioned.

Ian grinned at him. 'No one fights like an Irishman.'

Wyatt tied up to the dock and stepped out onto the pier, holding the boat steady while the GhostWalker leapt from the pirogue. Gator climbed out and stretched, rolling his shoulders and eyeing the club. The Huracan was one of the wildest and most popular clubs in the bayou. Accessible only by the waterway, mostly only the locals frequented the place. Once in a while some of the more astute music lovers in the business district discovered it, but for the most part, the Huracan belonged to those living in the bayou and they danced and drank and played hard there.

Music blasted out the windows and through the thin walls. The crowd sounded like thunder as individual conversations rose over the music. Ian leaned in close to Gator. 'Are you going to be able to hear what you need to hear in that place?'

Gator nodded. 'I can hear conversations through walls, Ian. It's just a matter of sorting them out. If someone is talking about Joy, I'll hear them.'

'It hurts though, doesn't it?' Ian's voice was pitched even lower to prevent Wyatt from hearing. 'I've seen your face when you're working with sound and it hurts like hell.'

'It's difficult to filter everything out. I can hear a great distance, but I have to concentrate on separating and identifying all the sounds. It's a lot of work and you know, when we open ourselves up for assault, we get slammed pretty hard.' He drew in a breath as he looked at the club. 'I've trained for this. Lily's exercises really helped. I noticed a difference right away, but I'll come away with a whopper of a headache.'

'Lily's exercises are to raise shields, not bring them down like you have to for something like this,' Ian pointed out. 'The trail is cold on this girl. I don't know that putting yourself in harm's way is very smart, Gator. I know you want to do this for your family but . . .'

'I want to do this because there's no one else looking

75

out for that girl. She didn't leave for the big city. She loves her family and she wouldn't cause them worry. Something happened to her – something bad and someone has to care about her.'

Ian nodded. 'I'm with you then, Gator. You pick up the information, any at all, and we'll be all over it.'

Shades of blue cast eerie shadows over the long strands of moss sweeping the water below the trees. The moon shed light across the bayou and the sound of authentic Cajun music traveled for miles. Flame stepped out onto the deck of the houseboat and flashed the old man sitting there a quick grin as she did a small pirouette. 'What do you think, *Monsieur le Capitaine*?' She held out her arms.

The faded blue eyes took in her form-fitting sheath of green with its kerchief hem, exposing one shapely thigh and hiding the other coyly. The dress clung to every curve, emphasizing her lush figure. The wide black velvet choker around her throat drew attention to her neck and the straight fall of silky red hair. Her eyes were enormous, a vivid green surrounded by long thick lashes. Most of all it was difficult to miss her sexy, pouting mouth.

The old man removed his pipe and cap, giving her a low bow. '*Cher*, you are too beautiful for words.'

She gave him a small curtsey. '*Bien merci!*' She did a small two-step across the deck to lean down and kiss his temple. 'I brought you a surprise.' She handed him a white pillowcase.

Burrell Gaudet glanced at her face and then pulled open the bag slowly. His eyes widened as he took in the cash. 'What is this?'

'You know very well what it is. Kurt Saunders stole your money. You had a legitimate business deal with the slimeball and he sent his men here to take your last payment so he could foreclose on your land.'

Flame had returned to the houseboat a week earlier, just after the place had been robbed. The captain was sitting with his head in his hands, his furniture smashed and his mattress torn apart. He'd blurted the truth out to her, that Kurt Saunders had sent his men over to steal the last of his payments for his land. Saunders was going to foreclose and he'd lose everything. 'I'm just returning what belongs to you.'

'Where did you get this?' he repeated, dazed, eyeing the bundles of cash.

She shrugged. 'I suggest you go to the bank and put it in an account immediately and get a cashier's check for Mr. Saunders. Otherwise, that money will be stolen just like your last payment.'

The captain sucked in his breath and peered around them, lowering his voice because sound traveled on the waterway. 'I told you to stay away from Saunders, Flame. He hurts people on the river. I told you before, I would find a better way to get the money.'

She winked at him. 'There is no better way. I'm good at what I do, *Capitaine*. He's been ripping you and your friends off for years. It was time someone taught him how it feels. Don't worry. No one saw me.' That wasn't exactly true, but she couldn't see Gator ratting her out. Whatever his agenda was, he would carry it out himself, not bring in Saunders. 'I didn't get caught and he'd never suspect me even if he sees us together eventually. I look too sweet and innocent.'

Burrell Gaudet shook his head. Flame looked anything but sweet and innocent. She looked a seductress, sultry and sinful, all curves and satin skin. Her mouth alone could provide a lifetime of fantasies. More than anything – the way she looked, the way she moved – it was her voice that turned heads. Sultry and velvet, pouring over a man's body until he remembered nothing else but that he was all man. Even at his age he wasn't entirely immune to her charm.

He closed his eyes briefly on the thought. He was an old man, but she had a way of moving, of talking, even smiling that was sheer come-on. The strange part was, now that he'd gotten to know her, she wasn't that way at all. She looked pure temptation, wild and untamed, made for the long slow nights on the bayou, but he hadn't seen her take up with anyone. He didn't know what was wrong with the boys in the parish, but if they didn't stand up when they saw her, he rated them fools.

'I told you not to be getting into trouble on my account, Flame. I won't have it.'

'I did it for the fun of it, *Monsieur le Capitaine*, no other reason. I like to stir the pot every now and then and see what floats to the surface.'

'Sometime, *cher*, it be best to leave the sludge on the bottom of the river.' Burrell looked down at his gnarled hands. There wasn't much left to him in the way of pleasure. He sat on the houseboat and listened to the music of the bayou, smoked his pipe, and played *boure* with his friends while telling old stories. The days of taking a ship up and down the Mississippi were long gone.

Flame had brought joy back into his life. Their meeting had been accidental. A young thief had stolen his wallet and his old knees wouldn't hold up to chasing the punk down. She had come out of nowhere, slamming a booted foot into the stomach of the fleeing pickpocket, taking the thief down in seconds and returning his property. They'd gone to the Café Du Monde and over beignets and café au lait he'd offered her a place to stay on his houseboat. He owned a small island, no more than swamp, mostly unusable, but it was his and it was going to stay that way. Unfortunately he'd purchased the land from Kurt Saunders and the man was determined to get the island back.

'Kurt Saunders has made a good living out of selling property and then taking it back when the balloon payment mysteriously disappears. We all know he steals the money, we just don' know how to catch him at it. I was warned not to buy from him, but I wanted my own land, *cher*, and I couldn't resist. He isn't going to take kindly to havin' the tables turned on him.'

'I saw the money, Burrell, you had the entire payment. And I followed them straight back to Saunders's private mansion in the Garden District. No wonder he lives like a king. He steals from everyone.'

'Should have kept the money in a bank. Thas why he sells to the river rats. He knows we don' trust the banks. I'm not the first he's swindled. 'Course none of us knew for certain it was him doin' the stealin'. We suspected, but none of us could prove it.'

'I told you before not to keep your money in the mattress with all that moss.' Flame rubbed his head affectionately. 'Some modern technology is really a good thing. And you don't fool me, Burrell. You had to be an educated man to captain a ship all those years on the Mississippi.'

'I was born and raised here, little missy, and I choose to fit in with my neighbors. It's the life I love, the one I want to finish out my days living.'

She grinned at him, unrepentant and pressing her point. 'If you're going to keep large amounts of money on your houseboat and you deal with sleazebags like Saunders, you should at least have some security on board. I can figure something out for you if you'd like.'

'No security system on my houseboat is going to

keep the likes of Saunders and his men from takin' what they want here on the river. You know that, girl.'

Her smile widened until she was smirking. 'Maybe not. But then he just got a good dose of his own medicine, now didn't he? He'd never suspect you, not in a million years. He'll just think his men missed one of your stashes and he'll be mad as hell at them, but he won't be able to do a thing about it.'

He took a long slow draw of his pipe, regarding her laughing face. The laughter never quite reached her eyes. There was something there, a hint of sorrow, a splash of wariness, whatever it was, that look was as addicting as the sultry heat of her voice. 'Kurt Saunders is a mean man, Flame. If he ever comes to suspect that you stole his money—'

'*Your* money,' she emphasized. 'I stole your money back.' A faint grin crept over her face. 'Of course, I grabbed everything in the safe and there might be a bit more than he took from you. Quite a bit more, but I have a few expenses of my own. And he had several disks in one of the briefcases, but no papers, nothing that should make him too upset. It was mostly cash and a lot of cash at that.'

'Loss of money will make him upset,' he pointed out. 'I should have known when you said you were thinking about taking the money back, that you'd do it. You shouldn't have, *cher*, but I'm going to take it to the bank and explain I've been holding it in my mattress all these years. Now that you've retrieved it, I might as well use it.'

'I thought you'd see it my way.'

'You can never tell anyone, Flame. Not ever. He'll come after you,' the captain cautioned.

She shrugged. 'Who would I tell? I'm not into bragging, *Capitaine,* just getting a little justice once in a while. Throw a bit of moss in the bag and mix it up a bit so it looks and smells authentic.' She glanced at her watch. 'I told Thibodeaux I'd be at his club tonight to do a little singing.'

'I don' like you going to the Huracan. That Thibodeaux, he runs a mean place. They're good people but they like to drink, dance, and fight. Or fight, drink, and dance, depending on how the day went. Looking like you do, Flame, you could be in big trouble with those boys.'

'I'm just going to do a little singing, Burrell, nothing else. There's no need for worry. I had a talk with Thibodeaux and he said he'd watch out for me.'

Burrell shook his head. 'This has something to do with Vivienne Chiasson telling you about her daughter's disappearance, doesn't it? I was watching your face when she told you about Joy and I didn't like what I saw.'

Flame sank into one of the tattered chairs beside him. 'Here's the thing, Burrell. I heard talk of a girl disappearing in another parish a couple of years ago. A couple of the men at one of the clubs mentioned it when they were talking about Joy. The cops said she left to find a better life, but her family and friends said she wouldn't do that. Isn't that what they said about Joy too? *You* told me yourself you didn't think she ran off.'

Burrell held up his hand. 'Everyone in the bayou, up and down the river, knows the story. The police don't believe the two disappearances are connected. Even most the families don' believe it. Joy was seeing a boy from the city. He was real sweet on her. His family has money and they think Joy isn't good enough. She broke it off, but he keep comin' around. I think he got mad when she say no to him one too many times.'

'A lot of the families around here think the same

thing, but what if they're wrong? What if Joy's disappearance and the other girl from a couple of years ago are related?'

'Why would you think so? They didn't know each other. They didn't look the same. There's no connection between them at all.'

'Yes there is.' She leaned closer to him, giving him a faint whiff of the fresh scent of peaches. 'They both had really distinctive voices. Like warm butter. Sexy. Sultry. Velvet. Smoky. Those words were all words used to describe their voices. All a sleazebag needs is a trigger to set him off, Burrell. Maybe these girls share that trigger.' She sat up straight and gripped the armrest of the chair tightly enough that her knuckles turned white. 'And maybe I have that same voice.'

'No! I forbid you doing this, Flame.' Burrell nearly dropped his pipe in his agitation. 'Those girls are gone. Some say dead, some say they ran, but I'm not going to let you risk your life to find out which it is.'

She shrugged. 'You're a dear to worry, *Capitaine,* but truthfully, I have a tiny problem with orders. I've never been good at following them.'

'You could get yourself into a bad situation,' he cautioned.

'Joy doesn't have anyone looking out for her. The cops buried the case and that means, wherever she is, whatever happened to her – she's alone. I have to find out for myself that this girl is off somewhere safe in a city, not dead . . . or being caged like a rat by some monster.'

He glanced at her sharply when her voice cracked. The boat creaked and rocked a bit with the lazy movement of the water. She held herself too still, her face without expression, and her eyes defied him to ask. He didn't. Whatever had happened to her went too deep, was there in the dark places of her mind and swirling for just a moment in her eyes. There was horror there – and knowledge of things he had never experienced and never wanted to. He reached out and patted her hand. 'Be careful.'

Flame forced a smile. 'I'm always careful. It's my middle name.' She turned her head to stare out over the water. The gentle waves lapped at the sides of the houseboat, creating a motion she found soothing. She was inexplicably tired lately. Instead of singing in a club with the crush of a crowd surrounding her, she wanted to lie in her bunk and pretend she had a home. Or maybe, even better, she'd go back to Gator's home and have tea with his grandmother.

'Why are you looking so sad, Flame?' Burrell asked.

'Was I?' She swallowed the lump in her throat. Why the hell was she so melancholy? Raoul Fontenot didn't matter. Nothing he said or did mattered.

'You never told me why a beautiful girl like you is all alone in this place,' the captain said, choosing his words carefully. 'Where's your family?'

'I don't have any family.' She was horrified to hear the words slip out aloud. She was gifted at making up stories, making them believable, and she never forgot her own lies. She could come up with a line of bullshit faster than anyone she knew, but she hadn't done that. She couldn't look at the captain. She didn't want to see pity in his eyes. Worse, in some ways, she'd compromised her own safety by telling the truth. She was a ghost, a chameleon, blending in with the local populace briefly and then simply vanishing. It was one of her greatest and most useful talents – and it was what kept her safe. She rubbed her temples to relieve a sudden ache.

'I don' have family either, *cher*. Maybe thas why we get along so well. You always have a place here with me, you know that don' you?'

She flinched at the compassion in his voice. It made her all too aware of what she was. Thrown away by a mother who didn't want her. Sold by an orphanage with too many children. Caged and treated more like an animal than as a human being. It never mattered how much she worked to educate herself, to improve herself, somewhere deep inside, in a place she protected and defended, she still felt like that unwanted child.

She forced a lighter note into her voice. 'Thanks, *Monsieur le Capitaine.*' Deliberately she looked at him, blew him a kiss. 'I'm a wanderer. I love to see new places. I can't imagine staying in the same place all the time. It's a good trait to have. If I didn't, I'd never have had the pleasure of meeting you.'

'You're good for an old man's soul, Flame.' His gaze narrowed on her choker. 'What's that on your neck? It looks like bruises.'

'Does it?' She fingered the choker, drawing it up closer around her trachea. 'How odd. I hope the dye isn't rubbing off. I'd better go check.' Before he could look again, Flame was already halfway across the deck to jerk open the door.

She inspected her neck beneath the choker. The bruises were darkening and spreading. Swearing softly, she tossed the choker aside and grabbed a scarf that nearly matched the color of her dress and wrapped it artfully around her neck. As long as she avoided Raoul Fontenot she'd be fine. Otherwise, he might very well take advantage and strangle her after what she'd said and implied to his grandmother.

Laughing aloud, she rejoined Burrell on the deck. 'It was the choker. Does this look okay?'

'Beautiful,' he replied, once more puffing on his pipe.

'You don't happen to know the Fontenot family, do

you? They live in this parish.'

The captain burst out laughing. 'Fontenot is a very common name in this part of the country, *cher*. I need a little more information.'

'I think the boys were raised by their grandmother. One of the boys is named Raoul and another Wyatt.'

Burrell sat back in his chair nodding. 'Good family. Oldest boy, Raoul took off to join the service but always sent his money to his grandmother to help care for the other boys. They're wild and Raoul had a certain reputation for fightin'.' He winked at her. 'All those boys have a way with the ladies, so you look out for them. Don' you go off with any of them and don' you believe their sweet talk.'

'No worries, *Capitaine*. I have no intention of ever getting that close to any of the Fontenot men.' She glanced again at her watch. 'I've got to go.' She leaned down to kiss the top of his head. 'You guard that money. Don't say a word about it until you have a cashier's check to give to Saunders. I'll go with you when you pay him off. You'll want a witness with you. And behave when I'm gone. I saw you giving old Mrs. Michaud that cute little come-on smile of yours.' She waved as she stepped off the houseboat into the airboat tied up beside it.

He waved her off with a dismissing hand and a pleased grin. The last she saw of him, he was happily puffing away on his pipe.

Chapter Five

Gator sat back in his chair, legs sprawled lazily in front of him, his fingers tapping a rhythm on the tabletop in beat to the music. The tapping allowed him to stay focused when each beat of the crashing instruments and the strands of conversations felt like nails pounding into his skull. He couldn't take much more. And it wasn't doing him a whole hell of a lot of good. He'd managed to hear two conversations regarding Joy. The first took place outside the walls of the cabin, whispered words of anger and conspiracy – brothers and friends wanting vengeance. In the second conversation two women had mentioned her in passing as they reminded each other to watch their drinks at all times.

He rubbed his temples, felt beads of sweat forming on his brow. Even his hair was slightly damp from the strain of sorting through the cacophony. Lily had been correct when she said the trick of listening to conversations at a great distance, even through walls, was to be able to sort out the multitude of noise. His head was about to explode. Even his teeth hurt. He needed to go somewhere quiet and peaceful, somewhere he could be alone to listen to the stillness of the night. He tried to suppress the sounds crowding in around him, but nothing worked. He reached inside of himself in an attempt to silence the myriad voices around him, to find the stillness in his mind that was his haven, but nothing could stop the noise from beating at his brain.

His stomach lurched. He was on serious overload. A stupid mistake. One he hadn't made since he'd first been psychically enhanced. He was going to have to get out of the club as fast as possible. He glanced at his brother, already talking up a pretty woman over at the bar. Beside him, Ian tossed peanut shells onto the floor along with everyone else, laughing as he did so. Neither seemed at all aware of Gator's predicament. Just as he pushed himself out of the chair, the door opened and Flame Johnson walked into the room.

Not walked. He couldn't say walked. She swayed. Gator lowered himself back into the chair, sliding farther into the corner, into the shadows, his gaze drinking her in. She was beautiful, sexy. Too sexy. Instantly he became aware of the other men, the way their hot gazes rested on her body and slid over her soft curves. She moved across the room, her dress molding to her soft skin and as far as he could tell, it didn't look like she was wearing panties.

Gator tried to drag air into his lungs, but there didn't seem to be a sufficient supply. Her head turned abruptly, as if she had radar, and her eyes met his right through the crowd. For a moment they were the only two people in the room. She frowned, her gaze moving very slowly over him, taking in the fine sheen on his skin and the dampness of his curling hair. She saw way beyond his easy smile. At once the noise receded and he became aware of a soft, soothing note humming through his mind. The pounding in his head eased along with his churning stomach. She turned away, talking with animation to Thibodeaux.

Gator sat very still, feeling the first astonishing wash of utter jealousy. He had never experienced the emotion, but recognized it for what it was. His attention narrowed until there was only Flame. He could see the smallest details there in the dim lighting and smell her scent in the midst of the crush of bodies. His every sense was acute, so sharp, he could almost inhale her. It was an experience he'd never forget, and he sat there, sprawled in his chair, unable to control his body's fierce reaction any more than he could his mind – and for a man like Gator, that was very dangerous.

His headache was gone, thanks to Flame. Why would she help him? Did she feel, in spite of herself, the same pull toward him that he felt toward her? He hoped so. He hoped he wasn't alone in his need to see her.

Flame stepped up the one stair to the stage. Thibodeaux considered the Hurican an upscale blues club because of the perfectly tuned piano he owned. The instrument sat in the midst of chaos and peanut shells, gleaming like black obsidian, highly polished, with white ivory keys, his shrine to the music he loved so much. No patron ever touched the piano, only the musicians. It was an unspoken rule, but they all understood Thibodeaux carried the baseball bat for a reason, and it wasn't because of the numerous fights that broke out. It was to keep the piano safe.

Flame went right up to the piano as though she owned it. She looked an elegant, classy lady as she seated herself on the bench, fingers poised over the keys, the uneven hem of her dress draped over her shapely legs. Thibodeaux hovered anxiously, bat wrapped in his meaty hands, his gaze on Flame as the first notes poured into the room.

Her voice was low and haunting, stealing into Gator's mind and holding him in some kind of thrall.

The first words of her song sank into his heart and soul, wrapping him up tightly, squeezing his insides so that her song was personal to him, only to him. Everyone else had dropped away. There was no other man in existence. Even the room dropped away so that they were wherever his imagination took them.

He could almost feel the softness of her skin as her voice beckoned to him, summoned him, trapped him in a web of sexual need and sensual stimulation. One song blended smoothly into the next, smoky notes transporting him into fantasies and making him weep inside for lost love and missed chances. It took effort to make his brain work when all he wanted to do was carry her off to a place where they could be alone.

His mind seemed sluggish, working at slow speed, and that bothered him. It made no sense why he couldn't turn his head and look at his brother to observe his reaction to her, he could only stare, transfixed at the woman playing the piano. He saw the silk of her red hair, individual strands begging to be touched. Her skin gleamed, impossibly soft and inviting. Her neck was slender, bare when she turned her head, driving him to the brink of insanity. All he could think about was pressing his mouth there and wandering, exploring, losing himself in the lushness of her body.

One song led into another while he struggled to control himself. His jeans were so tight he was afraid he'd burst, his aching, throbbing body hardened to the breaking point. In the end, he resorted to his old trick, tapping his fingertip on the table, establishing a counter beat, one he could concentrate on. Almost at once he realized how much power her voice wielded. Flame wasn't simply mesmerizing with her incredible, sultry voice, she was hypnotizing her audience with her music and he had fallen into the trap right along with everyone else.

He took a cautious look around. No one moved. No one drank. Every eye was on her, everyone entranced by the seduction of her smoky, sultry voice. She didn't look at them, didn't catch anyone's eye and flirt, she simply bent over the piano and allowed the music and song to carry her away. Her audience was transported right along with her into a world of satin sheets and steamy nights. He felt her under his skin, fingers stroking and teasing, her mouth hot satin . . .

Gator shook his head hard to clear his brain. She had an amazing gift, far too powerful for anyone, even Whitney, to conceive of. What would the doctor have done had he known she could captivate an audience the way she did? He was aware of the hypnotic effect of her voice, yet he still had to fight it. He tapped his finger harder on the table, counting out a rhythm in his mind to keep from losing himself in her voice. Lily would want to know. She maintained several contracts with the government along with a high-security clearance, and the government would definitely want to know what Flame could or couldn't do with her talent. It was no wonder there was a flag on a computer somewhere trying to monitor where she was and whom she associated with.

Where would that leave him? He rubbed his temples and hummed to himself to keep from drowning in her voice. He had the same gifts, the same talents. Once it was known, how much of a guinea pig would he become? And if his past experiments ever came out, if the government – or Lily – figured it out, what would they do to him? He'd probably be sitting right alongside Flame in a cage somewhere.

The last notes of music drifted away. Her haunting voice died away, and the patrons of the club began to come to life, glasses rattling, voices raising, feet shuffling, and the inevitable crunching of peanut shells. Flame rose gracefully and smiled at the band. 'I'm thirsty, any of you want a drink?'

'Oh, baby,' a man called out. 'I've got something for you to drink.'

Flame turned her head, her gaze moving over the heckler with bored tolerance. 'Lovely. But not happening.' She turned back toward the band, but Gator noticed she was in a defensible position and, although her head was averted, she was watching out of the corner of her eye.

Gator recognized Vicq Comeaux, one of a large family of brothers and cousins, mostly boys, he and his brothers had drunk and fought with since they were about fourteen.

Vicq yelled another lewd comment and pushed his way to the front of the crowd to stand directly in front of the stage. Something dark and dangerous swirled deep in Gator's gut. A stillness took over. His world narrowed, tunneled, until there was only the newcomer, him, and the red haze of temper riding him hard. The rest of the crowd disappeared. He stood up, a fluid easy motion that propelled him toward the heckler.

'Gator . . .' Wyatt stepped in front of him, put a placating hand on his arm. 'You don' want to be fightin' and me havin' to explain to *Grand-mere* what happened. She'll think I started it.'

Gator shook the hand off and stepped around his brother, brushing Ian's hulking frame out of his way as he proceeded toward the band. The crowd parted for him until he was standing directly behind Vicq Comeaux.

'I don' think you want to be sayin' anything else to my woman,' he said, his voice pitched low and soft, almost gentle. 'Not another word. You have anything

91

else you want to say, you do it my direction.'

There was instant silence. The music faltered as the band lowered their instruments and Flame turned back toward him. Gator barely registered the movement. His attention was completely focused on the man in the red shirt and cowboy boots.

'He's drunk, Gator,' Louis Comeaux said hastily, leaping up to defend his cousin. 'Vicq don' mean nothing by it.'

'She looks good enough to eat,' Vicq said, ignoring the men and taking a step up onto the small wooden platform that served to separate the band from the rest of the rowdy crowd. 'I'm hungry, baby. Come to Daddy.' He reached out to wrap his hand around Flame's bare leg.

The sound of flesh slapping against flesh was loud in the silence of the bar as Gator caught Vicq's arm to prevent him from touching Flame. Gator's hand squeezed Vicq's wrist like a vise, jerking him down and away from the singer. 'I guess you didn't hear me.' He enunciated each word between his teeth. 'You're about to become alligator bait. Leave my woman alone. Don' look at her. Don' talk to her and don' be thinking about her. I will tear you up and spit you out, do you understand what I'm saying to you?'

Vicq's first reaction was obviously to fight, but something in Gator's face must have given him pause. He shuffled his feet and looked toward his cousin, suddenly much more sober than he'd been minutes earlier.

'Gator.' Delmar Thibodeaux sidled up, baseball bat in hand. 'We don' want trouble. Not with you.'

Gator didn't glance at him, but kept his entire attention centered on Vicq. 'There isn't going to be trouble, Del, not unless Vicq here forgets to apologize to my woman for his big mouth. I don' take kindly to anyone speaking to her that way. Then he can sit quietly and enjoy the music and I'll buy him a drink, or he can leave and we'll call it good.' He never raised his voice, but it carried throughout the building.

Flame found she was holding her breath. Everyone's attention was so riveted on Gator and Vicq, they didn't notice the walls of the club expanding and contracting as if breathing. They didn't notice the vibration resounding through the wooden planks, or the peanut shells jumping on the floor. She saw a small crack begin to travel in the mirror behind the bar. Everything was going to go to hell fast, if something – or someone – didn't stop Gator.

She pushed past Vicq and slung one arm around Gator's neck. He didn't look at her, didn't break eye contact with Vicq. The floor trembled hard enough to be a small quake. Desperately, Flame circled Gator's neck with both arms, leaned her body into his and kissed him full on the mouth. She meant to get his attention. Nothing else. Only a small distraction.

Electricity sizzled and arced between his skin and hers. His mouth was hot and sexy, his arms coming up to trap her, to hold her even closer, so that his body was imprinted on hers. His strength was enormous. He took control of the kiss and damn him, he knew what he was doing. Fire raced through her veins, poured into her belly, and tightened her body. Her nipples peaked and she actually felt her womb contract.

She forced herself to pull away before it was too late, but even so, she had to cling to him like a weak-kneed groupie. Rubbing at her mouth, Flame glared at him for taking advantage of her. He knew his kiss affected her, she could tell by his quick, knowing grin and the sudden wicked glint in his dark eyes.

Gator slid his hands possessively over her rib cage to

her hips, leaned down and pressed kisses against her stomach.

'*Cher*. How is *mon enfant* this evening?' His voice was tender as if he cherished her. His breath was warm right through the thin material of her dress and his kisses incredibly intimate. 'You aren't giving your *ta mere* trouble are you?' His whispered words slipped inside her skin and wrapped around her heart to squeeze hard.

Flame froze. He was outrageous. She'd saved him. *Saved* him, the ungrateful wretch! And he was mauling her in front of the entire club. No one was going to make a move on her as long as he was around. It was clear even the infamous Delmar Thibodeaux with his silly baseball bat wasn't going to cross Raoul Fontenot.

She caught a fistful of his silky black hair and yanked his head up. 'What do you think you're doing?'

He caught her hand, pried open her fingers, and pressed another kiss to the center of her palm. 'I'm talking to our baby, *cher*. The doctors say babies can hear early. I want him to know the sound of his father's voice.'

She closed her eyes briefly, counting to ten. The chatter in the bar resumed as Louis Comeaux pulled his cousin away. Thibodeaux went back behind the bar and the band took a break. At once the jukebox was blaring. She noticed everyone was smirking. Gator was back in good graces. According to the law of the bayou, he had every right to protect what was his.

'Come outside with me,' Flame demanded.

Gator grinned at her, his dark gaze never leaving hers. 'I'd follow you anywhere, especially into the night.' Raising his voice he called to his brother. 'Wyatt, I'm leaving with *mon amour*. Catch you later.' His fingers shackled her wrist as she started toward the door. 'Stay right beside me.'

Flame shot him a venomous look. 'Don't think you can order me around.'

'You asked me to go outside with you, *cher*.' He pushed open the door but retained possession of her wrist. 'And I'm obliging.'

He was strong. She should have taken that into account, that whoever was sent after her would have had at least muscle mass enhanced. His body was fit. When he held her, he felt like iron pressed up against her, no give to his body at all. Flame let her breath out slowly, trying to swallow her anger as she moved away from the light and the possibility of anyone overhearing them.

'You can let go of me now.'

'Not quite yet.' His free hand slid down her back and over her buttocks, lower to her thighs. He pushed the hem of her dress up, his palm sliding over her bare bottom, finding the small tee of lace that disappeared between her bare cheeks. His hand moved lower still, between her legs to the inside, slipping over the soft skin of her thighs until he found the leather scabbard. Due to the uneven length of her dress, the knife was positioned high up on her thigh and as he removed it, his knuckles brushed multiple times against the most sensitive intimate spot between her legs.

Flame clenched her teeth together and refused to acknowledge the shock waves rippling through her body with each feather-light contact. 'Did you enjoy that?'

'More than you'll ever know.' He shoved the knife into a short leather scabbard looped through his own belt. 'My grandmother is expecting you for tea tomorrow. I told her I'd bring you.'

'I want my bike back.'

'Then I guess you'll be comin' for tea, won't you?' His grin widened. 'You do get yourself into scrapes, *cher*.'

'If you're referring to that drunken idiot, I could have handled him. I'm *working*. The last thing I need is for you to drive all the men off.'

His black brow shot up. 'Working? Working on what?'

She curled her fingers into two tight fists. 'It isn't any of your business what I'm doing. Suffice to say, I can't have you scaring men off.'

'Suffice to say, you're engaged to me and you're carrying my child. The entire bayou will know by morning. No other man is coming near you, not without me ripping his head off and everyone will think it's my right.'

'*You* told them all that.'

'I did announce the news,' he agreed smugly.

'Will you stop! This isn't funny. You know damn well I'm not pregnant and we're not engaged. So stop acting like a Neanderthal.'

'Oh, I beg to differ with you, *cher*. My grandmother believes you are carrying my child.' His palm slipped over her stomach, the lightest of touches, but it sent her pulse racing. 'She insists I do the right thing and marry you and I told her, of course I would. We're officially engaged.'

A sound of pure exasperation escaped. 'Look. Be reasonable. I know you may have a teeny reason to be upset over the knife at your throat, although you did steal my bike, but I can explain to your grandmother . . .'

He shook his head. 'She has a heart condition. I don't want her upset in any way. You should have thought about consequences before you told such a whopping lie. My grandmother values family and tradition. It would kill her if I didn't live up to my responsibilities, especially involving a child. And you can take responsibility for your lie. You told an elderly woman

96

with a heart condition something bad about her beloved grandson. She wants it fixed.'

Flame let her breath out in a long hiss. 'Listen, you lunkhead. You brought this on yourself, not me. All I wanted was my bike. You shouldn't have taken it.'

He glanced at the airboat, relatively rare for the patrons of the Huracan. 'That your rig?'

'Yes. And I didn't steal it, either.'

'No, just the money that paid for it.' He took her arm and propelled her toward the edge of the pier. 'Let's go.'

She resisted, stepping closer to the boat, more to get away from his touch than to obey him. 'I'm not going anywhere with you unless I have my knife.'

'Oh, for God's sake, get in the damned boat.' He picked her up, his hands hard, biting into her waist, and tossed her into the airboat. 'If I was going to kill you, Flame, you'd be dead already.'

She glared at him, rubbing her sides where his fingers had dug into her skin. 'You just think you're that good.'

'I know I am.' He deliberately crowded her, so close he could smell her faint perfume. She stepped away from him, just as he knew she would, giving him control of the airboat.

She stayed a distance away from him, watching him closely as he took them out into the bayou. 'You may as well relax, Flame. I can't very well kill you and dump your body in the bayou, as tempting as that may be for me. My grandmother comes first and she wants to see you tomorrow. I promised her you'd be there.'

'Why?'

He was aware she was listening intently to his voice. Sound was their world and it was also their greatest ally. He could manipulate sound waves and interject the exact notes needed into his voice to convince others of his utter sincerity – with the possible exception of Flame. He wasn't certain how to answer her because he didn't know what the truth was.

His grandmother wanted to see her again. Nonny was shrewd. She probably didn't believe for a moment that Flame was pregnant, but it suited her to make them all think she did. She was demanding he bring Flame home again. More than that, she wanted a firm commitment out of him to 'make things right'. He had no idea what she was up to, but he respected her judgment. He also realized Flame would never allow him close to her without a good reason.

'In spite of what you might think, *cher*, I love my grandmother. If she wants to get to know you better, then I'm bringing you home.'

It was the wrong way to put it. Gator could see that immediately. Her eyes flashed hotly at him, a quick glimpse of temper and then she turned her face away, obviously struggling for control. She brought out the worst in him, the need to dominate, the need to possess, traits he usually kept under wraps. He wasn't the easygoing man he presented to the world, and Flame was seeing the real Raoul, not the one he usually projected. It wasn't like he could take the words back and he meant them, damn it. He was going to bring her home, one way or the other.

'You go for the best, don't you, Flame?' He put genuine admiration into his voice. 'This is a nice rig. What kind of engine?' Anything to change the subject and judging by her motorcycle, the woman knew and valued good machinery.

'V-eight, very powerful,' she answered. Her eyes immediately went bright and she ran her hand over the seat. 'Runs through shallow water like butter and does the same on land. She's fast too, even hauling weight, and she turns on a dime.'

He took the opportunity to run the boat down the narrow channel and out into more open water. Neither spoke as he put the airboat through its paces, deliberately making a ninety-degree turn, giving Flame time to relax with him. She was a natural on the boat, the same way he was certain she was with the motorcycle. 'You like toys.'

For some reason, the way he lowered his voice, the note of sensuality, made her blush and lower her gaze. He was immediately aware of the tension stretching between them. His body still ached and it was a miracle he could walk. It was no wonder Vicq Comeaux had tried to approach her. He was surprised there hadn't been a riot.

'What was that all about?'

'I beg your pardon?' She tilted her head, slightly haughty, princess to peasant.

'At the club tonight. What was that all about?' He tried not to be angry. Or jealous. What the hell did he have to be jealous about? But she damn well had better not have been looking to take a man home.

'Is it any of your business?'

'I'm making it my business so pretend it is and answer me. Do you have any idea how dangerous that was? What if those men had gotten out of hand? There could have been a riot and quite frankly, *cher*, I wouldn't blame them.' He rubbed his hand down the front of his jeans in a casual display. 'I'm still feelin' the effects and I knew your song, your *voice,* was a weapon.'

Her color deepened. 'It's never been that strong before. That was your fault. You were amplifying my power.'

'I was not. Don' you go blamin' me for that little

99

exhibition. You were deliberately drawing men to you and you were very effective.'

'I'm telling you, it wasn't all me. I can keep everyone . . .' she hesitated, searching for the right word. 'Enthralled. I can soothe people and I can draw them to me, but it's never been like that before. You were amplifying me.'

'I'm not an amplifier,' he denied.

'How would you know? Are there others like us? With the same talents? You stopped the guard dogs from barking. You're just as capable of manipulating sound as I am. You let Whitney make a freak out of you when you had a family. A home. People who love you.' She stepped close to him, itching to slap his face, fury building so that the water churned around the airboat. 'You threw it all away. What did he promise you? Money? Power? What did he give in return for your family, Raoul?'

Gator guided the boat into the middle of the canal and cut the engine. There were only the sounds of the bayou, the hum of insects, and the splash of water. 'Tell me what you were doing in the club tonight and I'll tell you why I volunteered to be a genuine psychic guinea pig.'

'Why does it matter so much to you what I was doing?' Flame regarded him uneasily.

'It just does. You were deliberately stirring the men up. You wanted them obsessed with you. Why?'

'I don't trust you.'

'You don't have to trust me. We're out here all alone. Search me if you think I'm recording this. If I wanted you dead, you'd be buried in the swamp.' He swung away from her, an abrupt, angry movement, unlike his usual grace.

'Why are you so angry with me?' It shouldn't have

100

bothered her. She didn't care if he was upset with her – he was nothing to her – but it did. She could tell his inclination was to shake her. The sexual web between them was strong. She'd never experienced such a thing before and their antagonism toward each other only seemed to add fuel to the fire.

'What the hell were you doing in the club tonight?'

Flame waited until he turned back toward her, until his dark, angry, turbulent gaze met hers. He was smoldering with temper, his fist opening and closing, his easy charm obviously wearing thin.

'Do you have any idea what could have happened to you in there? Do you *want* men to be so obsessed they can't control themselves?' He took an aggressive step toward her.

She stood her ground, one hand steadying herself on the seat of the boat, refusing to be intimidated. She was never intimidated. She could easily protect herself, whether he had her knife or not. His eyes glittered at her with a kind of fury she found intriguing rather than terrifying. Raoul Fontenot was a man who liked to portray himself as easygoing but beneath the veneer was a man of intense passions, of dark secrets, a man he kept hidden from the rest of the world.

'I absolutely did not expect that to happen. Obviously you were affected and it's upset you. Did you think you'd be exempt from the effects? Have you checked out the weapons they have now or are in the process of developing? They actually have everything now, from acoustic beams and blast waves to my personal favorite, the acoustic bullet, high-powered, very low-frequency waves emitted from one to two meter antenna dishes that result in blunt-force trauma, affecting anything from discomfort to death. Surprise, Raoul, even the shooters can be affected if they aren't behind the device used to produce the sound. You and I, we're basically human acoustic bullets. We can get into and out of places fast and without being seen and we don't need an antenna.' Her eyes widened. 'You were created after me, weren't you? And you amplify my talent, don't you?'

'Don't you look at me like that.'

'Like what?'

'Like you suspect me of some conspiracy.' He swore in Cajun, a blast of words so fast she was hard put to keep up with him.

Flame remained silent, intrigued by the way he looked when his ancestry came out. He was a good-looking man, rough around the edges with his blue-shadowed jaw, but the thick black wavy hair and ready smile provided the killer charm. 'It simply occurred to me that Whitney wanted to see what would happen if we were together.'

'Whitney is dead.'

'You keep telling yourself that.'

'Tell me what you were doing at the club tonight.'

Flame sighed. 'You're like a bear with a sore tooth. I was trying to lure a particular person to me. A girl disappeared a few weeks ago. She was a singer, had a beautiful sultry voice. The cops think she picked up and left the area because it's convenient for them to think that. But her family and everyone who knew her think something happened to her. And I do too.' Her voice was pitched low, not in the least remorseful or defiant.

There was a long silence. Too long. It stretched out between them until she could feel the full weight of his disapproval. 'You're telling me, you set yourself up as bait for what could be a killer because a girl you don't even know disappeared? Have you lost your mind or do you just have a death wish?'

'I don't have to justify my actions to you.'

'You don't have backup. I don't go on a mission without backup. That's just plain stupidity.' He stepped closer, his fingers settling around her upper arms.

Flame felt the tremor running through him. 'Let go of me before I push your butt into the bayou. Talk about stupidity! You had everything and you threw it away. At least I have a good reason for the things I choose to do.'

'Like stealing from Saunders, who, by the way, I had investigated and he's about as mean as they come. He's suspected of having ties to the underworld—'

She jerked away from him. 'Like I didn't know that already? I do my homework.' Red hair went in all directions as she shook her head. 'I'm not exactly a team player. I make decisions based on percentages and the percentages were in my favor this time. The girl . . .'

'Joy Chiasson,' he supplied, his gaze on her throat. When she'd turned her head, the scarf she wore slipped. He moved even closer, crowding her, his body brushing hers. 'Our two families have known one another for years. I came here to find out what happened to her.' He broke off, his attention diverted. His fingertip brushed the dark marks on her throat. His fingerprints. 'Did I do this?'

She lifted a hand to hide the marks, but he stopped her, this time much more gently. 'I'm sorry, Flame. I didn't mean to hurt you.'

'I had a knife to your throat. I think the situation was a little tense.' Her voice was suddenly husky, a little too intimate. 'Did you really come to New Orleans to look for Joy?' Why hadn't she moved away from him? He was so close she felt his heart beat. And why was she whispering?

'Yes. My grandmother asked me to come. When she told me Joy was missing, I remembered another woman, a singer from another parish who disappeared a couple of years ago. I thought the fact that they both had incredible voices was worth checking into. And I don' like *Grand-mere* to be upset.'

'Because of her heart.'

'Because I love her and she rarely asks me for anything. But I'm not going to lie to you. Lily asked me to find you, if possible, and persuade you to join us.'

Flame stepped away from him, her eyes suddenly hard and sparkling with temper. 'And just how would Miss Lily know I was in New Orleans?'

'She ran the probabilities of you coming here through a computer.'

'She knew the fire at the sanitarium would draw me out. They made a hit on Dahlia, didn't they?' She turned completely away from him, but not before he caught the glitter of tears in her eyes. 'I didn't find her in time.'

'The GhostWalkers found her in time,' Gator said. 'Dahlia's alive and well and very safe. In fact she's married to a buddy of mine.'

Chapter Six

Flame sucked in her breath sharply. 'I don't believe you.'

'I don't care if you believe §me. She's married to another GhostWalker, Nicolas Trevane.' Gator raked a hand through his hair in agitation until waves spilled across his forehead. 'Okay. That was a lie. I do care that you believe me. Why would I lie?'

'To get me to go back with you. I'm never going back with you, not for any reason. You're a smart man. Do you think the government and Whitney are going to sink millions of dollars into experimental weapons and then just let them run around loose? You aren't that stupid. You're either up to your neck swimming in their cesspool or you've been brainwashed.'

'You could be wrong, you know,' Gator pointed out. 'You might consider that.'

'You might consider that Lily wasn't the only one of us with an enormous IQ. If I'm wrong, why do we have this thing between us?' She stuck her chin in the air and fiddled with the edges of her scarf, but her gaze was steady on his, almost a challenge.

'Which thing? The knife? The bike? The baby? Or the sexual attraction that, quite frankly, might be off the Richter scale?'

'The sexual attraction. That's what's really making you so angry, isn't it? You don't trust it any more than I do. And you're angry with me for making you feel the way you do.'

'Yeah. Maybe. But I'm not the only one royally pissed about it,' he pointed out.

'You're right, I don't like it. I don't trust you. Why the hell would I feel attracted to you?'

'My charm and good looks.'

'You aren't that charming. And you have the despicable reputation of being a hound dog. I know because I asked around *and* your grandmother told me.'

'No doubt to endear me further to you.'

She narrowed her gaze. 'You're a breaker of hearts. A rake and a playboy.' She made a face. 'A *disgusting* playboy who isn't even concerned with safety issues.'

'*Grand-mere* didn't say that, did she?'

She smirked at him. 'Well, you got me pregnant, didn't you?'

A faint smile stole over his face. 'I guess I did. I'm potent. Even from a distance.'

'That's a scary thought. Do you really know Joy Chiasson?'

'Yes. You can ask *Grand-mere Nonny* all about her tomorrow when you show up for tea. Our families have been friends for years.'

Flame spread her hands out. 'So what are we doing out here in the middle of the night?'

'We're talking truce, *cher.*' His slow smile matched the warm molasses in his drawl.

'Don't you think before we talk truce it would be a gesture of good faith to give me back my motorcycle?'

'Have you shoved my brother's Jeep into the Mississippi yet?'

'That was on the schedule for tonight.'

'It's my brother's Jeep,' he reminded her, fingertips tracing the smudges on her throat. 'Not mine. I just borrowed it.'

'Bad decision on his part to lend it to you.'

His eyes darkened as his gaze drifted over her throat. 'I'm sorry about this, *cher*. I could kiss it better for you.'

She remained absolutely still beneath his touch, her heart beginning to hammer in time to the blood roaring through her veins. The heat of the bayou enveloped them in the perfume of the night and the rich rhythm of life. 'You aren't going to seduce me into cooperating with you and, if you try, the Jeep definitely goes into the Mississippi.'

'It was a bad decision on his part to lend it to me.' Gator murmured the words against her soft throat, his body pressed against hers, although he didn't wrap his arms around her. He simply stood leaning into her, the warmth of his breath touching her skin.

She swallowed hard when his lips pressed against her throat, feather-light, velvet soft. 'So you're willing to sacrifice the Jeep.'

'Damn straight, *mon petite enflamme*. No sacrifice is too great.' His tongue swirled over the dark smudges as if to soothe them.

Her breath left her body in a little concentrated rush. 'Well then, you'd better do a very thorough job.'

He lifted his head, his gaze sweeping over her face. 'When I kiss you, what exactly are you planning to do?' Raw huskiness mixed with suspicion in his voice.

She could barely breathe. She had an unfamiliar urge to circle his neck with her arms and press her body tightly against his. 'You said no sacrifice was too great,' she reminded.

'That's when I thought the sacrifice was going to be

my brother's Jeep. Now, I think you have something
else in mind. What are you planning to do?'

'Retrieve my knife, of course,' she answered honestly.

His head bent an inch lower until she could feel the
velvet of his lips brushing hers. 'You don't think I can
distract you?'

'You've been distracting me all evening, but no, if you
kiss me, the knife is definitely back in my possession.'

He ached to kiss her. The temptation was overwhelming, but he wasn't nearly as stupid as she thought
him. Reluctantly he stepped back away from her, a faint
smile on his face. '*Cher*, we've got us a problem.'

Her gaze brushed the front of his jeans. 'You more
than me.'

His eyes darkened. 'Oh, I don' think so, *mon amour,*
and if you want me to prove it to you, just come
closer and let me touch you.'

'Try it and I'll definitely slap your face.'

His grin widened. 'You are wet for me, aren't you,
cher?'

She ran her tongue along her lower lip, her gaze hot.
'More than you'll ever know. Too bad you're such a
chicken.'

'You're playing a very dangerous game, Flame,' he
said.

'You're the one with my knife and motorcycle.'

'That's not why. You think this is all part of another
experiment, don't you?'

'Isn't it?' She moved into the heat of his body, her
hips pressed close. 'When you're with other women,
is it this intense? Do the women you meet make you
feel like tearing off their clothes right there, right that
moment, and the hell with everything you've ever
believed and valued?'

'If you know I feel that way, why the hell are you tempting me out here in the middle of nowhere when we're alone? What you did in that club was wrong and what you're doing to me right now is wrong and with another man, you could be in trouble.' Something dark and frightening burned briefly in the shadows of his eyes and was gone almost immediately.

Flame shook her head, her expression defeated. 'That's just it, Raoul, *I'm* not the one doing it. You are. We are. Don't you get it?' She pushed a hand through her hair, scattering pins so that strands of red hair fell in all directions. 'You do get it. You knew what I was thinking, because you were thinking the same thing. It's all part of Whitney's experiments. Take me back. It's been a long day and I want to go home.'

She did look tired. And sad. And very alone. Gator turned her accusations over and over in his mind. 'It would be impossible to manipulate the sexual chemistry between two people wouldn't it?'

'Why would it be? He manipulated everything else, didn't he? He was building the perfect army. The perfect weapons. The perfect agents.' She sank down, looking up at him from the seat. 'Whitney had years to work things out. And somebody knew he was doing it. Somebody helped him. He wasn't alone in this, he couldn't have been.'

Her twisted logic was beginning to make sense to him and that was alarming. 'I go out on missions all the time with the GhostWalkers. Of the missing girls, only Lily and Dahlia have been found. And now you.'

'What a shocker that is. Maybe we're all his little puppets and he's playing us. You don't want to consider that could be what's happening because that would bruise your ego. You think you chose what happened to you so that somehow makes me the poor victim and you the hero in charge of your life. If what I'm saying is this truth, that makes you a victim right along with me and you just can't stand the thought.'

Gator turned over the words in his mind. The logic of her argument. If she was right he was no more than a programmed robot, a marionette and Whitney was pulling his strings. Worse than that, she was right. On some level he had thought of her as a victim, hell, all of the GhostWalkers thought that way. The women had been bought and experimented on. The men had chosen to be heroes, to save the world. He erupted into another long passionate string of inventive and crude curses.

'I'm sorry to rock your world. But if you're in with Whitney, and you're doing what he wants you to do by coming here and trying to take me back with you, at least consider that he's playing you. Whitney never does anything that doesn't benefit Whitney.'

'Damn it, the man is dead.'

'Do you realize you didn't answer a single question tonight, Raoul?'

'Just don't talk anymore. Damn it anyway.' He was silent as the boat sped through the canal, his features etched in stone.

Flame couldn't take her eyes off of him. She felt sad for him. Sad for her. She didn't even know why.

There was a small silence as the airboat moved up the canal. As the pier came into view, Gator glanced at her, his gaze moving over her dress, her legs, the curve of her bottom. 'I don't want you doing it anymore.'

'It?' Her eyebrow shot up.

'Don' give me trouble. You know what I'm talking about. Don' go tryin' to lure Joy's fate to you. If someone took her, or killed her, the same thing could happen to you. You don't even have backup. You don't

110

have anyone to watch out for you.'

Flame shrugged. 'That's something I'm used to, Raoul. I'm not a team player.'

'I've searched for Joy for four weeks. My brother, Ian, and I have been all up and down the bayou. We've questioned everyone. We've even looked in shacks and investigated every tip we were given. Joy's disappeared and I'm not having the same thing happen to you.'

'I'm not Joy. I can take care of myself.'

His dark gaze flickered over her face and there it was again, that something undefined she couldn't quite catch, but that made her shiver. 'You couldn't have stopped me if I was a different sort of man.'

She shrugged her shoulders. 'Think what you like. Men always do.'

'I'm not arguing with you about this. And be at my house tomorrow by two for tea. *Grand-mere* expects you.'

'Why in the world would I show up?'

'Two reasons.' He jumped onto the pier and tied up the boat, reaching back to offer her his hand. 'You want your motorcycle and any woman who would risk her life to find out what happened to a stranger is not going to disappoint an old woman with a heart condition.'

'Does she really have a heart condition or are you making that up?'

'I don' lie about my grandmother. Don't be getting the men riled up again and don't be setting yourself up as bait, or you and I are going to have a fight you aren't going to win.'

She looked him in the eye, waiting for him to release his hold on her. 'I don't like you very much.'

'That's too bad. When you sleep with me, you'll just have to pretend.' His fingers reluctantly slid from her wrist.

'Who says I'm sleeping with you?'

Deliberately he crowded her body, aggression in every line of his much larger frame. 'Let's put it this way, you won't be sleeping with anyone else, so if you want to get rid of all that heat, you'd better be thinking of me, *cher*.'

She didn't back up an inch. 'Go fuck yourself.'

Palming her knife, he moved closer still, his hand traveling over the curve of her bottom, sliding beneath the hem of her dress to shove the knife back into the scabbard. All the while his knuckles brushed bare skin, the back of his hand massaging the damp heat between her legs. His breath was warm against her ear. 'I'd much rather fuck you and judging by your panties, I'd say you feel the same way.'

'I ought to make you eat that knife.' She didn't move away from him or his probing hand. She stood face-to-face, eye-to-eye, staring him down, a quiet fury burning in her eyes. She hated that her body burned for him. She hated that she might actually enjoy his stupid sense of humor. Most of all she hated that he was a puppet for a man who played God with people and moved them around like pieces on a chessboard.

'I'm going to kiss you. If you stick me with that thing, make it somewhere not important to me.' He gathered her to him, his arms locking around her, hands sliding up her back. His body was hard and hot and thick with need and he rubbed against her, massaging the terrible ache as he bent his head to hers.

Flame lifted her mouth to his, meeting him halfway, the slow burn igniting instantly when her lips touched his. His tongue swept into the moist heat of her mouth, the craving for her so strong it shook him. He felt an answering tremor run through her body as she melted into him, all soft flesh and lush curves. He tasted sex

112

and sweetness and fury mixed together in a powerful concoction.

She was addicting, potent, the chemistry between them highly volatile. He wasn't simply kissing her, he was devouring her, feasting on her, long, hard kisses over and over because it wasn't enough. Her breasts were soft temptations against his chest and when she rubbed her leg over his thigh, aligning their bodies more closely, the breath left his body in a mad rush.

It was torment, his body so tight and hard he thought his skin might burst. His blood pounded and thunder roared in his ears. 'Come to my cabin with me.' He bit her lip, sucked it into his mouth and teased with his tongue. 'Right now. Forget everything else and come home with me.'

Flame fought her every instinct to climb on top of his body. 'I didn't know you had your own cabin. You're staying with your grandmother.' The temptation of being alone with him in a cabin with a bed was more than she could think about. Her brain was on total meltdown.

'When I visit, I stay with her. The cabin is small, a hunting cabin but it has a bed.' He kissed her again, long, ferociously, a wicked combination of command and coaxing, his hands sliding down to her bottom to lift her closer.

Flame became aware of her leg wrapped around his waist, of her hands under his shirt caressing his bare chest, of the heaviness of her breasts and the terrible throbbing between her legs. She had never wanted any-one the way she wanted him. Her need seemed beyond lust, beyond attraction, bordering on obsession. She tore herself out of his arms, stumbling backward toward the edge of the pier.

It was more reflex than thought that allowed Gator to

reach out and steady her, preventing her from falling into the reed-choked water. They stared at each other, both fighting for control.

'Let's not do that again,' Flame said, shaken.

'I was thinking we should do that all the time,' he countered. 'You have the right name. I thought for a minute there I might go up in smoke.' His grin flashed at her, a quick teasing smile that made her heart do some silly flip.

Flame wiped her swollen lips with the back of her hand. She could still taste him in her mouth and feel him imprinted on her body, pressed deep into her bones like a brand. 'In case you aren't paying attention, they're fighting inside.' Her voice was so low, so husky she hardly recognized it. She couldn't look away from his gaze, held captive there like a hostage.

'I hear them. Ian and Wyatt can hold their own. They're fighting with Louis and Vicq, which isn't surprising. Our two families have been fighting since we were about five years old.'

The door behind them opened and Raoul spun around to watch as the crowd poured out of the Huracan Club. He took two steps to place his body between Flame and the throng of men, many still fighting as they spilled out into the yard and onto the pier. Several large men surrounded Emanuel Parsons and his son James as they pushed their way toward the relative safety of the end of the pier.

The older Parsons wore a long trench coat and with his silver hair and cane looked very out of place in the midst of the fighting crowd of men. His son, sporting a darkening eye and a swollen lip, shook off his bodyguard's hand as the group neared Gator and Flame.

'Raoul Fontenot,' Emanuel Parsons offered his hand. 'I met you at a fund-raiser a few years back.'

114

'I remember,' Gator said. 'This is my fiancée, Flame Johnson.'

Parsons's eyes flicked over her. 'You're quite lovely, my dear. I've heard you sing a few times. Have you considered singing professionally? I can make a few phone calls if you're interested.'

Flame flashed a perky smile, eyes wide with awe, her gaze flicking toward the bodyguards and the shadowy driver always in the background. 'Really? Do you think my voice is that good?' She took Gator's outstretched hand and allowed him to pull her to his side. He curved his arm around her waist rather possessively, but she let it stay there while she observed Parsons's son. This was the man who had been engaged to the missing Joy. The man who swore he didn't know what happened to her. Joy's brothers had obviously taken a couple of shots at him in the middle of the brawl.

James Parsons stood slightly behind and to the side of his father, avoiding the stare of the bodyguards, uncomfortable in his role as the son of a powerful man. He stole hot licentious glances at Flame, but didn't speak to her and his father didn't bother with introductions. James was a handsome man, but to Flame looked spoiled and petulant, bored with his father talking to the locals and irritated that he didn't get an introduction when he so obviously wanted one.

No doubt he got that spoiled, bored look from his father. The older man had worn the same expression the night she'd spotted him in the club in New Orleans when several businessmen sat at his table with him drinking, making certain he had picked up the tab. James didn't want to step forward on his own and introduce himself; it would lessen his importance in his own eyes. She wasn't going to pander to his ego by noticing him. Behind him, the driver, who obviously observed

James's sulky behavior, winked at her.

The crowd behind them fought ferociously, slamming one another to the ground and into the sides of the cabin. The porch creaked ominously as bodies hit the supports, and the sound of bottles breaking was loud in the night.

'Yes, I do believe your voice is that good and I have an ear for talent.' The elder Parsons ignored the raging fight around them as if it didn't exist. He snapped his fingers and his driver stepped forward to pull a card out of a slim silver case. Emanuel Parsons took the card and handed it to her. 'This is my private line. If you really want to see if you can make a go of it, give me a call and I'll see what I can do to make it happen.'

Flame smiled up at him, all white teeth and wide innocence, properly awed that he could have connections in the music industry. Gator's fingers dug into her wrist as she reached out and took the card, clutching it to her chest as if the man had given her a priceless gift. A large man slammed into the driver, was pushed off, and fell into the water with a loud splash.

The tallest bodyguard leaned in close to Emanuel Parsons to whisper in his ear. 'Sir, we should leave,' he advised. 'This is getting out of hand and there's a lot of sentiment against your son.'

Emanuel Parsons quelled the man easily with one look. The bodyguard retreated and James smirked, obviously enjoying that his father had reprimanded him publicly.

'What brings you back to the bayou, Raoul?' Parsons asked. 'I'd heard you were in the service. Are you out? I always have work for a good man.'

'No, sir.' Gator shook his head. 'Home visiting kin. My grandmother lives here and I have three brothers in the area.'

A large body flew past them to land hard against the post with a thud. Parsons smiled and shook his head. 'I remember the good old days whenever I came out to the Huracan. It's always a breath of fresh air. It was a pleasure to meet you, Flame.' He reached for her hand, carried it to his lips, dropping it just as quickly and turning away before she could reply.

Flame scowled after them, rubbing her knuckles against Gator's shirt. 'Ew. He tongued me.'

'Anyone would tongue you given the chance.' He took her hand and rubbed the pad of his thumb across her knuckles. 'I'll kick his ass for you if you want me to.'

'I'll kick his ass if I want it kicked. What did you think of his son?'

'If that was Joy's former fiancé,' Gator said, 'he didn't look all that broken up to me. He was eyeing you like you were whiskey and he had a long thirst.'

'Lovely way to put it, but I think you're right. He probably dated Joy to put his daddy's nose out of joint. There's definitely an elitist syndrome buried deep in that family.' She glanced down at the card in her hand. It didn't even have Parsons's name, only a telephone number in a raised black font on a pale linen background. 'Very elite.'

'I saw the videotape of James's interrogation when the police questioned him about Joy's disappearance. He appeared very broken up. I think our boy has acting skills.'

'Maybe he actually took acting classes,' Flame said. 'It would be easy enough to find out. Quite frankly he gave me the creeps. I don't know what Joy saw in him.'

'Flash. Money. He's smooth enough and if he has the acting skills to pull it off, he probably convinced her he was in love with her.'

117

'Until Daddy objected and humiliated her in front of his entire family,' Flame said, an edge to her voice. 'He did it on purpose. Her mother told me all about it.' She whirled out of the way as one of the Comeaux brothers staggered backward and nearly bumped into her.

'Maybe James needs his father to object to his choices to make himself feel more important or to enjoy her humiliation.'

'And prove to himself that he was above everyone else. He's a rat bastard,' Flame declared.

'We don't know for certain,' Gator pointed out. 'And for the record, have you ever referred to me as a rat bastard?'

'Yes, several times, but in a different way. He's a slimeball rat bastard. You're just a plain old garden variety man-type rat bastard.'

'Thanks for clarifying.'

'Anytime.' She smirked at him.

'Flame?'

'I'm going now.'

'Put the knife away.'

She glanced down at her hand. She'd pulled the knife without even being aware of it when Comeaux had nearly plowed into her. She held it low, blade up, close to her body, already in a fighting stance, light on the balls of her feet. 'You don't like it?'

'It's sexy as hell, *cher*, but I don' want these men to get the idea you're a wild woman. I'd be in a fight every night. Go home where I don't have to worry about you.'

She turned her back to the club and slipped the knife away, glancing over her shoulder at him. 'You mean they'd like it if they knew I carried a knife.'

'They'd be lining up to marry you.'

She flashed him a tentative smile, the first time she

looked less than assured. 'You're a little bit crazy, aren't you?'

'Yes. Keep that in mind before making any decisions to cheat on me after we're married with several children and you think life is too tame.' The moment the teasing words slipped out, he knew he'd blown it. A man named Whitney had taken her past from her and as far as he knew, the man had probably taken her future as well.

Her smile faltered for all of a microsecond and then it was back in place as she stepped aboard the airboat. 'Have fun, Raoul.' She waved toward the brawling men. Ian stood taller than most of them and stood out easily fighting at Wyatt's back. 'I know you're dying to join in.'

'You want me to escort you home, *cher*?' He didn't want her to go. He wanted to hold her, keep her safe somehow. Change her life. Change her mind about him.

She shook her head regretfully. 'I'm not falling for the gentlemanly act. You just want to know where I live.'

'Where do you live?' He watched her start the boat, his heart beating too hard and the urge to stop her so strong he was afraid to move, afraid he might actually try to stop her. She was heartbreaking and she was lethal.

She froze, turning her head so that her gaze met his squarely. 'Did you plant a homing device on the airboat?'

'Of course.' He flashed her a cocky grin and forced his body to move away from her, back toward the fighters. Behind him he heard her mutter something rude that sounded suspiciously like 'rat bastard,' but he didn't turn around. As he waded through the combatants, he heard the airboat retreating down the canal.

''Bout time you showed up,' Wyatt called, grinning

119

unrepentantly at him. He took a solid punch on the jaw that made Gator wince.

Gator spun around the man who'd hit his brother and landed a one-two punch combination that dropped him to the ground. Ducking a wild fist he shoved someone hard and managed to make it across the last couple of feet to Wyatt.

'So if you had to choose between being slimeball rat bastard' – he jerked his head aside to escape another fist and lashed out with his foot, dropping his opponent – 'or a common garden variety man-type rat bastard, which would you choose, Wyatt?'

Catching one of the two men driving his brother backward, he tossed him aside and went after the second man. Wyatt bent over, catching his breath, grinning as Gator easily dropped his adversary. 'Watching you fight is a thing of beauty, Gator.' He rubbed his sore jaw. 'I'd be the slimeball, bro. I wouldn't want anyone thinking I was common, you know?'

Gator hit him square on the jaw, dropping him like a sack of potatoes. Wyatt crawled over to the wall and fished around until he found the beer he'd brought out with him. Sitting on the ground he leaned his head back and grinned. 'Guess that was the wrong answer. You didn't score, did you, bro?'

'Shut up before I break that bottle over your head.' Gator shoved another victim out of his way and stomped inside.

The club was in a bit of disarray and he righted a couple of chairs on the way to the bar. 'Great night, Delmar,' Gator said. 'I could use another drink. Most fun I've had in a long time.'

'The boys needed to release a little frustration. You got yourself a beautiful woman there, but she goin' to bring you trouble. Lots of trouble, that one.'

120

Gator grinned at him. 'She's got a knife. A great big knife. I make her mad enough she shows me that knife.'

Delmar whistled softly. 'You're one lucky man, Gator. Don' go blowin' this one. I never understood why all the women find you so purty.'

Gator tossed back his drink and put the glass on the bar, winking at the owner. 'I'm charmin', that's why. Catch you later.'

Delmar snorted his derision. Gator stepped away from the bar, hesitated and turned back. 'Answer me this, Delmar. If you had to choose between being a slimeball rat bastard, or a common garden variety man-type rat bastard, which would you be?'

Delmar cocked his head to one side while he mulled it over.

'It isn't a trick question, Del,' Gator said. 'Just pick one.'

'Well then, that's easy enough. I don' want to be a common garden variety of anything. I'll be the slime-ball rat bastard.'

'That's just plain stupid.' Gator threw his hands in the air in exasperation. 'You want people thinking you're a slimeball?'

Delmar gave one of his slow nods. 'Yep.'

Disgusted, Gator stomped out, tipping over the two chairs he'd righted. 'Come on, you two,' he called to his brother and Ian. 'Get up.'

They were side by side sitting with their backs to the wall, legs out in front of them, beer bottles in hand. They exchanged a long look and both burst out laughing. 'Could be a problem, bro,' Wyatt said. 'I'm not sure we can get up.'

Gator scowled at the two of them. 'Well you've had yourselves a time. Did you start it?' He glared at his brother.

Wyatt took a long pull on his beer, contemplating the answer. 'I just might have, now that you ask.'

Ian nudged him. 'You threw the first punch and it sure was purty,' he praised. 'Vicq claimed your woman, Gator, and Wyatt here stood up for you.'

Gator felt the rush of black temper seething and boiling in the pit of his stomach. It came out of nowhere; just like every intense emotion he seemed to feel when Flame was involved. 'He has no claim on her. Hell, she's carrying my baby. He say he slept with her?'

Wyatt and Ian both took another drink from their respective beers. Gator observed their frowning faces with disgust. 'Don't tell me you can't remember. It's an important detail don't you think? If she's runnin' around on me, I should know about it.'

'Yeah,' Ian agreed. 'The baby might not be yours.'

'Damn it, Ian. The baby's mine. She didn't sleep with Vicq Comeaux. I don't care what he said.'

Ian and Wyatt looked at each other again and burst out with fresh laughter. 'Thought you said there wasn't a baby,' Ian said.

'Oh shut up. Did he say he slept with her?'

'I can't shut up and answer you at the same time,' Ian pointed out pragmatically.

'Not that I recall,' Wyatt said. 'Vicq's been following her from club to club. Bet he didn't work up the courage to ask her for a date. He's long on running his mouth but doesn't do much when it comes to the ladies.'

Ian nudged Wyatt. 'He was bragging about what he'd do with a little hot thing like Flame.'

'He wouldn't know what hit him,' Gator sneered. 'She'd slice him up his middle before he made the first move. I saved his worthless hide tonight.'

Both Wyatt and Ian blinked up at him drunkenly. 'That's right, man, she's got a knife.'

Wyatt pushed himself unsteadily up the wall. 'She had the biggest damn knife I ever saw and she actually had it against Gator's throat.'

'You don't have to sound like you admire the fact she put a knife to your brother's throat,' Gator objected. 'She nearly killed me. Did you ever think about that?'

'It was awesome.' Wyatt staggered forward and turned back to politely extend his hand toward Ian. 'Plain awesome.'

'Wish I'd seen it,' Ian said plaintively.

'The two of you need to get in the pirogue before I decide to leave you here. Fat lot of good the two of you are to me.'

Ian exchanged another long look with Wyatt, both looking as if they might erupt into another round of laughter. 'He forgot you defended his claim on the woman, but I've got a long memory, lad, and I'll be reminding him.'

'He's just really pissed at me right now,' Wyatt explained, rubbing his jaw again. 'I gave him the wrong answer to his question. Between Gator and Vicq, I got me a sore jaw. Vicq sure had a mad on for everyone tonight. He got himself into a heated argument with that city boy Parsons and then his bodyguards. I thought he was going to take all of them on.'

'Yeah, until the driver said something to him and he backed off.' Ian grinned. 'I thought maybe he offered to drive him around New Orleans in that big fancy car.'

The two staggered across the long wooden pier to the small pirogue, snickering together. Gator helped his brother into the boat and into the seat before turning back toward the larger Irishman. They all nearly ended up in the canal when he stepped off the pier into the

123

middle of the pirogue, slipped, and crashed down onto Wyatt. The two men sat on the bottom of the boat howling with laughter.

Gator glared at them, clearly disgusted as he caught up the long pole and pushed them away from the pier. 'You two are a pair of jackasses.'

That brought on another wave of laughter. Gator shook his head as he took them through the reed-choked waterway toward more open, but shallow water. The canal was fairly narrow and easy enough to maneuver. There was something very satisfying in the old ways, the digging of the pole onto the bottom of the canal, the jar that ran up the pole and into his shoulder, and the familiar play of muscle driving the pirogue through the reeds. He could have enjoyed the night a little better if he could pretend he was alone, but his imagination wasn't good enough to drown out the noisy singing of his brother and friend. He shoved again with the pole.

'Hey, Gator. Just what was the question you asked my buddy Wyatt,' Ian asked.

In the sudden vacuum of silence as both men went quiet, sound poured in. The hum of insects, the murmur of other conversations as men made their way home along the same route, the splash of water as larger reptiles slid into the waterway, and the whisper of something moving along the shore, matching the progress of the pirogue.

Gator turned toward the sound, heard the snap of a branch and crackle of dried moss. Something shiny spun toward him, caught for a split second in the faint light of the small crescent shaped moon. He knocked it away with a quick flip of the pole and it hit the water with a splash, sinking below the dark surface immediately.

Forcing air through his lungs, he waited for the next

attack. There was a rustle in the brush, branches in front of him swayed and then the sound of a heavy thud followed by silence. He didn't move until the insects resumed humming.

'What was that?' Ian asked, sounding more sober than drunk.

'I think someone just tried to kill me,' Gator answered.

'Put us ashore,' Ian definitely didn't sound drunk.

Gator glanced down at his brother, clearly feeling the effects of the alcohol. 'I don't think so. Not tonight. We'll come back in the morning.'

'Was it the woman?'

'Well that would be the question, now wouldn't it?' Gator replied thoughtfully.

Chapter Seven

'You didn't tell Lily you found Flame,' Ian said.

Gator looked up, one eyebrow raised in inquiry from the papers strewn around him in a semicircle.

'At the briefing. You didn't tell Lily you found Flame.'

'I guess I didn't. I must have overlooked that bit of information.' Gator tapped the pictures of the evidence of both girls' disappearances. 'I don't see anything here that can help us, do you?'

'No. And we aren't finished talking about Flame. She might have tried to kill you last night. She was there – I'm sure of it.'

'What did you see that I didn't see, Ian?' Gator asked, tossing the pictures into a heap. 'I searched, the same as you. I didn't find a single print that might have been hers. I did find several men's prints. And the same brand of cigarette Vicq Comeaux smokes.'

'She was there and you know she was there. She's like a GhostWalker. She moves through the shadows and she leaves nothing behind, but we both felt her.'

Gator met Ian's gaze squarely. 'She *is* a GhostWalker. She's the same as we are, not different, the same.'

'She still may have tried to kill you. I think maybe you're thinking with the wrong part of your anatomy.'

'She wouldn't have made noise, Ian. She wouldn't have snapped twigs and made the branches sway. There was no wind. Someone human did that. And whoever slipped in the mud was large.'

'I'm just saying to watch yourself. She's beautiful, but she's not coming in. You won't be able to bring her in.'

'Don't sell me short, my friend. I can be persuasive when the situation calls for it.' Gator reached for his coffee cup. 'There's nothing quite like Cajun coffee. I miss it when I'm away from home.'

Ian snorted. 'You could take the skin off a skull with that stuff. And she was on that island. I'm not saying she tried to take your head off, but she was there last night.'

Gator swallowed coffee. Yeah. She'd been there. He'd felt Flame's presence, just the same as Ian. She'd been watching him, but he had no idea why. He'd lain awake most of the night thinking about her – the way her skin felt, the way her mouth was hot with the same carnal lust that he felt raging in his own body. Had it been her mesmerizing voice that had ensnared him? And whoever took Joy Chiasson, had they obsessed about her in the same way he obsessed about Flame – the crawling need under his skin, his body hard and aching no matter how many times he tried to rid himself of her scent and touch? Had they obsessed day and night until looking and fantasizing wasn't enough and they helped themselves?

'Gator!' Ian raised his voice. 'I'm just saying you've got to get a handle on this thing. I'm covering you with the captain, but if they call us back about the problem in the Congo . . .'

Gator shook his head. 'I can't leave right now. Someone else will have to handle this. Our teams have gone to the Congo, Iraq, and Afghanistan eight times in the last ten months for extractions. We've completed every mission, but someone else will have to take this one.'

'Ken Norton and his team were sent in to pull out some hotshot scientist and his people. Ken covered them as they ran to the helicopter, but he was wounded and they had no choice but to leave him and get the civilians to safety. GhostWalkers don't leave their own behind, and not with that particular band of rebels. They've tortured and killed every prisoner they've ever held. We're not leaving him there and you know it, Gator.'

'His team got the prisoners out so the rebels are going to be more than pissed,' Gator agreed. 'But we're halfway around the world. They'll need someone at the ready. Get ahold of Rye and see who they're sending. Tell him we've got trouble here and that I'd rather stay on this if we have a choice.' He glanced at his friend. 'And don't think you have to cover for me.'

'They've got a team lined up, but he's still going to ask what the trouble is.'

'Tell him my gut is saying there's trouble.' A small grin escaped. 'We're supposed to be psychic aren't we?'

'Oh, he'll get a huge kick out of that. And he'll know we're not being straight. We've never once backed away from a mission.'

'It wasn't offered to us.'

'No, Jack Norton, Ken's brother, is leading a rescue team. Nico and Sam and a couple of Jack's guys are going in,' Ian agreed. 'But we were standby.'

'Just give him the message. He'll handle it for me.

If you feel you need to go, believe me, I'll understand.'

'I'm not leaving you behind.'

'And I'm not leaving her. Whether you like it, whether she likes it, she's one of us and I'm not willing to let her go.'

'Is that the GhostWalker in you talking, or the hormones?'

'How the hell would I know?' Gator shoved the pictures away and stood up, pacing across the room to stare out the window. 'I don't know, Ian.'

'Well you'd better figure it out fast, Gator,' Ian advised. 'I'll call Ryland and let him know we're needed here for a while longer.'

'Are you going to tell him Flame is here?' Gator didn't turn around, but kept his gaze fixed sightlessly on one of the huge trees out in his grandmother's yard.

'Not unless he asks me.'

Gator didn't reply. He didn't know why he was so reluctant to let the others know Flame was in New Orleans. Had Lily known for certain or had it really been a computer guess? He didn't know. In the beginning it didn't matter all that much to him. Like being physically enhanced. It had been cool to run faster and leap over a fence. The feeling was one of power, of exhilaration, but all of a sudden, his future mattered to him.

He wanted to live in the bayou close to his brothers and their families. He wanted his children to play with their children. He wanted his grandmother's face to light up when he put his son or daughter in her lap. Had he traded his future away and been careless about it? As careless as Flame thought him to be?

And what of Flame? He seemed to know her far better than he should with only a couple of brief meetings between them. They thought alike. It was eerie to *feel*

129

emotion and know it was hers, not his. And she felt his. He knew it without being told. There was a strong connection between them, every bit as strong as the volatile chemistry. How could he ever explain to Ian that it wasn't that he didn't *want* to leave her behind, it was that he *couldn't* leave her behind.

It was scary to think that she might be right, that Whitney had developed her as a weapon first and then somehow developed Gator to complement and amplify her powers. It would make sense, the entire point of psychic engineering and genetic enhancement was amplification of power, but what about the physical – no, it was far more than physical – attraction between them? Had that been deliberate or a by-product of the engineering?

He touched the glass on the window, feeling her close. Feeling her just the way he had in the early morning hours when he and Ian had slipped out of the house and had gone back to the island near the Huracan to examine the tracks left by whoever had stalked him the night before.

Flame had been there. He hadn't found a single thread from her dress or a track from her high heels, but she'd been there. He and Ian both knew it instantly, in the way all GhostWalkers seemed suddenly aware of each other's presence, almost as if power called to power. He didn't want to believe that she had stalked him through the trees attempting to assassinate him – not that he doubted Flame was capable of killing, but it didn't seem likely that she would attempt to kill him in that manner.

He rubbed his hand over his face trying to clear his thoughts. Ian was right, that was the worst of it. He couldn't think clearly when it came to her. He was bringing a very dangerous woman into his grandmother's home.

It had been a small game to him, one he thoroughly enjoyed, but it wasn't fair to put his family in danger.

'Rye didn't ask and I didn't volunteer,' Ian announced. 'But I want you to promise me something. If I determine you're in over your head, we pull back until we both feel comfortable with the situation.'

Gator shot him a brief, hard glance, but finally nodded his head in compliance. He had to trust someone's judgment if he couldn't trust his own. The first thing he was going to do was assure himself that Flame's knife was still in her possession rather than beneath the murky water of the canal.

Flame pulled on thin leather gloves and glanced at herself in the mirror. She looked pale, her eyes too big. She hated the sunken look she sometimes got when she didn't get enough sleep. She'd lain awake most of the night thinking about Raoul. Wanting him. Despising him. It was the dumbest thing she could imagine and she felt like an idiot for being so pulled in two directions. He worked for Whitney, her worst enemy, and she just kept fantasizing all kinds of erotic and shocking things about him. She liked being in his company. She liked his idiotic sense of humor. She liked the feel of his hands on her skin and his mouth on hers.

She closed her eyes and gave a small groan. She would *never* go back. Not to Whitney, and not to Whitney's daughter. She didn't trust any of them. She'd spent her entire life being an experiment and she damned well was going to make her own choices for the rest of her life – even if that meant she had to keep moving forever. Raoul, for all his charm and sexy smile and hot mouth and bod, was not going to persuade her, capture her, or otherwise entice her into returning.

'You goin' somewhere, *cher*?' Burrell asked as he

stuck his head in the open doorway and whistled softly. 'Cuz you look mighty good.'

She blew him a kiss. 'You always cheer me up. I was just thinking I looked pale and uninteresting or worse, pale and zombielike.'

He paused. 'Flame, did you meet someone last night?' His grin was teasing, but his gaze was worried. 'I know all the boys in these parts. Who'd you meet?'

Her heart contracted. He sounded like a worried father. She'd never had a worried father and for a moment, tears were close. 'I asked you about him last night. His name is Raoul Fontenot.' She couldn't help it. She knew it was part of the fantasy she was acting out, a home, someone who cared, people she could call friends and neighbors, but she wanted his concern, *needed* to feel like she mattered to *somebody*.

'I heard he was home visitin' his grandmother. He's a good boy. Rough. He don' be a man you mess around with.'

Flame burst out laughing. 'What does that mean exactly? Is that some kind of warning that he's a lady's man and he'll break my heart? Or does it mean he's a fighter and likes a good brawl?'

He frowned at her, trying to look severe. 'It means Raoul Fontenot is a man who will never turn away from trouble. Don' be rilin' him up, cuz he won't stop comin' after you.'

Flash grinned at him. 'Should I be scared of him, do you think? Because he seemed sweet and cuddly to me.'

He snapped a towel at her. 'That's it, girl. You be teasin' me one time too many.'

Flame allowed him to chase her around the houseboat, the two of them laughing together. She liked the captain. Burrell had never married; he'd been too much of a river rat, a man who needed to run the perils of the river as often as possible. Now, retired and living alone on his houseboat, he enjoyed Flame and her antics as much as she enjoyed his company and stories. She finally ripped the towel out of his hand and turned the tables on him. He sat in the tiny kitchen catching his breath as she leaned against the sink, her eyes bright with shared amusement.

'You went to the bank this morning, right, *Capitaine*?'

'Yes, ma'am. I called Saunders and offered to mail the payment. He's always asked for payments in person, but I thought he might want me to save him the trouble. He told me to meet him late, so I'm going to visit Vivienne Chiasson for a couple of hours this afternoon, then I'll meet with Saunders and maybe go see the widow tonight.'

Flame sighed. 'I'm sorry I'm no closer to finding out what happened to Joy than anyone else. I still don't believe she ran away, Burrell. Don't say anything to the family, but I'll keep looking into it.'

'I don' want anything to happen to you, *cher*. Don' do anything dangerous.'

Her slight frown turned into a small mischievous grin. 'I'm going to meet Raoul's grandmother this afternoon. That ought to be very safe, don't you think?'

His eyebrow shot up. 'Why are you going to see Nonny?'

'Apparently she asked her grandson to invite me and he was rather adamant that I go. He claims she has a heart condition.'

'I heard that a while back. All the Fontenot boys be very protective of her.' He tilted his head and studied her face. 'That's a big thing, having her ask you to visit, Flame. She don' just ask anyone, you know.'

'No, I didn't know that. I met her a couple of days

ago briefly and I guess she wanted to finish our conversation.'

'Nonny Fontenot is a friend of mine.'

'Now you're being protective. I'm not stealing from her.'

'Don' go trying to break that boy's heart, Flame. You're a nomad, you said so yourself. Raoul don' know it, but he's a family man.'

She turned away, unexpectedly hurt although she knew he spoke the truth. 'Maybe he'll be breaking my heart, Burrell.'

'I have a shotgun. If he messes with your heart you just tell me and I'll pay him a visit.'

In spite of herself, she laughed again at the idea of the captain trying to threaten Raoul Fontenot. 'I think I can take care of myself. I'll see you this evening.' She blew him a kiss and watched him leave before going back to the mirror and her makeup. She didn't like dark circles under her eyes. Raoul would notice and he'd make some comment. And it would hurt.

Flame scowled at her reflection. 'He has no power over you. None. He can't hurt you even if he says you look like a zombie.' She felt like a zombie lately. Chasing Burrell around the small houseboat had worn her out. 'Too many late nights,' she scolded and tidied up the houseboat. She waited to be certain Burrell was gone before she began to take care of her other business.

She'd already removed the contents of the four slim briefcases she'd stolen from Saunders. Most held cash, but one held a couple of discs hidden inside a large manila envelope. Everything had been dumped into a plastic bag the night before, and she'd stuffed the waterproof bag inside her duffel bag. The four briefcases had been filled with rocks and dropped deep underwater in the middle of one of the canals. Other than the money she'd given to Burrell, there was nothing to connect her to the break-in once she hid the duffel bag.

Sound penetrated the thin walls of the houseboat. A squish followed by a sucking noise as if something was pulled from the mud. The sudden silence of insects. Birds rising fast from tree branches. She had company and it definitely wasn't Burrell returning.

Without haste she went through the houseboat, making certain there was no incriminating evidence and nothing to reveal her real identity. Sliding open a window, Flame emitted a sound pitched far too high for the human ear to hear. The response was immediate. The buzz in the marsh grew loud fast as thousands of mosquitoes blackened the early afternoon sky. The moment she heard the sound of palms slapping at flesh, she slid out a window on the opposite side, landing lightly on the deck, duffel bag in hand. Using the furniture as cover, she made her way to the edge and stepped onto the small island Burrell called his 'yard'.

Flame slipped into the trees, staying low to keep from being seen as she sped through the marsh away from the sound of mosquitoes and curses. Using the trail leading around the outside edges of the marsh along the waterway, heading back in the direction of the houseboat, Flame stayed close to the foliage in case she needed cover. Several cars, including the Fontenot Jeep she'd commandeered, were parked near a rotting pier on the small strip of land that connected the bridge to the frontage road. Her airboat was tied up there along with two small fishing boats. She was relieved to see Burrell's boat gone. Flame shoved the duffel bag in the back of the Jeep beneath a dirty tarp and a box of tools.

She drew a cap over her hair and emitted a second

high-pitched sound to drive the mosquitoes away as she made her way back to the edge of the marsh. She needed to know who was after her. Raoul had admitted he'd slipped a homing device somewhere on her airboat and, although he'd sounded as if he'd been teasing her, she believed him. She certainly would have done it.

Flame skirted the edge of the cypress trees until she could hear the men shuffling back and forth, talking in whispers, crunching cans and muttering curses as insects bit and stung. One man scanned the canal continually with high-powered glasses while two others checked the interior of the swamp and the outer edges. None of them were very thorough, which led her to believe they weren't military. She couldn't tell exactly what they were doing or why they were there.

She had no choice but to head inland using the cover of brush and trees to get close enough to see them. With each step she sank into the mud nearly to her ankles. Behind her the dark water filled her tracks so it was impossible to see which direction she'd come from. She muted the sounds of her feet going through water and mud so there was no chance of giving away her presence to the intruders.

There were four men. Two shifted position continually, obviously uncomfortable in the humidity and spongelike surface of the marsh. Each time they moved, the mud made a squishing sound around them. The man with the binoculars would glare at them occasionally, annoyed by their constant motion. He objected when the fourth man lit a cigarette and it was put out instantly when he snapped the command to do so.

The men never approached the houseboat, simply observed the comings and goings on the water. They hadn't staked out her airboat or the Jeep. In fact none of them checked on the vehicles in the parking area, or the boats tied to the pier. She watched them for a long time, unable to ascertain what they were doing. After about a half an hour, the group of men entered the swamp, carrying what looked like supplies. They didn't look like trappers or hunters, but it was possible they were scientists. She knew several studies of the marsh were being conducted. 'It's possible, Flame, even probable, that you are becoming paranoid.'

She scooted backward until it was safe enough to stand in the concealment of the trees. As she made her way back to the Jeep, she tried to rub some of the mud from her clothes and kick it out of her shoes, but it was impossible. Swearing under her breath, she drove along the frontage road until she saw an older woman walking along with her groceries. She offered her a ride and quickly accepted the offer of a shower and a change of clothes. She drove very quickly to Gator's house. She was fifteen minutes late and he jerked open the door before she could even knock.

'About time you showed up,' Gator greeted, stepping back to allow her into the house. 'I was getting worried about you.'

'I had to take care of a little business. I'm not normally late.' *Why* had she said *that*? Flame nearly groaned aloud. She didn't need to explain or apologize.

She followed him into the kitchen. The room smelled of corn bread and jambalaya. A large pot on the stove simmered and a tea towel covered a plate of cookies. She couldn't help inhaling the scent of freshly baked bread and cookies she couldn't identify, but her mouth watered.

Only then did she notice the house was strangely silent. Her muscles tensed with sudden suspicion. 'Where is everyone?'

Gator didn't answer. His gaze drifted over her,

almost as if he were drinking her in. The intensity of his perusal caused a strange reaction in her body, her heart doing funny little flips and her womb clenching tightly. Up close, in broad daylight, she found him unbelievably attractive. There was a quirk to his mouth and a hint of laughter she found as sexy as all get out. His fingertips brushed her face, feather-light, his touch so gentle she was nearly disarmed on the spot.

'You've been doing recon.' She stood very still, holding her breath as he brushed at another spot on her chin. 'You didn't get this near my house.'

'No. Someone was nosing around the houseboat. I thought it might be you, or a team sent by Whitney to assassinate me.'

His eyes narrowed and his mouth hardened perceptibly. 'Who was it?'

She was inexplicably pleased with his reaction but forced herself to give a casual shrug. 'You don't want anyone stepping on your toes?'

'Absolutely not. If anyone gets to do you in, believe me, honey, it's going to be me after all the grief you've given me. Who was it?'

She frowned. 'I'm not sure. They didn't look military or particularly skilled as fighters. Only one of them seemed competent in the bayou. The rest made too much noise. I didn't recognize any of them.'

'What did they want?'

'I have no idea. I left them to a hot afternoon in the swamp. They're sitting on Burrell's little island and it's going to be uncomfortably muggy. If they're looking for me ...'

'Is it possible Saunders had homing devices in the briefcases?'

She scowled at him. 'I'm not an amateur. That was the first thing I checked for. In any case, the briefcases are at the bottom of the canal.'

'I don't like this.'

'I didn't like it much either,' she admitted. 'On the other hand, they didn't seem interested in the houseboat or the cars so more than likely they were trappers and had nothing to do with me.'

'I'm coming home with you after you visit with *Grand-mere Nonny* to see what these bums are after.'

'No one invited you,' she pointed out.

'So invite me because I'm going home with you.'

'Be still my heart. I feel absolutely faint. Your charm is just overwhelming me.'

'Let me see your knife.'

She rolled her eyes. 'You're obsessed.'

He was, but not with her knife. 'Stop stalling. Put the weapon on the table.'

'Weapon?' Her eyebrow shot up. 'Why would you think I only had one? I brought a freakin' arsenal along just in case you wanted to go a round or two.' She leaned close so her breath was warm against his ear. 'Does it turn you on?' She pulled a long knife from her boot and spun it in her hands, smirking a little at him. 'Nice balance, but not the best for throwing.' She laid it on the table.

It wasn't the same blade she'd had the night before, but he was beginning to think he had a kinky streak because something was turning him on. 'Just how good are you with that?'

'I only carry it for show.' She reached behind her neck and withdrew a second blade. It was quite a bit smaller. 'This is a *great* throwing knife. One of my favorites.' She placed the knife beside the larger one.

It wasn't the one she'd had strapped to her thigh the night before either. 'Is that all you've got, *cher*?' He quirked an eyebrow at her in challenge.

139

' 'Course not. I knew you might have a couple of friends along, you know, just in case things got a little too hot for you to handle. I'm not afraid of you, but you do so hate being alone with me.' She withdrew a thin wire, placed it beside the knives and added three small throwing stars. Her belt yielded a small tool kit that had two lethal-looking instruments beside the pick tools, and she pulled a small metallic round disk, innocent looking until she popped open the curved blades.

'Anything else?' The knife from the night before still wasn't on the table. He scowled at her, but she simply flashed him her killer smile, totally unrepentant.

'You wouldn't want me to strip naked, now would you?' She reached for the largest knife. 'A girl has to have her secrets.'

'The idea has possibilities.' He pinned her wrist to the table while his other hand slid over her jean-clad bottom to the inside of her thigh. Even without the feel of her skin he found himself getting hard. 'Where is it?'

Her gaze turned turbulent, a dark smoldering promise of trouble. 'I don't like being manhandled so I'm going to *once*, that would be *one* time, ask you politely to remove your hands. If you don't, you're very liable to lose them.'

He removed his hands, but crowded her close. 'Don' be threatening me in my grandmother's house,' he reprimanded. 'Where is it?'

'If you act like an ape in your grandmother's house you can expect to be threatened a lot. Where is what?'

'The knife. The knife from last night. You were wearing it in a very intriguing place and I'm rather fond of it. Where is it, *cher*?'

'You really believe that you're utterly charming, don't you? I'm not wearing a dress. It's my dress-up knife. So sorry. Let me know what you want in the way

140

of accessories next time and I'll try to accommodate you.' She turned her head. 'We're about to have company. I'm putting my toys away now. I don't share well with others.'

'You don' do much of anything well with others,' he observed.

A slow, heated smile curved her soft mouth. Her gaze drifted up and down his body in deliberate inspection. 'There are a few things I do well with others,' she corrected, 'depending on who that other happens to be.'

He groaned softly. 'That's just not right.'

She bent over to shove the long blade down into her boot scabbard. The action sent his heart racing. He found himself staring at the smooth line of her jeans curving over her bottom. As she straightened, she caught him staring and shook her head. 'You need help.'

'Don' I know it, sugah.'

She lowered her voice to a mere wisp of sound. 'Does your grandmother know she raised such a perv?'

Knives were the least of her weapons. She was a fighter, well-versed in martial arts and more than that, her voice alone was a devastating weapon should all else fail. Gator stayed close to her. 'I'm only a perv when I'm around you.' He swept his hand down her back, more to touch her than to frisk for additional weapons, but he felt the thin scabbard between her shoulder blades.

She merely raised an eyebrow. 'Find what you were looking for?'

His hand continued the sweep, molding the curve of her bottom almost lovingly. 'You're wearing one of those sexy little thongs, aren't you?' He whispered the question as his grandmother, Wyatt, and Ian entered the house and started down the long hall toward the kitchen.

She leaned into his shoulder and turned her face up to his until their lips were a breath apart. 'Am I?'

Heat shot through his body, blood pounded in his veins straight to his aching, thickening groin. He had to stop touching her. The alternative was unthinkable, not with his grandmother coming through the doorway with a welcoming smile on her face. He nearly groaned, catching the back of Flame's shirt to hold her in front of him. 'That's just so not fair,' he said.

Her soft laughter taunted him, teased his senses as she deliberately moved back until her bottom rubbed up against him, a mere brush, but it was enough to send a jolt through his entire body.

'How wonderful to see you again,' Nonny greeted. She reached out and tucked her hand in the crook of Flame's arm. 'Let's sit in the parlor, *cher*, and get to know one another. Raoul, you can bring the tea in.'

'I'm sorry I was so late getting here, Mrs. Fontenot,' Flame apologized. 'It was unavoidable.'

Nonny patted her hand. 'Thas' just fine, no worries,' she assured. 'I understand you're staying with Burrell on his houseboat. He's a good friend of mine, child.'

'That's what he said.' Flame cast Gator a smoldering look over her shoulder promising retaliation. She knew he'd really put a homing device on the airboat, that he'd already checked up on her. 'He's a wonderful man.'

Gator sent her his quick, easy grin, balancing the tea tray easily in one hand as he trailed after them.

Nonny sank down onto the couch and patted the seat beside her. 'Sit here, *cher*, and tell me all about your family.'

'My family?' Flame echoed, a sudden sinking feeling in the pit of her stomach. She didn't want to lie to this old lady the way she lied to everyone else. Why hadn't she considered that it would be the first thing the woman asked her? Nonny Fontenot was all about family. She was concerned for her grandson and wanting Flame to be the mother of his future children.

Gator watched the color fade from Flame's cheeks. She glanced up at him almost helplessly and his heart turned over. She actually pressed backward into the pillows of the couch as if to get away from the question. 'Flame's an orphan, *Grand-mere*. No blood relatives.'

Nonny clucked her sympathy. 'That don' matter, *cher*. When you marry Gator, you'll have all kinds of family. More family than you know what to do with.' She patted Flame's hand again, more of a stroking than a pat.

Flame had a foolish desire to cover the back of her hand with her palm, to hold that small gesture against her skin and take it out later to feel it all over again when she was alone. She flashed Gator a look of anger. How could he have betrayed his family for Whitney? She wanted to slap his face. Wake him up. Shake him. This wonderful, sincere woman loved him and surrounded herself with his pictures and drawings. She'd probably fixed him chicken soup and read him stories when he was sick.

'How long have you known Burrell?' She needed a good, safe topic.

Nonny gestured to her to pour the tea. 'Oh, a lifetime. We both grew up in this parish. He was so handsome and smart, but the river claimed him. All he wanted to do was travel the Mississippi. Of course he came to every *fais do-do* when he wasn't on the river and all the ladies wanted to dance with him.'

Gator made a sound of pure shock. Nonny quelled him with a stern look. 'I'm not dead, Raoul, just old. Of course I noticed how handsome Burrell was. He brought me flowers every couple of months after Rene died. Sometimes he'd come over and we'd sit a spell on the porch and smoke a pipe. He's the only man I ever smoked a pipe with.'

'I love the smell of his pipe,' Flame admitted. 'I tell him smoking is bad for him, but I do inhale a lot when I'm around his pipe.'

'In your delicate condition,' Gator said, 'do you think you should be inhalin' *cher*?'

The teacup rattled on the saucer as Flame handed the cup to Nonny. She gave Gator a swift, scowling reprimand, but he simply grinned at her. 'I do hope you have pictures of Raoul when he was a boy. I'd love to see what he was like. I imagine he was curly-headed and strong-willed.'

Nonny nearly clapped her hands. 'He still has that wonderful head of hair.' She raised her voice. 'Wyatt. Bring me the family album.'

'No. *Grand-mere*,' Gator groaned. 'Don't do that to me.'

'Great idea, *Grand-mere*,' Wyatt said cheerfully. He went to a large antique sideboard and pulled open a drawer. The album was wrapped in a hand-crocheted shawl. Wyatt carried it over to his grandmother with obvious care.

Gator sank down onto the couch beside Flame, deliberately crowding her, his thigh tight against hers as he leaned forward to grab a handful of cookies off a hand-painted plate. 'I was a cute kid,' he admitted. 'Everyone said so.'

'There's a naked picture of him in there,' Wyatt pointed out with glee as his grandmother opened the album cover, her hand smoothing over the pages with near reverence.

Flame leaned toward Nonny, away from Gator to

144

peer at the picture of the baby happily throwing water into the air. He sat in an old cooking pot with two handles, looking joyfully at the camera in the first picture. In the second he stood waving chubby arms, hair dripping water into his face, laughing while giving a full frontal view. He looked about eighteen months to Flame.

Gator nudged her. 'Even as I child I was well-endowed,' he teased, feigning pride. He shifted his weight so he was wedged tight against her again.

Flame peered at the pages, listening to the pride in his grandmother's voice as she told stories of his childhood. Wyatt leaned over her shoulder and pointed to a black-and-white picture. There was five-year-old Gator with a torn shirt and ragged knees. He'd been protecting one of his younger brothers from a neighbor. The seven-year-old Gator had a black eye and a big grin. Nine-year-old Gator had tape over his nose and two little girls staring at him with wide-eyed wonder. Eleven-year-old Gator had two black eyes and a grin as wide as the Mississippi as he swept off his straw hat and bowed toward three little girls sitting on a pier.

'There seems to be a pattern emerging here,' Flame said. 'Was he always in fights? And was there always a female audience around?'

Nonny laughed. 'Oh my, yes. He was a fighter, that boy. And a charmer.'

'I still am,' Gator said and lifted Flame's knuckles to his mouth.

She snatched her hand away, shocked that she was holding his hand and didn't even realize it.

Chapter Eight

The afternoon seemed entirely surreal to Flame. She kept forgetting to stay on her guard, relaxing and laughing with Nonny before she realized she was doing it. Nonny talked about the four Fontenot brothers, her voice spilling over with love. Both Wyatt and Gator talked in low, affectionate voices, and they leapt up to get Nonny whatever she asked for. Often they addressed her as ma'am. Flame found it very quaint and endearing.

She rose reluctantly to go. It was the first time she'd ever really felt at home and she was aware she probably would never get to have the feeling again. 'I had a lovely time, Mrs. Fontenot,' she admitted. 'Thank you for the tea and cookies. Your home is wonderful.'

'Come back soon,' Nonny urged.

Gator took her hand as she stood up. 'I'm going with you,' he reminded.

Flame shot him a quelling glance as she made her way to the front door. 'It's quite all right, Raoul. I'm perfectly fine on my own.' She leaned close to him. 'I've had enough of your company and you'll only get in my way.'

He retaliated by kissing the nape of her neck. 'I can run circles around you, babe. I'll follow you with your bike and we'll make the exchange at the houseboat,' Gator added as he escorted her out the door.

'It's my bike. I'll take it home.'

'You'll take off like a bat out of hell and I'll never see you again. The Jeep can't possibly keep up with that bike and you know it. I'm coming home with you.'

Flame glared at him. 'I hope Burrell has his shotgun out. He warned me about you. He said you were a lady's man and a bunch of other not so nice things.'

He grinned at her. 'Betcha you got all jealous and snarly on him.'

She tossed her head, hair spilling around her face. 'Get over yourself.'

His grin widened. 'You did, didn't you? No worries, *cher*, I've sowed my wild oats and am ready to settle down to wedded bliss. You're the one and only for me.'

'I ought to insist on marrying you. You'd run screaming for the hills. Wedded bliss, my ass. You couldn't maintain your façade of charm and the image of an easygoing nature full-time.'

He pressed his hand to his heart. 'Honey, that plain hurts. Everyone in the bayou knows I'm easygoing and charmin'. I think you have the pre-wedding jitters. Don't you worry your pretty little head . . .'

'You're about to get kicked. Hard.'

He laughed aloud. 'Talk like that turns me on.'

She turned away before he could see her answering smile. She wanted to think of him as an enemy, but it was becoming more difficult. She actually *liked* the lunatic. She especially liked how gentle he was with his grandmother. And, God help her, his warped sense of humor. It was one of her worst failings. She enjoyed people. She knew it was because she wanted to fit in somewhere. She wanted to belong.

Raoul Fontenot had the family Flame always wanted. They loved one another and teased and treated each other affectionately. She craved that, needed the feel of a home and family, and he had shared his with her. Flame walked away from him with a lump in her throat and tears burning behind her eyes, away from his smiling grandmother and his perfect home.

'Hey!' Gator came up behind her and slung his arm around her shoulders. 'You all right? I thought we were joking around.'

She would *not* cry in front of him. She was going home to Burrell. Maybe it wasn't the same thing, but the river captain needed her company almost as much as she needed his. Flame shrugged Gator off and picked up the pace, practically running to the Jeep. It was a cowardly thing to do and she was ashamed of herself, but what the hell? She didn't owe him an explanation. And she damn well didn't want him being nice to her. Because she felt like a fool, she leaned out of the Jeep to look back at him.

Raoul was watching her, rubbing his shadowed jaw with a perplexed look on his face. He looked sexy in his tight jeans with his shirt stretched across his broad shoulders. 'Try to keep up,' she called to him and started the engine.

He flashed her a boyish, heart-stopping grin and made a run for the house. Flame tore out of the yard, raising a cloud of dust as she sped out the gate. She knew the capabilities of her motorcycle and even with a head start, Raoul was going to catch her, but she wasn't going to make it easy for him.

Racing down the highway, she spotted the open field that would give her a huge advantage. The shortcut would take her along the edge of a marsh, and through a series of small wooded areas, but she'd shave off several miles. She took the narrow dirt road and sped

148

the Jeep across the overgrown field, dodging a couple of trees. The vehicle slid through a bog, slinging up mud behind her as she cut through a narrow patch of the marsh at high speed.

Laughing out loud she spun a doughnut in the next patch of mud, just because it was exhilarating and she knew Gator was roaring down the highway on her bike. She *felt* him. The connection between them was strong, strong enough that she knew if she reached, whispered, called to him, he would hear her.

She was in the risky area now, the Jeep slipping around turns as she let up just a hair on the gas going into the curve and punching hard, sliding nearly sideways through the turns. The Jeep was decked out for all terrain and she used every bit of skill she possessed to drive at breakneck speed along the faint trail. The Jeep caught air and slammed down, the front end tipping to the left and throwing her forward, only to catch air a second time, this time tilting to the right. She braced herself using the steering wheel, but the seat hit her back several times as she was thrown back and forth. Mud sprayed the air behind her, throwing up a dark trail and covering the Jeep in rich goo.

She didn't dare let up on the gas; in the heavy mud she'd be stuck immediately, so she pushed the Jeep to its limit, powering through the spongy ground and bumping over the nearly invisible road. Twice she dared the lower creek beds. Wyatt had a snorkel on the Jeep, but she didn't want to take a chance using it in deeper water because it would definitely slow her down so she only went for the shallower beds, crossing fast and driving hard up the bank before shooting onto the frontage road that would take her along the canal leading to Burrell's island.

The Jeep was black with mud even with the speed

she was going, the wind spraying the dirt behind her. She smirked and waved as a car tried to stay up with her only to back off when mud spattered it. A black town car was heading in the opposite direction, and she recognized it as Parsons's private vehicle. There was a certain satisfaction in seeing mud spray up and over it as she blew past. As she sped along the frontage road, she glanced toward the highway and her heart slammed hard in her chest. Gator was low over the motorcycle, his shirt rippling in the wind as he raced toward the exit to the extensive waterway system.

Flame couldn't believe how excited she got just spotting him. Her stomach did a series of little flips and her heart began to beat wildly. She hadn't had so much fun in a long time. He was just as determined to win as she was, his jaw set, his mind focused. She knew it because he was a competitor through and through, just as she was. They were so alike in so many ways, yet so different where it counted.

She tore up the frontage road along the canal, glancing back to see the motorcycle already exiting. Raoul had to have seen her even with the dust flying. She bent low over the steering wheel, her foot hard on the gas, urging the vehicle to greater speeds. The engine screamed at her, but over the top of it, she could hear the purring of her beloved motorcycle. The bike flew past her, tearing into the small dirt parking lot just moments ahead of the Jeep.

She parked next to her bike, leaping out, laughing, because she couldn't help it. He sat on the motorcycle, swinging one leg, looking lazy and cool despite the humid heat of the swamp.

He pulled off his dark glasses and winked at her, holding out the keys to her bike. 'I do believe, Ms. Johnson, I kicked your pretty little ass.'

She took the key chain from him and dropped the Jeep keys in his palm. 'I do believe there must be at least ten cop cars chasing after you.'

'I lost them somewhere near the bridge. If they're coming after me, they're mighty slow. What's my prize?'

'You think you deserve a prize for speeding? You were breaking the law. That was cheating.'

'I'm a rule breaker, *cher*. You'll have to get used to it.'

She quirked an eyebrow at him. There were flecks of mud on her clothes and some on her face, but all he could focus on was the laughter in her eyes. Everything male in him responded to her, but when she laughed because of him, he felt almost as if he could fly.

'I can't imagine you as anything *but* a rule breaker. You were a little outlaw as a child and you're still one as an adult. You get away with too much because you're so charming. It isn't good for you.'

His grin widened and he poked her with his finger. 'Aha! I knew you found me charmin'. Even the toughest ones fall eventually.'

'You're not nearly as charming as you think.' She started back toward the Jeep.

Gator trailed after her. 'Yes I am,' he teased. 'You're trying to escape me now, but I'm going to say hello to Burrell and declare my honest intentions so he won't be comin' after me with that shotgun of his.'

She stopped so abruptly he ran into her and had to catch her shoulders to keep both of them from landing on the ground. 'Your *only* intention toward me is to get me back to Whitney's little laboratory,' she reminded.

'Well now, I wouldn't say that was true,' he denied, heat gathering in his eyes.

'*Hello*, you idiot. I'm not pregnant. We haven't slept

together. We're not engaged to be married. You're here to drag my ass back to Whitney.'

He tilted his head to inspect the curve of her bottom. 'And a nice ass it is too. You've got me wondering again about those pretty little panties of yours.'

'Stay on track here, Raoul. I think you have ADD.'

His hand slipped from her shoulder to slide the length of her arm, trailed to the curve of her hip. She glared at him. 'And keep your wandering hands to yourself.'

'You like my hands.'

'Not that much.' She faced him squarely. 'You're making this hard.'

'Well, that's fair. You make me hard.'

She threw her hands into the air in sheer exasperation. 'Go home, Raoul.'

'Not a chance, *cher*. I introduced you to *Grand-mere*. Why don't you want to introduce me to Burrell?'

'You already know Burrell. And don't give me your puppy-dog look. It isn't going to work. I'm not taking you home to him. If you give him your ridiculous story about pregnancy and engagements I'll never hear the end of it.'

He grinned at her. 'Of course he's going to hear about it, Flame. This is the bayou. We have our own newscasters. *Grand-mere* has announced to all her friends and they've called all their friends. The news has traveled throughout all the parishes by now.'

'Great. Just great.' Her eyes met his. Sober. Penetrating. 'Why did you insist on me going to see your grandmother? She's a lovely woman and I really enjoyed meeting her, but why would you do that?'

'I told you why.'

'That wasn't the reason. I saw you with her. You're very protective of her, of your entire family. Why would

152

you give me ammunition like that?'

There was a small silence. She held his gaze. Gator sighed and shoved a hand through his thick wavy hair. 'I wanted you to know who I really am.'

She inhaled sharply, lips parting as if to speak. She shook her head. 'I have no idea who you are, Raoul. You . . .' Her voice trailed off and she swung around to face in the direction of the swamp. She went very still as if frozen and stiff.

In spite of the distance, he heard it too, the sound of someone running, crashing through reeds and branches. The impact of a bullet, so distinct even with a silencer. The thud of a heavy body falling. The soft cry of pain was muffled, but the reverberation of a second bullet cut off the sound abruptly.

'Burrell.' She looked stricken, her eyes wide with shock. 'Raoul, that was Burrell.' They stared at each other for one heartbeat of time – for an eternity. Her expression changed, became a mask of determination. She sprinted away from him, heading toward the island Burrell owned.

Gator caught up with her, signaling for silence and caution. She held up four fingers indicating four assailants as she ran across the narrow strip connecting the mainland to the island. He split his fingers and made a circle. She nodded and veered off, breaking away from him so they could approach from two directions. Gator increased his speed.

Burrell was probably dead and he didn't want Flame to find the body. The ground turned spongy and dangerous. He had lived in the bayou most of his life, even taking a boat to school, and he knew better than to run haphazardly through a swampy area but he did it anyway. He dodged low-hanging branches and jumped over fallen logs, landing up to his ankles in mud. Cursing, he continued, batting aside the low-hanging moss, slowing enough to stay quiet and watch out for deeper bogs.

He found where Burrell had tied up his boat and walked to the site where he was planning to build. The cabin was laid out with string and Gator could see where Burrell had worked on adding fill to a small area around where he planned to put the house. He had walked over toward a cove where he must have done most of his digging. A wheelbarrow was overturned in the muck and a shovel lay a few yards from it as if it had been flung aside.

Gator knelt beside the wheelbarrow, looking for tracks. In the fresh dirt Burrell had dumped around the area, he could see several footprints of various sizes.

'That's Burrell's track,' Flame said softly as she came up beside him and touched one boot mark. 'He comes here every day to build up this area because it was too low and flooded every year.'

'Did you see anyone?'

Flame shook her head as she examined the ground. 'They shot him here and he fell over the wheelbarrow. He tried to crawl away from them.' She pointed to the twin furrows in the dirt and one handprint. Blood stained the tracks. 'That's where they shot him the second time.' There was a much larger pool of blood seeping into the dark water oozing up from just below the surface. 'This is the one.' She indicated a boot print. 'The big guy in charge. He shot him. The others dragged him by his ankles off that way.' She didn't look at Gator. Her voice was tight, but rock steady.

They followed the drag marks in the mud. Water was already filling the crevices, but it was impossible to hide the bright splashes of blood on the leaves and vegetation. The trail led around the side of the island to a natural basin. The mud bank had a distinct slide indicating an alligator used the area. Judging by his tracks, the reptile was large and had been there for some time. The four men hadn't tried to hide the evidence, dragging the body through the mud and water to the edge of an alligator hole. There were knee marks where two of the men had dropped down beside the body wrapping a cord around it.

Flame picked her way through the fortress of exposed roots, while Gator circled the dark waters of the basin. He slipped twice on the muddy bank. 'Over here, Flame. They must have used something to weigh him down.'

'Can you get him out?' She stepped into the murky water, sinking up to her knees. 'Can you see him?'

'I can't see anything including the damn alligator. Get the hell out of there. You know damn well he isn't alive. You can't save him, Flame.' He waded toward her, gut churning with a mixture of rage and fear for her safety.

'This is my fault. I should have seen this coming. I thought they were after me, and then I just dismissed them. This is my fault.' She continued to wade out into the black water, feeling for the body.

Gator went after her, his fingers settling around her arm like a vise, yanking her with him toward the shore. 'That's bullshit and you know it. Get the hell out of the water. You think dying is going to help him now?'

Her face remained a stiff mask. She didn't even wince at his harsh question. She'd seen the massive amount of blood. She knew Burrell was dead. It was the thought of Burrell being fed to the alligator that made her crazy enough to try to get his body out of the basin. An acrid scent drifted to them through the trees.

Flame used a low-hanging branch to pull herself onto the shore. She felt sick to her stomach. 'Can you find him? Can you get him out of there? Use a branch and see if you can feel him.'

'Who were they, Flame?'

'Do you smell smoke?' She turned suddenly toward the canal. 'Damn them. They're burning his houseboat.' She took off running, more to get away from the reality of Burrell's body in the water with the alligator than to save Burrell's home. There was no way to save anything. Once again the bad guys triumphed and a good man lay dead.

She heard Raoul shout, but his voice was far away, competing with a strange roaring in her head. Her lungs burned for air and her stomach gave a sickening lurch. She stumbled, her vision blurring as the roaring in her head grew to a long wailing scream. For a moment, she thought she'd actually screamed out loud, but the sound only reverberated over and over in her head, so much sorrow, so much rage wanting to get out. Flame fought it back, held it in, all too aware of Raoul's close proximity. She could inadvertently hurt him – kill him. She fought for control, the effort making her head pound and her stomach churn.

She emerged from the trees to stare in horror at the black smoke and orange and red flames leaping into the air. The houseboat was completely engulfed by the fire. Birds rose, shrieking alarm, fleeing the area. In spite of the roar of the conflagration and the noise of the retreating wildlife, she caught the sound of a Jeep and, above that, a triumphant yell.

'Wait, Flame!' Gator commanded.

She glanced back and saw him pulling at his boot where he had stepped through the thin layer of earth and sunk into the mud. Celebratory laughter blended with the noise of the vehicle drawing her attention. She caught a glimpse of an open Jeep, four men bouncing on the seats as they tore down the road.

Without hesitation, Flame switched directions, using every ounce of speed she possessed, hurtling her body through vegetation, splashing through muck and water recklessly. Branches slapped at her, needles caught at her clothing, but she felt nothing as she sprinted back to the parking lot where her motorcycle waited. It fired up immediately, roaring to life as she kicked it over and spun, racing down the road after the killers.

Gator swore as he extracted his boot. Damn the woman. Damn the situation. There was no way he could catch her in his Jeep. And she'd definitely catch the murderers with her rocket of a motorcycle. He stood in silence, listening to the sound of the engine until he was certain of the direction. They weren't heading for the highway; they were going across country, not wanting to be seen, taking one of the old hunting trails. He could hear the whining of the engine and the whooping of the men as they raced inland right into the preserve.

He dragged his satellite phone from his belt and punched in a number. 'I've got trouble here, Ian. I'll need a clean-up crew fast so make the call. This one is going to be bad. No time to explain, but track me. Get here like yesterday and bring Wyatt.' He slammed the phone back into his belt and took off running through the swamp, heading for the interior. He had to get back on the frontage road, off the island and head across the canal to cut them off inland. He knew exactly what Flame was going to do because he would do the same thing.

He cursed as he ran, setting a punishing pace that was double what a normal man could do. He didn't care if he was spotted, he had to intercept and the only chance he had was racing through swampland cross-country. In any case the only people likely to spot him were hunters and fishermen, people of the bayou who would mind their own business. He was Raoul Fontenot, one of their own and they would never volunteer information about him.

He was well aware of the dangers, the snakes and poisonous plants not to mention the sinkholes, but this was no time to be careful, he couldn't afford the delay. The best he could do was to try to stay on animal trails whenever possible. Moss, branches, vines, and leaves hit him in the face. Brambles tore at his clothing, raked his arms and face until he could feel blood dripping as he ran. Startled birds flew up, raising a ruckus. He didn't bother to try to control them, not wanting to waste his energy.

He barely avoided a snapping turtle sunning itself and had to virtually leap over a small alligator as he skirted the edge of a waterway before heading inland again through bald cypress and tupelo gum trees. As he ran, leaves and petals and twigs settled in his hair and clothing and fell down his back. Sweat coated his body and drew insects to him.

Nothing mattered but that he get to her. The faint animal trail intersected with the Jeep trail at one point and he had to make it to that spot before, or at least at the same time, as the murderers and Flame. They had no chance of making it past that point without her catching them. His pounding footsteps began to slap a harder surface, carrying him deeper into the interior away from the faint whine of the engines. He hadn't realized he'd been unconsciously keeping track of the two separate sounds until he was running alone in the interior of the preserve.

He focused his mind on the beat of his feet. His heart and lungs easily handled the punishment of his increased speed and the long leaps over debris. There was no question of enhancement. No normal human could maintain a sustained run at his current pace, and he was barely winded. He became aware of a heavy weight on his mind. Grief beat at him. Guilt and horror ate at the edges of his thoughts. His connection to Flame was growing and he could feel her ferocious struggle to maintain control when she wanted – even needed – to rage at the universe.

Flame muted the sound of the motorcycle as she trailed the Jeep over the dirt road at breakneck speed. She was closing in on them; following in the wake of the clouds of dust rising behind them. They were so drunk on the success of their mission, not even the driver checked the rearview mirror once they had turned onto the dirt road leading through the preserve. She could hear them whooping it up and laughing as they retold the story of Burrell's death over and over, making fun of him trying to run from them. One of them even went so far as re-creating the drama of shooting him.

They were coming up on a small junction where the road widened considerably. The trail through the preserve was one of the many escape routes she'd planned before she'd moved in with Burrell in case she had to leave the area fast. She'd made this particular run three times, liking it the best. It had the least number of people and offered the most cover. As she raced along the dirt track, she tried to recall the exact details of the junction. She needed enough room to maneuver.

She pulled out her throwing knife and slipped it between her teeth as she came up alongside the driver just as the Jeep approached the junction. The driver glanced at her as she appeared out of the dirt, his eyes widening in shock. One of the men in the back lifted

159

his gun but she had already seen the movement out of the corner of her eye. Flame threw the knife hard, burying it to the hilt in his throat. He went over backward with a ghastly gurgling sound, landing in the dirt and muck to lie still.

With the motorcycle parallel to the driver, Flame balanced for a split second before kicking the man in the head as hard as she was able. Her boot connected with a sickening crack, but the force drove her off the bike and into the soft dirt. She landed hard, the breath knocked out of her lungs, every bone feeling as if it had shattered in the fall. She kept rolling away from the sound of the Jeep, coming up on her knees, pulling the knife from her boot.

The Jeep careered off a rotted log, scattering bark and wood in all directions as it mowed down a patch of saw-weed before slamming into a large cypress and coming to an abrupt halt, spilling passengers in all directions. The tires continued spinning, throwing more dirt into the air, obscuring all vision. Simultaneously the motorcycle veered the opposite way, away from the trees into the muddy bog where it fell over onto its side into the mud.

Flame caught a glimpse of movement in the cloud of dust, saw the flash of a muzzle and threw herself forward into the dirt. She scooted back toward the trees, staying on her stomach, using her elbows to move fast into the deeper cover of the vegetation. She stayed still, listening for the sounds of the others to tell her where they were. One man groaned over by the Jeep. That had to be the driver. Her right leg and ankle throbbed painfully. She hoped the driver's head hurt as badly.

A second man rattled bushes to her left. He wiggled backward into a nettle bush and yelped. The third man was totally silent and that told her everything she needed to know about him. Flame began to work her way through the foliage toward the driver. His groans were loud and long. He interspersed the noise with inventive curses and pleas for help that were more growling and spitting than actual words.

'Shut up, Don,' the man to Flame's left burst out. 'I can't see anything and you're making so much noise I can't hear anything either.'

The driver spat out more curses before managing to get a couple of distinct phrases out. 'My jaw. She broke my jaw.'

'Who the hell is she?'

'Don' know,' Don returned, the words slurred and accompanied by more groaning.

Flame shifted position again, worming her way through sedge and marsh grasses. Water soaked into her clothes as she eased through the marshy land, and carefully muted the sound of her movements as she displaced the water.

The driver of the Jeep crawled to the nearest tree, an ancient oak with wide sweeping branches. He sat with his back propped against it, holding his jaw and rocking back and forth. He nearly went right over the top of Flame, his hands and knees inches from her body as she slithered toward him. He began to move and she froze, lying prone in the muck, holding her breath as he shuffled past her. She remained motionless while he jerked out a knife and began stabbing at the dirt and tree roots around him. For a moment she feared he saw her lying among the reeds and grass, and her hand tightened on the hilt of her knife. The driver continued to stab at the same ground over and over making strange animal noises as he hacked up the plants and sent mud into the air.

Flame eased her body over the plants and muck to

get within a few feet of Burrell's killer. The branches of the oak tree hung low to the ground, moss and ivy weighing them down. Catching movement, the driver turned his head to stare at a snake hanging eye level to him. The long thick body curled along the limb of the tree. The snake was olive-brown, close to five feet in length with a tapering tail and a broad head much wider than the neck. There were no dark cross bands on the stout body, but there was a distinctive band extending from the eye to the rear of the jaw. The snake had a drooping mouth and protective eye shields making it look particularly glowering.

Mesmerized, the man stared at the snake, going suddenly silent as it drew its body into a loose coil, tilted its head upward and opened its mouth wide to reveal the whitish interior lining. His scream reverberated through the bayou as he threw himself sideways in an effort to get away from the snake. The driver's cries stopped abruptly as his legs jerked and kicked, his body thrashing in the reeds before going still.

Silence settled over the swamp. Flame lay stretched out, the top of her head nearly brushing that of the driver, her gloved hands tight on the garrote around his neck. She breathed slowly and evenly, making certain not a ripple of grass betrayed her presence to the other two men who had guns trained on the exact spot. She waited, listening to her heartbeat, listening to the hum of insects. After a time, above her head, the snake slowly retracted its head to settle once more on the branch.

'Don? You snakebit?' The hoarse whisper came from several yards away. 'Rudy? You think the snake bit him?' A slight shifting of the foliage straight ahead of Flame accompanied the voice.

Rudy didn't reply. Flame waited. Rudy was the dangerous one, obviously highly trained and skilled in combat situations. He knew better than to give away his position and he obviously had been using Don as bait. He would have done better to spray the entire area around the driver with bullets and then move quickly to a new position. Flame would have taken the chance, but Rudy was more concerned with his safety. Most likely trying to puzzle out who was attacking them, he was lying low, waiting a clear shot while he let the third man, the talker, become the unwitting bait.

With her ear pressed to the ground and her hearing acute, Flame became aware of Gator's approach. He was coming in from the east, through the interior of the preserve and fast approaching the marsh, sprinting at top speed. She couldn't let him run into the waiting Rudy.

Flame slowly relaxed her grip on the thin piece of wire wrapped so tightly around Don's neck. Keeping every movement snail slow and deliberate, so as not to disturb the vegetation around her, she used her elbows to push herself backward away from the body and into deeper cover.

Once she was screened by the root systems and twisted, knobby knees of several larger cypress trees, she emitted a sound pitched just above the level humans could hear. Using directional sound, she sent Gator as much information as possible, confident that he would hear her warning. She'd never used directional sound with a partner before, certainly not under such extreme conditions, but she had every confidence he, and he alone, would hear her. She waited, crouched in the small circle of trees, lying in the heavy cover of reeds and grasses.

She could no longer feel or hear the faint vibrations through the earth, signaling Gator was stationary or had, like her, begun a stealthy approach to the enemy. The third man, the talker, lit a cigarette, the smell drifting upward. The scratch of the match gave his position away. Flame skirted around a rotting log, making a face as several species of beetles and stink bugs scurried close to her. A snapping turtle was sunning himself on the log and she was especially careful not to disturb him. Concentrating her attention on him, she wiggled at right angles to the log. Immediately several Peeps lifted into the air.

Flame rolled instantly and kept moving fast, water soaking her clothes and hair. She felt crawfish against her skin as she rolled in the shallow water. They hurried to get out of her way, but she kept on the move, heading toward the only real shelter, a small depression in the midst of the taller reeds. Bullets smacked into the mud and water inches from her body. Two guns, not one. Two directions. She immediately identified the smoker. She had a clear idea of his location, but not Rudy.

That made no sense. Echolocation should have revealed his hiding place immediately. She couldn't even hear his heartbeat and she could hear Gator's. Adrenaline raced through her system, a rush of fear and sudden recognition. This man wasn't like the others.

She rolled into the depression and sank into soft mud. It oozed around her neck and into her hair. The smell made her want to gag but she controlled the urge waiting until the barrage of fire ceased. Timing it for when Rudy stopped firing, she reared up on her knees and threw the knife blindly at the smoker. The perfectly balanced blade cut through the air with the force of her enhanced muscles and the pure adrenaline rushing through her system fully behind it.

The knife connected hard, the sound loud in the stillness after the gunfire. The smoker toppled over backward, crashing heavily into the brush, breaking small branches as he went down. His rifle clattered to one side, hitting a chunk of rock. Birds shrieked as they rose into the air, fleeing the scene of violence.

'That's three, you son of bitch,' Flame called. Rudy knew exactly where she was. He just wasn't in a position yet to get a clear shot. If he wanted to kill her, he would have to move. And if he moved, he would be every bit as vulnerable as she was.

Sound reached her, a blast of command, the same pitch she used when talking to Gator, but he was telling her to shut the hell up. The man had a mouth on him when he was angry. He had a good idea where the last killer was hiding and was working his way around to get in place behind him. He wanted her to stay put, not provoke the man and let him do his thing.

She responded by offering to draw fire and keep attention fixed on her. The barrage of distinct commands coming back at her made her wince and dig down deeper into the mud. Gator was really, really angry.

Chapter Nine

Gator fought down the unreasonable anger churning in his belly. *Stay where you are and keep your head down, or I swear I'm going to beat you within an inch of your life*. He used directional sound to give her the command, uncaring that the notes were pulsing with rage. The spongy ground undulated slightly and birds shrieked an alarm, taking once more to the air. He wasn't concerned about the sniper hearing him. Directional sound waves were powerful enough to go through walls, yet they could be directed specifically to one recipient. He had worked on the ability in the field often and wasn't in the least surprised that Flame was as adept at it as he was.

Be still my heart.

His fingers itched to shake her – or strangle her. She had to know the sniper had a bead on her. Gator couldn't spot him and that made the man dangerous. He had training and he was just lying in wait, biding his time, waiting to get a shot at Flame. All she had to do was stick her head up and the marksman would kill her. She knew better. She should have waited! It was illogical to rush off after four murderous gunmen when she had only knives – and it was really, really stupid to get pinned down.

I can't hear him. Not even his heartbeat. Can you?

That brought him up short. She was right. He should hear breathing, at least the beat of the sniper's heart, but he heard nothing at all. He could *feel* him, but there was no sound – and there should have been.

Gator moved with deliberate slowness, forming a makeshift Gilly suit by shoving reeds, leaves, and moss through his shirt. It didn't take long to construct a hood for his head and back, cover it with the foliage and begin a slow stalk through the swamp. Somewhere nearby, the sniper lay silent, targeting Flame, rifle steady and waiting. Gator had to find him before he managed to get off a clear shot at her.

He studied the area where he knew Flame lay in the reeds and water. He couldn't see her. She was adept at becoming a ghost, using the camouflage around her. No doubt she was still digging deeper into the muck. Their two big advantages were that the shooter didn't know Gator had joined the hunt and that they could communicate with each other.

Do you have a bead on his location? Gator asked.

That last shot came from directly in front of me, somewhere near the cypress with the one branch sweeping to the ground, but he moved immediately. He doesn't have a clear shot at me or he would have taken it.

Gator considered the information. What would he do under the circumstances? The swamp offered several good places for concealment and a professional sniper could lie for hours waiting for that one moment to take his shot.

Gator worked his way in a wide semicircle using Flame's position as his reference. The going was slow and methodical. He had to inch his way, careful not to disturb the reeds or bend any foliage.

He has to be enhanced. He has to be sent by Whitney.

Not necessarily. But he didn't know. What the hell kind of sniper could mask his heartbeat? His breathing? Was he the same as they were? Gator and Flame muted any noises they might make. Could the sniper do the same?

Raoul? It's going to rain any minute. I can feel moisture above us, can't you?

Was there a tremor in the sound coming to him? Her voice just slightly wavering. She was probably stiff and sore from falling off the motorcycle, and lying so still in the mud and water she'd be cramping up. She was looking for reassurance and completely unaware of it. His every protective instinct grew stronger.

A little rain never hurt anyone. You aren't worried I'm going to leave you, are you, cher? A man doesn't leave the mother of his child. And after this, I expect you to address me as your hero.

Her soft laughter reached his ears coming toward him on the precision sound wave she generated.

The clouds suddenly burst with an ominous rumble of thunder and rain poured down from the sky. Gator kept his head down, but his gaze moved ceaselessly over the terrain. He was looking for anything that might reveal the presence of the killer. With the rain coming down, it was much more difficult to see, but he strained his eyes, feeling rather than seeing that something was moving closer to Flame.

He's shifting position. Flame's warning came on the heels of his own radar. The man was good. Even with the rain flattening the reeds in places, there was nothing to give him away. Gator looked for telltale 'tree cancer,' a small dark spot on either side of the tree that might mean a sniper had set up shop, but there was nothing, only his warning system blaring at him.

My ear is planted in the mud and I can feel the earth vibrate. He's using the cover of the rain to get a better angle. I'm going to roll to my left. I think he's to my right.

No! Gator's command was sharp. *He's deliberately trying to get you to move. Stay still. I'll get him. You need patience for this kind of hunt. Don't panic on me, cher.* The thought of Flame moving terrified him. His heart actually jumped in his chest and something squeezed hard on his lungs. He didn't know how he knew the killer was trying to spook her into movement, but he was absolutely certain. And while he didn't think that Flame's training had included sniper school, Gator would have bet his cabin that the killer's had.

As if! I never panic.

He hoped that was true. Playing cat and mouse with a professional killer took nerves of steel. Flame knew the killer had a scope on the spot where she went down. If he managed to get a good shot off, she was dead. It took a lot of guts to lie still when a high-powered rifle was pointed right at you. Snipers didn't miss. He knew the odds. Where many soldiers fired off hundreds of rounds in a battle, a sniper used one to three shots per kill.

The rain poured from the skies, through the canopy of trees, so heavy it obscured vision. The water would help obliterate the tracks when it came to clean up, but it also provided a conductor for sound. He muted noise and sent out sonar, using echolocation in an attempt to pinpoint the location of the sniper. The man had to be concealed in the network of tree roots. Gator willed Flame to remain still as he crawled through the reeds and muck toward the last known spot where his adversary had been.

He scooted through a water-filled depression before realizing it was a man-made trench, narrow with just enough space for a man to lie in. He froze. He had to be almost on top of the sniper. Carefully, only allowing his eyes to move, he searched the area around him, quartering every section of ground. He barely allowed his breath to escape, waiting for something, anything at all to give the sniper's position away.

Time crept by. The rain poured down. Gator felt the rhythm of the marsh now, the teeming of insect life and the whisper of movement as frogs and lizards darted out from cover to grab a quick meal. His watchful gaze poured over the terrain again and again. The log to his left had split apart, rotted with age and was home to various life forms. A small green lizard skittered toward the log in small stops and starts, dashed forward and abruptly stopped before going up and over a slight mound.

Gator's breath caught in his throat. That mound, no more than ten feet from him, was the sniper. He hadn't moved, lying so completely still, covered in reeds and mud, he appeared part of the landscape. If he turned his head and looked, he would be able to spot Gator as only Gator's head and shirt were camouflaged. His jeans were muddy, but no way, at such a close range, would he escape detection. He didn't have a gun, which meant he would have to use a knife – and that meant working his way without detection until he was within striking range.

What's wrong?

He heard the anxiety in Flame's voice clearly.

Nothing. Stay down.

Your heart rate just went through the ceiling. Don't give me nothing. Fill me in. I'm not some pansy ass that can't take bad news.

No, she wasn't that. She'd coped with bad news most of her life. *No, you're a hothead and you might get yourself killed.*

I knew that weasel Whitney wanted me alive. Give it to me straight, Raoul. I need to know what's going on.

He weighed his options. He'd only have one chance at the sniper. She had to know the danger. *He's a few feet away. If he turns his head, he'll see me. Don't move, Flame. This guy knows what he's doing. He hasn't moved a muscle and he's had his eye to the scope the entire time.*

There was a small silence. He found himself holding his breath. *Raoul. I'll be really angry at you if you blow this and get killed.*

Now cher, *make up your mind. I thought you wanted me dead.*

You haven't had time to take out an insurance policy for the baby and me.

Nothing's goin' to be happening to me.

Flame was silent again. *I could kill him using sound. It's risky, but better that, than taking a chance . . .*

No! He forced calm into his voice. She was shrewd. He'd just given away too much to her, but it didn't matter. He wasn't going to chance it. He wouldn't let her chance it. *No. We'll do it the old-fashioned way.*

Count off. On every fifth second I'll use sound to move the reeds off to my right.

Was there relief in her voice? He couldn't tell. *Damn it, no.*

Damn it, yes. Just enough to make him worried I might be on the move. He'll be concentrating on me and it will give you a chance. I'm not stupid enough to let him get a shot at me. There was determination in her voice. *You can't have it both ways. Either we use sound or we take the chance together.*

171

Gator counted to five and propelled his body forward through the mud using his elbows. He silenced the sucking sound as muck dragged at his body in an attempt to hold him in place. He gained two feet. A few more and he could launch himself onto his target. He would have to go from a crouch to a full-on attack, leaping the distance before the sniper could turn and get a clear shot.

The second count he pushed forward only to see the sniper shift ever so slightly, shoulder hunching.

He's taking his shot.

He sent the warning simultaneously as the gun went off. The sniper rolled to his left, came up on his knee, rifle to his shoulder for the second shot. Gator sprang, more than grateful for the physical enhancement that allowed him to smash into the sniper, driving him face-down into the mud.

The man must have sensed his presence at the last second because he tried to turn, tried to keep the rifle out of the mud. Gator drove his knife into the man's side just as the sniper slammed the rifle stock against the side of Gator's head. For a moment, everything faded in and out. The sniper heaved him off, but Gator caught the rifle, hanging on and kicking at the other man's crotch.

Flame! Are you hit? He felt frantic, needing reassurance, needing to hear she was alive and well even as he was fighting for his own life. The sniper fought savagely, fear and anger lending him strength as they struggled for possession of the gun. *Answer me.*

'I'm here,' Flame called out to him as she pushed up out of the muck. The wet ground sucked at her, tried to hold her in place and her leg was throbbing and painful as she tried to stand. Gator had jerked the rifle from the sniper's hands and it went flying away from them. Both men pulled knives and began to circle.

She dragged herself out of the mud, willing her leg to work when it buckled under her. It didn't matter, nothing mattered but that she get to the gun. Gator leapt back avoiding the slice of the sniper's knife by a hair's breadth, feinted with his right hand, and moved in, going for the kill with his left hand. Flame launched herself into the air, landing hard beside the gun, going down as her leg collapsed under her, but she wrapped her fist around the rifle and brought it to her shoulder. The sniper was already stumbling backward, Gator's knife in his heart. He toppled over slowly, landing face-up in the rain, eyes wide open, shock on his face.

Gator turned and looked at her. Her gaze clung to his. She looked worn. Beat up. Shocked. Both heard the approach of a four-wheel-drive vehicle, but they didn't look away from each other. Gator walked over to her and pulled her to her feet. She stumbled, lacking her normal fluid grace and he caught her arms, steadying her, then reached out to wipe the mud from her hair. Streaks of brown and red ran down her pale face as the rain tried to wash her clean.

'Did you plan this?' Her voice was low, barely discernible, but her gaze remained locked with his. Steady. Demanding. There was pain there. Sorrow. Betrayal. All of it mixed together and it tore him up inside that she could think he might have been part of killing Burrell. Her body shook almost uncontrollably despite the heat and warmth of the rain.

Gator sucked in his breath, his fingers curling into two tight fists. 'What the hell are you accusing me of doing?'

She shook her head. 'I'm asking. Tell me the truth. I need the truth.' Her arms swept out in a semicircle to encompass the swamp. 'Did you do this? Set it up?'

173

The SUV screeched to a halt and Wyatt and Ian jumped out, looked around at the dead men, then to the couple, but they didn't approach them. Something in the way Gator and Flame stood so close, one body protective, the other fragile, yet both seemingly combative, warned the two men off.

'Damn it, Flame. Are you asking me if I killed Burrell? *Grand-mere*'s friend? *My* friend? What possible motive could I have?' Gator demanded.

'A field exercise to see if we worked well together. If we did what we were created by Whitney to do. We did, you know. We just performed a perfect combat mission.'

'Get the hell out of here. Go with Wyatt and stay with Nonny until I can get home.' He raked a hand through his hair. 'That's a hell of a thing to accuse me of, Flame, when I just saved your life. You have a real knack for getting under my skin.'

'I need to hear you say it.'

'Or what? You're going to shove a knife down my throat? You can't be here when they come to clean up. I've got to take the heat for this. I'm not about to stand here defending myself to you.' He took a step closer, gripping her upper arms before he could stop himself from giving her a little shake. 'You're being completely unreasonable and illogical . . .' His voice trailed off. Was she? Could he say with certainty that someone hadn't set them up to test their skills? The sniper had had exceptional skills.

He dropped his arms, suddenly wary, gaze working the area. 'Damn it, now you have me thinking conspiracy theories.'

'At least you're thinking. I can't stay with your grandmother. Don't argue with me, I just can't. I'll find somewhere, a motel, a room, it doesn't matter. I'm not being difficult, I need – space. Downtime. You know what I mean.'

He did. It didn't sit well with him, but he knew exactly what she meant. 'I have a cabin out in the bayou. It's far away from everyone. I'll have Wyatt take you there.' She turned away from him but Gator caught her arm. 'I expect you to be there.'

'I hear you. It isn't like I have too many places to go.'

'I didn't. Set this up I mean. There was no field exercise that I know of. I have no idea who these men are or who sent them, but I'll find out. I didn't do this, Flame.'

'Just out of curiosity, who'd you call for help with the cleanup? I'll bet it wasn't the local authorities. You called Whitney, didn't you?'

He almost wished she sounded angry. Instead, she sounded weary, exhausted, defeated even. 'Not Whitney. Lily.'

She shrugged. 'It's the same thing, Raoul. If you're talking to one, you're talking to the other, you just can't admit that to yourself.'

He reached out to brush mud from her face, his touch gentle, tender even. Flame stepped back, pushing at his arm, her gaze jumping to first Wyatt and then Ian. 'Don't.' Her whisper barely reached his ears. 'You can't be nice to me right now. I wouldn't survive it.' Her voice broke and she turned her face away from him.

Pain knifed through his heart. She looked broken, so fragile every protective instinct he possessed rose up to overwhelm him. He needed to hold her, to comfort her. 'Flame.' He drew her to him, uncaring of her mud-soaked clothes or her brittle resistance. 'I want to go with you, but I can't. We can't just leave a bunch of

175

dead bodies out here.' She trembled and he pulled her even closer, trying in vain to warm her body. Not even the heat and humidity of the bayou seemed enough to drive away the icy coolness of her skin.

'Why? They left Burrell to the alligators.' Her voice broke and she ducked her head, resting her brow against his chest.

Gator wrapped his arms around her, uncaring that Wyatt glanced at his watch and then up toward the sky. The helicopter would be arriving momentarily and somebody would be demanding answers to questions. All that really mattered at that moment to Gator was comforting her. 'I'm sorry, *bebe. Je vais faire ce droit. Je jure que je ferai ce droit.*'

She lifted her head to study his face. 'You can't make it right, Raoul. You can't bring Burrell back. Nothing can make this right.'

He brushed his lips over her eyebrow, a soft caress meant to comfort. '*Je suis desolé, le miel.* I wish I could make this right. Please go with Wyatt.'

His voice was a drawling sexy tenderness that nearly was her undoing. She blinked up at him, aware of her wet clothes, of the fact that she smelled like the swamp, that she was covered in mud, but most of all that tears shimmered in her eyes. She looked away from him, not knowing what to do or say. She needed desperately to be alone.

His hands covered hers. 'You were wearing gloves. Good girl. Ian's retrieving the knives and we'll lose them somewhere in the bayou a great distance from here. I don't want them traced back to you. He's replacing all sign of your being here with that of his own. These men killed Burrell, we chased them and fought.'

She shook her head. 'Forensic people are too good for that.'

'Not if they want to believe what they see. Our people aren't going to let the locals in on this. I'll say I wrecked the bike kicking the hell out of the driver. I did kill the sniper and the others are guilty of killing Burrell. I just want your name kept out of it. It's safer for you.'

'Why are you doing this for me?'

'Don't ask me that. I don't know the answer. Just get out of here and go with my brother.' He tipped her head back and brushed her lips with his. He didn't care that they were both covered in grime. 'Don't make me come looking for you tonight, Flame.'

'Come with me.' Wyatt jerked his thumb toward the swamp. 'We don't want to leave any tracks they can't cover. You've got my Jeep stashed somewhere. We can take that.'

'What about my bike?' She wasn't certain her leg would stand up to a run through the swamp, but the SUV would be sighted from the air. Ian would say he had driven it to the scene when Gator called him. 'If they check it . . .'

'I stole it, remember?' Gator said. 'Don't worry, I noticed it isn't registered to Iris Johnson. No one is going to make the connection, Flame.'

'Lily will. Whitney will.'

'Get out of here.' He wasn't going to argue with her anymore. Hell, she was sounding more and more like she was making sense. He frowned as he watched Wyatt and Flame start into the swamp. She was running, but she seemed to be limping. He almost called her back but Ian cleared his throat.

'This guy burned off his fingerprints. No ID on him at all, Gator. What the hell is going on here?'

Gator let out his breath. What was going on? Was it possible Flame was right and Whitney was still alive?

No one had seen the body. Only Lily claimed he was dead. Would she lie to protect her father?

When he was certain Flame was out of earshot, Gator turned to Ian. 'There may be something to Flame's suspicions. I couldn't even hear him breathe, Ian. You know I can hear just about anything.'

'You think he was one of us? One of the other team?' Ian asked.

Gator shrugged. 'I have no idea. Is there the slightest chance Peter Whitney is still alive?'

Ian swallowed his first instinctive answer and thought about it. 'How the hell would I know? There was no body. He disappeared and Lily told Rye she connected with him as he was being murdered. I suppose it's possible.'

'Do you think Lily would help him disappear?'

Ian scratched his head. 'No. No way. She's torn up over the things he did. If he's alive, she doesn't know it.'

Gator frowned. 'Lily's psychic, Ian. How could he fool her? She 'saw' his death.'

Ian shrugged his massive shoulders. 'Whitney was on the cutting edge of experimentation. No one knew more about psychic enhancement than he did. He experimented on children, on us and on at least one other team we know of. What's to say he didn't do a few experiments on himself?'

'Why? Why would he just disappear?'

'Higgens wanted him dead. The service was bound to be closing in on him. Most of his experiments were illegal. Even his money wasn't going to keep him out of harm's way. What better way to get out of it than to 'die'? He had more money than he knew what to do with. It wouldn't have been that difficult to bleed off a few million to a secret account and establish another residence and lab outside the States.'

'Flame thinks he's alive. She even thinks this might have been some kind of field operation to see how we work together.'

Ian's eyebrow shot up.

Gator nodded his head. 'Flame, *Iris*, has this idea that Peter Whitney is alive and directing everything from behind the scenes. I thought she was crazy at first, but now little things are bothering me. For one, I'm so damned attracted to her I can't think straight. It isn't just lust or emotional, it's a powerful combination of both and it borders on obsession. When I'm with her, I would do almost anything to have her, and I feel like killing any man who comes near her. That isn't me, Ian, and I don't trust it. *She* doesn't trust it. She feels the same way and she thinks Whitney managed to pair us somehow.'

'That's a little far-fetched, don't you think? How could he do something like that?' Ian stepped away from Gator, putting a small distance between them in an unconscious effort to deny what he was saying.

'Is it? I'm acting out of character. Even more, out of training. I knew she was dangerous, but I led her straight back to my house. To my family. Wyatt and Nonny. To you. Why would I do that when every instinct I possess would lead me to do just the opposite? I make illogical decisions around her. Why? Because I *have* to see her. The need is as strong as any drug. Look at Ryland and Lily and Nico and Dahlia. It's the same with them. And if that isn't enough our psychic gifts complement each other. My psychic talent matches hers. I can even amplify her. As a weapon, the two of us are probably unstoppable in an environment where we could destroy a large number of targets with no risk to civilians. Flame thinks Whitney did that on purpose and now he's sitting back testing us.'

'What do you think?'

'I don't know what the hell to think. There was a military sniper in this group – one with a very questionable background. He didn't belong with the others, he was light-years ahead of them in training. None of them carried IDs. His fingerprints are burned off. That's a hell of a lot of trouble to go to just to kill a retired riverboat captain.' He cocked his head to one side, listening. 'The helicopter is on the way. Who do we trust, Ian?'

'Each other. Just the way it's always been.'

'Do we warn the others? We don't have any facts, just pure conjecture.'

'It really doesn't matter if this was a field operation or whether it was something altogether different,' Ian said. 'The others need to know there's a possibility Whitney is still alive.'

'Then they ought to know we were physically enhanced as well as psychically.'

Ian nodded. 'I suspected as much. I didn't think being able to see through walls was going to help me jump over them. The physical enhancement just seemed a bonus.'

'He infected Flame with cancer more than once when she was a child. Enhancement can sometimes produce cancer and he wanted to find ways to avoid that. She was used as his lab rat. And Ian . . .' Gator waited until his friend looked at him. 'She was never adopted out any more than Dahlia was. She says if any of the girls were, it was only one or two of them, which means Whitney planted false stories for Lily to find. Lily is very suspicious already.'

Ian whistled. 'It never occurred to me that Peter Whitney might be alive.'

'Do you realize what that would mean? He's yanking on our strings. Setting us up. Still using us for experiments, only this time we don't know it.'

'We're in the service, Gator. It isn't like we don't expect to conduct field operations. It's why we agreed to the enhancement in the first place. We all thought we'd cut down on casualties and better serve our country. He could just have someone following us on assignment and document what we do. Going to this kind of trouble seems overkill.'

'Not if he wants to see us working with the women. If Whitney is alive and he's conducting secret experiments by putting us into other positions using the women, that changes everything. We didn't volunteer for that and that makes us . . .' He trailed off, unable to actually voice the word without bile rising in his throat. 'Damn that son of a bitch, Ian.'

'I'm not a damn victim, if that's what you're getting at,' Ian responded, his brilliant green eyes suddenly going flat and hard.

'Yeah, that's what I'm getting at. Do you think we feel superior to Lily, Dahlia, Flame, and the others because we made the choice? We volunteered for psychic enhancement. Do we pity them?'

Ian opened his mouth, then snapped it shut again. 'I wouldn't say superior. But the pity might be true. Although how anyone can pity Flame is beyond me. She's beautiful and she's lethal. And sexy as hell.'

'Thanks. You don't ever need to be saying that again. Or thinking it.' Gator let his breath out slowly. 'We didn't agree to physical enhancement and as cool as it has been, it also means we could get cancer just like Flame. For all I know the son of a bitch could have targeted us just like he did her. Once he realized gene enhancement could stimulate a mutant cell, he deliberately caused the mutation in order to figure out how to beat it. So he gave Flame cancer and then put her into remission a couple of times just as if she were a lab rat. Who's to say he hasn't done that to us?'

Ian swore softly. 'Cancer? Is that for real, Gator?'

'Yeah, it's for real. Lily thinks it may recur in Flame. Whitney used viruses as the vector for the enhancement. Sometimes the enhancement stimulated a cell that shouldn't have been messed with and there you go. Cancer. Of course Lily explains it all a lot better, but it boils down to the fact that Whitney deliberately used Flame for medical research.'

'What about children?' Ian asked. 'How do we know we're not going to pass something on to them?'

'Exactly. Lily says the gene doping shouldn't be passed on, but she's worried.'

'She's worried that he deliberately experimented at least on the women to see if he could,' Ian guessed. 'Because the question would occur to him as well. And knowing Whitney, he wouldn't be satisfied until he had the answer.'

'And that means the women had to grow up and find a partner,' Gator said. 'If Whitney conducted some other kind of experiment to match us all up, he'd be in a great position to get his answers.'

'If he were still alive,' Ian added.

'Exactly. If he's still alive.' Gator shoved a hand through his dark hair. 'That sniper was too well trained to be a civilian like the others. I swear, Flame's theory is beginning to make more sense than I want to admit.'

'How'd Flame get away from Whitney if she wasn't adopted out? And when? How long did he have her?'

Gator shook his head. 'She hasn't confided in me yet. She thinks Whitney sent me to bring her back.'

'Well. In a way that's the truth, isn't it?'

'Not like this.' Gator looked around him. 'I don't want them to trace any of this back to her. It's another gun aimed at her head.'

'Then we have to make certain they think you were on the bike, that you threw the knives, and had the garrote. We have to remove every trace of her, and we don't have much time.' He was working as he spoke. 'If they're looking for her, Gator, and they suspect for even a moment she's been here, they'll crawl through this place to find a strand of her hair. I'm laying down my prints and my tracks everywhere she was, but you need to be all over that bike. A child could read what went on here. And they'll be sending experts.'

'Chopper's already landed.' Gator cocked his head to one side listening. 'A couple of our boys, Kadan Montague and Tucker Addison, are heading this way. What would they be doing in this vicinity?' He hurried to help obliterate all signs of Flame's participation.

'Come on, Gator. Kadan and Tucker are with us. You can't suspect them of being part of a conspiracy.'

Gator met Ian's gaze squarely. 'Just to be on the safe side, until we know what's happening, let's be careful what we say.'

'She's going to be royally pissed about you claiming that bike,' Ian warned. 'She has a thing about that motorcycle.'

'Well she'll have to get over it. Until we know what's really going on, I'm going to assume she's in danger. Whether Lily or anyone else likes it, Flame is a GhostWalker and is under our protection.'

Ian laughed as he turned to walk back toward the small clearing where the helicopter had landed. 'You've got it wrong, Gator. That woman thinks you're under her protection. She's going to kick your ass for this. You're taking advantage of the fact that she was a little bit shell-shocked with Burrell's death. When she recovers . . .'

'Stop trying to give me nightmares.' Gator righted the bike, not an easy task when it was half buried in mud and the front tire was completely twisted. It wasn't going to be easy, in fact, it was probably impossible to hide the fact that Flame had been there from Kadan and Tucker. He trusted them with his own life, but he wasn't so certain he trusted them with Flame's. He didn't know exactly how to explain that to Ian.

'I think you're in over your head,' Ian tossed back over his shoulder, striding away, his long legs covering ground fast.

'That's an understatement,' Gator admitted aloud.

He lifted the motorcycle out of the muck, for the first time really paying attention to the superhuman strength of muscle in his body. He could run twice as fast and twice as long as he could before the experiments. He could jump and clear unbelievable heights, but it was really his tremendous strength that astonished him. He knelt beside the motorcycle and looked as if he were examining the bent frame and wheel.

'Nice mess,' Kadan greeted as he stepped around the Jeep. 'What the hell happened here, Gator? It looks like you went hunting.' His sharp gaze was already touching on the water-filled tracks in the mud.

Kadan had trained in Special Forces, served a couple of years, joined the FBI, and had a reputation for solving very difficult murder cases. He'd volunteered to join the psychic team and retrain with the rest of them when he was approached. It was common knowledge Kadan had been far more psychically gifted prior to the enhancement than any of the rest of the GhostWalkers.

'Four men killed a local retired riverboat captain. He was a good friend of mine. Knew him since I was a kid.

184

They hunted him on his island, murdered him, and threw his body in with one of the big alligators, weighted it down so no one would find him. Then they burned his boat. Burrell wasn't a troublemaker, just a nice man who deserved a hell of a lot better than that.'

Kadan's steel blue eyes never shifted from Gator's face. 'And you happened on them afterward?'

Gator nodded. 'I was actually going to the houseboat, had parked the motorcycle I was using when I heard the shots coming from the island.'

Kadan glanced at the Jeep wrapped around a tree, at the body of a man with a knife buried to the hilt in his throat and the driver garroted, his weapon lying beside him. 'You lost your temper, Gator.'

Behind him, Tucker Addison snorted. 'I'd say that was a hell of an understatement. This is a war zone. And it didn't do much for your motorcycle either.'

Gator didn't crack a smile. He didn't feel like smiling. He *had* lost his temper and that was a dangerous thing. And he hadn't been the only one. Flame had shown restraint. It didn't much look like it with four men lying dead in the swamp, but she could have flattened everything within a five-mile radius had she not been disciplined enough to focus on only the four assassins.

He ducked his head, the memory of his own loss of temper, his own lack of discipline a lifetime ago washing over him before he could stop it. The blow felt like a punch in the gut and he choked on shame and guilt. He had to turn away from Kadan and his all-seeing eyes. He could never look at any of the GhostWalkers, not straight in the eye, when he recalled the early events of his training. He slammed the door closed on ugly memories the way he always did, but he wondered how many ugly memories Flame had. It was another thread tying them together.

Without conscious thought, his hand stroked the seat of the motorcycle. He only became aware of it when he felt Kadan's gaze following the movement. Abruptly he pulled his hand away. 'I couldn't let them get away with it, Kadan. They were whooping it up and I followed them. We fought and they died.'

'Sounds simple enough, doesn't it, Tucker?' Kadan asked.

Gator glared at him. 'They had their chance at me. The big guy over there,' he gestured with his thumb toward the sniper, 'nearly killed me.'

'Did you try to take them in?' Kadan stared at the Jeep and the dead man with the knife shaft sticking out of his throat.

'There were four of them and they didn't exactly say they were giving up.'

Kadan's sharp eyes slid over him. 'Not with a knife sticking out of their throat, I'll just bet they didn't. Why aren't you telling me the truth? What happened here?'

'Why were you in New Orleans?' Gator countered. 'The last I heard you were recovering from a mission and holing up for a while.'

The tension shot up. The rain poured down. Kadan's blue eyes grew colder, turned more gray than blue. 'What the hell's going on here, Gator?'

Tucker moved up beside Kadan, his features hard and still. Ian shifted position until he was shoulder to shoulder with Gator, facing the other two GhostWalkers.

Kadan's cell phone jangled. He let it ring twice before he pulled it out and snapped it open. 'Make it fast. I'm in the middle of something.'

'Tell me what's going on out there, Kadan.' Lily's

voice could clearly be heard. 'Does this have anything to do with Flame? With Iris Johnson?'

'As far as I know Gator came out here to find Joy Chiasson. I don't know anything about the Johnson woman. I don't know if this is related to Joy's disappearance or not, but four men, one highly skilled and definitely trained in the military, probably special ops, from the evidence I see, murdered an old man, a friend of Gator's. That's what this is about. You know of anyone running a field op down here, Lily?'

'I'll find out. Is everyone okay?'

'All the good guys. The bad guys are in a hell of a mess.' Kadan hung up, pocketed the phone, and looked directly at Gator. 'This is about Flame, isn't it? You found her.'

Another silence settled over them so that the rain seemed loud as it beat down on them. Gator shrugged his shoulders. 'She's here in New Orleans. She was staying with Burrell in the houseboat.'

'You think she was the one they were after?' Tucker gestured toward the dead men. 'You don't really think they were sent to assassinate her, do you? Who would know about her? Who would send them? And why would there be a son of a bitch just as trained as we are and most likely just as enhanced psychically?'

'You think Whitney is alive.' Kadan made it a statement.

Gator shook his head, a slight, humorless grin tugging at his mouth. 'You're good, Kadan, and you weren't even touching me. Yeah, I think the bastard just might be alive. And I'm thinking he might be setting us up to see how we match up in the field with the women he experimented on.'

Kadan frowned, thinking it over. 'No one saw his body. I suppose it's possible. He could have fooled Lily and set her up to do his work for him.' He looked around him with suspicious eyes. 'Gator, you didn't think Tucker and I were part of someone else's team, did you?'

Gator shoved a muddy hand through his disheveled hair. 'I don't know what the hell I'm thinking anymore. Who can I trust when her life is on the line? Lily wants her back, but I can't exactly force her to go back when all she's ever known there is pain and suffering. She doesn't trust Lily.'

'What about you, Gator? Do you trust Lily?'

'Well, that's the question, isn't it?'

Chapter Ten

Flame was weeping. Gator's belly knotted. The sound was soft and muffled, probably by a blanket, but he could hear her even through the pounding rain and it broke his heart. He tied his skiff to a post beside the airboat and jumped onto shore. The ground was spongy and his boots sank a couple of inches into muck. In his life, he had never imagined the sound of a woman quietly crying would tear him up the way it was doing. He should have come to her immediately instead of taking the time to shower and pick up a few supplies.

He paused outside the door. What was he going to say to her? Kadan, Tucker, and Ian had all agreed with him that it was possible that Peter Whitney was still alive. They had no idea why Burrell had been murdered. If the one obviously enhanced sniper hadn't been with the others, Gator would never have suspected that Burrell's death had anything to do with Flame or the Ghost-Walkers – now he just didn't know.

The other GhostWalkers were with his grandmother and he felt far better about her having protection after Burrell's death – especially as he needed to be with Flame. A shower had helped stave off exhaustion for a short time while he packed a few supplies, but he was feeling the effects of psychic and physical fatigue.

Gator pushed open the door to find Flame straight ahead, leaning against the wall, a throwing knife in her hand. She looked as if she'd been crying for hours, but she faced him with determination. Her hair was still damp from her shower and she wore jeans that were too big and an oversized men's plaid shirt he recognized as belonging to Wyatt.

'I'm alone,' he assured her.

The tension went out of her and she relaxed visibly. At least she hadn't thrown the knife at him. That was some progress.

'What did you find out?'

'Not much. A couple of men from my squad showed up and helped Ian and me clean things up. Burrell's been reported missing and I told the police you were with *Grand-mere* and me all afternoon and when we came back, we heard shots coming from the island and while we were investigating the shots, someone started the houseboat on fire. I stuck to the truth as closely as possible.'

Tears shimmered in her eyes again. 'I can't believe he's dead. That someone would murder him. All he wanted to do was live on the waterfront and listen to the music in the bayou while he smoked his pipe. He never hurt anyone in his life. This isn't right, Raoul. It just isn't right.'

'No, it isn't right,' he agreed, the lump in his throat threatening to choke him.

'We just left him there in the alligator hole.'

'He would have wanted us to cover for you. We don't know who we're dealing with yet, Flame. I was going to track for the forensic people tomorrow if they hadn't figured it out. It's been raining heavily and the rain may have wiped out most of the tracks. Burrell's island is a good distance from where we took down the killers and nothing will lead them to the preserve. The bodies are gone. Even if they find the wrecked Jeep, none of us touched it.'

Another sob escaped, but she choked it back, turning away from him. 'I hate this. I hate being out of control.'

He didn't know how to comfort her. Strange when he'd always been so good with women, but now, when it mattered to him, he didn't know the right thing to say or do. He rubbed her arm awkwardly. 'You have every reason to cry.'

She shrank away from him, glaring. 'I'm not crying.'

'*Cher.*' His tone was incredibly tender and her eyes filled up all over again. He watched her wipe at them with the back of her hand. 'It's okay to cry. It's good to cry.'

'No it's not. Why do people say that? Crying is a complete waste of time. It doesn't do any good whatsoever. Your face swells up and turns red. Your eyes burn and you get the headache from hell. Will crying bring Burrell back?' She sank down onto the bed, back against the wall, drawing her knees up. 'I cried once in a while after I learned to screw up Whitney's camera and recorders. It didn't make me well. It didn't get me out of the cage he put me in. It didn't do a damn thing but give him satisfaction when he found out. I'm *not* crying.'

Gator shoved a bag, the one he recognized from the first night he'd met Flame, into a corner of the cabin out of the way before stripping off his shirt and tossing it onto the back of a chair. He pulled a bottle of water from his pack. 'Here, drink this.'

'Thanks.' She took the bottle, watching as he tugged off his boots and tossed them into the corner of the room beside the large bag. 'I'm not sleeping with you so you may as well take the bed. I can sleep on the floor.'

Gator sat down beside her. She flinched when he jarred her leg. 'I didn't ask you nor was I going to seduce you, *not*, mind you, that it wouldn't work.'

'You were going to ask me. And seduction wouldn't have worked.'

'I wasn't going to try,' he repeated.

She frowned. 'Why not? What's wrong with me? I think you'd try with an alligator so why not me?'

'An alligator? I draw the line at reptiles.'

'Fine, I take it back. Why aren't you going to *try* to seduce me?'

He raised his eyebrows at her. 'You mean why aren't I *going* to seduce you? *Grand-mere* raised a gentleman. You're too upset for me to take advantage of you right at this moment. We can both sleep on the bed and I'll behave myself.'

Her gaze moved over his face. 'But you *would* have tried to seduce me if I wasn't so upset, right?'

'W-e-l-l,' he drawled. 'I don' know if I would have or not. You have a thing about knives.'

She made a face at him. 'You like my knives and you know you do. It turns you on every time you think about them.'

He didn't deny the obvious. 'Did you huck one at me the other night after you left the club? Inquiring minds want to know.'

'Huck? Is huck a word? No, I don't *huck* knives; I throw them with deadly accuracy. If I threw a knife at you, you'd be in the bottom of the bayou. I saved your ass, actually.' She wiped at her eyes again, took a drink of water, and twisted the cap back into place.

'What the hell does that mean?'

'It means you aren't quite the Mr. Invincible you like to think you are. You got someone mad at you the other night and he was just drunk enough and mean enough to try to take you out. You've grown complacent, and complacency can get you killed.'

'You were following me?'

'I was *baby-sitting*. You and your drunken idiot brother and friend. Someone had to do it and I didn't see anyone else volunteering. Personally, I don't think you have all that many friends.'

'It was Vicq, wasn't it? He waited for his chance and threw the knife.'

She shrugged. 'I was pretty certain he wasn't going to just walk away quietly. He isn't the quiet type. Did you know that he dated Joy? They went out twice. She called it off when he gave her a black eye for looking at another man.'

Anger churned close to the surface. 'How the hell did you find that out? If Wyatt had known he would have been gunning for Vicq.'

'Word is, everyone is afraid of the man.'

'I'm not.'

'Which is why I was baby-sitting you.' She sent him a look of censure. 'Just because you're enhanced doesn't mean you can't be killed. You dismissed him because he isn't combat trained. He's dangerous, Raoul, and you should have known that. I could see it in his eyes. He *likes* violence and he gets away with it. I'll bet he's very abusive toward women as a rule. He's going to beat his wife and children and he'll have fights all the time hoping to hurt or do worse to the men he picks the fight with. He *likes* it. He likes hurting people and probably animals as well.'

'How'd you find out he went out with Joy?'

'I talked to her mother. She told me Joy came home

crying and had bruises on her face. They didn't want her father or brothers to find out because Vicq has such a bad reputation. Joy's mother mentioned it to the police but they didn't even question him.'

'It wasn't in the police report, I read the report myself.'

'What a shocker. You said Vicq's last name was Comeaux. Did you notice the police officer's last name on the report? Everyone is related to everyone.'

Gator swore softly in Cajun. 'I should have caught that. So Vicq Comeaux is actually a suspect. You haven't tried to question him, have you?'

She frowned at the sharpness in his voice. 'I'm not that stupid. I don't think anyone would get anything out of him by questioning him, and certainly not a woman. The best way is for someone to get drunk with him and talk trash about women. He's going to brag.'

'You know a lot about people, don't you?'

'It's a survival technique. I learned it early on. Whitney was a hell of a teacher.' She turned her face away from him, but not before he caught the glimpse of pain in her eyes. 'My bet is on the boyfriend. Parsons's son,' she continued, leaning her head against the wall and stretching her right leg out in front of her. 'Something isn't right about him.'

'I had the same feeling. Take the jeans off.'

Her gaze leapt to his, held there. 'You said you weren't going to try anything.'

'I'm not. For God's sake, woman, you're beautiful, but don't flatter yourself. I'm not after your body. I'm after your leg. That's a single body part.'

'You are too after my body. There's heat in your eyes and' – she waved her hands around – '*evidence* elsewhere.'

He leaned close until his breath was warm on her

194

lips. 'I'll let you in on a little secret, *cher*. I'm a man. When I get near you, there's going to be a lot of evidence that I want you. Now get rid of the jeans. I want to see your leg.'

'I'm not showing you my leg.'

'Do you have any idea how stubborn you can look? Our children better never give me that look, although I won't mind if they give it to you. You'd deserve it.'

'Where's my motorcycle?'

He groaned and leaned back, hands behind his head. 'Don' be askin' me questions that are going to get you all riled up. You're tryin' to get out of strippin' for me and it won't work. I'm going to look at your leg so you might as well just get it over and take the damned jeans off. They're too big for you anyway.'

'I don't have anything else to wear. My clothes were on Burrell's houseboat.'

The little catch in her voice made his stomach flip. '*Don'* start crying again. I can't take it.'

'You just got through telling me it was good for me.'

'I was being manly and comforting you. Now it's just plain self-preservation. I'll buy you clothes tomorrow. You can get ten pairs of jeans for all I care.'

A faint smile curved her mouth. 'You're crazy, you know that?'

He continued to look at her pointedly.

Flame heaved a sigh. 'I don't have any underwear on. I wasn't going to wear your brother's. My leg is sore. I kicked the driver to make him wreck. Well,' she hedged, 'I was hoping to break his neck and eliminate him altogether.'

He reached for the waistband of her jeans. 'We're going to have to do something about that temper of yours. You can't go around killing people because they piss you off, not even when you have reason to be pissed off.' His fingers brushed bare skin. Soft skin. Her belly was firm, but so damned soft he wanted to lean forward and press his mouth against it.

She stiffened, her hands covering his, stopping the movement but holding his fingers against her stomach. He could feel the tremor running through her. 'I'll do it myself.'

'And I was having such fun.'

'Look the other way. I'm not putting on a show for you, perv.'

He closed his eyes obediently and lay back on the bed again, suddenly tired. It had been a long, frustrating day. He had more questions than answers. Burrell was dead. He was no closer to finding Joy Chiasson than the day he'd arrived in New Orleans, and he was certain when Flame peeled off her jeans, and he got a good look at her injured leg, he wasn't going to like what he saw.

She wiggled against him as she dragged off the jeans. Twice he heard a gasp escape as she tried to be careful removing the garment. He opened his eyes just as she dragged a sheet around her.

'Fils de putin!' He bent closer to inspect her leg. *'Maudit!'*

'You're looking.'

'Hell yes, I'm looking.'

'Stop swearing. It's not that bad. A few bruises, a little swelling. What did you expect? The bike was going fast, so was the Jeep and I kicked him as hard as I could. It wasn't all that soft when I landed either.'

'How did you manage to make it back through the swamp on this leg? You were running full-out, I saw you.'

She shrugged. 'I found out a long time ago, you can endure anything if you have to. Whitney didn't defeat me, Raoul. I learned a lot of very valuable lessons.' She looked him straight in the eye. 'He isn't going to get me back. I'd rather die. If you or anyone else managed to get me there, I'd take down his house and everyone in it. I mean it. Think long and hard on that before you decide to try bringing me back.'

He looked down at her mottled leg. From knee to hip her thigh was black and blue with ugly swollen blotches that might indicate internal bleeding. '*Fils de putin.*' He swore again under his breath, his hands going to her leg, lifting it onto his lap as if he could magically take the pain away.

'Are you listening to me?'

'I heard you. You need to see a doctor, Flame.'

'I meant it. I can't go through that again. I really meant it.'

'I know. What the hell are we going to do about your leg?' His palm stroked down her skin, his touch featherlight, barely there, but she felt it all the way to her bones. 'I'm taking you to *Grand-mere.* She knows the *treateur* – the healer. They've been best friends for years.'

'Take me tomorrow. I can't be around anyone tonight.' Her chest hurt. She felt as if someone had dropped a hundred pound weight on her. A part of her wanted to scream and scream, another part wanted to flood the world with tears, but the worst part of her, something cold and dark and ugly, wanted to go hunting. 'Did you tell Lily you found me? She's the one who sent you after me, didn't she? If you or your friend told her . . .'

'Lily doesn't know we've had any contact. No one told her anything. If Whitney is alive and he's aware of your presence here, it didn't come from any of us.'

She believed him. She rarely believed anyone, not

really. Not all the way. But with Raoul, she felt almost as if she knew him intimately, the real Raoul, not the one everyone else saw. And God help her, she actually believed him. 'Maybe I'm just tired.' She murmured the words aloud.

'You didn't do this, Flame. You didn't cause Burrell's death.'

'How do you know that? Whitney's capable of anything, even killing a kind old man just to get the end results of his experiment. He must have changed a lot over the years to have you think he wouldn't do it, or he hid that side of himself well.'

'I didn't much like him. None of us did. He was cold. Inhuman.' He shifted her as gently as possible until they were turned around in the bed. 'Lie down.' He waited until her head was on the pillow before he pulled a blanket over her. 'I never could understand how Lily loved him. She didn't know he wasn't her biological father. She found out after he died.'

'He isn't dead.'

'Maybe he isn't. In all honesty, you've got me halfway believin' the man is out there somewhere recording every move we make.' Gator switched off the lights and stretched out on the bed beside her, careful to avoid touching her leg.

'I should leave.'

He heard the sound of his heartbeat accelerate. He knew she heard it too. The protest surged up, a strong tidal wave of denial. The walls rippled with a low pulse of dissent. She laid her hand over his.

'I'm not going. I have to find out who did this to Burrell. I'm just saying, it's the smart thing to do. And there's Joy. Someone did something to her. I wish I could believe she was dead, but I don't.'

In the darkness he turned his head to look at her.

'You don't think she's dead? Why? What makes you think she's still alive?'

She would never have told anyone else. Ever. She would have gone to her grave and never told a single soul. 'Sometimes when I go places I hear echoes of sounds.' She waited for him to snicker. To laugh. To say she was crazy.

He twisted his fingers through hers and brought her hand up to his chest, over his heart. 'Go on.'

'I think plants sometimes absorb the sound. It gets trapped there in certain plants and I can hear it.'

'You think the sound is trapped in the plants?' The pad of his thumb brushed idly over the back of her hand. 'I've heard it too, the echo of screams, or laughter. The murmur of voices. At first I thought it was because my hearing was so acute, but then I realized that I was hearing something that had taken place in the past, minutes to months earlier. I thought it could be pockets of space, like the air pockets in a car when it sinks under water. But sound disperses. That didn't make any sense at all. But plants don't have ears. How the hell would they hear?'

'The echo of the past in certain places really bothered me.' She sniffed, still trying to get a handle on her emotions. It helped that Gator had bantered a little with her, but she still wanted to cry a river of tears for Burrell. For Joy. For herself. She forced control, wanting to share something of herself with Gator, just because he cared enough to comfort her. The casual rubbing of his thumb over her hand should have been trivial, but it wasn't.

'I did consider that maybe Whitney had managed to drive me out of my mind, but then I remembered it had happened a couple of times when I was really young, before I realized just what a monster he really was, so

199

I did some research. I wrote down each time I heard the sounds and tried to remember everything that was around me at the time. The one thing each incident had in common was that there were plants there. Not a single plant, but a large group of plants.'

'I never thought of plants. How would they hear things?'

She was acutely aware of his thumb on her hand, stroking caresses back and forth. It wasn't sexual. She almost wished it were. There was comfort, an intimacy, the small gesture tying her to him where any other touch might have driven her away. She stared up at the ceiling, shocked she was talking about things that mattered to her, revealing secrets she'd never dared to tell another soul – things she'd never *wanted* to tell another person.

'There's an Asian plant with transparent leaves called Hydrilla verticillata. Under a microscope you can see live streaming protoplasm. And before you think I'm brilliant and a scientist, I looked it up and someone else had conducted an experiment. In the research I read about, Huxley used a tuning fork and managed to speed up the protoplasm by using sound.'

'And this relates to the voices we hear, how?'

'I love the sarcasm in your voice. You're such a skeptic.' She laughed softly, a small sound that actually held humor when deep inside she was weeping. Flame had a difficult time analyzing why she wanted to share her theories with Gator and why he could make her smile in the midst of overwhelming grief. She didn't even know why it was okay with her to be lying in the dark, his body solid and warm and so comforting she wanted to cling like a small child to him. The sound of the rain beat down on the roof and only added to the surreal feeling.

'Well come on.'

'We can destroy things with sound, why not make them grow? For years scientists have believed songbirds contribute to plant growth by singing all the songs in the early-morning hours. A French physicist conducted a very successful experiment exposing how plants respond to sound waves. He composed musical note sequences that helped the plants grow. Each note is chosen to correspond with an amino acid in a protein with the full tune corresponding to the entire protein. It's done with electromagnetic energy . . .'

'Sound waves.'

'Exactly. He also warned musicians not to play the notes because they might become ill.' She loved the sound of his voice, the way he drawled his words. She could lie in the dark and listen to the combination of his voice and the rain forever.

'So low frequencies. You think the plants absorb and possibly retain low-frequency notes in their makeup?'

'As well as high acoustical sounds. Like laughter. Like screams. The low murmurs we hear and the edge of violence.'

He brought her hand up to his mouth, his teeth nibbling gently at her knuckles. He seemed unaware of his action, but she felt it all the way down to her toes. Her stomach did a series of interesting little somersaults. She tried to be analytical about the strange sensation, but all she could think about was the feel of his teeth and tongue on her skin.

'So you caught something repeating back from the past that had to do with Joy? Where? What?' His teeth nipped the end of her finger, a tiny stinging bite instantly gone when he drew her finger into the warmth of his mouth.

Her breath hitched but she couldn't quite bring

herself to pull her hand away from him. She heard her accelerated heartbeat, but it meant she was alive, *living*, able to experience whatever she could before time ran out. She wanted to be with Raoul Fontenot, tonight, this night, when her world had once again crashed and she'd failed yet another human being. She wanted to lie beside him and feel his heat and his solid body, to let him comfort her in the darkness.

'I heard Joy cry out. She begged someone not to hurt her. Most of what he said was very unintelligible, but I caught something about her coming to enjoy the things he would do to her. I don't think whoever took her meant to kill her, at least not right away. I think if we work fast enough, we have a chance of finding her alive.'

'But you have no clue who the man was?'

'None. The more I tried to listen, the less I heard. The bottom line is, we have to find Joy Chiasson. I won't be able to live with myself if we don't. I believe she's alive and I think she's in the hands of a monster.'

'Then we have to search together. Where did you hear this?'

'Just outside the Hurican before I went in to sing. She was there.'

'Everyone knows that, she never made it home from the club. You're not going back to the Hurican to try to tempt every pervert there to follow you home.'

'I wasn't tempting perverts.'

'That's *exactly* what you were doing.' His teeth nipped a little harder at her finger but before she could protest, his tongue swirled around to ease the slight ache. 'You were trying to draw out whoever took Joy and make them come after you. You had no backup, no real plan, no help whatsoever.'

'So what's your big plan? I don't see hanging out in

the clubs did you much good. You had less information than I had.'

'I found out that James Parsons lied his ass off to the cops. He isn't the least bit broken up over Joy's disappearance, other than the attention it's gotten him.'

She gave a little sniff of pure disdain. 'You didn't find that out in the club. You met him and we discussed it.'

'Briefly. It was a brief discussion. I have sharp perception when it comes to readin' people, *cher.*'

'Only after *I* said he was a good suspect,' she reminded. 'Was there a fire in here? You have scorch marks on the windowsills and around the door. What happened here?'

'Dahlia was here. After the attack on the sanitarium, Nico, one of the men in the GhostWalker squad, brought her here. She has this little problem with energy although she's working on controlling it.'

Dahlia. Flame remembered Dahlia, a rebel, so very much like herself. Whitney had despised them, even in the early ages when they were barely five years old. Dahlia had been in so much pain, rocking back and forth, the nurses begging Whitney to let her be with Flame or with Lily. Either of them could ease the pain, but Whitney had isolated her, just as he'd isolated Flame. The terrible memories crowded in, memories of unbearable loneliness, of fear and rage. Memories of the slow realization that Peter Whitney, the man who held absolute power over her, was a monster. Worse, that one moment in her childhood when she'd become aware that a monster had begun to grow inside of her. A small sound of despair escaped. She never opened those doors, never looked back. But it was all there, reaching out with greedy claws to suck her down into a dark hole she remembered all too well.

Flame yanked her hand away from Gator and pushed at him. 'Leave. You have to go.' She was going to cry again, she could feel the choking in her throat, the burning in her eyes and the weight pressing hard on her chest. 'Hurry. Get out of here.' Because if she sank into that darkness, she couldn't trust herself and she wasn't going to take a chance on hurting Raoul.

'*Maudit!* Stop pushing me away. I'm not going anywhere.'

She buried her face in the pillow. 'You have to. You don't understand how dangerous it is for me to lose control. I can't stop crying and I'm so angry with Whitney. I try never to think about him because I don't know if I can maintain discipline. You *have* to leave. Please, I'm asking you to leave. You don't know what I've done. What I'm capable of doing. I don't want to hurt you.'

'Do you think you're the only dangerous person here, Flame? I'm like you. I'm worse than you. He developed me into a damn weapon and sent me into a field to test the results without having a clue what would happen. I went like a good little soldier and I did what they told me to do. I killed five people. One was a friend of mine. I injured nineteen others. Try living with that on your conscience. Whatever you've done is nothing, *nothing* compared to that.' He pulled the pillow from her face, bracing his hands on either side of her head to stare down into her eyes. 'I *murdered* them. Men I'd sworn to protect. Don't talk to me about discipline or danger. I smile and I swallow anger and I back away from anything that might make me lose control. Not now. Not this time. I'm here to stay. You got that? Are you hearing me? I'm not leaving this time. I'm not giving up something I want as badly as I want you because that *fils de putin* did this to us.'

She shook her head, her fingers brushing his face. Lightly. With tenderness. There was regret on her face. 'I don't even care if he did something to make us want to be together. You're an incredible man, but you're a family man, Raoul. You know you want it all. You want a wife and a house filled with children. You deserve that. Wyatt will get married and your children and his children will all be best friends. You can't want me the way you're looking at me. You don't even know me.'

'Flame.' There was a stark ache in his voice. Heat. Desire. He had never wanted a woman in the way he wanted her. 'Don't say I don't know you. I've known you forever. You see me. The real me. You see me where no one else does, where no one else ever will or could. You can't ask me to give that up. And I know you. You don't have to be afraid or hide from me.'

'I had cancer. Not once, but several times. I can't have children, Raoul. I don't have a future with a family.'

'We'll find a way.'

'There is no way and you know it. And Whitney isn't going to let me have a happy ever after. He invested far too much time and money in all of the girls he brought over from the orphanages. And if you think Lily isn't involved, tell me why she hasn't figured it out yet. She's smart. She's very smart.'

'Not when it comes to her emotions.' He leaned forward, lowered his head. Just enough to brush his lips against hers. He didn't know if he was comforting her – or comforting him. It was just imperative to kiss her. To feel the softness of her mouth against his. To feel her response to him, as natural as breathing. He wanted to gather her into his arms, hold her against him and just shelter her there.

Flame kissed him tentatively, reaching a little to

complete the contact between them. She felt the heat of his mouth spreading through her body, just that one touch, but it was enough to warm her, to push back the cold of death and grief and the fear of being a monster. Her arms slid around his neck to pull him closer to her.

Gator sank his mouth into the heat of hers. His body blanketed hers, a slow stretch over the top of her, so that he felt every soft curve of her body. Her tears were damp on her face and her mouth was fiery hot. 'Stop crying. Nothing's going to happen right now.'

'Maybe that's why I'm crying.' She kissed him again, rested her forehead against his. 'I don't want to be anything like her, have anything in common with her – or with him.'

'Flame.' It was a protest, swift and sharp and shocked. 'You're nothing like him. Nothing like Lily. Why would you even say that?' He eased his weight off of her, settling next to her, his arms surrounding her, holding her to him when he felt she was on the verge of flight.

'Why do you think he chose us, Raoul? Even then we were different. He could see it in us.'

'You had psychic gifts.'

'It was more than that. I'm a freakin' genius, Raoul. There isn't a whole hell of a lot I don't understand. I have a need of knowledge, a love of it, and I'm driven to feed that need. I have to have answers. I'm smart in every area until it comes to my emotions. That's where I make all my mistakes. How did he know? How did he figure out by looking at infants he could take control of their lives and hang on to them forever?'

'He couldn't know that, Flame. And you aren't anything like him. He may have been smart, but I didn't see that much emotion in him.'

'You didn't?' She shook her head. 'There was such

rage in him. It consumed him. He was in terrible pain and he wanted everything and everyone around him to feel the things he was feeling. He had emotions and he wasn't in the least bit of control of them. That's what he hated the most.'

'I didn't think about it like that.'

'Peter Whitney is my enemy. I studied him. I studied everything there was to know about him. I found every newspaper article about his grandparents, his parents, and about him. He was unwanted just the way all of us girls were unwanted. His family was all about politics and money. They had him because it was expected, not because he was wanted. Nothing he did was ever good enough for them. He was ignored and shoved aside in spite of his brilliance. And he hated that. He wanted to do something to make them stand up and take notice. Maybe he even wanted to embarrass them. Buying orphans overseas and experimenting on them would definitely do that. Especially since his parents frowned on his outrageous beliefs when it came to psychic ability. He had rage all right. And he sowed that same rage in me. In most of the girls. Probably all of them.'

'How long did he have you, Flame?' He felt the breath catch in her throat. She turned away from him, settling her head on the pillow, stretching her bruised leg with care, her back to him. 'You never talk about it. Why is that?'

'What's there to say? He had you, didn't he? Do you talk about what he did? What you did? The training he gave you? I probably could have escaped sooner, but there was that terrible need for more knowledge. Until I realized it was what he counted on. How much I was becoming like him. All that rage and all that pain buried so deep I couldn't find it. The focus was always on the training and the knowledge.'

'How did you escape?'

Instantly, as if he'd thrown a switch, she retreated, physically drawing back, her face carefully blank, her eyes cloudy and unreadable. She let out a small, forced sigh and rubbed at her temples as if they were throbbing, averting her face. 'I'm so tired, Raoul. I need to sleep.'

Gator wanted to protest, but he could see it wouldn't do him any good. She had shut down completely. He kissed the nape of her neck and lay listening to the steady rhythm of the rain. Eventually her body relaxed and he heard her soft breathing indicating she really had fallen asleep. She didn't want to answer him. She was exhausted, that was true, but she had cut off communication immediately when he'd asked the question. He'd felt her instant withdrawal. He was coming to know her, the slightest nuances, and Flame hadn't been about to tell him how she'd escaped.

Outside the cabin, frogs set up a chorus and once an alligator bellowed. Inside, he lay awake, wondering how he was going to keep the woman in his arms, the only one he'd ever wanted, for his own.

Chapter Eleven

'Essayez-vous *de vous echapper de moi, ma petite flamme*?'

Flame paused in the act of shifting carefully off the bed. She should have known she would disturb him. 'I'm not escaping. I'm not your little flame either. I've got business this morning.'

Gator groaned and sank his head back onto the pillow, fingers curled around her wrist, anchoring her to him. 'Is it morning? It's still dark.'

'You have your eyes closed. You're not a morning person, are you?'

'I could be if you snuggled with me,' he said hopefully.

'I don't snuggle. I don't even know how.' She leaned over and pressed a kiss against his forehead. 'Thanks for last night. I'm not usually so – pitiful.'

'You were grieving for Burrell. That's human, Flame. You are human, aren't you?' His eyes were open now. One kiss, a featherlight brush over his skin at that, and he was wide awake.

She frowned. 'How would I know? For all I know I have the DNA of a tiger. Let go. I've got work to do and I don't have much time. It occurred to me that whoever sent those men is going to be wondering what happened to them. The police know all about Burrell and the houseboat, but they have no idea all four men were killed too. So someone will be looking for them. And they'll be hunting for evidence before too many people start stirring.'

'It's too damned early in the morning to be killing anyone. And you certainly aren't going off alone.'

'I can handle it.' She twisted her wrist to remind him to loosen his grip. 'It's just recon. I want the person behind this, whether it's Whitney or someone else. I'll just follow them and see where they go.'

'We'll follow them,' he corrected, reluctantly letting go of her. He watched her scoot off the bed, fish around for her jeans, and drag them on. He caught a brief glimpse of soft curves and his body reacted with a rush of need.

'You could have looked away.'

'Yeah. I could have.' He'd be damned if he was repentant. He'd been a saint all night, lying awake in too tight clothes, with her bare skin and silky hair and soft breathing. He'd been as hot and as aching as a man could be without shattering. And then she cried in her sleep. It was enough to make a tough man turn into Jell-O. 'But the view was too nice. You have beautiful skin.' Although her leg was worrisome. It was very bruised and for some reason, that raised a red flag in his mind. He wanted to bring her to his grandmother immediately.

'Thanks. Good genes, you know.' Sarcasm dripped.

Gator groaned again and buried his face in the pillow. 'I need coffee.'

She gave a small sniff of disdain. 'I'm leaving. Right now. If you're coming, get a move on.' She caught up the duffel bag. 'Afterward, I've got to go shopping for some clothes.'

'Afterward, I'm taking you to my grandmother so she

can have her friend treat your leg,' he called from the bathroom. He glanced at her through the open door. She was strapping knives on. The sight of her working so efficiently, so casually, to arm herself, sent another rush of heat through him. She was someone to contend with, a woman to stand with him in the midst of a crisis. He was grateful he'd thought to provide her with her favorite weapons after she'd sacrificed her own.

'You could close the door.'

'I could, but then you wouldn't get a good look, would you, *cher*?'

'Don't flatter yourself. And you'd better not be slowing me down because I'm not waiting for you.'

She flounced out of the cabin and slammed the door. It was a nice exit, but the duffel bag got caught between the door and jamb. Gator followed her out. 'I'm drivin'.'

She glared at him over her shoulder. 'You're not touching my airboat. You already destroyed my motorcycle.'

'Woman, forget about the motorcycle. I'll get you another one.'

She ducked her head, the mass of shiny hair covering her expression. 'I hid things in the bike. Stupid little things. I guess they really aren't all that important. My getaway money was in it too, but I've got more.' She held up the duffel bag she'd stuffed with money.

He followed her to the airboat, took the duffel bag from her and tossed it aboard while she untied the rope. The 'stupid little things' weren't really stupid at all – they were important to her. It meant going out to the swamp and retrieving the bike any way he looked at it, because she was getting her things back. He caught the rope she threw and held out his hand to help her aboard.

She hesitated before taking his hand. A slow grin

came over his face and crept into his eyes. 'You like me.' He pulled her up against him until her soft breasts were crushed tight against his chest. 'You don' want to admit it, *cher*, but you like me. You think I'm charmin'. And handsome. And sexy.' He drawled the words in her ear, his breath warm and his lips soft against the little shell of a lobe.

She sucked her breath in and her breasts shifted, rubbed right through the thin barrier of their clothing until his jeans were suddenly uncomfortably tight and he wanted to groan with need. He wanted her with every fiber of his being. His arms slid around her, aligning their bodies more closely, so she could feel the painful hard-on stretching the front of his jeans. His mouth found her neck, her throat, his lips trailing kisses, his teeth taking tiny nips.

'I could devour you.'

'Well don't.' Her voice wasn't as controlled as she would have liked it to be. 'Show some restraint.'

'Someday, I swear to you, Flame, you'll be begging me not to show restraint.'

'Well it isn't this morning.'

'If I can't have coffee, maybe sex would do the trick.' She hadn't pulled away from him. In fact, her body moved restlessly against his. He bent forward just a bit, enough to use his weight to bend her body backward away from his. His fingers slipped beneath the material of the old plaid shirt, settling on her narrow rib cage. Her skin was definitely as soft as it looked.

'I'm sure we have plenty of time. Don't you think we have time?' He meant to tease her, swore to himself it started out that way, but *Dieu,* he wanted her. Maybe he even needed her. His body was so damned hard he was afraid of taking a step, afraid of moving. He couldn't ever remember having such a raging hard-on

212

or such a painful need to relieve it.

The sun was coming up, spilling light through the cypress trees and over the water's surface. Her face was bathed in the early-morning light as it scattered through the trees, highlighting the confusion in her eyes. She still hadn't pulled away from him and he allowed his knuckles to brush the underside of her breasts. 'You're so beautiful, Flame.'

His hands cupped the soft weight of her breasts, thumbs sliding over her taut nipples. A small sound escaped her throat and he felt the sound vibrate through him. He bent his head very slowly to the sheer temptation of her body, giving her time to protest. He felt her first reaction, stiffening, her hands pushing at his shoulders as if she might thrust him away, but the lower half of her body moved against him, rubbing subtly, sending small electrical charges flashing through him. His jeans were already stretched to the maximum without bursting, but impossibly he felt his body tighten more, harden more.

Her breath escaped in a little rush as his lips touched her bare throat, moved lower to nuzzle along the swell of her breasts where the button was open. His hands held her possessively as his mouth found her right through the material of her shirt, teeth scraping gently, sending sensations shooting through her bloodstream. Her womb clenched and welcoming liquid heat rushed to bathe her entrance. His mouth settled over her breast, suckling strongly, his hands sliding down her bare skin, tracing her waist to her hips until he found the curve of her bottom. Without stopping his assault on her breast, he lifted her so that the throbbing heat of her mound met the thick bulge at his groin.

'Raoul.' His name came out somewhere between a plea and an invitation. Her arms went around his neck to cradle his head. 'I thought you weren't going to seduce me.' She arched her back to thrust her breast deeper into his mouth.

'Unbutton your shirt.' He murmured the command around her breast, the material of her shirt wet from his ministrations, her nipple aching and tight from the combined sensations of his mouth and the rough material.

Her hands slid the button loose, then a second one before bunching in his hair. His hair was silky soft, as black as night and curled around her fingers as if holding to her as tightly as she was holding to him. She closed her eyes as his warm breath teased her bare skin. When his mouth closed around her breast she cried out, pulling him closer, her fist bunched in his hair. Her knees went weak and heat rushed through her body like a fireball, pooling low and wicked so that she sought relief by rubbing harder against him.

'You have too many clothes on,' he whispered. 'We both do.'

'Kiss me again.' She needed his kiss, craved it with the same terrible ferocity as his touch. She wrenched at his hair in an effort to pull his head up, in an effort to retain reality. Teeth tugged her nipple, his tongue laved, easing the sharp bite of pain that only seemed to add to the fire building in her.

'I want your clothes off.' His teeth nibbled and scraped around the mound of her breast, underneath, tormenting her until she was desperate for him, her leg wrapping around his waist in an effort to ride him.

The things he could do to her body with his mouth and his hands were incredible, unbelievable things she had never experienced or thought would heighten her pleasure. He was by turns rough and then tender, his hands hard then soothing, his mouth biting, then hot silk. She would lose herself in him, lose her sanity, need him. She would *need* him. Flame stiffened, jerked back, stumbling, nearly falling off the airboat.

'What am I doing?'

There was terror on her face. In her eyes. Gator drew in a ragged breath and attempted to force his body under control. She was trembling, shaking her head, looking at him as if he had suddenly become her enemy. Her hair was disheveled, spilling in wild abandonment around her face, her lips were swollen from his kisses, and her breasts gleamed at him from her gaping shirt, faint red marks of his possession on them. It was impossible to control his body when everything in him urged him to take her right there in the bottom of the boat.

'Nothing happened, *cher*,' he assured, keeping his voice low.

'What do you mean nothing happened? Something happened here and we can't take it back.' Her voice shook.

She was right. He knew she was. He would never, ever, as long as he lived, stop craving the feel and taste of her. He wouldn't walk away satisfied from another woman. He wanted Flame. Only Flame. All of Flame. Her heart, her body, maybe even her soul, whatever he could take for himself and hold on to. The same knowledge was in her eyes and she looked so scared he couldn't stop the step toward her.

'It's addiction. Obsession. Everything but what it should be.' She couldn't back away from him but she shrank against the seat.

His fingertips deliberately caressed her breasts. 'What should it be if not this?'

'Simple physical attraction. *Normal* physical attraction.'

'I'd rather have this. I'd rather have you.' His hands

215

cupped her breasts possessively, his thumbs stimulating her nipples. 'Normal is never going to be enough for you, Flame, any more than it will be for me.' He leaned in to her to claim her mouth.

The moment his lips feathered over hers, his tongue teased the seam of her mouth, she felt an electrical charge running from her mouth to her breasts and to her groin. His fist was suddenly in her hair, holding her in place as his teeth tugged at her lower lip, demanding entrance. Her brain went into meltdown as she allowed his tongue to sweep inside her mouth, to tangle with hers. They seemed fused together, so hot and so addicting she couldn't stop kissing him. Her bare breasts mashed into his chest and she could hear their combined heartbeats, smell the musky scent of their combined need.

His mouth became rougher, more demanding, his hand tightening in her hair, but it only added to the intensity of her desire for him. Fire raced up her belly to her breasts, spread through her body until she wanted to cry with need. He tasted hot and wild and it was almost more than she could bear. To want him. To be made to want him. It should be her choice. *Hers*.

Flame pushed at his shoulders until he allowed her to escape. Dragging the edges of her shirt together she wiped at her mouth. It didn't help. She could still taste him there. Her body felt swollen and achy and unfulfilled.

'Why?' Gator could barely breathe. Barely think. It took every ounce of willpower, of discipline and control to keep from taking what she wouldn't give him. He knew she wouldn't be able to resist him if he persisted.

'Whitney.' She whispered the name.

She may as well have shouted it. Dead or alive, the

216

man haunted them. Gator fought to drag air into his lungs as he stared at her, fighting back the need to just overrule her decision. Her shirt was pulled together over her breasts, but had slipped off her shoulders. He could see a hint of darker smudges marring her skin. He stepped closer to her, a small frown on his face. 'Flame?'

She glanced at her shoulders and jerked the shirt over her skin. 'It's nothing.'

'It isn't nothing. How did you get those bruises?'

'I told you, I bruise easily. I got a little beat up driving the Jeep over rough terrain.' Flame buttoned up her shirt, wincing as the material brushed against her tight, sensitive nipples. His gaze dropped to her breasts, clearly seeing the outline. He licked his lips and turned away from her to start the airboat.

Wrapping her arms around her waist, Flame refused to look at him as the boat skimmed over the water toward Burrell's island. She would not be used as an experiment, not ever again. Certainly not for some perverted sexual experiment. She'd never responded to anyone like she had Raoul. She'd never wanted or needed anyone the way she did him. The ache in her body refused to subside and she simply didn't trust the intensity of her craving for him.

Raoul didn't believe Whitney was alive. He certainly didn't believe he'd somehow found a way to make them addicted to one another. But she knew what the doctor was capable of doing.

She stared at the passing landscapes. The bayou was a beautiful place. She didn't even mind the humidity so much. She loved the wildlife and the way it sat there, right out among the midst of civilization as all around it the city built up. Normally she didn't care to be in cities, people crowding in where she couldn't stop the

217

continual assault of noise, but she liked New Orleans and the French Quarter. She thought the aboveground cemeteries looked like miniature cities, beautiful and different and perfect for New Orleans. Mostly, she liked the people with their smiling faces and their various accents and ready laughter. She didn't want to leave any of it, and she especially didn't want to leave Raoul.

As if reading her mind, Gator's fingers brushed her arm, slid down to tangle with hers until he was holding her hand. 'I'm not going anywhere.'

'You had all this. How could you think whatever Whitney did was worth the trade?' She nearly choked on the question. She wanted his life. His grandmother and brothers and his wonderful home.

'At the time, I didn't think I was trading it away. I had some psychic talent and a huge sense of responsibility. I thought by getting more training I could save more lives. I'd already had so much special training in so many areas, Flame, it just felt like one more. Then it all went to hell.' He shrugged his broad shoulders, his gaze watching the waterway.

With his foot standing on the gas and one hand on the stick controlling the rudder he had to be alert. The trail was narrow and the plants slick as they skimmed the surface of the marsh. He didn't dare let up on the gas going over the mud because he didn't want to get stuck. When navigating an airboat, he looked out for everything from other boats, to alligators and the knees of cypress trees, anything that could damage the bottom of the boat. The airboats were top heavy and could flip rather easily and he was very aware Flame was riding with him. He didn't want anything to happen to her.

Gator kept his fingers tangled tightly with Flame's as they raced over the waterway and marsh to reach the small island Burrell had loved so much.

'Do you regret your decision?'

He glanced at her. 'Not anymore. No.'

Flame sucked in her breath. He just accepted what was between them. He didn't care if Whitney manipulated them or not. He had no idea how protective he could look, how possessive and how intense the desire that shadowed his eyes was when he looked at her. She detested Peter Whitney and everything he stood for. Whitney believed the end justified the means and that humans were small sacrifices to make for the greater good of knowledge. She had seen so much pain inflicted on the other girls he'd bought from the orphanages as well as experienced it herself.

Throwaways he'd called them. She still flinched inwardly every time she thought of it, every time she recalled the contempt in his tone. Joy Chiasson was not a throwaway. Neither was Burrell. Flame could stand up for the ones like her, the ones no one else would stand up for. Whitney with his billions might get away with his monstrous experiments, but she would bring down the ones she could.

'Flame.'

She shook her head. 'Don't, Raoul. I have to think about this. Give me time to think things through. Something is going on here and I have to figure it out.'

'Why? What does it matter if he manipulated us sexually or emotionally or whether we're just attracted because we know each other like no one else could? We have a chance at something few people ever have.'

'What? Great sex? He'll put us in a cage and watch us.'

His fingers tightened around hers. He'd been in a cage, waiting to be murdered. 'I'm not going to let that happen. We're worth millions of dollars to the military.

I go out on missions when they send me and I come back and report and take my leave. That's my life. It has nothing to do with Whitney. No one is going to lock us up when they need to use us. What would be the point of that?'

'You keep telling yourself that.'

They were nearing the island and Gator throttled down, taking the airboat right up onto the island into dense reeds. 'This is where we get off. You're going to get muddy.'

'I have to buy new clothes anyway.' Flame jumped onto a small patch of what looked like solid ground, but sank up to her ankles. 'Ugh. Why is it every single time we recon, it's always in the mud or in water?'

'It's going to rain too.'

'I didn't need you to tell me that.' She worked her way carefully through the sludge until she was on more solid ground, then began to make her way across the island toward the small basin where Burrell had always kept his houseboat.

There was little left of it, mostly the smell of burnt wood and the blackened remains of one part of the deck. She could see Burrell's favorite chair partially burnt lying in the reeds near land. She stumbled, pressing her hand to her mouth.

'I can do this, Flame,' Gator offered. 'There's no need for both of us to be here. We don't even know if anyone's going to show up.'

She lifted her chin. 'Burrell was mine. I didn't have him very long, but he was mine. He didn't deserve to get chased out into the swamp, shot, and thrown to the alligators. I'll take these people down, and if I'm a little uncomfortable so be it.'

Gator kept his face completely expressionless. She did things to him, to both his body and mind when she talked like a warrior. He respected her, wanted her, admired her courage. Her leg had to hurt like hell, but she was barely limping. He had the sinking notion he was beginning to fall in love. Judging by the look on her face, she wouldn't welcome the admission so he simply stayed silent.

Wanting a clean sweep of the surrounding area, Gator chose the high ground. They didn't have long to wait. A car slowly made its way along the narrow ribbon of road leading to Burrell's island. The driver parked in the small widened area where Burrell's old truck still remained. Three men pushed the doors open, all the time looking around them warily.

Flame's fingers closed around Gator's wrist. 'I've seen the man in the plaid shirt before. He works security for Saunders.' Could Saunders have had Burrell killed? He couldn't have known she'd taken his money. There was nothing to trace the robbery back to her. What had Burrell said that morning? He was meeting Saunders later in the afternoon to pay him with a bank draft rather than cash.

She sank down, uncaring that she was sitting in muddy water. Her legs wouldn't hold her. She never considered Saunders might kill Burrell if the riverboat captain made his last payment and took possession of the island. She looked around her. 'Look at this, Raoul. This is a tiny piece of land, mostly uninhabitable. The ground is spongy, the water table is high. It's worthless. There isn't even enough wildlife to hunt for a living here, or trees to harvest. Saunders can't want it badly enough to kill for it.'

Gator stroked a caress through her hair. 'I have a feeling Saunders doesn't like to lose. He's a high-stakes player. Parsons has been trying to get something on him for a long time and from what I understand, they know

221

Saunders is dirty, they just can't nail him. And it isn't because he's that careful. His people are too afraid of him to ever testify against him and everyone who's ever tried to go up against him has ended up dead.'

'What about Parsons? Is his cover really that good? I found out he was DEA. If I could, why couldn't Saunders? A good computer hacker can find most anything.'

'Parsons resides here. He doesn't really hide what he does. He's a businessman and he lives in the same area as Saunders. They struck up a friendship and go to the same clubs. Saunders likes to rub elbows with the politicians and the hotshots in town. Parsons is only one of them. Saunders knows the mayor and even the governor.'

'But why would Parsons investigate here, in New Orleans, a man who would kill not only him, but his entire family?' She rubbed her forehead, a little frown on her face. 'If he's pretending to be friends, he's playing a very dangerous and stupid game. And if they are friends, then he's dirty right along with Saunders.'

'Who else did the agency have? They couldn't get anyone near Saunders and Parsons was already here and he knew Saunders socially. He had no choice.' His hand dropped to the nape of her neck, easing the tension out with his strong fingers. He kept his gaze on the three men as they tried without much success to read signs. The rain had been heavy all through the night and it was already beginning to drizzle again. It was obvious from the way they moved in the mud, the sweat on their clothes, and the way they slapped at all the insects, that the men weren't used to the heat and mud of the bayou. They wouldn't last long.

'You got all that information from Lily, didn't you?'

He glanced up at the recrimination in her voice.

'We're just goin' to have to agree to disagree about Lily, sugah. Peter Whitney can burn in hell for what he did to you, but Lily is as much a victim as you are, maybe more. She believed he loved her. She even thought he was her biological father.'

Flame turned her face away from him. The rain came down harder, drenching them in spite of the canopy of trees. The three men jumped back into their vehicle, obviously consulting with one another before driving up the frontage road a short distance, past the remains of the burnt-out houseboat. The men looked at the blackened ruins and then pulled a U-turn and proceeded back toward the freeway.

Flame started to rise. Gator's fingers tapped her wrist and he shook his head, holding up his hand for silence. He held up two fingers and pointed back toward the interior of the swamp.

Flame remained crouched in the mud, listening. She'd been so focused on the three men she hadn't paid much attention to anything else. The familiar rhythm of the swamp was off-key. There was the hum of insects and the croak of frogs, even the scurrying of lizards through the brush, but something was slightly off-kilter. She closed her eyes and heard the soft whisper of material against bark. Someone was stealthily climbing down from a tree. It took a few minutes to pick up the steady heartbeat.

'Now who do you suppose has come looking for us?' she asked softly.

'Don' jump to conclusions, *cher*. I'm going to circle around and see if I can spot him. I don't want you killin' anyone before breakfast.'

'You know he's probably enhanced, Raoul. He's here looking to find out what happened to his buddy. We can follow him when he leaves. Don't go giving him a

223

target. And *don't* tip him off that we know he's here.'

Gator laid a hand over his heart. 'You think so little of my abilities. I may be charmin', *cher*, but I know my stuff. He isn't going to see me.'

The tightness in her chest increased tenfold. She grabbed his arm to keep him with her. She couldn't, *wouldn't* lose him. 'You can't go, Raoul.'

The little catch in her voice was his undoing. He ran missions all the time, most of them in the deadliest hot spots of the world, but here she was, looking up at him with fear in her eyes, fear for him, and he couldn't move. 'Kiss me.'

'What?' She scowled at him. 'Are you crazy?'

'Right here. Right now. You kiss me.'

'Or what? You're going to go play hide-and-seek with more killers? Don't be ridiculous.'

Gator caught her arms and pulled her to him, his mouth coming down on hers. 'He's spotted us and he's coming toward us. For God's sake, don't kill him. Can you get a good jump off your leg?' He whispered the words into her mouth, breathing into her, his tongue teasing even as he issued the warning.

'I'll go left,' she said.

'We need him to escape and lead us back to whoever sent him,' he reminded, tightening his grip on her.

She kissed him back, leaning into him, pretending to be oblivious to the approaching man. She couldn't help enjoying Raoul's mouth or the subtle way his body moved against hers. All the while she listened for the approach of the man stalking them.

He was right on them when she felt rather than heard Gator say 'now' against her lips. Simultaneously they crouched and leapt, pushing off each other, springing up into the air and backward, Flame to the left, Gator to the right, somersaulting in perfect synchronization to land behind their enemy. Flame saw the gun in his hand and he instinctively turned toward Gator, thinking him the bigger threat. She launched herself in the air again, this time wrapping her legs around the man's neck in a scissors hold.

They both went down hard. He lost his grip on his rifle, reaching back to try to break her hold before she strangled him. Flame locked her legs together, exerting more pressure in an effort to subdue him fast. He pounded on her leg with his fist, three short, hard punches that took her breath away. Her leg was already damaged from the day before and she couldn't focus away from the pain enough to keep the pressure on him.

Gator kicked their assailant in the head hard as he reached down and jerked her to her feet. 'He's got partners. Get out of here. There are more of them.' He shoved her toward the canal. 'Run, damn it.'

She didn't hear anything, but she felt the telltale rush of her senses, a heavy dread that signaled far more danger. Flame ran, but her leg was throbbing, every step jarring her. She tried to hide it, jumping over the fallen logs in their way and racing toward safety. Gator dropped behind her, covering her back as they zigzagged through the trees and brush to leap into the reed-choked canal. He shoved her underwater as bullets spit into the water around them. Keeping contact, they dove as deep as possible, using the rotting logs and plants on the bottom to pull them away from the island and out toward more open water.

With the enhancement of their bodies, both could stay underwater far longer than normal so they swam away from the island and the debris of the houseboat. Gator directed her with hand signals on her body and she followed him until her lungs were burning. She

225

tapped his shoulder to signal she needed to go up for air. They were in much deeper water. He signaled that they needed to make it a few more feet ahead.

Flame knew Raoul had a specific spot in mind, somewhere safe, but her body was wearing out. She'd noticed that lately she didn't have the stamina she usually had. She caught his belt loop, afraid she'd try to surface before they were safe and she'd get him killed. She'd always worked alone and having someone else to worry about was frightening – especially when she liked him so much. Too much.

She gasped as they came up, gulping for air, dragging it into her burning lungs. Gator came up behind her, his arm circling her waist. They were screened from the island by both a rise in the contour of the island as well as plants growing along the edge of the basin they were in.

'Are you all right?'

She nodded, controlling her heartbeat and the adrenaline charging through her system. 'Why the hell didn't we hear them? We should have known they were there. What's going on?' She hadn't been afraid of the first hunter, but something about the eerie stillness, the complete silence of the others had given her the willies. It hadn't even been the same feeling as with the sniper the day before. She'd known he was there. The swamp had known it. But these men had been able to hide their presence not only from Raoul and her, but also from the swamp itself.

Gator studied the shore surrounding the island. There was only one man he knew of that could be that silent. That scary. That much of a ghost. Kadan Montague could move through the world almost as if he were invisible. No one really knew how he did it – not even the other GhostWalkers. He was quiet and dangerous, a strong telepath and a man few argued with. He had gifts none of them really understood and even Lily wasn't talking much about them. One of Kadan's strongest talents was his ability to shield the entire team from detection. Had that talent been duplicated in another man? Gator had the sinking feeling it could be so.

'Do you know them?' Flame asked.

She was shivering in the water. The rain had begun again, a relentless downpour that added to their misery.

'I don't know. I didn't catch a glimpse of any of them. Did you?'

She shook her head. 'The big one is heading back toward the road. I can hear him. He's limping.' There was satisfaction in her voice.

It couldn't be Kadan. Gator was almost certain of that, but the fact remained, whoever was in the swamp was trained in Special Forces, and they were enhanced.

Chapter Twelve

'Come on, Raoul. He'll get away from us. Let's get to the airboat.'

His arm clamped her to his side. 'He's bait. The others haven't left with him. They're out there, watching the surface of the water for one small change, one shift in the way the reeds wave. The *only* thing we have going for us is the rain.'

'I can make my way to the airboat and follow the other one to see where he goes. I'll swim underwater. I'm not losing my chance at finding out who's behind killing Burrell. You stay and fight the ghost, I'm out of here.'

His arm pressed hard into her side. 'You already know that Saunders had Burrell killed. You just want to see who this one reports back to, and we both know it won't be Saunders. I'm telling you it's too dangerous to move until we get a direction on his partners.'

For a moment she stiffened against him, then slowly relaxed, letting her breath hiss through her teeth. 'Now do you believe Whitney's alive?'

'Maybe. Something's going on here and it isn't connected to Burrell or Joy. We've stumbled into something on . . .' Gator trailed off. Maybe it wasn't about any of them, not even Flame. He glanced at her. She didn't look intimidated, she looked determined – and as mad as hell. 'If I knew where they were, I could use sound to draw them out, but I have no idea of their direction.' He said it more as a warning to her than as an option.

'I can't even get them with echolocation, the same as the first sniper. These men have to be enhanced, Raoul.'

There was something in her voice he didn't like. Rising suspicion perhaps. She had been beginning to trust him. He couldn't exactly blame her if she suddenly was thinking conspiracy – he was beginning to think it as well. 'I'm going to try something.'

Gator wasn't the strongest telepath in the GhostWalker squad, but, if necessary, he could reach out to someone who was strong. He either believed in Kadan or he didn't, and the truth was, Kadan was one of the GhostWalkers. He would always be. No one was going to buy him off, blackmail him, or threaten him. Kadan would stand with his own. Flame wouldn't see it that way, but he knew now she wasn't ever going to come around voluntarily to the idea of belonging to the GhostWalkers. And he wasn't going to let her influence him when he knew absolutely his friends were above suspicion.

Kadan. I'm in trouble. We're pinned down and need help.

He waited, drew Flame's shivering body a little closer to him. Her arms slipped around his neck and she leaned more of her weight against him. He turned his head to rub his face against her neck. 'It takes patience. Most of the time, whoever moves first, dies first.'

'I know. I was just thinking of Burrell. Those three men who came looking were Saunders's men. I know they were. He's definitely involved. And poor Joy, I'm really not any closer to finding her than before. I haven't done very much for anybody and now you're trapped here with me.' She pulled her head back and looked into his eyes, a small smile curving her mouth. 'Don't worry, baby, I won't let anything happen to you.'

He didn't know whether to laugh or to scowl at her. Any other woman would be teasing, but he had the feeling she meant it. 'First of all, *I'm* the man and I do man things, like take care of my woman in a bad situation.' He ignored her rolling eyes and continued. 'Secondly, there's always the possibility that these men have nothing to do with you and everything to do with me, so don't take any responsibility yet. I've made a few enemies here and there; it comes with the line of work I'm in. Everyone is still searching for Joy. Wyatt, Ian, and I spent the last month combing the bayou for clues to her disappearance and trying to piece together information. I think we're closer than we know, especially after our conversation last night. I want to take a good look at Parsons's son. I think he had more to do with her disappearance than any of us first thought.'

I had a bad feeling when I woke up. We're already on our way. The voice came out of nowhere, calm, reassuring, very Kadan.

Gator breathed a sigh of relief. It was an eerie feeling to know they were trapped in the water with a sniper's rifle possibly already targeting their area. One mistake could get them both killed. *Burrell's island. Whoever these bastards are, they're enhanced. At least one is like you – has your talents. I can't spot any of them, not even with echolocation and that means he's shielding them in the way you shield us. I couldn't even detect their presence at first.*

There was a moment of silence while Kadan digest-

230

ed the information. *Well. Well. That's interesting.*

Gator felt the tension leave his body. That was so Kadan. Nothing ever ruffled him. He didn't sound surprised or confused and he didn't argue. He was just simply on his way.

'You're the man? What does that mean? I hope you don't mean what I think you did. I'm a soldier and I can fight every bit as well as you.'

Flame sounded a little hot under the collar at his remark, but he was pleased to see she kept her awareness, muting her voice so the sound came only to him.

'Now you're finally admittin' to being a soldier. *Cher*, you keep up that sweet talk and I'm goin' to be gettin' all hot and bothered and hard right here in the battlefield.'

'You're so crazy, Raoul. You *are* getting turned on. We're in danger of getting shot and you're acting like an idiot.' He was rubbing his groin over her, back and forth, right there in the water with marksmen scanning for a target. 'Do I need to remind you at least one of those men is a sniper? You deserve to get shot.'

'We can't move for a few minutes and we may as well make the best of a bad situation. In any case, the contour of the basin is providing us with cover. They can't see us here. They'd have to wade out into the water, into the open to actually sight us. Don' worry, sugah, I've got the rhythm of the waves and my mind tuned for battle.'

She hadn't noticed that the water was lapping at the shore. Part of her wanted to laugh and part of her was getting turned on. 'You're making me into a perv.' Flame pressed closer to him, cautious of not changing the natural, gentle movement of the water around them. 'You'd better keep your mind tuned for battle.'

'Did I mention you smell so sweet?' He rubbed his

231

face in her neck again, his teeth tugging gently at her skin, enough to send a shiver of excitement through her body.

'I smell like a swamp rat. You're so crazy. Only you would get like this in the middle of rain and mud while we're being hunted.'

His hand cupped her breast right through her soaked shirt, his thumb stroking her nipple. 'Did I mention I'm partial to your breasts? I want to lie down beside you and just suck and play to my heart's content.'

'Not only are you a perv about knives, you have an oral fixation.'

'*Cher*, I have a lot of fixations. Just saying the word *oral* conjures up that beautiful mouth of yours fixating on my very hard cock.' He kissed her ear, his tongue doing a little foray that sent another shiver through her body. 'Did I tell you I love your mouth? Hot and velvet soft and very moist. I don' know if I can survive just thinkin' about your mouth and tongue and all that heat.'

Flame wrapped her legs around his waist, moving with infinite slowness, very aware he was one hundred percent alert to their danger. His gaze moved ceaselessly along the opposite shore, studying every detail of the cypress grove. She was careful to align her body perfectly with his, her aching mound stretched tight over the bulge in his soaked jeans. He turned her on so easily and she didn't even have his full attention. What would happen when his intensity was strictly tuned to her?

'That's not fair, *cher*,' he chastised softly, his breath hitching just a little. 'I'm concentratin' here.'

She let her mouth wander down his neck, soft little kisses and teasing nibbles. 'You were distracting me so I'd do what you wanted and stay here. I'm not stupid,

Raoul, just susceptible to a Cajun's charms.'

'Not any Cajun,' he corrected, 'just me.'

'You sound so utterly confident. What makes you so sure?'

'You left the homing device on the airboat and you don' make mistakes like that. Why do you think you did that, sugah?'

'Why'd you lead me to your grandmother's house?' she countered.

You two okay?

Gator started to respond to that faraway voice talking in his head, but stopped, his muscles freezing into position. He tapped Flame on the shoulder and held a finger to his lips. She nodded, puzzlement in her eyes as she slowly unwrapped her legs and allowed them to fall carefully away from his waist. Gator replayed the words in his head, listening to the sound, the choice of words.

That hadn't been Kadan. But it was a direction. Gator tuned to it immediately and sent a blast of low-level notes, enough to make everyone in its path very sick, but hopefully not kill every living thing. He knew there were no other normal humans in the immediate area because he didn't hear their heartbeats, but there were animals.

Obviously their enemy wasn't exactly like Kadan. Kadan would never have opened his mouth and given away his location.

Flame suddenly slammed all her weight against him, taking him underwater. Bullets spit around them, boring through the water like angry bees. The shots had come from above, slanting down, indicating the shooter was in the treetops. She kicked away from the reeds, tugging at his hand to bring him with her. They swam out to deeper water, going against the current in the middle of the waterway as they looked for safer ground.

The easiest and most logical thing was to let the current aid them, but the hunters would know and expect that.

The water was murky and it was nearly impossible to communicate even with hand signals so they used touch as they kicked strongly heading around the length of Burrell's island. They swam for several minutes until their lungs forced them toward the surface. There was no real cover, so both only allowed their mouths and noses above the waterline to suck in the precious air before sliding back down into the depths again.

Twice they came up for air, circling around the island until they were certain they could approach without the hunters' knowledge. As they began to move into the shallower, reed-choked water, Flame felt something grab hold of her arm. It squeezed like a vise, yanking her down, tumbling her into the rotting debris and muck on the bottom. She actually heard the snap of her bone as the force of the spin broke her arm. *Alligator.* Without conscious thought she pulled the knife from her belt loop and began punching the leathery hide as hard as she could with her free hand, the hilt of the knife tight in her fist as she pounded her way up the head of the animal to the top. She sank the knife as deep as she could, going for the eye, driving it deep with every bit of strength she had.

Gator saw the tail of an alligator rise to the surface and then the water roiled and churned, debris, blood, and muck rising like a boiling volcano. Immediately he pulled his knife and dove below the service, his heart in his throat. The alligator was coming out of its death roll, surfacing, jaws still clamped around Flame's arm, dragging her to the surface with it. She gasped for air, still pounding on the thrashing head. Gator struck from below, slamming his knife repeatedly into the underbelly. The alligator opened its jaws wide and Flame jerked backward away from the bellowing reptile.

Gator caught her around the waist and, kicking hard, took her toward the shore. She was still wildly swinging with her good arm, trying to punch toward the alligator, almost fighting him to go back. 'Stop it,' he hissed. 'You're safe, *cher*. Safe.'

'I'm killing the damned thing. It broke my arm. He can just die for that.'

Gator dragged her up the muddy embankment, through the weeds and brush, a safe distance from the water where he could examine her injuries. She jerked away from him, furious, in shock, blood running into the ground, her feet kicking toward the water as if she could attack the alligator.

He trapped her with his legs, holding her still, tearing his shirt with his teeth. 'Stop fighting me, Flame. I'm on your side.' *Damn it, Kadan. Where the hell are you? We're in trouble here. I need a medic now.* He tied his shirt around the wound. She was lucky. The alligator had been big enough to have pulled her arm off.

'That hurts. The son of a bitch broke my arm.'

'They hunt for food in the early morning. He's a big boy and we just happened to be in the wrong place at the wrong time. Hold still. You're bleeding all over the place. This is going to get infected. You know that. I have to get you to a hospital.'

If she could turn any whiter, she managed. 'No. Once I'm in their computer system Whitney will find me. No way. I can handle this. Take me to your grandmother's friend.'

'There's no way that attack wasn't heard for miles. I didn't mute it and neither did you. We have to move, and we have to move fast. Can you do this?' He used directional sound, throwing voices, the sound of running and heavy breathing to the east of them, trying to buy time.

Flame didn't respond. She swayed against him, looking pale and frightened.

Gator cursed under his breath, spewing Cajun cusswords as fast as he could think of them, expecting a sniper's bullet any moment. She was shaking uncontrollably, in shock and not even realizing it. 'Listen to me, Flame.' He caught her face and turned it toward him. '*Listen to me.* We're in trouble here. There are several of these hunters and they aren't just going to let us waltz out of here. I have to find them and take them out so I can get you safely out of here. They've probably rigged the airboat, so we can't use that. I want to move you to a safer place and then I'm going after them.'

She blinked rapidly, her body swaying against him, the fight going out of her. 'It hurts like a son of a bitch. Do you have a medic kit on you? If I have something for the pain, I can back you up.'

'I want you to stay quiet. Kadan and the others are on the way and we'll have help in a few minutes.' He could feel her body beginning to stiffen again. Again there was that brief flare of suspicion she couldn't hide from him. He couldn't blame her. Their stalkers were ghosts, unseen, unheard, only felt and that was suspect. He'd called in the others without consulting her and she was extremely vulnerable.

Flame flexed her fingers to see if she could move through the pain. Her arm and hand were useless to her. 'Let's go then. I'll feel safer a bit farther from the bank.'

Gator hadn't expected cooperation. She'd lost a fair amount of blood and her arm was definitely broken. The teeth had gone through her skin and, between the muddy water and the alligator's diet of rotten meat, there was bound to be major infection. She needed medical attention immediately whether she wanted it or not. He didn't wait for Flame to change her mind, but helped her up. She clenched her teeth, no sound escaping, and it occurred to him she hadn't made a single sound during the attack.

'Come on, *cher.*' His tone was on the husky side, but he couldn't help it. Everything about Flame appealed to him – even her fierce independence and her stubborn streak and her unfailing courage. They moved over the uneven terrain as quickly as possible, her breathing labored and her face twisted with pain, but she didn't say a word. 'This looks good.' It was a small area, covered in brush. Flame would be hidden and he could go on the attack.

Gator helped her settle onto the ground and crouched beside her. 'This won't take long. You goin' to be all right without me?'

'I'll be fine. Don't worry about me.' She waved him off. 'Just watch your back.' She didn't meet his eyes.

He caught her chin. 'I'm coming back for you, Flame.'

'I know.' Her voice sounded strangled and she leaned forward to press her lips against his. It was no more than a brief touch, very light, but he felt it through his entire body.

Gator stood up and looked around. Watching him, Flame noted his entire demeanor changed. He looked fluid, powerful, and suddenly very much a warrior, not at all her charming Cajun. His expression was hard. Resolute. His eyes were as cold as ice. He turned and ran lightly through the brush – and she didn't hear a sound.

What goes unseen, unheard and unknown. Gator

237

repeated the mantra to himself. He was a GhostWalker. It mattered little that the hunter was a phantom. So was he. The bayou was his backyard. He'd been born and raised in these waterways; he'd hunted the islands and gone to school in a pirogue. More than anything else, the woman he was falling in love with was injured and needed his help. He wasn't going to play field games anymore. Things had taken a serious and deadly turn.

He worked his way back toward the other side of the island where the hunters had been, stopping several times to listen. Sometimes it was the lack of sound that could betray presence. The rain fell steadily, small animals scurried, and the leaves rustled. He couldn't hear a heartbeat, not even Flame's and that meant she was shielding the sound.

Dropping into the brush, he used deference tones, projecting the murmur of voices coming from the opposite side of the water. The sound was muted as if the slight wind had picked up whispers. Instantly a hail of bullets from several semiautomatic weapons burst out over the water toward the sound. He listened carefully, trying to sort out the various sounds and which direction each came from.

Gator pulsed high-power, very low-frequency sounds straight toward the shooters, keeping the field narrowed toward the locations he thought each of the men were most likely to be. The sound waves could easily produce blunt force trauma or death to anything in its path. He'd seen the results after he'd lost control once and it had sickened him. He'd promised himself he'd never go for a kill using sound again, unless he had no other choice. He'd never gotten over the nightmares and now he'd be sweating the full force of night terrors after using the weapon again.

He heard the sound of repeated retching, even as

bullets slammed into trees all around him. More vomiting. Coughing. Another spray of bullets. The hunters were shooting blind, but their instincts were good. Several bullets splintered tree branches around his head. Fragments of wood embedded in his skin. Gator dropped to his belly and began to worm his way through the weeds and brush toward the area where the most firing was coming from. He thought maybe there were three men, not more than four and at least two of them had stayed close together.

Sound ceased again. The hunters were back in control of themselves and one of them was shielding, masking the heartbeats of his team members in the way Kadan did for the GhostWalkers. The game of cat and mouse had begun in earnest. They all knew it was life or death for them. There could be no mistakes. Gator moved with infinite patience and care, uncertain what he was facing in the way of enhancements.

Peter Whitney had bought orphans from various countries and enhanced them first. No one thought he had tried his experiment again until a few years earlier when he was backed by the military – but they found they weren't the only ones. There had been a second military team. There had to be a third. Had Whitney created his own private army? It was beginning to look that way. And if Peter Whitney was dead, who was in command and what was the agenda?

Gator sent another blast of sound, along with a silent prayer Flame had stayed where he'd left her and wasn't in the target zone. He had to keep the hunters off balance, sick, and on the move. He didn't want to give them a chance to surround him and he wanted to push them toward the marsh, out of the interior of the island. The outer edges of the island were far spongier and more treacherous. His familiarity with the bayou gave him a huge advantage over his enemies.

He pulsed sound through the thin layer of ground covering, looking for what he needed. Setting a trap for psychically enhanced soldiers had to be done with precision timing; the slightest shift in the wind could tip them off, anything could. When he found the spot he was looking for, where the ground was thin and just barely covering the high water table, he worked his way out about ten feet and deliberately twisted a leaf and snapped the tip from a weed. He left a very small drag track, no more than his heel sliding in the mud and a splatter of muck on a rock. He found a hollow reed and cut the ends off right before sending out another pulsing call, this time directing it to the water and shore in search of alligators.

Gator lay in the mud, his body stretched out in the muck waiting. The rain fell steadily adding to the already high water table. Within minutes he heard the brush of clothes against plants. The shield was coming apart as the two men hurried back toward the center of the island. Grunts and bellows began almost at once. The pad of reptilian feet hitting the spongy ground. Snapping jaws. A curse. The protection was gone. He'd gotten lucky. One of the men was the shielder and he was distracted.

Gator sent out another pulsing wave, directed at the alligators in the area. The sound traveled through water and over land herding several of the reptiles right at two of his enemies. Once he was certain he had the reptiles on the move, he sent wave after wave of low-frequency sound to keep the hunters sick and disoriented. The men moved inland, their attention divided between the powerful jaws of the alligators and the continual assault on their nervous systems.

The first man wore desert camouflage clothing and

stuck out easily in all the greenery. That told Gator they hadn't been expecting trouble; that it had been a recon mission and nothing more until he and Flame had been spotted. The man moved in standard two-man pattern, covering and signaling his partner forward. The second man was in regular camouflage, greens and browns, and much more difficult to spot. Gator was certain he was the shielder. It was difficult to see him through the downpour and several times Gator had to fight back the impulse to wipe at his eyes and clear his vision.

A small alligator shot past, scooting out of the way of his much larger brethren. Without Gator driving them, the reptiles seemed as disoriented as the hunters, stopping and grunting, looking around for a slide back into the water. A long tail covered in thick scales swept around, nearly knocking into the man in green and brown. He jumped forward and let out a startled yell as he fell through the thin crust of earth separating him from the high water table. The ground around him sank, pouring into the hole and water bubbled up as he disappeared completely.

'Ed!' The first man in the desert camouflage raced forward. Before he could reach the hole, the large alligator suddenly rushed in front of him, intent on getting back into the water. He flipped into the hole headfirst. At once muffled gunfire erupted and the water turned red. The second man peered down the hole, trying to see to help his buddy, afraid of firing and hitting him.

Gator came up out of the mud, only a scant couple of feet from him, knife in his fist. The man spun around, swinging his rifle hard in Gator's direction to drive him back so he could bring the weapon up to get off a shot. Gator caught the rifle before it could hit him, his palm slapping the barrel hard. He jerked and the hunter went sailing over his head. Gator followed

him, kicking the rifle out of his hands as the man |
somersaulted back onto his feet and faced him in a
fighter's crouch.

The man looked familiar. Gator sucked in his breath.
'I know you. You took the psych test the same time I
took it. Rick Fielding, right? Why the hell would you
come after me?'

'Because you're a dumb shit and you're fucking
everything up,' Rick snarled.

'Good reason, Ricky,' Gator said, stepping to his
left, careful to place his weight where he knew the surface was spongy but stable. Moving forced Fielding to
step also. 'I hope you think it's all worth it because
your sorry ass belongs to me.'

'I don't think so. You and your little slut are the only
ones here. You're going to be very dead and she's going
to be entertaining tonight.'

Gator laughed, the sound soft and taunting. 'That
woman would entertain you, Ricky boy, but not the way
you think.' He feinted with the knife, crowding close,
forcing Fielding back another step. 'You'd be wearing
a happy smile right around your throat, you mess with
her.' He moved left, pressuring the soldier with another slight maneuver of the knife.

Rick's gaze dropped, following the action of the
knife, and he took another step to the side. The thin
ground gave way under his weight and one leg dropped
into a hole. Rick sank to his crotch. Frantically he dug
at the collapsing mud, clutching at the ground, trying
to keep from slipping beneath the surface. Fear super-
seded the anger in his eyes as more of the ground gave
way and mud began to pour into the hole with him. His
other leg slipped in.

It was the sudden widening of Rick's eyes, hope
flaring for a brief instance that had Gator spinning

around, hands up to defend himself. It was the only thing that saved his life. Ed stood behind him, soaked, covered in mud, a knife in his fist as he shoved it toward Gator's kidneys. Gator deflected the blade, stumbled in an effort to keep away from the thin layer of ground and was forced to jump over Rick to avoid the thinner crust.

Rick sank up to his chin as mud continued to pour into the hole around him, effectively burying him. 'Ed.' He coughed, tried to wiggle free but the mud held him prisoner, pinning his arms so he was helpless as he continued to sink into the sludge.

Gator pulsed sound directly at the shielder, driving him back. It would have knocked another man unconscious, or even killed him, but the shielder only dropped to his knee, face contorted, one hand up in an effort to deflect the blast of low-frequency sound coming at him. He vomited twice, and fought to regain his feet. His glance shifted once to his partner, but it was too late to save Rick; he had disappeared beneath the mud, his air cut off.

Ed backed off another step, this time paying attention to where he was stepping. Gator was certain Ed had panicked when the large alligator had plunged down on top of him. The alligator had just wanted to get back in the water, he hadn't been attacking, but Ed had fired and the wounded alligator had most likely thrashed around, knocking the rifle from the shielder's hands.

'Why did you come after us?' Gator asked, hoping for a better answer than Rick had given him.

The shielder threw the knife with blurring speed, suggesting genetic enhancement. Gator twisted his body in an effort to avoid the blade, feeling it slice through his torn shirt and shave off skin along his left

243

bicep. He answered with another pulsing wave of sound, this time stronger than the last. Mostly he listened to the sound of running footsteps, still a distance away, but coming fast.

The shielder turned his head as the wave hit and Gator jumped, slamming both booted feet hard into the thin crust of earth separating the ground from the water. He went in fast, the water closing over his head, the downpour of rain driving mud in after him. He managed to get the hollow reed to his mouth and the tip to the surface, allowing him to breathe under the water and muck.

Beneath the surface, he felt the vibration of heavy footsteps. Gator waited for them to come close, to edge out onto the thinner crust. One pulse of sound could break it down and send the entire group into the water, but the shielder must have warned them off. The vibrations ceased just steps from the thinner layer of earth, then they retreated, heading inland away from the marshy region.

Gator was certain two men had approached and three walked away. Using his hands, he broke through the layer of mud plugging the hole so he could push his head up. The rain and air never felt so good. He turned his open mouth up to allow the rain water in. Rinsing and spitting several times, he began the slow work of fighting the pull of the thick mud.

A bird called and another one answered. Gator sifted through the noises of the bayou and heard multiple heartbeats. Ian. Tucker. Maybe Wyatt or Kadan, although Kadan could mask the sound. The hunt had turned even deadlier. He fought his way out of the hole, taking care to distribute his weight evenly so as not to break through any more of the surface. It took time to drag himself out of the thick mud around the surface.

Dirt and mud fell into the water widening the break-through point, but he worked patiently to extract himself until he lay flat, arms and legs spread wide while he took in great gulps of fresh air.

Gator. Give me a signal to lock on to.

I took out one of them. There's at least three more. The shielder is injured and they're looking to run. He could sense the GhostWalkers close now. They moved with stealth, but Kadan didn't shield them, wanting Gator to know they were coming to him. He knew Kadan had locked on to him the moment he'd spoken telepathically. Relief swept through him. Not that long of time had passed since he'd left Flame, but it felt like a lifetime. He wanted to get her to a hospital immediately. With the other GhostWalkers there, they could sweep the area with quick efficiency and then get Flame medical attention.

They'll be coming at you north, northwest.

We're coming to you. Kadan's voice was confident.

Gator rolled over and stared up at the pounding rain, allowing it to wash most of the sludge from his face. He lay for a short while to get control of the raging headache that always accompanied the use of psychic talent, before turning back onto his belly and scooting forward much like a lizard. He used small stops and starts, keeping his weight evenly distributed at all times until he gained solid ground.

Gator leapt to his feet and began his pursuit of the other soldiers. No one had answered his question, but they were enhanced and Rick Fielding had definitely been in the same room with him while he took the test to determine psychic talent. Gator had assumed, obviously erroneously, that Fielding hadn't made the cut.

The GhostWalkers drifted out of the trees, pacing alongside of Gator, checking his condition out. Ian

MacGillicuddy. Tucker Addison. Kadan Montague. They were in full combat gear and tossed him a rifle and several clips of ammunition.

'You okay?' Kadan asked. 'I brought a medic kit.'

'Flame needs it. Alligator attack. It broke her arm, but she fought it off. We've got three men left here. One's a definite shielder. I'm using low-frequency sound waves to keep them sick and disoriented so they don't have a lot of fight in them. They just want to get the hell out. We need someone alive so we can follow them back to whoever is running them.'

They kept on the move, covering ground as fast as possible. 'You're certain these men aren't part of Jack Norton's team?'

Gator shook his head. 'Jack's team works mainly NCIS when they aren't running ops. These men are more like mercenaries. I'd met one of them. His name was Rick Fielding. He took the test in the same group I did. I don't know who they work for, but they aren't very pleasant. And the dead one threatened Flame.'

Kadan shot him a quick glance. 'No wonder he's dead.'

The GhostWalkers spread out across the small island, several feet between them as they began to stalk their prey. The men ahead of them would have no choice but to keep moving or turn and fight. They wanted to regroup. And they didn't want to take on a skilled army no matter how small it was. Gator continued to pulse low-frequency waves in front of them, not hard enough to kill, but to make the men sick.

'They're splitting up,' Tucker announced, pointing to tracks. 'Can you hear them, Gator?'

Gator shook his head. 'Their shielder is strong. He's been very resistant to the sound waves. I figured they'd split up. It's the only chance they really have for any of them to get out.' With the sound waves coming at them, they knew if they split up, they had a better chance to elude the pulsing waves Gator was sending at them.

Ian indicated he was climbing. He slung his rifle around his neck and went for the tallest cypress tree in their vicinity. As he climbed, Tucker, Kadan, and Gator looked over the tracks carefully.

'That's the shielder,' Kadan said, indicating a path to their right. 'He's moving fast.' For the first time there was a note of worry in his voice. 'He's locked on and is hunting.'

Gator felt a sudden cold chill go down his spine. 'Flame's back there.' He indicated the other side of the island. 'I'll take the medic kit to her.'

The sound of rifle fire reverberated through the swamp. Birds rose shrieking their annoyance. Ian joined them on the ground. 'Knew one of them would get the clever idea of lying back to wait for us. He was sitting in a tree a few hundred yards from here.' He nudged Tucker. 'Must have not liked your looks. He had his sights set for you. Guess I saved your life.'

Tucker gave a derisive snort. 'Guess you're full of yourself. Bullets bounce off me. I've got my superman shirt on today.'

'Is that where my shirt went? You thief. I been looking for it ever since I did laundry.' Even as they wrangled back and forth good-naturedly, they were scanning the ground for more tracks.

Kadan dropped down to examine a footprint. It was small and right over the top of it was the shielder's print.

'There's blood here, Gator, and it isn't from one of their team,' Kadan announced.

Gator crouched down to touch the smears of blood on the leaves. 'She left me. Damn her for this. She left me.'

The earth vibrated beneath their feet and shook the smaller puddles of water gathered in several depressions, drawing his attention. He sucked in his breath and fought back the need to express his anger and growing fear. Already the trees around him were shaking. He drew in a hard breath. 'One of them is tracking her. When I catch up with her, I'm going to shake that woman until her teeth rattle.'

'That'll help,' Ian agreed. 'Betcha that will get you a lot a points. Where'd you ever get the rep for being charming?'

Gator flashed him a single warning look. His stomach churned with alarm for Flame. She was on the move and she was losing too much blood. He had held on to his control every moment of the hunt, yet now he felt wounded, a terrible hole torn through his gut and he wasn't so certain he could hold back the intense emotions crowding in, all conflicting with each other. 'I'm not letting her go.' He made the announcement between his teeth.

Ian shrugged his broad shoulders. 'No one expected you to, bro.'

'She expected me to.'

'She doesn't know what a stubborn son of a bitch you are,' Tucker pointed out.

'Let's go get her,' Kadan said.

Chapter Thirteen

Flame sat in the mud with her back against the tree, breathing through the pain shooting down her arm. 'Rat bastard alligator. I don't care if you were just looking for a meal. I should have made a purse out of you.' She glanced down at her muddy boots. 'And shoes. Real alligator leather shoes too.'

Her arm hurt like a son of a bitch, but that wasn't the reason tears burned behind her eyes and her throat felt clogged. She was leaving New Orleans and Raoul Fontenot. It wasn't safe for her to stay. She wouldn't be able to find poor Joy Chiasson or avenge Burrell's murder. And there would be no making love to Raoul Fontenot. She closed her eyes briefly, regret pouring through her. She'd never wanted a man the way she wanted him. Just the simple sound of his Cajun drawl made her body hot. She even liked his swearing.

Flame groaned. She was a lost cause. Raoul was a dream, a life out of her reach and she wasn't going to die for something she knew she couldn't have. Whitney was too close. She could smell him. He had locked on to her presence and he was sending in the troops to retrieve her.

Raoul had never been her enemy and he would try to

protect her. After spending time with him she felt she could only do the right thing for both of them. As long as she was around he would be torn between the people he loved and her. He believed in the GhostWalkers – and maybe he even had reason to – but she would never be comfortable with them.

Gator wanted and deserved a home and family, a woman to take home to his grandmother, one who would produce babies he could put in her arms. That woman could never be Flame. If she stayed he would need to defend her and no matter what his dreams of family, he would never leave her. That was the kind of man he was.

Flame gritted her teeth and forced herself into a standing position, holding on to a tree trunk to steady herself. Waves of dizziness washed over her. She fought back the feeling and looked around her, trying to get her bearings and pick the safest way back to the frontage road. She couldn't get in Raoul's path. He was bound to use low-frequency sound waves and they would affect her in the same way they would their enemies.

'You can do anything for a short period of time. Control. Discipline. Patience.' How many times as a child had she recited the same familiar mantra when Whitney had made her so ill? How many times had she knelt on the cold bathroom floor near the toilet, rocking back and forth to ease the nausea brought on by the chemotherapy treatments?

She'd slept on the bathroom floor, a thick blanket under her with Dahlia and Tansy pressed tight against her on either side. She hadn't thought of those days in years, hadn't allowed herself to think about the other girls. It hurt to remember them. Their voices and laughter. The sound of their sobbing when the pain of

250

working with their psychic talents became too much.

Tansy had brushed her hair for her when they were allowed to be together and when it all fell out, she'd cried with Flame. Who else had been there? Dahlia. She'd been fairly good friends with Dahlia, the other 'bad' girl. And Lily. Flame sucked in her breath sharply. She remembered laying her head in Lily's lap while she stroked Flame's bald head, rocking gently and whispering that everything would be all right.

Back then, she'd believed Lily. And maybe that was why her betrayal went so deep. Flame worked for months on her first escape plan, hoarding the secret closely, confiding in no one. Until that one moment of weakness. She'd been up all night retching from the aftereffects of chemotherapy, helplessly weeping over the loss of her hair, and the other girls had sat with her, holding her hands, washing her face, and sharing her tears. Stupidly, foolishly Flame had confided in the other girls. Lily protested vigorously, claiming she feared Flame would die without treatment – but Flame didn't care. She'd figured Whitney was going to kill her anyway.

Lily hadn't allowed Flame that freedom. She'd gone to her father and told him of Flame's plan. Whitney's men were waiting for her when she escaped. She'd been punished, kept locked up for weeks without seeing the other girls. She'd been so sick and Whitney forced her to take the medicine, even giving her shots while strong men held her down. Lily had crept in once to admit what she'd done and whisper she was sorry, but Flame turned her face away and never spoke another word to her.

Pain shot through her head momentarily taking away the pain in her arm. It robbed her of breath and she bent over, dragging air into her lungs to keep from fainting. It was odd, but she always associated pain with her memories of the other girls. She tried never to think of them, not as children, not when they were with her.

Flash wiped her mind blank, pretending it was a chalkboard and she could just simply erase all thoughts. She wouldn't think of her past. She wouldn't think of Raoul and her bleak future, and she wouldn't feel the broken bones in her arm or the raw flesh where the alligator had taken hold of her. She would concentrate only on walking.

The rain seemed endless, as if the storm had stalled right over the island. She was soaked and muddy, blood running down her arm, hair plastered to her face. She stumbled again and stopped, the jarring pain making her sick. She looked around carefully, frowning as she did so, all senses going on alert.

All she really wanted to do was lie down and go to sleep. The kick came out from behind a tree, slamming into her hard, driving her back and down so that she landed on her butt, cradling her arm protectively. She actually saw white stars as she fought to keep from fainting. When she could control the pain she forced her head up to look at her assailant. A man dressed in military-issue camouflage clothes stood over her pointing his rifle at her face.

She started to laugh, the sound slightly hysterical. 'You know, this hurts like a son of a bitch. You'd be doing me a favor. Go ahead and shoot.'

'Get up.' He glanced right and left and then reached down, grasping her good arm and yanking her to her feet.

She went boneless, turning into a helpless rag doll. The barrel of his rifle dipped low as he used his strength to drag the dead weight of her body up. Blood dripped steadily down her useless arm and hit the reeds with small splatters. She concentrated on the pattern of the drops, focusing to keep from feeling the pain pumping through her, making her sick as he jarred her broken bones. The moment her feet were under her, she lashed out, kicking the rifle from his hands with enough force to send it spinning into the water.

He swore at her, circling a safe distance from her feet. 'You're losing a lot of blood. Eventually you're going to go down and then I'll just drag your ass through the swamp.'

'You can't wait. They're hunting you and this time there's a pack after you. You don't stand a chance and you know it.' She reached back between her shoulder blades and slid a knife out. The hilt was familiar and oddly comforting in her palm.

'I think I have more time than you do. You're going to pass out.'

She drew in air, slow and even, watching him, turning in a slow circle to stay facing him, using the minimum amount of energy. 'Men always underestimate women.' She watched the middle of his chest, able to see arms and legs, his entire body as he continued his slow stalking circle. 'You shouldn't have come after me. You can walk away from this right now. Whitney will never know. If you don't, I'll have to kill you.'

He spat on the ground. 'So you're a tough chick.'

'Oh, you have no idea how tough.'

He moved with blurring speed, kicking out at her broken arm in an attempt to quickly end the standoff.

She stepped aside, just barely, just enough to allow the booted foot to miss her by a hair's breadth. As she stepped she slashed his calf with the knife, slicing through his heavy clothes to cut deep.

'You bitch!'

'That was me being nice,' she contradicted.

He rushed her, fists clenched, the promise of death in his eyes.

She stood her ground, let him come, the knife held low and close to her body. She knew he expected her to try to bring it up when he was in close, but he was far too big and she was in bad shape. She didn't dare let him get his hands on her. When he was two feet from her, she threw the blade straight and hard, using every bit of enhancement Whitney had given her. She stood unmoving when he clutched at the knife, blood bubbling around the shaft, a shocked look on his face. His legs crumpled and he went down hard, face in the muck.

'That was me being a bitch,' she said. She swayed, wanting to retrieve the knife, but knowing she didn't have the strength to turn him over and pull it out of his chest.

She had to get off the island before Raoul found her gone. She couldn't go into the hospital. She'd thrown Whitney's name out to the hunter and he hadn't even flinched, hadn't questioned her. He knew Whitney and he definitely was part of the doctor's experiments. 'I'm sorry, Raoul,' she whispered. 'But I'm never going back there. Never. Not even for you.'

She began walking toward the small strip of land that connected to the frontage road. If she could find one of the bayou people, someone older, someone maybe versed in treating injuries, she'd hole up there until she could make it out of New Orleans. It was a temptation to go to her airboat. She had everything she needed on it, but if anyone was watching, or it was rigged to blow, she wouldn't have the strength – or time – to find out. She'd have to rely on the bayou courtesy to help her escape.

Most of Burrell's friends knew her and they would treat her injuries and give her a place to stay, but unfortunately Raoul was part of their community – she doubted if they would hide her presence from his grandmother or him. She would have to find a way to keep the gossip from getting out until she could leave.

Light-headed, she stumbled over several rocks and plants before finding the small narrow trail leading to the strip of land. She'd lost too much blood. Flame recognized the signs. She had to hurry to get onto the road where someone might stop for her before Raoul came out of the marshland.

She threw up twice as she made her way toward the frontage road. She just kept moving, one foot in front of the other until she was on the road. She walked toward the bridge, swaying, making a great effort to keep her feet under her and praying for a car to come by.

It wasn't a beat-up old pickup truck, or one of the older cars that passed her, but a shiny new town car complete with a chauffeur. The black car slammed on its brakes and backed up until it was beside her. The driver's door burst open simultaneously with the passenger's door. James Parsons and his driver both rushed to her side. James caught her good arm to steady her and the driver circled her waist to keep her from falling.

'Let me help you into the car,' the driver said. 'I'm Carl. Carl Raines, Mr. Parsons's chauffeur. You remember me. My God. What happened to you?'

Flame heard his voice as if in the distance trying to soothe her. She shook her head. She couldn't go to the hospital. There was no way she could protect herself if they took her there. She was too weak to stop the two men from putting her in the car. James Parsons slid in beside her and slammed the door closed.

Out of energy and unable to turn her head, Flame just stared at the closed door. All around her was rich leather and mahogany. She slipped farther down on the seat unable to hold herself upright. Her line of sight was below the seat. It took a moment or two before she noticed small details. Leather ties anchored to the seat. The scratches in the leather. There were three of them, one deep and two much more shallow. Her hand fell heavily to the floor between the seat and the door. Her eyes followed. There was a small distinct earring, one she was certain she'd seen before. It was a gold hoop with silver footprints on it. The same earrings Joy Chiasson wore in the picture her mother had given Flame. She'd told Flame all about giving the earrings to her daughter.

Flame managed to bring her head up, her movements slow and uncoordinated. Across the leather seat her eyes met James Parsons's. He was smiling. She became aware of the musty scent of sex. Both James and the driver wore evening clothes, as if they were returning from a party.

She smiled back, sliding deeper into the seat. Her gaze shifted around the car, taking in the neat bar and the plasma screen. The player was tiny, a mini DVD player. Beside it was a disc much like a CD but smaller. 'Thanks for helping me.' Her gaze drifted toward the front. A small red eye blinked back at her.

'James, get her something to drink.'

The order came from the driver and there was a distinct command to the voice. James reddened as he leaned forward to pour amber liquid over ice in a small Waterford tumbler. 'I know what to do,' James snapped under his breath. He thrust the glass into her hand. 'Drink this.'

Flame swirled the liquid over the ice. She'd bet her last dollar that the drink was doped. 'I'm dripping blood all over your seat. Do you have a towel?' No matter how hard she reached for her voice, it wasn't there. She sounded thin and reedy.

James's smile stretched wider, but didn't reach his eyes. His expression remained flat and cold and empty. Flame glanced away from him to the front where the driver sat. His eyes stared back at her from the rearview mirror. Not cold. Not flat. Not even empty. There was cruelty there – worse – evil. And there was a carnal lust she'd never encountered. Not normal, not even kinky. Just raw depravity.

James leaned into her, pushing the drink toward her mouth. Still staring into her eyes, he yanked at the front of her plaid shirt, ripping it away to expose her bare breasts.

She threw the contents of the drink in his face, followed the liquid up with a hard slam of the Waterford crystal tumbler to the side of his head. 'Back off you slime bucket.' She tried the door, found it locked and slammed the tumbler against James's head a second time when he lunged at her. 'I'm not sweet little drugged Joy, am I?'

She might not be drugged and she might not be Joy, but she was definitely going to get sick again. The bones in her arm grated together, this time taking her breath away.

'What the hell!' Carl exclaimed.

Flame glanced at him and her eyes widened as she saw the GhostWalkers materializing out of the gray rain. They stood in a line across the frontage road, semiautomatic rifles to their shoulders, muddy, wet, barely discernible in the driving rain. Behind them, a helicopter set down making it impossible to get past them. Carl slammed on the brakes instantly.

He shoved open his door. 'I've got a woman hurt here. I'm trying to get her to the hospital.'

Gator and Kadan split off from their group, walking up from either side of the car, the rifles rock steady. 'Where is she?' Gator asked.

'In the back,' the driver said. 'She's bleeding all over the place.'

'Did you call an ambulance to meet you?' Kadan asked. 'Unlock the back door,' he added when Gator stepped back as if he might drive the butt of his gun through the window.

'I just picked her up. I was calling when I saw you.'

'We'll take her from here. We'll airlift her to the hospital.' Kadan never once lowered the barrel of his rifle.

Gator yanked open the door and stared at Flame. She was covered in blood and mud. Her shirt was torn open, her breasts exposed. She was so pale he thought she might have already bled out. 'God, baby,' he whispered.

She turned her head, the movement obviously painful. 'I'm okay. You ought to see the other guy.'

'I did.' He reached in and drew her out to him, careful of her broken arm. It was only when he was settling her against him that he realized the man in the backseat was James Parsons and his face was split open above his eye. Flame still clutched the bloodied crystal tumbler in her hand. 'You son of a bitch. What did you do?'

'Nothing.' James put his hands up. 'I swear. She was hysterical. Her clothes were ripped, she was bleeding. We put her in the car and were taking her to the nearest hospital. I tried to get her something to drink, but she went crazy on me.'

'The thing is, James,' Gator said, 'I know where you live.' He kicked the door closed and carried Flame to the helicopter.

Kadan stayed at his back, rifle trained on the driver of the car. The other GhostWalkers were motionless until Gator was safely in the helicopter and then they followed, one by one, rifles still trained on the black town car's occupants.

Gator covered Flame with a blanket, his throat tight, his heart squeezed hard in his chest. 'I'm really pissed at you, *cher*. You should have stayed where I put you.'

Her hand twisted weakly in his shirt. 'Whitney will come after me in the hospital, Raoul. I won't be able to protect myself. Swear to me you won't let him take me. Swear it.'

He looked down at her face. Her eyes were closed, her breathing shallow. Beads of sweat formed on her face under the mud. There was still strength in the hand gripping his shirt. Gator leaned close, pressed his lips against her ear. 'You have my word, Flame. I swear it.'

Her fist relaxed slowly and she turned her head into his chest, giving up the fight against unconsciousness.

Flame smelled the stench of the hospital first. She could hear the murmur of the nurses talking. Someone leaned over her and adjusted the IV in her arm. Fear choked her and she tried to struggle awake. She heard groaning and again there was a soft murmur, this time a man's voice soothing her. She wanted to open her eyes, but the command between her brain and her eyes didn't seem to be working.

'Flame? Can you hear me, *cher*? They operated on your arm, set it, and are pumping you full of antibiotics. Everything looks good.' That was definitely Raoul's drawling voice. 'You're in the recovery room.' He leaned closer. 'You were never alone. We were in the operating room with you.'

'She won't remember anything you say,' the nurse advised, 'but it's good to talk to her. It will help bring her out from under the anesthesia.'

Flame felt his hands on her and a part of her relaxed. Raoul was there with her, just as he promised. 'You sure she won't remember?' he asked.

The nurse must have shaken her head because Raoul leaned closer to her and pressed a kiss against her ear. 'Can you hear me?'

Flame nodded her head.

'I think I've fallen in love with you.'

Flame stayed very still. She almost held her breath as his soft drawling voice went straight to her heart. It wasn't commanding, or cajoling, it was a voice filled with fear and wonder.

'You sure she won't remember anything I say?' Gator raised his voice again.

'They never do.'

She waited, her heart beating hard in anticipation. She felt the warmth of his breath against her ear. His lips touched her. 'You scared the hell out of me, *cher*. If you ever do something like this again, I'm goin' to turn you over my knee and beat your pretty little ass until you can't sit down and you beg me for mercy.'

Laughter bubbled up out of nowhere. She was smiling as she succumbed to the drugs in her body.

The second time she woke she knew she was in a hospital room. There was that same choking fear, amounting almost to terror. She smelled Whitney, his drugs and his experiments. They were all around her. She wanted out. She *needed* to be out.

'Raoul?' She whispered his name. Her guardian angel. He'd slipped past her guard somehow and she'd let him in. When had she gone from thinking him her enemy to believing in him so strongly?

'It's all right, you're safe.' That was definitely Raoul. She tried to pry her eyes open. She frowned. Nothing made sense. She could swear the male nurse was Wyatt.

She seemed to be drifting so maybe she was caught in a dream.

The nurse leaned over her talking overloud. 'Did you say Wyatt? Cuz you can't be whispering my name with my brother in the room.'

There was no doubt in her mind that the voice was Wyatt's. She focused on him. 'What are you doing dressed like a nurse?' Maybe she really was dreaming. He was in green scrubs.

He winked at her, reminding her all too much of Raoul. His dark curls fell into the middle of his forehead. 'I'm undercover.'

'Well you look ridiculous.'

'I look fetchin'. I've got Gator all hot and bothered worrying you're goin' wake up and fall in love with me.'

'You look ridiculous,' she repeated.

'All my patients think I'm cute,' he argued.

Gator snickered. 'You don't have any other patients.'

Flame kept her focus on Wyatt. Nothing made any sense. 'You're giving me a headache. What exactly is your job?'

'I'm guardin' you, babe.'

Flame turned away from him to find herself looking into Gator's eyes. He was sitting beside her, both hands holding hers, his thumb rubbing back and forth over her skin in a long caress. His eyes were shadowed and dark. He leaned forward and brushed a kiss on the corner of her mouth.

'You scared me.'

'I'm sorry.'

'Don't ever do it again.' He stroked back strands of hair from her face. 'I mean it, *cher*, never do that to me again.'

'Take me out of here, Raoul. Anywhere else. The cabin. Take me out of here.'

'Don' be breakin' my heart, Flame. You need more antibiotics. And they're giving you strong painkillers. Believe me, *cher*, you need them. The team is here and we're covering you. No one's goin' to be takin' you away from me. Go back to sleep now.'

She tried to be reassured, but the idea of Whitney finding her was terrifying. 'He'll know I'm here. The computers . . .'

'Have been taken care of. Go to sleep and let me handle this. You're a ghost, honey, just like the rest of us.'

She dreamt of the other girls. Young girls rocking back and forth in pain. Girls laughing together, stolen moments of happiness. She dreamt of a room with no windows and no comfort and being so alone. She dreamt of betrayal – and Lily.

It was dark the next time she opened her eyes. She looked around the room. A small woman with dark hair was adjusting the IV. 'I don't like the look of all the bruises, Ryland. I should be getting the blood tests back soon. She looks so worn down.'

A man moved into her view, his fingers going to the nape of the other woman's neck. 'She'll be okay. Gator isn't going to let anything happen to her, Lily.'

Flame's breath caught in her throat. Her gaze darted around the room until she found him. He was sitting close to the bed, his legs sprawled out in front of him. He looked tired, and his five o'clock shadow was getting unruly. 'I don't like you being here, Lily. You shouldn't have come.'

Ryland turned at the edge in Gator's voice. 'There's no need to talk like that. Lily had to come. Flame is her sister, just as Dahlia and the other girls are. Of course she had to come.'

'Flame doesn't trust her.'

'She has no reason not to trust her,' Ryland snapped.

'Shh,' Lily cautioned. 'Don't wake her. And she does have reason not to trust me.' She moved closer to the side of the bed to touch Flame's arm. 'She was going through chemotherapy and she planned to escape. I told him. She would have died without treatment.'

Flame opened her eyes to stare up at her, wondering why she was all grown up instead of Lily the child. 'I wanted to die. I wanted to get away from him that much.'

Lily drew in her breath. Her gaze met Flame's. 'I knew you wanted to die, but I couldn't let you. You were my family. I loved you, Flame. I know you felt it was a betrayal to tell him, but I had to save your life.'

Flame closed her eyes. 'I can't remember those days. They're too painful and I've wiped them from my memory.'

'No, Flame. You didn't. *He* did. He didn't want us to be close. He didn't want us to have memories of one another. That's why it hurts to look at our pasts or try to remember one another. It's why we don't. He even took that away from us.' There was a sob in Lily's voice. 'I didn't realize until I tried to remember why you never liked me. I knew there was something between us, but I couldn't remember. It hurt to remember.'

'I'm not going back.' Flame sounded tired even to her own ears. Maybe she really was dreaming, otherwise she'd be telling Lily what she really thought of her. 'How could you side with him when you knew what he was doing to us? Did you tell him I was here?'

'He's dead, Flame,' Lily assured in her most soothing voice. 'You're perfectly safe now.'

Flame turned her head away from Lily to find Raoul. He was her only hope, even if she was caught in a dream. 'He's not dead,' she whispered.

Raoul caught her hand and held it to him. 'I know, baby. I know. Everything's in place. He can't get to you.'

'You can't possibly think Peter Whitney is alive, Gator,' Lily gasped. She threw out her hand to Ryland, who immediately took it. 'He's dead. I felt him die. I saw it, even though I wasn't there. He disappeared, no one has found a trace of him.'

'I don't think he is dead, Lily,' Gator said. 'I'm sorry, I would have told you differently, but something's not right. The men who attacked us are trained, just as we are. They're all enhanced both genetically as well as psychically. I think Whitney has a private army and we either got in his way when he was trying to reacquire Flame, or he was running a little field operation to see how his boys stacked up against us.'

Pressing a hand protectively to her stomach, Lily felt behind her for a chair. 'This can't be happening. I feel like he's taken everything from me. *Everything.*'

She had to be dreaming, Flame decided. Lily wept so quietly, so hopelessly it nearly broke Flame's heart. And she didn't feel for Lily. She would never trust her again, never be her friend, never call her sister. But if she didn't stop crying, Flame was going to have to find a way to drag her butt out of bed and comfort her. 'Men are so freakin' useless,' she muttered.

'I'm pregnant, Ryland. It's too late to stop trying. I'm already pregnant. What if he is alive? This is a nightmare.'

Ryland crouched beside his wife's chair. 'Listen to me, honey. This doesn't change anything. We have a mission. We're going to find the other girls and protect them. We'll find them.'

'But what if this is all about the next generation? What if . . .' She trailed off, weeping again, this time into her hands.

Flame felt the choking terror rise. Whitney was just monster enough to have created such an experiment. It would explain why she was so attracted to Raoul. Why he was in her thoughts every moment, why she dreamt about him at night. Why her body burned for his. She couldn't have children, since the treatments had left her sterile, but all the others would have to be protected.

'Raoul?' She slipped her hand under her pillow, needing to feel as if she could defend herself. Her fingers found the smooth edge of the hilt of her knife encased in a leather sheath. She looked at him and smiled, some of the tension leaving her body. 'Thanks.' She looked through the open doorway of her room and saw a man mopping the floor. He looked familiar. She was certain it was Ian, Raoul's friend, but why would he be a janitor in the hospital? She had to be dreaming.

Gator eased his body onto the bed, stretching out beside her, careful of her broken arm as he wrapped his arm around her waist. 'You're welcome. I like you with knives.'

'You're such a perv.' She snuggled closer to him, already drifting, uncaring anymore if she was dreaming or if Lily was real. She only cared about the warmth of Raoul's arms.

The sound of whistling woke her. It was off-key and hurting her ears. She opened one eye cautiously. Raoul was asleep beside her; although how he could sleep through the noise she didn't know. It was morning and there was no Lily or Ryland in the room.

'Wyatt, what are you doing now?' Raoul asked, his voice grumpy. 'You're hurting my ears.'

'I was warning you. We've got company coming. You don't want everyone seein' you lookin' like a jackass, do you?'

'I look like a jackass?' Raoul sat up slowly, careful not to jar Flame.

'You're besotted. Whipped. Had. You can't leave the woman alone even after she's had surgery.'

'Who's coming?'

'*Grand-mere.*' Wyatt straightened his scrubs. 'She went shoppin' for Flame, got her all kinds of clothes. And Kadan went over the airboat, retrieved the duffel bag and put it in the cabin. Everything's locked down the way you asked. Are we movin' her tonight?'

'I *am* awake,' Flame declared. 'Someone could ask me. And I have to go to the bathroom before your grandmother comes in. Does someone have a tooth-brush?'

'I'll help you,' Gator said.

'I'm her nurse,' Wyatt said. 'There's no need for you to be doin' my job.'

'Go away, Wyatt,' Flame said. 'I have to ask your brother something and I may have to shove a knife through his heart when he answers me. I don't want any witnesses.'

'You take all the fun out of my job,' Wyatt said and winked at his brother as he went out.

Flame sat up slowly, feeling a little dizzy. 'They're giving me pain medicine, aren't they? You have to stop them. I have to be able to function.'

Gator slipped his arm around her. 'Just sit for a minute on the side of the bed.'

'Was Lily here last night? Lily Whitney?' She turned her head and looked him directly in the eyes.

Gator glanced down at her hand, making certain she didn't have the knife and wasn't about to pull it out from under the pillow. 'I couldn't keep her away. She wanted to see you and Ryland brought her. I told her how you felt, but she came anyway.'

'Was it necessary to tell her I was here in the first place? Couldn't you have waited?'

'Ryland is my commanding officer as well as my friend. I was using Lily's private equipment and he asked Kadan what the hell was going on. I wasn't going to put Kadan in the position of having to lie for me. We told the truth, but we took precautions. You were never, at any time alone. I was in the operating and the recovery rooms. The others guarded the doors. Once you were moved to a private room, we took over all care. And you aren't in their computers.'

'She took my blood.'

'She's worried the cancer has returned.' He hesitated. 'So am I, Flame.'

'You should have just asked me. Of course it came back. It was meant to come back, remember?' She slid off the bed, trying to wrap the flimsy hospital gown closer around her. 'Don't look. I may be weak, but I can still kick your ass. This is humiliating and I'm already irritated with you. She had no right to come into my room when I was so out of it.'

He was still reeling from her casual affirmative answer to the cancer question as he watched her walk to the bathroom. 'Flame.' He couldn't quite catch his breath.

She paused by the door. 'I don't want to talk about anything important here.'

'We are going to talk about this.'

'I love it when you get all alpha male on me, Raoul.' She flashed a smile at him. 'A lesser woman might be intimidated.' She disappeared into the small room, closing the door behind her. 'Did you beat that nasty little weasel James Parsons into a bloody pulp for me?'

'Not yet, but he's on the list. What the hell was going on in that car?' Gator looked down at his hands.

He wanted to smash something. James Parsons would do.

'I think he was trying to drug me, as if I wasn't already a mess, but it's all a little hazy.'

'You smashed his head in with a glass.' Gator leapt off the bed as his grandmother entered the room.

'Did I? Good.' Flame's voice purred with satisfaction. 'He's such a slimy little bastard.' She opened the door and came waltzing out, at least until she caught sight of Nonny. Color washed immediately through her face. 'Nonny. I didn't know you were here.' She sent Gator an I'm-going-to-strangle-you-with-my-bare-hands look before flashing a tentative smile. 'Sorry about the language.'

'No bother. I raised me four boys and I've heard it all. Which slimy bastard were you talking about?'

Chapter Fourteen

Someone had tried to fix up the cabin to make it less of a hunting cabin and more of a home. Flame suspected Nonny had paid a visit while they were gone. A homemade quilt, the craftsmanship beautiful, covered the bed and there was a tablecloth on the small makeshift table.

'Are you tired? Do you need to get into bed?' Gator asked.

'It's a broken arm. I've spent more time in bed than I ever have.' She wandered over to the window and looked out. 'I love this place. The bayou is so peaceful. I think I love the nights like this the best.'

'We're alone,' Gator announced.

She glanced at him over her shoulder. 'I'm very much aware of that. You're still angry with me.'

'Damn right I'm angry. You took off.' He threw his gloves and everything else in his hands on the table and crossed the room to stand behind her. 'You know how casual you sounded when you told me you knew you were sick again?'

Flame turned to face him, resting her back against the wall. 'There was no question that the cancer would come back. Dr. Whitney made certain of that.'

His gaze darkened. 'You knew that?'

'Not at first, not until I realized he'd coordinated my escape.' She shrugged. 'Oh, it wasn't all that easy. I was kept in a laboratory in Colorado for years. I escaped when I was nineteen. He made certain my escape was difficult so he could record it and see what I could and couldn't do. He soundproofed everything so I couldn't use sound against him. He made it hard enough, but after I managed to get out, it occurred to me that he wanted me to escape. How else could he test me in the world? In the field? Unlike his beloved Lily, I wasn't cooperative. He didn't give me any run of the mill cancer; he made up his own. He needed to find a way to ensure I would have to come back to him. It didn't occur to him I'd be willing to die.'

There was absolute resolution in her voice. Gator felt something hard grab his heart and squeeze until he thought his chest might implode. 'That's not an option.' He forced the words out when his lungs burned for air.

'It's the *only* option. I'm not ever going back where he can get his hands on me. He's evil. I don't care how much he spouts that his work is invaluable to science and will save thousands, maybe millions of lives. He's evil.'

'Flame . . .'

'Don't.' She cut him off, her features set. 'I weighed my options before I ever escaped. I knew he wanted something from me and if I left, maybe I'd be giving it to him. He didn't think I'd be smart enough to figure it all out. He placed a microchip in my body to track me. It was here.' She pushed the low-riding jeans his grandmother had bought for her down farther so he could see the arc of flames along her hipbone. The tattoo covered an ugly scar.

He heard a hoarse shout of protest echoing through

his mind and for a moment was afraid he'd yelled out loud. He made himself breathe. 'You cut the chip out of your body yourself.'

'Damn right I did.'

He wanted to hit something. Smash it. Drive his fists into something solid until he felt the physical pain. Maybe that would take away the churning rage and the terror of losing her.

'Raoul.' She leaned close to him, laid her hand gently, almost tenderly on his chest, right over his heart. Her voice was soft, so low he barely caught the words. 'The cabin is shaking. You have to calm down.'

He let his breath out, his hand coming up to cover hers, pressing her palm closer to him. 'I'm sorry. I didn't realize I was losing control. You were just going to walk away, walk down that road and head out of town, weren't you? Knowing you could die from an infection or from cancer. You were going to let it happen.'

'I was protecting you. Both of us, really, but you're in an impossible position. You're so . . .' She searched for the right word. 'Gallant. I can't let you lose everything you have in the world when there's no saving me. It's not logical.'

'Sometimes I want to shake you until your teeth rattle.'

'Well try to control the impulse.' Flame moved around him to pace the length of the cabin restlessly. She knew the painkillers were making her anxious, but she couldn't help it. 'There are so many things I need to do. Burrell's killers. Keep away from Whitney. Find Joy or at least find out what happened to her.'

'We've been looking for Joy, but we haven't turned up any information that will help us yet.' He jammed his hands into his pockets as if to keep from grabbing ahold of her. 'We're not finished talking about this.'

271

'Well talk all you want. I'm finished. I'm really, really angry that you let that woman into my room when I was . . .' She broke off.

'Vulnerable? You were vulnerable. Say it. It happens to all of us at one time or another. I'm not going to let you die because you're too damned stubborn to see the truth when it's staring you in the eye.' He had to work to keep his breathing slow and even. She could make him angrier than any other person on the face of the earth.

'What truth? Yours? You didn't even know Whitney was alive. You're too trusting, Raoul, and it's going to get you killed.'

'Maybe, *cher*, but lack of trust will definitely get you killed.'

'I'm going to get ready for bed after all. It's warm in here.' It was warm just being in the same room with him. And for some reason, when he was angry, she found herself getting damp with need. Even her breasts ached. Maybe *she* was the pervert.

Gator snatched up a bottle of beer and uncapped it, using the edge of the table. He sank into the one good armchair and took a long swig of the cold liquid, hoping it would cool his temper. She damn well wasn't going to die on him. And he couldn't get the vision of her scar beneath the tattoo out of his mind. He wanted to kiss it better. He just plain wanted. He pressed the beer bottle to his brow. It was going to be a long night.

'Don't you want to know why I bashed James Parsons in the head with his little crystal tumbler? The bastard.'

He turned his head and wished he hadn't. She had her back turned to him and was in a man's plaid shirt. He was certain this time it was his shirt. His grandmother's version of nightwear? She was awkwardly

272

shimmying out of her jeans, shoving them down with one hand and kicking at them to get the material away from her.

'Are you just going to sit there or are you going to help me?' She glared at him.

'Oh, *cher*. I'm goin' to sit here. I'm not getting near you when you're in such a mean mood.' He leaned back in the chair and stretched his legs out in front of him. 'I rather like the show.'

'You would.' She gave a final kick to her jeans and they went flying off.

'So tell me about Parsons. I didn't believe his story, but I didn't have time to beat the truth out of him.'

She shook her head. 'You aren't the type of man to beat the truth out of anyone. You're too nice.'

He took another pull of the beer and looked at her over the bottle. 'Don' you go thinkin' I'm all that nice, *cher*. If that man did what I think he did, he is accidentally goin' to die. He ripped your shirt, didn't he?'

'Yes.'

Something deep inside him he kept hidden from the rest of the world began to unravel. He felt rage. Cold. Absolute cold rage. He set the beer bottle down carefully on the floor and looked at his hands.

'Raoul.'

He heard her say his name softly, from a great distance. He curled his fingers into two tight fists. The man had been so close and on some level, Gator had known. Flame would never have sat in a car with her breasts bared to the world no matter how much blood she'd lost. If some other man had ripped her shirt in the swamp, she would have covered up before getting into the car. She had presence of mind to bash Parsons, she sure as hell would have covered up. He was going to kill the man with his bare hands.

'Raoul.' This time her voice was sharp. 'You're doing it again. The cabin is old. Do you want it to come crashing down? He's a skanky little punk.'

'He's a dead man walking.'

She sighed softly. 'There's more. I saw scratch marks in the leather and there was an earring. The earring was very distinctive. Joy's mother sent away for the pair when she saw them in a magazine. They had silver footprints over gold. The footprints represented a poem Joy loved about Christ carrying her in times of need.' She frowned, trying to remember more details. 'It was strange. I felt dizzy and everything seemed so dream-like.' She wiped at her face. 'I still can't remember very much.'

'You've lost a lot of blood and they have you on heavy painkillers.' His voice had a hard edge to it. He swallowed his anger and picked up the beer bottle, try-ing to distract himself from the memory of her covered in blood, in mud, bruised, battered, and her rescuer ripping her shirt open. He couldn't drink enough to erase that.

'I'm all right now. You got there in time. My arm's fine.'

Gator took another swallow then pointed toward the table because he couldn't think about it now. He had to change the direction of the conversation and his thoughts or he would be in jail by morning. 'Take a look at those pictures. Kadan pulled those out and said to have you take a look at them. He thought you might see something the rest of us don't.'

'Pictures?'

'On the table by my gloves.'

Flame leaned over the small makeshift table to study the pictures strewn over the tablecloth where they'd fallen out of a manila envelope. The shirttails rode up to reveal the underside of her bottom, her cheeks firm and smooth and curving deliciously. Gator repositioned his legs in an attempt to ease the growing ache in his groin. He wasn't about to call her attention to the fact that she was showing bare skin and giving him one hell of a hard-on.

'Joy's mother said she was a wonderful photographer and she's right. These must be the pictures Joy took of the bayou and wildlife. Have you looked at them? They're quite good. Joy took these photographs right before she disappeared.'

'Yes, *Grand-mere* told me her family developed them and took them to the police in the hopes that they'd see a clue to her disappearance. The other photos were taken of the other missing girl's bedroom. Lily had duplicates made for us.' His voice had gone husky and he could feel his body beginning to pulse with awareness.

'There's something here I'm not getting, Raoul. I can feel it.' She didn't look back at him but bent closer to the photographs. 'Maybe we should enlarge these. There's a small ripped piece of paper on the corner of this nightstand.'

He couldn't tear his gaze away from her. She was far more exposed now. He caught glimpses of the inviting entrance between her legs barely covered with a scrap of black lace. She brought up her foot and absently rubbed her calf with it before putting it down, her stance a little wider. The hem of the shirt was halfway up her bottom, exposing the globes of her ass to him. His air ran out and his lungs burned.

'You know what I think this is? Remember when Parsons's driver handed him his business card to give me? I think this is part of his card. He only had a number on it and I can make out part of a number on this ripped piece. That means that other missing girl had contact with Parsons, his son, or the driver at some point.'

'That makes sense, especially if that snake had the balls to rip your shirt. Good aim, by the way.' His voice was husky. 'You tore up his face.'

'With the drink. I thought he was trying to drug me.' She leaned her elbows on the table to study the various photographs. 'I can't believe how foggy my mind is. I keep trying to remember the details about what happened and to be honest, I just can't quite remember everything. It's so freakin' frustrating I want to scream. I should stop taking the painkillers. They're fogging my brain.'

'Give yourself time, *cher*, it will come back.' He set the bottle aside and got to his feet, drawn by the smooth temptation of her skin. His breath came in ragged gasps and his voice was hoarse. He stood directly behind her until he could feel the heat of her body. He pressed one hand on her lower spine and the other slid over the bare silky skin of her bottom. The feel of her took what little breath he had left. 'I have to see this black thong.'

She didn't protest. He heard the hitch of her breath and she went very still beneath his exploring caresses. He pushed the shirt up farther until he could see the three rows of black rolled string with the tiny bows down the middle disappearing between the firm globes of her bottom. '*Mon Dieu!* Is this your idea of nightwear?' He couldn't keep his hands off of her, rubbing and massaging almost compulsively. He had no idea he was virtually holding her down with his other hand.

'Not exactly. Remember, all of my clothes were burned.'

'*Grand-mere* didn't buy these.' He made it a statement as he tugged at the thin lacy strip covering everything he wanted.

'Like hell she didn't.' Flame closed her eyes, suddenly frightened of the things he could do to her body when he wasn't even trying. She couldn't move, didn't want him to stop, yet paradoxically, was terrified of where it would lead.

'She buys these sexy panties but gives you a man's shirt to sleep in?'

There was a small telling silence. 'I can't possibly wear what she sent.'

'She sent you a nightgown?' The hand at her spine began to make small circles to match the stroking on her bottom.

Flame closed her eyes, pushing back against his hand, feeling damp liquid heat pooling low in response. 'Not exactly.' It was the only response she could manage to get out. Her brain was melting right along with her body.

His hand spread the massaging circle wider, moving up her back until he suddenly stopped. A flare of excitement arced between them. '*Femme sexy.* You're wearing a knife.'

'I always wear a knife.'

He pushed her shirt up until he found the small leather sheath snuggled along her back. Gator bent forward and pressed a kiss against her bare spine. 'You know how much that turns me on.'

'Everything turns you on.'

'Baby, I'm so turned on I'm about to burst out of my jeans.' He bent forward, right over the top of her, his hardened groin pressed tightly against her buttocks as he pulled the knife out of the sheath and laid it on the table. 'I want to see the outfit.'

His voice was so damned sexy, his soft drawling whisper. Flame thought her legs might turn to rubber. She could feel the blush starting somewhere at her toes and consuming her entire body. He moved away from her and she straightened, almost afraid to turn around, but she couldn't stop herself.

Gator pulled open the shopping bag and dragged out the tiny scrap of mesh and leather. 'This is it? This is what *Grand-mere* sent you to sleep in?'

She nodded wordlessly, her hand on her throat.

He glanced down into the bag. 'What else is in here?'

'Don't look. Whatever you do, don't look in there.' Her voice was strangled.

He pulled the shopping bag wider and withdrew a small paddle covered in fake leopard skin. Flame groaned, her color deepening. He pulled a wireless strand of three small vibrating eggs with a little remote and some furred handcuffs. She covered her face. 'My, my. Looks like we're in for a long night of fun and games, *cher.*'

'What was your grandmother thinking?'

'She was thinking she needed to move us along in our relationship. She wants action obviously.' He held out the garment. 'Put it on.'

'Look at it. I can't put that on, it's crotchless.'

He smirked at her. 'I know. She chose it because it has no straps and you can easily get into it.'

'You're such a perv.'

'Put it on for me, *cher.*' One hand went to the front of his jeans. Her gaze followed as he stroked unself-consciously, a soft groan of excitement escaping.

Flame stood motionless looking at the impossible scrap of leather and mesh and the man holding it out to her. Stark desire was so intense, so raw, it deepened the color of his dark eyes to almost midnight black. She shook her head, knowing she was going to give in to him, knowing all that mattered to her in that moment was pleasing him.

278

She took the outfit and retired to the bathroom, refusing to struggle into it one-handed in front of him. If he looked into the bag he was going to find the whipped cream and the oils and the scented candles. And she knew he was going to look into the bag. Why that excited her, she had no idea, but maybe being a pervert was contagious. She mulled it over while she dressed, or rather undressed. There was no doubt that she was getting even more turned on at the idea of his reaction to seeing her in the very revealing and risqué outfit.

'You coming out anytime soon, or do I have to come in and get you?'

Flame looked at the little pile of clothing, the over-sized plaid shirt, the black thong, the leather sheath and harness for her knife and she took a deep breath. Once she stepped out that door there was no turning back.

'Cher.' He sounded impatient, sexy, hoarse with need. 'The suspense is killing me. You want me to come to you?'

Flame opened the door and sauntered out, pretending to be confident and casual and that a million men had seen her with nothing on but leather and mesh. The leather part of the bustier pushed up under her breasts into the black mesh that ended just under her nipples, so that she was completely exposed. The mesh was open around her belly button and crotch and buttocks, but clung to her waist and ribs.

The room was dark other than the glow of several candles. She was grateful for that, particularly when she saw that Raoul was completely naked. He was very well endowed. She couldn't help staring. There were a couple of things she should have mentioned to him before she ever put on leather and mesh, but now, when she had his undivided attention, she was afraid it was too late. He stood beside the bed, the silly sex toys laid out on the end table as if he intended using every one. Her heart accelerated at the sight and she knew he could hear it because he held out his hand to her.

Gator moistened suddenly dry lips. '*Mon Dieu.* You have a beautiful body.' He made a small circle with his fingers.

She forced herself to turn around slowly for him, showing off the outfit and the bare body beneath it. With him watching, her nipples hardened into tight peaks and her breasts ached for attention. She watched as he circled the rigid length of his shaft with his fist as he said something in French she wished she understood.

'Come here.' His body shook with wanting her. He had been with other women, but he had never felt like this. He'd never needed like this. In that moment, when she'd emerged from the bathroom looking so damned sexy in her outfit, the realization that he'd been isolated for so long came to him. She was sunshine. Laughter. Fine wine and silk sheets or beer in the bayou with the setting sun. She was secrets and sex and his very own warrior. She was his equal. She was everything he could want standing right in front of him.

She could hardly breathe, but Flame wasn't a woman to back down once she'd made up her mind. He was looking at her, his face etched with desire and his body as starkly aroused as it could be, holding out his hand to her and she took it, allowing him to draw her close.

Careful of her broken arm, Gator bunched her hair in his hand and, tilting her head, caught her soft sigh in his mouth. The hard peaks of her nipples pressed tightly into his chest as her body melted into his. His tongue tangled with hers, hot and moist until a river of need burst free in him. He wanted her so much he couldn't breathe, couldn't think straight. Her skin was incredibly soft against his and her throaty little moans nearly drove him mad.

He kissed her over and over, rough with desire, until she was pressing her body against his, rubbing her soft belly against his arousal. The mesh brushed against his ultrasensitive groin until he was afraid he might explode. His mouth left hers to trail down her throat, nibbling along her neck until he found the creamy mounds spilling out of her costume. He thumbed her nipples, watching her eyes darken with desire.

She cried out when his mouth closed over her nipple, suckling hard while his fingers tugged at her other breast through the mesh. She arched her body into his, wanting more of him. His hand slid down between her legs, to cover her dampness and she jerked in his arms, her need nearly as strong as his own. He took his time, lavishing attention on her breasts, rubbing the mesh over her skin with his chin, teasing her belly button with his tongue, all the while, moving her backward to the bed.

When the edge of the bed hit the back of her knees, he lowered her, his mouth once more on hers, hard and insistent, refusing to allow her a moment to think. She had taken him to the very edge of his control and they'd only gotten started. She kissed him back, every bit as hungry as he was, but her eyes contained a hint of fear. She moaned in his arms, her body moving naturally against his, yet her touch was unsure.

'You want me.' His lips left hers and returned to her breasts, his teeth and tongue teasing, mouth suckling, pulling strongly, hands tugging and massaging. He loved the animalistic sounds coming from her throat. He looked at her body, flushed with desire, breasts swollen and nipples hard peaks, her breathing as ragged as his. Beneath his wandering hand her stomach muscles contracted and her hips moved restlessly. 'But I want more from you, Flame. I want you crying for me. I want you needing me the way I do you. I need more.'

Flame couldn't imagine there being more. More might kill her. He wanted her crying? She was nearly sobbing for mercy. His mouth was so hot, blazing a trail of fire along her tummy. He paid particular attention to her tattoo, licking along the flames, kissing her scar, driving her crazy. His hand slid up her thigh, drowning her in sensations she'd never experienced.

His eyes met hers as his tongue paid lavish attention to her belly button, and then began to track lower, dropping little kisses and teasing bites all the way down to the end of the mesh. His fingers brushed her mound and she jerked beneath his hand, a moan escaping, one that brutally hardened him to the point of agony. He wanted to sink into her heat immediately, but not before she was writhing mindlessly. Flame was a warrior woman and he needed to keep her involved, because if she changed her mind, he'd have a fight on his hands. He lowered his head and inhaled her scent.

'Raoul.'

There was a catch in her voice. A tremor. He heard it as he flicked his tongue along the flowering moist seam. She nearly came apart as he widened her thighs to accommodate his shoulders. He pushed his tongue inside her with a slow deliberate stroke. Her hand twisted in his hair and she pushed forward into his mouth.

She tasted sweet, like honey and he couldn't stop himself from diving deeper, taking his fill. He flicked and stabbed with his tongue, sucked and teased until she bucked against his mouth, sobbing for release.

Flame tried to find an anchor, something, anything

at all to hold her to earth. She wasn't prepared for his expertise and Raoul was sweeping her away before she could catch her breath, or think or analyze or do any of the things she needed to do for control. His mouth was insistent, drinking her, eating her, shattering her every erotic fantasy and replacing it with something far too real. He seemed to savor her taste, groaning with need, hot and hungry and desperate for more.

Flame couldn't catch her breath as pleasure crashed over her, wave after wave of it, her body not her own, but his to do with as he wanted. She screamed as her entire stomach contracted, her belly, and breasts and her thighs. 'I can't take any more.' She gasped the words, wanting more, needing more, but afraid it was going to kill her.

'There's so much more,' he whispered. 'I want to be inside you, Flame. I can't wait any longer.'

The sound of his voice, the look on his face, the harsh hunger for her nearly sent her over the edge. She widened her legs as he knelt between them. Her heart began to pound and fear edged up into her throat. She wasn't giving herself to him. It wasn't like that at all. She repeated it over and over to herself, waiting. Feeling the large head of his erection pressed tightly against her. He pushed slightly, but he didn't enter her, making her wait.

'Look at me.'

She swallowed hard, her eyes meeting his. He wasn't even in her and he felt too big. She should have started with something much smaller.

'You've never done this before, have you?' His voice was harsh with the struggle for control.

Flame shook her head. 'Who was I going to do anything with?' Her fist tightened in the quilt. If he stopped, she had no idea what she was going to do. She knew so much in theory, but he was light-years ahead of her.

It shouldn't have made him feel more possessive to know that no other man had had her. It was a primitive way to think, but he was beyond all reason, it seemed, when it came to Flame.

'This is us. You and me, Flame. And this is *my* choice. I want you because of who and what you are, not because of an experiment. You're in my heart. You have to understand that. This is only between us.'

She could hardly think or breathe, her body not her own anymore. His features were set and determined. He was waiting for a response. She didn't have one, didn't know what was real when it came to her life. She'd never had a man want her the way Raoul did. His hunger was so raw, so intense she almost couldn't believe it was for her. She managed a nod, lifting her hips, searching for more, searching for relief. She need-ed him inside of her *now*.

He watched her face as he began to push into her body. 'You're so fuckin' tight you're killing me, Flame.' And hot and slick and velvet soft yet gripping him like a fist. He stretched her slowly, terrified of hurting her, but far too close to losing his own control.

She thought he had it the wrong way around. He was killing her, stretching her impossibly. It stung, burned, yet it felt so good. She didn't know if she wanted to fight him off of her, or drag him closer.

'Don't move.'

She realized she had been moving, pressing closer, trying to take more of him, wanting all of him. She could feel her muscles clenching around him, gripping him tight, beginning to spasm with the hard slide of his body. She moved again, an enticing little wiggle she couldn't quite stop. He groaned and surged forward, past the thin barrier to lodge deep. The bite of pain mingled with a burst of pleasure and the breath exploded out of her lungs in a single rush.

'It's all right now.' His voice was strained. He moved, withdrawing from her, so that she held her breath at the first feel of fiery friction. He surged into her deep and hard, making her cry out. His arms looped beneath her thighs giving him a better angle so each time he pistoned forward through her tight folds, he could hear that breathless little cry over and over. It seemed to vibrate through his body and center in his groin adding to his own pleasure.

Her body squeezed tightly around his until he felt sweat beading on his forehead with the intensity of the sensations pouring over him. She was so hot and the sight of her, lying under him, her body sprawled out for his pleasure alone was enough to send him into oblivion. With every hard stroke as he thrust into her, her round breasts swayed, nipples hard with desire – for him. Her eyes were slightly glazed and her breath was ragged. Her soft little moans drove him crazy, vibrating through his body, swelling his cock more than he'd ever experienced.

Gator didn't want to stop, wanted to be forever just like this, his idea of paradise, thrusting in and out of her tight body with hard, deep strokes, watching the effect of his body on hers, the near ecstasy washing over her and the idea that she was his. Only his. That she opened to him, body and mind and heart when she never let any other so close. That alone was a huge turn-on to him.

The walls of her channel tightened impossibly around him with hard deep spasms, contracting and squeezing, the orgasm exploding over both of them, robbing him of what little control he had left. He swelled impossibly bigger, his balls drawing up painfully and then he was surging hard, pounding into her, a single long note of ecstasy escaping from his throat. His orgasm seemed endless, a merciless volcano pouring through his body and into hers while she sobbed, clutching at the quilt, trying to ride out the exquisite torment.

Flame didn't think her body would ever stop the rocketing spasms. Wave after wave of sheer pleasure rippled through her body, and when she thought it would subside, he moved, just a bit, and aftershocks instantly took over, shaking her and throwing her into another quaking round. She clung to him, shocked that he could make her body so responsive, so sensitive and so incredibly hot.

Gator stared down at Flame in awe. '*Mon Deiu, cher.* Just kill me now and I'll go happy.' He collapsed on top of her, sliding the top half of his body to one side to avoid her injured arm. 'You're amazing.'

'I was, wasn't I?' Flame said, smirking with satisfaction. 'And don't let me forget to mention to your grandmother that mesh is not the least bit comfortable.'

He kissed her neck. 'What about the leather?'

'It itches when it's sweaty.'

'I don' sleep in clothes anyway. You don' need to either.' Gator propped himself up on one elbow and proceeded to rip the mesh away from the leather. It came away in his hand after a little wiggling on her part to get it out from under her, leaving her rib cage wrapped in leather.

'Now I look like a sausage,' she announced and burst out laughing.

He rubbed his face against her breasts, his shadowy jaw rough on her nipples. 'I wouldn't say that. I think you look sexy.'

She couldn't stop laughing, even though the movement sent aftershocks rippling through her body. 'You're so crazy. Unzip it.'

'I don' know, *cher'* His accent thickened. Her body reluctantly released his from her snug sheath and he sighed softly. 'I think you look good in leather.' His tongue flicked her nipples and he nuzzled his face into the valley between her breasts.

Still laughing, Flame reached for the knife on the end table beside the bed at exactly the same moment he reached for the can of whipped cream. 'You're such a freak, Raoul. Just what do you think you're doing with that?'

'Expanding my horizons.' He traced the flames of her tattoo as he shook the can. 'What 'ya going to do with that knife?' His tone lowered, was husky, frankly sensual.

She slid the tip of the razor-sharp blade along the edge of the leather and cut herself free of the offending material. 'Nothing thrilling, believe me.' Laughter was beginning to overtake her again. She couldn't help it. He looked so eager. 'Put your little can of whipped cream down, I'm going to sleep. You wore me out.'

He outlined her tattoo with the whipped cream, leaned down and licked it off. 'Good brand.'

'Well that's all right then.'

'Stop squirming. I'm drawing a masterpiece. This is art.' He used the whipped cream to draw a happy face on her lower belly. This time when he licked it off she closed her eyes and he could feel the shudder of pleasure running through her. 'I got me lots of toys to play with, Flame. You just go ahead and go on to sleep and when I think I need to wake you up, I'll find a way to do it that you'll like.'

'I can't go to sleep with you spraying whipped cream all over me.'

This time he outlined a bikini top on her breasts and bent to lick it off. His tongue rasped over her skin and around her nipple. There was a small tug of his teeth. Her womb contracted and clenched hard in response. Flame tangled her fingers in his hair and closed her eyes, giving herself up to the sensations of his tongue and teeth, the moist heat of his mouth and his exploring hands. 'You're not planning on really using those ridiculous toys, are you?'

'Hell yeah, we're using them.'

She opened one eye. 'I call the handcuffs and paddle.'

'Not a chance, *femme sexy*, I'm stronger than you.' His hand caressed her bottom. 'I've got me plans.'

'You're such a goof.' For the first time in her life, she felt truly happy. And she hoped it would be a long, long night. 'Just remember who has the knife.'

Chapter Fifteen

Flame woke with her heart thundering in her ears. Nightmares had invaded her sensual dreams and left her gasping. She lay still, looking up at the rough ceiling knowing dawn was just an hour or so away. She had never allowed herself to be so close to anyone. She'd formed friendships, let herself enjoy people, but she never took a relationship far enough that she needed anyone. She never risked wanting any thing so much that she couldn't leave it behind, so it didn't make sense to her that wanting to be with one person would ever be important enough to risk her freedom.

She rubbed her broken arm absently as she listened to the sound of Raoul breathing. His arm was around her body possessively, his hand under her breast. She could feel the rub of his knuckles and even that small contact sent excitement skittering through her body. He had power over her whether he knew it or not. Flame tried to be ruthless in her dealings with her own feelings. She didn't want to let go of Raoul. She tried to be analytical and logical.

What real future together was there for them? She could seek help from a conventional doctor. It might buy her time, but it wouldn't cure the cancer. Only

Whitney could do that. And going to a doctor would reveal her genetic enhancement and everything else Whitney had done. It would put her square in the limelight and the government would swoop in and retrieve her. She was worth too much money and frankly, they would think it would be too dangerous to allow her to run around loose.

She eased her way out from under Raoul, sliding to the edge of the bed. The moment she sat up, she was aware of her body, deliciously sore, strangely stimulating as if deep inside something moved against her most sensitive parts. Raoul had been so eager to get at her body, to keep nothing between them, his hands roaming over her even after his sexual appetite was temporarily sated. And he never seemed to be sated for very long, waking her over and over in the night.

As if reading her thoughts, his arm snaked around her waist. 'It isn't light yet.'

She closed her eyes at the sound of his voice, savoring his Cajun accent and the velvet smoothness of his tone. 'Almost.'

'We didn't get to finish playin' with all the toys, *cher*,' he cajoled, pressing a kiss against the scar in the midst of the flames arching over her hip. 'I was thinking we could spend a little time with the handcuffs.'

She turned her head to regard him with what she hoped was a stern look. Unfortunately, he always made her want to laugh. He looked sinfully sexy, a little bit wicked, yet still managed a boyish anticipation. 'Not in your wildest dreams.'

'Now, sugah. The entire concept behind handcuffs is a control issue. I like control. And the thought of you kneeling in front of me, hands behind your back, helpless so I can do whatever I want to your body makes me as hard as hell.'

She did burst out laughing, 'You really are a freakin' pervert, Raoul, and honestly, just about everything makes you hard as hell.'

'You don' know the half of it, *cher.*' He reached casually for the small remote on the nightstand and turned the switch.

Her breath caught in her throat and she spun around, wide-eyed as the small eggs deep inside her body began to vibrate. 'What did you do?'

'You were sleeping so sound, exhausted from all the playin' we did and I didn't want to wake you up. It was so damn sexy putting those eggs inside of you. Do they feel good?' He licked the scar, nibbled his way up her rib cage. 'Tell me what it feels like.' He laid back again, his dark eyes drifting moodily over her face, watching her expression. 'Even in your sleep you get damp and taste like honey. I wanted to do so many things last night, but didn't want to scare you off.'

Each movement of her body sent the eggs bouncing around until they were vibrating over her most sensitive spot, triggering a flood of liquid heat. Her womb and her stomach muscles contracted, an unexpected orgasm beginning to wash over her so that she gasped.

'Oh, yeah, they feel good,' he whispered and flicked his tongue over her nipple. 'Lean down here.' His hand circled the thick length of his erection, holding it up for her. 'Every time I see you, or smell you, or even hear your voice, this is what you do to me. Put your hands on me, your mouth. I want to have your mouth on me.'

'I don't know how.'

'Don' worry, *cher*, I'm a hell of a good teacher.' Using the remote, he changed the setting, so that the eggs were subtly vibrating against the walls of her tight channel. His fists curled in her hair and guided her head down to him. He closed his eyes as her tongue

291

flicked the pearled drops from him. 'Son of a bitch, Flame. I might not be able to survive the lesson.'

Flame looked up at his face, and the breath rushed from her lungs. She had such power over him. It was amazing to her and all he wanted was what she'd been curious about anyway. He knew her body intimately, she wanted to know his just as intimately.

He used his fists in her hair to guide her movements, as she slowly licked, kissed, and nibbled, building up her courage before taking him deep into the heat of her mouth. He groaned, unable to stop the sound from escaping. Flame had good instincts and it didn't take her long to figure out just from his reactions what he liked and what he loved.

Gator threw his head back, a low, strangled moan emerging from his throat. Flame never did anything in half measures and she was a fast learner. She started out so sweet and tentative. She was a mixture of innocent and siren and already she was taking him deep, suckling strongly, using her tongue to torment and tease. He had planned just a very short little lesson, but her hand caressed and squeezed his balls, circled his shaft and did the same all the while her mouth worked hot magic on him. Twice he felt the squeeze of her throat as she did a slow, heart-stopping slide. He could feel his balls drawing tighter and tighter until he was certain he would explode.

He did the only thing he could think to do to save coming too soon. He wanted to be in her body, giving her so much pleasure she wouldn't think of ever leaving him. He had time for everything else. Years, he hoped. Years of her mouth and body and her soft, sexy laughter and her sass. He hit the switch on the remote controlling the eggs so that they buzzed to vivid life, moving and fluttering and pressing against sensitive nerve endings.

Flame rocked back on her heels, crying out as her muscles spasmed and contracted. A tremor went through her. 'Raoul.'

He caught her waist and gently tugged until she was bent over the side of the bed. 'Watch your arm, *cher*. I want you comfortable.' He stood behind her, his hand caressing her bottom. 'I love your ass. I fantasize about it all the time.'

'Stop talking and do something.' She nearly sobbed the order, unable to stand still, her body rippling with orgasm after orgasm.

He switched off the remote and reached down to tug the string. She gasped as one by one the eggs slid over her heightened nerve endings causing a second shudder of pleasure. 'You're so wet, Flame, so hot.' He pressed against her, catching her hips and drawing her back while he slammed forward. 'So damn tight.'

The moment he plunged inside her, driving through her tight folds, so hard and thick, filling her, rubbing against her overstimulated nerve endings she couldn't stop from trying to take control of the pace. She was frantic, pounding back against him, riding him hard while her body seemed to wind tighter and tighter. She felt it everywhere, her legs, her breasts, but especially between her legs, the fierce pleasure spiraling out of control. Wave after wave shook her.

Suddenly he went still, his hands on her bottom, massaging, kneading, his body deep inside her while she pushed back against him desperate for relief.

'What are you doing?'

'I just can't help myself, *cher*. I'm a weak man and the temptation is too much for me.'

She could feel him swelling inside her, his excitement obvious. He felt too big again, hitting her womb, too thick, stretching her tight channel. Flame glanced back at him over her shoulder. Her eyes widened when she saw him pick up the leopard-skin paddle. 'If you want to live, you won't dare.'

'Then I'm going to die in paradise.' He smacked her bare bottom with the paddle.

Flame gritted her teeth. 'You do that again and I'll break that thing over your head.'

The paddle went flying. 'I didn't much like it, either. 'Course,' – his hand massaged her bottom again – 'if I were to give you a spankin' I'd want to do it with my hand so I could feel you – and you could feel me. That would be sensual, not impersonal. That's what was wrong.'

'Raoul!' Flame wailed his name, riding back against him, moving her hips to try to force his compliance, grinding her body against his with small sobs of need. She was going to have to hurt him if he didn't get on with it.

His hand came down on her bare butt bringing a flare of unexpected heat and then a caress as his palm rubbed over the spot. Her tight muscles contracted around him and a fresh flood of liquid bathed him. Before she could form a protest, he thrust, driving mercilessly through her hot sheath hard and deep, over and over.

Flame couldn't breathe, couldn't think. Only feel. A sob of pleasure escaped as her climax tore through her body with such force she would have fallen if Raoul hadn't been holding tightly to her hips. Her muscles clamped down on him, gripping hard, squeezing so hot and tight she heard his breath explode from his lungs.

He swore in Cajun, a long growling, guttural curse while his body swelled thicker and thicker until he was rising on his toes and gritting his teeth, shuddering with pleasure as his body jerked with his own violent, explosive release.

Flame lay facedown over the side of the bed, Raoul's thick erection buried deep inside her, his body blanketing hers, while they both gasped, searching to draw air into burning lungs and calm the wild storm crashing over their bodies. Spasm after spasm tightened ruthlessly on him, rocking them both, even as they lay quiet. She could feel her body pulsing around his, greedy for more, yet she was exhausted.

Dawn had crept into the room, the early-morning light spilling over them, bringing with it some semblance of sanity. She felt the burn of tears. She wanted to spend her life here, in this cabin, far away from the insanity of who and what she was, but it was impossible. How could she stand knowing what it would have been like to stay with him? To have him? To have a family?

Raoul would bring her pleasure beyond measure. And he would always make her laugh and feel safe and protected.

'Are you crying?' His hands stroked her hair. 'I didn't hurt you, did I?'

She shook her head. How could she tell him the truth? Of course it hurt. He had shown her paradise and she was going to have to walk away. His hands ran down the length of her body, lingered on the sides of her breasts. Even that small touch sent another small aftershock rippling through her. His mouth teased the nape of her neck, his hands massaging her bottom, fingers dipping into her heat and rubbing to send another much stronger aftershock through her.

'I love that,' he whispered against her spine. 'I love how hot and wet you are for me and how when I touch you, and I'm deep inside you, all your muscles clamp down on me as if you're holding me inside you and don't want to let me go.'

She turned her face to the side, resting it on the quilt. She looked exhausted, sated, drowsy, and sexy all together. The sight of her made his throat ache and his eyes burn. He had felt empty for so long, needing something and not even knowing it. Flame was a miracle, a once in a lifetime gift, and he wasn't going to be fool enough to let her slip through his fingers.

His body relaxed slowly, allowing him plenty of time to enjoy the ripples of pleasure coursing through her. He helped her sit on the edge of the bed, a slow grin stealing over his face as he surveyed the room. It smelled of sex and candles and he inhaled to remember the heady aroma forever.

She looked fragile when he knew she wasn't. Everything male in him rose up to want to protect her, which was funny, because when she got him riled, everything in him wanted to dominate her. She brought out extreme emotions in him, made him feel alive, made him want to be alive.

He drew a finger across her breast and leaned close to take the tip into his mouth, biting down gently and tugging, before laving with his tongue. He felt a shiver run through her. Male satisfaction was instant.

'We can't stay here all day,' she said.

He felt her withdrawal, a small feminine retreat, her body moving inches from his, but definitely telling him something. He caught her chin in his hand. 'Sure we can. You just got out of the hospital and you're entitled to a day or two of resting. Even with painkillers I know that arm has to hurt.'

A faint smile curved her mouth, but didn't reach her eyes. And she avoided looking at him. 'Is this what you call resting?'

Deliberately, to prove to himself he could, he bent his mouth to her breast again, this time suckling strongly, his hand on her stomach to feel the contractions sweeping through her at his touch. He loved the power of it, the way she shuddered with instant need when he'd just had her. It took him a moment or two to realize what that meant. She was still trying to withdraw and he was asserting dominance. Frustrated, he sat back, regarding her averted face while fear and anger began a deadly mix. 'What is it, Flame?'

She stared out the window, refusing to meet his gaze. 'This doesn't change anything you know.'

'*What* doesn't change anything?' Gator couldn't keep the challenge out of his voice. She damn well wasn't going to sleep with him and *dismiss* him.

Flame finally turned her head and looked at him. 'You know exactly what I mean. We . . .'

'Don't you *dare* use the *F* word. I made love to you all last night *and* this morning and you knew that was exactly what I was doing. Don't you even think about calling it anything else.'

Her eyebrow shot up. 'The *F* word? You weren't so afraid of using the word the other day or last night for that matter. I was going to say *slept* with you. You're such a hothead. We slept together, that's all.'

'I swear, Flame, I've never had anyone make me as crazy as you manage to do. I'm not letting you just dismiss me after last night.' His dark eyes glittered at her.

She shrugged as nonchalantly as she could. 'I'm certain you've rejected lots of women after sleeping with them. Don't act so outraged.'

He was angry. He could feel the anger churning in his gut, riding him hard as he struggled for control. He turned away, paced across the room when his fingers itched to shake her. She could pretend to be casual about what was happening between them all she wanted, but that's what it was – pretense. 'You're being a

297

damned coward, Flame, and that's beneath you.'

Her breath hissed out between her teeth and she whirled around, her eyes fairly shooting sparks. 'Don't you dare call me a coward. You don't know the first thing about me. Your ego is a little wounded because I'm not falling at your feet like all the other women you took to bed and then walked away from.'

He stepped closer to her, uncaring that the walls of the cabin expanded and contracted and beneath his feet, the ground shifted ominously. 'You think I don't know you want me as much as I want you? Hell, honey, you don' have near the experience I have.'

Flame sucked in her breath and quickly turned her face away from him, but not before he saw the hurt in her eyes.

'Fils de putin!' Gator passed his hand over his face. This was his fault, not hers. He was the experienced one, yet he'd been so out of control, wanting her so badly, he'd acted like a buck in rutting season. How would she know he'd been making love to her when he hadn't been tender and gentle?

'Flame . . .' he began, at a loss for words. He didn't talk about feelings. He just *felt*. 'I made love to you. That was me making love to you and maybe you deserved a different initiation, but I meant it as loving you. I'm not all that civilized and I can't say what I'm feelin' right all the time, but . . .'

She turned her head from him and he caught the glitter of tears. 'Don't, Raoul. This is me freaking out, not you doing something wrong.' She drew the sheet around her, suddenly feeling vulnerable. 'I'm afraid of you, of how you make me feel. When I'm afraid, I have a tendency to run. And if I can't run, then I go on the offensive.'

'You're not embarrassed with me, are you? Because

298

the things we did are natural. We didn't do anything wrong.'

She shook her head. 'No, I'm not embarrassed.' And God help her she wanted to do them all again with him. 'I'm just – confused. I've always had a plan and I've always kept on the move. I don't know how to stop. I don't know if I can stop, or even if it's safe to stop, even for a little while.'

'It's okay to be confused, *cher*. I can live with confused. I just can't take you leaving me. Maybe we're both a little afraid, but I say we give it a try.'

He was standing in front of her, totally naked and comfortable with it, such a temptation to her. It was impossible to be embarrassed around him because he made her feel beautiful and comfortable in her own skin, with her own sexuality. He made no excuses for the things he wanted from her body, but more than that, with the way he looked at her, the look in his eyes hungry and possessive, she couldn't help but respond.

He held out his hand. 'We need to shower. Don' be worrying about what we can't change, *cher*. You don' throw something like this away.'

'Like this?' she echoed.

He sighed. 'Why do women always make you say things?' He took her hand and tugged her to her feet. 'If I'm makin' love to you, sugah, it's because I'm *in* love with you. Come on, you're still a bit sticky from all that whipped cream.'

Flame didn't let herself think about the future as the hot water poured over her. Raoul insisted on shampooing her hair, using her broken arm for an excuse, and then he soaped her body, his hands lingering in intimate places. His lovemaking was far gentler without the wild, frantic pace, but no less intense. She wanted to cry with the way he made her feel.

299

'It's going to be all right,' he whispered, holding her close to him.

She knew a sound must have escaped without her realizing it. Life wasn't as easy and laid-back elsewhere as it was in the bayou, but she wasn't going to think about it anymore. She'd stay with Raoul as long as she could.

The clothes his grandmother had chosen for her were very tasteful and in stark contrast to the strange leather and mesh attire. She wiggled into a powder-blue tank top and frowned at Raoul. 'Are you *certain* you had nothing at all to do with that bag of sex toys? I just can't imagine your grandmother in an adult store. I mean, you are a perv, and it had to come from somewhere, but it just doesn't seem like something she'd do.'

Gator drew his jeans over his hips and buttoned them up, as casual dressing in front of her as he was with his nudity. 'Now that you say that, I've never had an inkling she even knew there were such things as adults stores, but don' be selling her short. She wants us together and she's very shrewd.'

Flame ducked her head. 'She wants you to have children, Raoul. She doesn't want you to be with *me*. I'm going to tell her the truth. She deserves to know.'

Raoul paused, hands on the last button of his jeans. 'Don' be getting all hot and bothered, *cher*, but she already knows the truth. I told her a little bit about you when you were in the hospital and I made certain she knew you couldn't have children.'

'Then why . . .' She pointed to the candles and the remnants of mesh and leather. 'Why would she want us to have any kind of a relationship let alone a permanent one?'

'Because you make me happy.' He said it simply, his dark eyes meeting hers.

Flame shook her head. 'You're such a goof, Raoul. I have no idea why I make you happy. You're not a very logical person, are you?'

He grinned at her as he scooped up the fur-lined handcuffs. 'We've still got these, *cher*. You'll make me very happy when you're my little sex slave.' He leered at her and dangled the cuffs.

She started laughing again, shaking her head just like he knew she would. 'You're going to have to help me with the zipper on these jeans.' They were just a little tighter than she normally wore them.

Raoul dropped the cuffs on the bed and crossed the room to stand in front of her, obediently doing the enclosure up for her. She suddenly sucked in her breath. 'Too tight?' He stepped back to look at her. 'They don' look too tight.'

'Sex slave.' She repeated the words aloud. 'There were tie-downs in that car. And a recorder. It was on when James tore my shirt open.' She looked up at him, knowledge blossoming. 'That's what they're doing. They drug the girl, have sex with her, and record it, probably really humiliate her and they keep her locked up while they get her addicted to drugs. They're using her as their own personal sex slave, Raoul. She's got to be somewhere in the bayou.'

'You think they'd keep her alive all this time?'

'Why not? The bayou's a big place. They use her for a while, make a few recordings, keep her hooked on drugs and then . . .' She trailed off.

'Then kill her?'

'Maybe. Maybe not. Remember the mini-discs I found in Saunders's safe?' She rubbed her temples and sank down onto the edge of the bed. 'It's all coming back to me now. I saw those same discs in the car. What if they turn the girls into porn stars or prostitutes

301

or sell them as sex slaves? Keep them, terrorize them, hook them on drugs, degrade and use them, threaten them with the movies, eventually the woman might do whatever they say.'

'That's a big leap, Flame.'

'The car was a trap for a woman. It can't be just date rape, Raoul. The driver's in on it. The camera installation alone would require big bucks. It's well hidden. I heard the hum or I wouldn't have ever noticed it. These stupid painkillers. If I hadn't been so foggy from the operation, I would have remembered every detail.'

'If more girls were missing we'd know about them.'

'Why would you? My guess is, they don't usually grab women close to home. The first girl was probably taken because her voice triggered the need and whoever is the ringleader couldn't resist.'

'And then Joy did the same thing.' Gator shoved his hand through his hair in agitation. 'You think the old man knows?'

'How could he not? His son. His driver.'

'We could be wrong about this, Flame. We have to go slow and make sure. Parsons has a lot of political contacts. If we make a mistake, we could be in trouble. James Parsons could just be a common garden-variety sleazebag. I don't see him as the type of man to be involved in a crime of this magnitude.'

'I agree. But he wants to feel important. And he'd love to put one over on his father, if I'm any judge of people. He's a spoiled kid who wants his own way. The driver is the brains. And he drives Emanuel Parsons everywhere, so he probably knows every private thing in their lives. If he could get James on camera, drugging and raping a woman, what do you think Daddy would do to protect his son?'

Gator shook his head. 'This is a big jump, Flame.'

'You weren't in that car. I know that was Joy's ear-ring.'

'And James Parsons would say that she was his girl-friend and they had lots of sex in the backseat of the car. Or he could just say she rode in the car.'

'Well, maybe we should go to your grandmother's house and play these discs. I have a firm belief that slimebags hang out together. There's a reason Emanuel Parsons is visiting Saunders.'

'He's investigating him for laundering money.'

'That's the official version. What's the real one? Why go to his house late at night? There was no party, no social event going on. I've thought a lot about that night. I was distracted knowing you were there, but Parsons didn't go for dinner. Saunders was in his ivory tower working late. No one else came. It wasn't a let's-get-together-for-drinks atmosphere and Saunders found out *before* Parsons left that the money was miss-ing. I heard the guards talking about the robbery, so whatever business he had with Saunders that night involved whatever was in the safe.'

They looked at each other. 'The discs,' he said.

She nodded. 'It has to be. He couldn't have opened the safe for papers because there weren't any papers, I would have taken them. And why would Saunders be paying Parsons unless he was paying him off, which I'll admit is a possibility.'

Gator shook his head. 'Unlikely. Saunders is a killer, plain and simple. When something, or someone is in his way, the first thing he thinks about is removal.'

Flame went very still, one hand going defensively to her throat. 'Like Burrell,' she whispered. 'I gave Burrell the money to pay off his loan. He called Saunders and was going to meet him to give him the check.'

There was a small silence. Flame pressed her fingers against her eyes. 'Saunders probably didn't show at the meeting and his men were waiting in the swamp to kill Burrell. I thought they were there for me. How could I have missed that? Oh, God, Raoul, I got him killed by giving him the money for his last payment. He would have been better off losing the money. He'd have his life and his houseboat and he'd be sitting on the river smoking his pipe and laughing with his friends. Instead he's Saunders's lesson to others not to cross him.'

'If Saunders had him killed, *cher*, you had nothing to do with that decision.'

'I recognized one of Saunders's men in the swamp before the others came. I'd seen him at the back of Saunders's property. He brings in the women for Saunders.'

Raoul retrieved the discs from the duffel bag as she swept up the photographs and stuffed them back in the envelope.

'Let's go.'

Flame's breath caught in her throat as she observed the stark, grim lines etched in his face. There were times looking at him, like now, that he was intimidating. She followed him out to the airboat, placing her feet carefully on the undulating boards of the pier. She reached out to rub his arm in a soothing gesture.

'Remember when you told me about losing control? You didn't tell me everything, did you?'

'Why would you suddenly think that?'

'Because the pier nearly shook apart just now. What else happened, Raoul?'

He glanced at her as he helped her on board. 'You don't want to know.' As she brushed up against him he felt the knife concealed along her rib cage. Instant heat spread through him. He caught her arm on the pretense

304

of steadying her and inhaled her scent.

'Of course I want to know. It's what's made you who you are.'

'Well I'm not telling you. I can't afford to lose you. Maybe when you're eighty, so if you want to find out, you'll have to stick with me that long.'

'I made a few mistakes.'

'Drop it, Flame. Ask me anything else, but leave that alone.'

She leaned into him, her hand cupping the side of his face, her eyes staring into his. 'You're a good man, Raoul. Whatever happened, you're a good man. I've seen evil and I know the difference.'

He kissed her because he had to. It was a need. An obsession. It was a claim. His mouth descended on hers, his tongue demanding entrance and the moment she opened for him, he swept inside, taking control. He loved the taste of her and he loved the feel of her soft, silky skin. Her mouth was hot and addicting, so that he didn't, *couldn't* stop. His arm swept around her waist and dragged her closer. Her arm bumped his chest and she flinched. Gator pulled back with a sigh of regret.

'I love your mouth.'

She smiled at him. 'I would never have noticed. I take it you're driving.'

'I have two hands.'

The airboat skimmed over the water for several minutes, birds rising into the air, shrieking in annoyance. He deliberately maneuvered the boat close to the shore so she could see the alligators sliding into the water and the turtles sunning themselves. This was his home, had been a good portion of his life. 'When I was a young boy, we lived in the cabin. All of us. *Grand-mere* and my three brothers. We fished mostly and Nonny did quiltin' and the like to get by. We were happy, *cher*. We didn't know we were poor. And at school, if any of the kids teased us about our raggedy clothes, we'd just beat 'em up. It was a good time.'

'How'd you manage to get so much property and that beautiful house your grandmother lives in?'

'My brothers and I worked. I joined the service and I still send most of my pay home. My brothers send a good portion of their paychecks as well. She raised us and loved us when she could have said it was too much for her. We were wild, Flame. She's a good woman.'

'I know that, Raoul. It was a wonderful thing that you and your brothers did.'

He shook his head. 'Naw, it was wonderful what *she* did for us.' He took the boat out into the open water so he could go much faster.

She looked around her at the beauty of the bayou and laughed with sheer joy. 'I love it here.'

Gator expertly swung the boat into a narrow slough, one the boat barely fit through. 'Me too. I'm not much for the city, *cher.*'

Her eyebrow shot up. 'You think you're shocking me with that admission? I had you pegged as a country boy, through and through.' She frowned, wishing he'd slow down as they rounded a corner and nearly hit the stump of an old cypress tree rising out of the shallow water. He zigzagged, scooting around the obstacle and shot back into the open channel.

'You having fun? I like this boat. You already tore up my motorcycle.'

'*You* tore up that bike,' he reminded.

'But it was your fault. You shouldn't have given me the keys.'

He laughed as they made another turn onto marsh-land, the airboat slowing to go over the watery land.

'What are you doing, you crazy man?'

His hand brushed hers until their fingers tangled together. 'We've got a tail, Flame. He's havin' a hell of a time tryin' to keep up with us, but he's following for sure.'

'Who is it? I could jump off here and wait for him,' she offered, all business.

'With your one arm?'

'Don't you worry about me, Raoul. I can take care of myself, one arm or not. You keep that in mind the next time you want to try smacking my bare bottom.'

'Damn, *cher.*' He grinned at her, almost making her heart stop. 'You're giving me a hard-on just thinking about your pretty little ass. Now's no time to be gettin' me all hot and bothered.'

'Will you be serious? This is the perfect place for me to ambush him.' She pulled her hand away from his and curled her fingers around the hilt of her knife.

His grin widened. 'You're so damned sexy, sugah. I love it when you talk dirty.'

'Raoul! Swing back around and let him get close enough so we can see who we're dealing with.'

'I know who it is. I recognize the boat and the way he drives it. That's Vicq Comeaux. He's about as mean as they come, but he isn't part of any of this.' Gator took the airboat back to the open water and poured on the gas so that they left the second boat far behind.

'He tried to kill you.'

He nodded. 'So did you. It seems to be a hazard I have to deal with quite often.'

She frowned at him. 'Maybe you should brush up on your people skills.' She glanced back at the boat. 'Really, Raoul, let me have a go at him. He could creep up behind you someday and you'd never see it coming.'

His arm circled her neck, drawing her close enough that he could find her mouth again, kissing her hard and deep. 'That's what I love most. You're such a blood-thirsty little wench.'

'Do you ever take anything seriously?' she demanded.

He pulled back to look into her eyes. The grin disappeared and something dark and cold and lethal crept into his eyes. 'I take what James Parsons did to you seriously. And I take what Whitney did to you *very* seriously. Don' you worry, *cher*, when it counts, I'm deadly serious.'

Chapter Sixteen

Nonny hugged Flame, dragged her into the house, and clucked over her broken arm. 'Did Gator take care of you, *cher*?' she asked, with a quick smile for her grandson.

Flame blushed, uncertain what Raoul's grandmother was asking. Surely she wasn't inquiring as to whether or not he'd taken care of her sexual needs? It didn't help that Raoul pressed against her back, his breath warm on the nape of her neck, both hands cupping her bottom right through her tight jeans. She smiled at Nonny and slapped at Gator's hands behind her back.

'He was – unbelievable.' She found herself stammering.

'Unbelievable?' Wyatt echoed, his eyebrow shooting up. 'He was unbelievable?'

Flame's color deepened and she cast him a glare. 'Astonishing.' That was worse. What was the matter with her? It wasn't her fault, Raoul was distracting her with his roaming hands. He had a fixation with her butt and she was going to have to do something mean right there in his grandmother's home if he didn't stop. Did one get aroused in front of other people? She never had, but then that was before she met the Cajun king of perverts.

Gator put his lips against her ear. 'Mind-blowing?' He helped her out. 'Or maybe that was you.'

Flame cleared her throat. 'I couldn't believe how attentive he was last night, Ms. Fontenot.'

Wyatt burst out laughing. He nudged his brother. 'You were *attentive*. Just how attentive were you?'

'Remember, *cher*, you were going to call me Nonny.'

'Yes, of course.' Her temperature was rising right along with her color. It was so hot she wanted to fan herself. She kicked backward with her heel, driving it into Gator's calf with a satisfying thud. 'Thank you so much for the clothes, Nonny. They fit beautifully, even the shoes.'

Gator's breath exploded out of his lungs and his hands came down on her shoulders hard. At least she knew where they were and he couldn't distract her.

'My friend told me about a nice boutique for young women and they had everything. It made it easy to shop,' Nonny said. 'I just made a cup of my special tea. Would you like some?'

Gator's fingers began a slow massage along her collarbone and up toward the nape of her neck.

Flame's face was bright red. She could feel the color, hot and bright, glowing like a neon banner for everyone to see. What nice shop? Did it specialize in sex toys? Did she dare drink the tea? It could contain an aphrodisiac. 'I'd love a cup of tea.' Her voice nearly croaked.

'Are you certain you're all right, *cher*?' Nonny asked. 'Maybe you've gotten out of bed too soon. Raoul, maybe you should take her back to bed.'

Wyatt nudged his brother, winking. '*Grand-mere* wants you to take her back to bed.'

'Thas no way for a gentleman to talk, Wyatt,' Nonny reprimanded.

310

Wyatt grinned at her, clearly unrepentant.

Flame let out her breath in a long hiss promising retaliation. It had to be Wyatt who provided her night attire and the sex toys. She'd find a way to get even, but at least it enabled her to relax a little around Nonny.

'The kitchen is a mite crowded. The boys have been eating since they got here, Raoul. I don' think those boys have had a good home-cooked meal in a long while.'

Flame stiffened. This was getting worse and worse. She had a feeling the 'boys' weren't Gator's other two brothers.

'*Grand-mere*,' Gator said, kissing his grandmother on her forehead, 'those boys have never had cookin' like yours. You're the best of the best and everyone in the bayou knows it. I can't blame them for eating so much.'

'They're good, polite boys,' Nonny said. 'I don' mind cookin' for them.'

'That's a good thing, Nonny, because Tucker never gets filled up,' Gator said.

Kadan and Tucker stood up as the women entered the room, Tucker grinning at Nonny a little sheepishly. 'I finished up the gumbo, ma'am. I've never had anything so good.'

Kadan nodded his agreement. 'Thank you, ma'am.'

'No need for that, boys,' Nonny said, looking pleased.

Flame felt the impact of the two GhostWalkers's gazes. Hard. Penetrating. As if they were looking straight through her to see *inside* of her. She became aware of Raoul's hand then, his fingers stroking hers, covering her fist curled around the hilt of her knife. He was very close to her again, his body deliberately crowding hers so it would be difficult to draw the knife and throw in one smooth motion.

311

'They're my family, *cher*,' he reminded, his lips close to her ear.

Flame felt the stirring of his warm breath, heard the reassurance in his voice, but her gaze immediately covered the room, noting all exits, windows, and every single item she could use as a weapon should she need it.

'Flame, this is Kadan Montague and Tucker Addison. Both are my friends and work with me,' Gator said.

'It's nice to finally meet you,' Tucker greeted.

Kadan registered the fact that she hadn't loosened her grip on her knife and Gator's hand held hers stationary. 'I hope you're feeling better. Gator told us you won a fight with an alligator.'

She forced a smile that didn't reach her eyes and made a conscious effort to open her fingers and let go of her lifeline. 'Well, I don't know about that. He lost an eye and I nearly lost an arm, so I'd say it was a draw.'

'Rye called this morning and said the man you identified as Rick Fielding died four years ago running an ops in Columbia,' Kadan announced.

'That's impossible. He took the psychic test the same time I did. I'm not mistaken,' Gator protested. 'It was the same man.'

'You probably aren't mistaken,' Flame said. 'If I had access to a good computer I'd run a list of names of soldiers who took that test, supposedly didn't make it in but were listed as dead or missing a few months later. My guess would be they've become part of another team and someone with a lot of money and a lot of contacts is running them.' Kadan's gaze had such an impact she hunched, but refused to look away from him. She brushed her palm over the hilt of her knife for reassurance.

312

'I'd agree that running that list of names and comparing them to men who are supposed to be dead is a very smart idea,' Kadan agreed. 'I'll pass it on to Rye and see what he comes up with. He also mentioned that a couple of days ago a U.S. registered Falcon 2000 executive jet landed at the airport here and remained until yesterday. The jet is owned by a company called Lansing International Consulting.'

'Where's this company based?' Gator asked.

'They're out of Nevada.'

'I don't understand,' Wyatt said. 'Why would a jet be important?'

'Those men we encountered in the swamp,' Gator said, choosing his words carefully, 'had to have been flown in.'

Kadan cleared his throat and continued, 'One signature appears on the company's annual report, an Earl Thomas Bartlett. Ryland ran a search of all commercial databases and there is no record whatsoever of Mr. Bartlett. No residence, driver's license, Social Security number, or even evidence of a vehicle, yet Mr. Bartlett signs reports and sends jets to various locations all over the world.'

'Who was the jet purchased from?' Flame asked.

Kadan's strange, glittering gaze met hers, sending another chill through her. 'You're smart. That was the first thing Lily asked too. The jet was purchased from another company, one called International Investments. Like Bartlett, the owner of that company doesn't seem to exist in any public records.'

'He's alive,' Flame whispered. She looked at Gator, stricken. 'He is alive. I was right all along.'

Gator held out his hand to her and after a moment, she took it.

'Unfortunately, Flame,' Kadan said, 'I'm beginning

to think you could be right. This aircraft, as well as a few others like it, owned by private international consulting, investing, or marketing companies, appears to be able to fly into restricted areas and that takes clearance. The companies Rye's looked into all have the same low profile, claim to make small profits, turn in their annual reports, and each has one man who doesn't appear to exist at the helm. Ryland's still investigating and it will be a while before we know anything else, but in the meantime it would be a smart move to be on high alert.'

'Any news out of the Congo on Ken Norton?' Gator asked.

'Not yet. No one's heard anything,' Tucker said.

'Come sit down,' Nonny said, pulling out a chair at the table. 'The tea's done and we could all use a cup.'

They complied quickly, although Tucker hung out by the stove, inhaling the aroma of the fish stew slowly cooking. Gator sat between Flame and his grandmother, afraid the next subject would distress her. 'Flame and I have a theory about Joy's disappearance,' he announced. 'And we'd like to run it by you.' While his grandmother poured tea, he filled the others in on the details.

Flame liked the fact that Gator didn't try to hide anything from his grandmother. She had a strong feeling that Nonny could help them given the right information. She was shrewd and very knowledgeable regarding the bayou as she'd lived her entire life there. 'I think Joy's still alive and being held somewhere. Now that they're worried about me blowing it for them, they very well could move her – or even kill her,' she concluded.

There was a small silence. Tucker paced across the length of the kitchen. 'Emanuel Parsons is a huge

314

political nightmare. If we move on him, we've got to have proof beyond a shadow of a doubt.'

'James Parsons is a follower,' Gator said. 'No way is he the brains. I'm guessing someone fed his need to be important. He has a deep sense of entitlement and obviously feels superior to everyone, particularly women, so it wouldn't be all that difficult to entice him into deviant behavior. Once they had him on camera, they'd not only have him, but his father as well.'

'Emanuel has a good reputation in his department,' Kadan pointed out. 'Lily checked him out thoroughly when his name came up and we knew there was a connection to Saunders.'

'All the more reason for Saunders to compromise him,' Gator said. 'We brought a couple of discs Flame found in Saunders's safe.'

'Saunders's safe?' Kadan echoed. 'You just happened to be browsing there?'

'Something like that,' Flame said, sipping at her steaming tea. She glanced at Gator and sure enough he was grinning. 'I'm a little uncomfortable having everyone watch the discs. I suspect we're going to see Joy being raped in Parsons's car. For her sake and that of her family, I just think it would be better if we kept the viewers to a minimum.'

'I agree,' Nonny backed her up. 'I've known Joy since she was a baby and she'd be horrified and humiliated to know anyone saw a movie of her. Her parents would feel the same.'

Wyatt stood up fast, knocking the kitchen chair over. 'You really think that disc shows Joy being raped?'

Gator leaned over and righted the chair, his movements slow and deliberate. 'I think there's a good chance of it, yes. Worse, they probably put a drug in her drink so there's a possibility she cooperated with-

315

out knowing what she was doing.' He might as well get the worst out in the open. He'd long suspected Wyatt was concealing feelings for Joy. It had been Wyatt who insisted Nonny call Gator home.

Nonny wrung her hands together. 'Guess I should do it, but I don' know if I've got the heart for it.'

Gator swept his arm around her. 'Not you, *Grand-mere*. Kadan, Flame, and I will watch it. Kadan can sometimes see things we miss. Flame might be able to remember details from the other day when she was assaulted, and I'm hoping to recognize where they might have taken her.' He looked up at his brother's set features. 'We could be wrong about all this, Wyatt.'

Gator's hand found Flame's and he gripped her fingers hard. They weren't wrong. Flame was too certain of what had been in the car. She recognized evil when she saw it – she'd certainly been exposed to what a madman, who believed himself above the law, could do.

'I feel like I should be helping,' Nonny said.

'Me too,' Wyatt added, coming up behind his grandmother and circling her waist with his arm.

Flame had the feeling it was as much for his comfort as for comforting his grandmother. 'Well, I brought the photographs with me. Some of them are pictures taken from Joy's camera and they're of various places in the bayou. Maybe if the two of you looked at them, you'd be able to figure out where the photos were taken.'

'That would help?' Nonny asked, patting Wyatt's arm.

'Absolutely,' Flame said and passed the manila envelope to her.

Gator led Flame and Kadan into a small room they used for a television room. Nonny was very strict about entertaining versus entertainment. One didn't view tele-

316

vision with company present. She believed in visiting. Gator popped the first disc into the player and turned it on. No one sat down. Kadan leaned against the wall and Flame stood close to Gator near the screen. She had a wild idea if she was right and the disc exposed Joy's humiliation and the crimes against her, then she would jump in front of the television to shield her.

The sound of a door closing opened the homemade movie. Joy Chiasson slid onto the backseat of the car. She looked startled to see James and actually reached for the door handle. It was locked. 'I thought your father was meeting me to take me to see his friend.' Her voice was rich and smooth.

'He couldn't make it,' James said. 'He asked me to get you to the meeting. He thinks there's a good chance you'll come away from this with a recording contract.' The tinkling of ice could be heard. 'Here, drink this. It will help calm you down. I'll bet you're nervous thinking about auditioning.'

'I'm a little nervous,' Joy admitted. The camera panned the backseat allowing them a view of Joy taking the tumbler of iced liquid from James – allowing them to see the smirk on his face and the bulge building in his lap.

'Sleazy little bastard,' Flame muttered. 'I should have killed him when I had the chance. They must have been coming back from being with her all night judging by their clothes and the smell.' She pressed her hand to her stomach in a small protest. 'I remember now James smelled of sex. It was early morning. Why did it take me so freakin' long to remember the details?'

'Give yourself a break, *cher*. You'd lost a lot of blood and then you were operated on,' Gator soothed.

Flame tried to see the details objectively. The camera never panned to the windows, but focused on the backseat. Once Joy's hands and ankles were tied and she lay helplessly sprawled out, James was particularly vicious, slapping and humiliating her, telling her he would never consider marrying such a slut.

When the walls of the room began to undulate and the floor shifted, she wasn't certain if she was doing it or if it was Raoul.

'You both need to step out of the room,' Kadan advised, his voice calm.

Flame didn't wait for a second invitation. She rushed out of the room, through the hall and stepped outside, drawing fresh air deep into her lungs. She heard footsteps, but didn't turn around.

'Did he rape her?' The tone was low, but extraordinarily deadly. For the first time, Wyatt sounded exactly like his brother.

'We have to find her,' Flame replied. 'We have to find her right away.'

There was a long silence. She didn't look at Wyatt, not wanting to intrude when he was so obviously struggling for control. The scene from inside the car had been bad enough. She was terrified to think what might be recorded on the other two discs.

'*Grand-mere* recognized one of the photographs as having been taken in a small clearing on one of the islets. She said the Comeaux family has an old trapper cabin out there somewhere. She knew the old man, and he trapped and fished the bayou. He often stayed there for months on end and his wife would finally send one of the boys after him to bring him home.'

'The Comeaux family?' Flame repeated. 'But if she's being held there, why would they take her out there, let her take pictures, and then bring her back? That doesn't make any sense at all.'

'You think one of the Comeaux brothers would touch Joy? They're our people. They'd never lay a finger on that girl.'

'What about Vicq? I've heard he's as mean as a snake and brutal with women.'

'Vicq? He's mean all right, but he . . .' Wyatt trailed off.

Flame did turn then, catching the sudden rage on his face. 'Don't go running off on your own before we know what we're doing. If we tip them off, they'll kill her and we'll never find her body. We have to be very certain and go at this the right way. Come on.' She caught his arm. 'Let's go back inside and tell the others what your grandmother said.'

Wyatt went with her reluctantly, but at least she got him in the house. They interrupted a heated argument between Ian and Gator. Ian wanted to bring in the police and Gator absolutely refused, afraid Parsons would be tipped off.

'We're only going to have one chance at a rescue, only *one*,' Gator emphasized. 'If we hit the wrong place, she's dead. I say we go in quiet, get her out, and just take care of this. Let them all figure out from the evidence the why of it. They'll say vigilantes in the bayou did it.'

'You can't leave those discs of Joy behind,' Wyatt decreed.

'No one's going to see those discs, Wyatt,' Gator assured.

'Did Nonny tell you she recognized a clearing where the Comeaux family owns a trapper cabin way out in the bayou?' Flame asked. 'I think it's a big coincidence that Vicq tried to kill you the other night at the Hurican Club and then he followed us today. He dated Joy once and she broke up with him.'

319

'He got into a really heated argument with James Parsons at the club,' Ian added. 'And strangely enough, it was the driver who stepped in and calmed everything down. The minute he spoke to Comeaux, the man backed off.'

'Vicq Comeaux doesn't back off anyone,' Gator said, 'unless there's a reason.'

Kadan came in, poured himself a cup of the rich, thick coffee Nonny kept hot, and turned around to regard them all. 'That was some of the sickest stuff I've ever seen. They're hooking her on drugs, but they evidently like filming her frightened and fighting, so whatever they gave her in the car to calm her, they aren't doing anymore. I think they're stringing her out so she'll cooperate. They're using terror tactics, beating her, most of the time in some sexual display. I saw two men, but there was at least one more in the shadows, who stayed out of the view of the camera. She stared at him a lot, very frightened.'

'You recognize the men from any of the photos or files you've looked at?' Gator asked, avoiding looking at his brother.

'One was the Parsons kid. He's a real piece of work. The other is the driver.'

'Carl Raines,' Flame supplied.

Kadan nodded. 'He's the one who I think must have arranged the grab. He spends a lot of time with her. Most of the video clips are of him.'

'No evidence of the old man participating? You get the idea it was him in the background?'

Kadan shook his head. 'Couldn't say one way or the other, but whoever it is, she's very afraid of him.'

'If she's at the Comeaux cabin, why would she have pictures of the area?'

'Maybe they were going to grab her then and something went wrong,' Tucker offered.

'Or that sleazy kid got high just bringing her close to the cabin, knowing what was coming,' Kadan said. 'He's really screwed up and he'd savor the idea of showing her around, all the while knowing what he was going to do to her.'

Flame felt sick. Joy was caged up with monsters torturing her. She had no hope left by this time and she would be sick and confused. 'If we pull Joy out of there, she can tell us who else is involved. She won't be as afraid of me. I can check out the Comeaux cabin and if she's there, go in quietly while you all . . .' She hesitated, glancing at Nonny. 'Secure the place.'

'She'll have to go to the hospital,' Kadan advised.

'We'll notify the doctors and her family when we have her,' Gator said. 'I don't want to wait until dark.'

'If Vicq Comeaux is guarding her out there, he'll kill her and dump the body if he hears you coming,' Wyatt said.

'He won't hear us,' Gator assured. 'We know what we're doing.'

'I'm coming with you.' It was a declaration and Wyatt looked every bit as stubborn as Gator.

Gator shook his head. 'You can wait nearby, Wyatt, but you'd be a liability we can't afford. This is what we do. One mistake and it's all gone to hell.'

'How could something like this be goin' on in our backyard, Raoul, and we not know it?' Nonny asked. 'Do you think they took that other poor woman?'

'I don't doubt it for a minute,' Gator said.

'Don't worry, ma'am,' Tucker said. 'We'll do our best to get a lead on finding her if she's still alive.'

Gator's grandmother appeared very agitated, wringing her hands together, her back ramrod straight and her features very set. Flame rubbed her hand over

Nonny's arm. 'We'll bring her back to safety, Nonny,' she reassured gently. 'I've seen your grandson in action. He's very good – and so am I. We're not leaving her there and we're not messing this up.'

'Should I call her family?'

Nonny's thin body was trembling. Flame put her arm around the woman and led her out of the kitchen to the more comfortable couch in the sitting room, mouthing the word *tea* over her shoulder to Gator. 'No, I don't think that would be a very good idea. No one can know what we suspect until she's safe.' She helped her to sit down and Gator put a cup of tea in front of her. 'We'll do this. I promise you, we'll do this.' Flame pushed the tea into her hands. 'Will you be okay until we get back?'

'I'm fine, *cher*. Just a little shaken up to think this could happen here.' She patted Flame's arm. 'Don' worry about me. You just make sure Joy is safe.'

Flame stood up, feeling tears burning behind her eyes and clogging her throat. Joy would never be the same again. She would be forever isolated, eventually smiling and talking and walking around with her friends and family, but deep inside, deep where it counted, she would be forever cold and scared and filled with rage.

She looked at Raoul because she couldn't stop herself. She knew he would see the shadows and the demons and she would feel even more vulnerable for turning to him for comfort, but she couldn't help it. Why did it always seem as if evil prevailed? Life wasn't anything like the fairy tales and just once, she'd like a damned happy ending.

Gator's heart nearly stopped when he saw Flame's expression. He pressed his hand to his chest to make certain it was still beating. She could knock his legs right out from under him when she looked so sad, so openly fragile. He wanted to wrap her up in his arms and hold her close to him, where nothing could ever hurt her. Flame was a woman who kept one hand on her knife and would scoff at his notion that he had to protect her, but that didn't stop his need to do so.

He flung his arm casually around her neck, drawing her to him, pretending not to see the tears so close, pretending her body didn't tremble against his. She'd *kill* him if she cried in front of the others, so he was walking a fine line, using his body to shelter her while taking care that he didn't trigger a flood of tears. 'Let's go to work,' he said gruffly. 'I know where the Comeaux trapper cabin is located.'

Flame walked close to him, allowing the brush of his hard body against her to give her control and focus. She'd never relied on anyone but herself and it was a strange feeling to allow herself to be comforted by a man. A GhostWalker. She tasted the word as she slid into the four-wheel drive Jeep. Were they all ghosts, just as she was? She glanced around her at the other men. They all looked hard. Battle-scarred. And they all had shadows in their eyes. It didn't matter that Tucker Addison ate Nonny's food with gusto and was polite and gentle when he spoke to the older woman. Flame could see those same shadows, the light never quite reaching his eyes. Sharing something in common with them made her feel a little closer to them all.

The men murmured in low tones, developing a plan for making their way to the Comeaux trapper cabin. They would get as close as possible using the Jeep, take a pirogue the second part of the way and then go through the water. Wyatt would stand by with the airboat and when they signaled to him, he'd bring it in to remove Joy quickly.

None of the men protested when Gator said Flame would enter the cabin alone to check if Joy was there. She only half listened to them, knowing they were a team. She was odd man out. They had trained together and worked like a machine, each knowing what the other would do. Kadan was a shielder and he would make certain no one would hear or see them coming. Gator and Flame could silence any noise, adding extra protection.

The pirogue was flat-bottomed and made of cypress. Gator pushed the canoe through a sea of purple water hyacinths. Great egrets fed, walking through the water on stiltlike legs. A few fluttered their wings as the pirogue moved through them, but they didn't appear too disturbed. The boat passed groves of cypress draped in Spanish moss, tupelo gums and dramatic maples all turning shades of red or russet. It seemed a lost world with the tangle of brilliantly colored flowers on the swamp floor and the prairie grasses swaying gently with the slow flow of water. Flame had never been this far into the bayou and was astonished at the beauty of it all. It seemed obscene to her that somewhere a woman was held captive, drugged and tortured in the midst of so much splendor.

The skies darkened as another storm front moved over them. Gray clouds swept the blue from overhead and a fine drizzle began, turning the horizon into a silvery haze. Gator pushed the boat through the thick fields of *fourchettes*, using sheer strength to get through the marigold marsh. Flame silenced the alarms of the birds as the pirogue moved inland to shore.

The men all stepped out of the boat and held the sides, politely waiting for her. Flame took a slow, careful look around, trying to see if there were any telltale bubbles or even the rigid eyeplates of an alligator marring the surface of the water. In the thick field of *fourchettes,* it was virtually impossible to tell. She hesitated only a second before stepping out of the boat into the knee-high water. Her heart pounded and she had to work at controlling her breathing. Gator glanced at her, obviously able to hear and, to her shame, Kadan did as well.

Automatic rifles were slung over the men's shoulders and Kadan held out a small revolver. 'Would you like a gun? We should have asked. I'm armed to the teeth.'

Flame shook her head. 'I'm better with a knife.'

Kadan nodded and gestured her to follow Gator, who led the way. The others fell in line, walking single file in the water, sometimes up to their waists as they wound around the shore of the islet. The marsh was thick with flowers, nettles, and stumps and it was slow going as they made the approach toward the Comeaux hunting camp.

Gator held up his hand and the line stopped. He gestured toward land and Ian immediately broke off from the group and waded through the thicker foliage to solid ground. Within minutes, Tucker and Kadan had taken to shore so they could approach the cabin from every direction, spreading out like a giant net to encompass the large area around the hunting camp.

Gator and Flame continued creeping through the water until she could see the rickety planks of wood that served as a deck and walkway to the cabin. Two cypress trees rose up through the deck and several cans of gasoline sat in front of one of them, just a few feet from a generator. A single plank led past the trees to the cabin. A crab pot lay tilted on its side near the trees and an airboat was tied to a pole between the deck and the cabin.

'Vicq Comeaux,' Raoul said, keeping his voice only

to her. 'It started to rain so he decided to forget fishing.'

'He's not alone with her,' Flame said, her stomach beginning to knot up. She could hear inside the cabin now. The low cries of a female voice, the slap of something against flesh. The pleading and sobbing that followed. She quickened her pace. 'I can hear other voices.'

'Don' go getting yourself killed, *cher*. We want them all together. It will be easier that way.' He caught her arm. 'Someone's coming out.'

The door to the cabin opened and Vicq Comeaux shoved James Parsons out. James teetered and nearly fell. 'Get the hell out of here before you end up gator bait,' Vicq yelled.

'You wouldn't even have her if it wasn't for me,' James snapped.

Gator signaled Flame forward, out of the water and she went in low, allowing the water, even the shallows, to creep up to her neck so she slithered out on her belly. She began to crab crawl up the slope toward the side of the cabin using a slow, steady movement designed not to draw the eye or move the foliage around her too much.

She heard the call of a bird. A second one answered. A bullfrog croaked. The men were in place. It was up to her to get inside and protect Joy.

'You sniveling piece of city boy shit. You wouldn't have the balls to grab a woman. Carl took her, just like he took the last one. The only reason you were let in on it was to get your pappy offa Saunders's back. That's the only thing you're good for and we already got the tapes, so as far as I'm concerned if you turn up dead, nobody's gonna care one way or the other.' Vicq took a step toward him and James backpedaled, misstepped and tumbled into the shallow water.

Gator immediately sank beneath the surface of the water and headed toward James. Vicq burst out laughing, slapping his knee as he watched James trying to regain his footing in the soft muck on the bottom.

Flame crept up to the window. The cracked glass was coated with years of grime, making it nearly impossible to see into the room. An old piece of burlap hung inside, at one time intended perhaps to block the light, but it was ragged with age and torn almost in half. Moving around to the back of the cabin she discovered a much smaller window. One flimsy strip of board slashed across the open space at the back. There was no glass. It wasn't going to be easy with a broken arm, but she would endure anything to make it into that cabin and protect Joy.

Looking inside, Flame could see a bed directly under the window. Joy was standing, both hands tied above her head to a hook hanging from the ceiling. Her body was covered in bruises and welts.

'Don't look up, Joy.' Flame sent her voice directly to the woman. 'I'm a friend of Nonny Fontenot. She sent me here to get you out.' She wiggled the board free, and tossed it behind her before jumping up to catch the windowsill with her good arm.

Joy frantically nodded her head toward the door several times, obviously fearful that Vicq and James would return.

Flame was grateful for her physical enhancements, which enabled her to pull herself up so she could wiggle through the small opening. She had to go in headfirst, but she landed on the bed and somersaulted onto the floor in a crouch, knife already drawn. A jolt of pain ran through her arm and crashed through her body. Breathing deep to ride it out, she took a quick sweep of the cabin, noting there was only the one door.

A butcher knife lay on the counter alongside several stacks of dirty dishes. Flame stepped over a long thick staff and reached up to cut through the leather ties binding Joy's hands to the hook.

Joy crumpled to the floor, her legs unable to support her. Flame reached down to her, grasping her shoulders when the cabin shook slightly, and she knew immediately Raoul was warning her.

Vicq Comeaux stepped inside and quietly closed the door, a huge grin spreading over his face. 'Nothing I like better than to see two women on their knees in front of me. Go ahead and touch the bitch, everyone else does.'

Flame's eyes widened. She started to stutter an apology, standing, backpedaling – drawing him to her. Vicq stalked her across the small room, toeing Joy out of his way to get to Flame. Flame went for the helpless look, cradling her broken arm, making herself look even smaller until Vicq reached out with one meaty hand, grabbed her breast, and yanked hard to bring her to him. She went, using his tremendous strength along with her own, burying the largest knife she owned as deep into his gut as she could get it and jumped back out of his reach.

Vicq roared with pain, both hands going to the hilt as he stared at her. 'What have you done?'

'That one was for Joy. This one's for putting your filthy hands on me you son of a bitch.' Flame pulled the second, smaller throwing knife from inside the cast on her arm, watching his eyes widen with the certain knowledge that she wasn't small and helpless. That she wasn't tied up. That he couldn't stop the inevitable. Even as he staggered toward her, she threw the knife with deadly accuracy, burying it in his throat.

Vicq went down hard, shaking the cabin as Joy tried to struggle to her feet. She began to sob quietly. 'There are more of them. How are we going to get out of here?'

Chapter Seventeen

Gator used the debris along the bottom to pull his body through the shallow water yet keep him submerged at the same time. He heard Vicq and James shouting at each other. Water churned around him as James lost his footing and fell, his butt landing inches from Gator's hand. Gator swept his knife free of his belt as the man scrambled to his feet, rushing out of the shallows up the slope toward the cabin.

Gator found the roots of the cypress trees growing through the deck and came up for air, keeping his gaze focused on the two men. James struggled up the slope, his hands curled into tight fists, his face flaming red, but he stopped just out of Vicq's reach.

'Go play with yourself,' Vicq said. 'If you come back inside I'm going to play with you. We'll see how you like being my bitch.' He turned his back on Parsons, clearly unafraid of him.

Gator immediately bounced a sound wave through the cabin walls to warn Flame the man was returning. There was no call for help from inside so he kept his focus on James. The man was muttering to himself angrily as he stomped across the plank to the deck. Gator heard him dragging something. Before he could

330

move into place to grab the man, he heard the sound of a boat coming toward them fast. He sank back into the water to assess the new threat.

'What the hell are you doing?' The shout came from the motorboat as Carl Raines swept into view.

James ignored the question, lodging a heavy piece of timber against the cabin door and picking up one of the cans of gasoline. He doused the walls of the cabin as quickly as possible, soaking the dry timber with gas.

'Are you crazy?' Carl tied up the boat and leapt into the shallow water to race up the slope.

James didn't even turn around, picking up the second can and methodically covering the side wall, walking around the building until he was out of sight.

Carl stumbled, sliding in the mud a bit, turning slightly in his effort to recover and found himself staring eye-to-eye with the man lying half in and half out of the water. Gator's face was streaked with mud and he blended into the shadows of the deck and roots, but Carl was nearly on top of him. As Raines pulled his gun, Gator shot him twice. The first bullet went between the eyes; the second went through his crotch. All around the hunting cabin, birds rose into the air, flapping wings and shrieking loudly.

Gator came up out of the water, his rifle to his shoulder as he emerged. James couldn't have failed to hear the shots or the alarm of the birds and neither would Vicq, if he were still alive. Gator kept his mind firmly from dwelling on that possibility. His job was to clear the outside of any threat. Flame would do her job, which was to protect Joy. He ran up the slope to circle the cabin.

The smell of the gasoline combined with the *whoosh* of the fire as it ignited was overpowering. *Anyone have a bead on that bastard? I have to get Flame and Joy out of the cabin.* He sent the call immediately even as he raced around the side of the building to get to the front.

You're covered. The sound of a rifle shot reverberated through the swamp and set the birds off a second time. Gator removed the large plank propped against the door just as the fire raced over the cabin, quickly engulfing it, the intense heat driving him back. He tossed the plank and then his rifle and ammunition aside. His clothing and hair were already soaked from lying in the water so he didn't waste time, kicking hard at the front door with his boot, so that it sagged on the rusty hinges. A second kick took it all the way out, but flames licked along the floor from the wood splintering. Black smoke rolled into the cabin in waves.

Gator leapt through the ring of fire to Flame's side. She'd already rolled Joy in a wet sheet and awkwardly hefted the woman onto her back in a fireman's carry – difficult to do with one arm, even enhanced. The other woman appeared to be too weak, or too drugged, to stand on her own. She sobbed uncontrollably but clung tightly to Flame, even when Gator tried to remove her.

'Joy! You know me. Let me take you so we can get out of here.' His eyes met Flame's as he hoisted Joy to his own shoulders. She looked frightened, but calm. Both looked at the doorway. The flames were hot and greedy, pieces of wood falling off. 'You ready?'

She nodded.

'You stay right behind me.' Without hesitation, Gator rushed the ring of fire, leaping over the flames on the floor and through to the outside. The wind generated by his body made the flames flare as he leapt over them.

Flame followed him through. She jumped, drawing her knees up to her chest, uncaring of the landing so

332

much as not getting burned. She landed in a crouch and somersaulted down the slope nearly into the water, landing facedown in the mud. She lay there, listening to the crackle of the fire, the lapping of the water, and her own heartbeat. Mostly, she felt the pain crashing through her broken arm, sending shock waves through her body.

Gator's hands were gentle as he helped her up. He wiped mud from her face. 'You're always such a mess.'

'I don't like you very much.' She pushed his hand away and sat on the slope waiting for her strength to return.

'You're crazy about me.'

She scrubbed her hand over her face. 'I'm just crazy.'

'I know, but that's what I find so attractive.' He leaned in close and brushed his mouth gently against hers. 'Joy's in bad shape. Wyatt's bringing the airboat, but she's in shock. She won't talk or look at me and she can't stop shaking. I know you're hurt.' He touched her arm gently and brushed his fingers against hers.

'It's not that bad. I'll stay with her while you all do whatever it is you do to secure the place.' She allowed Raoul to help her up, mostly because she was suddenly so exhausted she wanted to crawl into a bed and sleep for hours. She even leaned on him as he walked her to a small clearing away from the burning cabin. She recognized it from the photographs that Joy had taken.

She sat down beside the woman and put a steadying hand on her shoulder, mouthing to Gator to go away. 'They can't hurt you anymore, Joy,' she said. 'Everyone's been looking for you. No one gave up hope.'

There was a small silence while the wind fanned the

flames. Overhead the gray clouds began to drizzle rain on them again. 'I did,' Joy said. 'I gave up hope.'

'Wyatt Fontenot sent for his brother to come find you. Raoul took a personal leave from the military and has spent weeks tracking you down.'

'What am I going to do?' Joy shuddered visibly. 'How can I ever rebuild my life? I'll never be the same.'

'No, but you'll be stronger. You're a survivor. You think you gave up, but you were right there, trying to fight Vicq Comeaux right along with me.' Deliberately she used his name. 'I saw you try to grab his ankle when he came at me. That's a fighter, Joy. They had to keep you drugged because they couldn't break you. Whatever you did in that room with those men, you did to survive. That's all. You came out of it alive.'

'I heard Carl say to be more careful with me than they were with Francine. I think she's dead. She disappeared a couple of years ago. There were four of them.' Joy began to sob again, covering her face. 'The worst one wasn't here. He'll find me and he'll kill me. He'll beat me to death.' The words tumbled out of her, an expression of fear and loathing.

'We know all about Saunders,' Flame assured her. 'He had a very good friend of mine killed. I'll be very surprised if he makes it to trial.'

'Trial? Oh God. Everyone will know. They'll show the movies they made. My family will be humiliated.'

'Joy,' Flame stroked back her hair. 'Look at this place. It's burning to the ground. Carl, James, and Vicq are dead. There won't be anything left to show anyone. Tell me about Saunders. Are you sure he was the boss?'

Joy nodded several times. 'Everyone seemed a little afraid of him. He and Carl are related somehow. They hired Vicq to guard me and . . .' She sobbed again, this time more hysterically. It took her a few minutes to regain control. 'Soften me up. Train me. That's what Saunders said. He would strangle me until I couldn't breathe while he raped me. I think that's how Francine died. Carl and Saunders reminded him several times not to kill me.'

Flame rubbed her back, wanting to keep physical contact. She noticed Joy seemed to need the reassurance of her touch. 'Nonny, Raoul and Wyatt's grandmother, was the one who pointed us to this area. You took pictures of this clearing.'

'James brought me here on a picnic. Now I know he must have planned to kidnap me then and turn me over to Vicq.'

'Why didn't he?'

'Some trappers came by I knew. They're friends with my brothers and they stopped to talk to me.'

'Of course,' Flame said. 'James would be afraid they could identify him as the last man seen with you way out here and alone. He wouldn't want that. Those pictures were a big help, Joy.'

Joy turned and looked at her for the first time. 'What am I going to do?'

'Live. One day at a time. Heal. One day at a time. You have a wonderful family and amazing friends. You're smart enough to know not all men are like Vicq and the others. It won't be easy and you'll need help, but you'll find a way to live a happy life. I know you will.'

Joy shuddered. 'I just want to see my mother's face again. I prayed I'd see her face again.'

'You will. Wyatt's here now. We've got to get you down to the airboat so we can take you to the hospital. Someone has to carry you. Raoul or Wyatt?'

'Wyatt Fontenot is here?' Her voice rose to a small wail. She bit it off, catching her lower lip between her

335

teeth. 'He knows what went on here? How can I face him? I don't want him to see me like this.'

'Wyatt hasn't stopped looking for you, not for one moment. Yes, he does know what happened here, but it only makes him want to keep you safe, the same as Raoul. The Fontenot brothers are very protective.' Flame glanced up to see Wyatt striding toward them, his face set and hard. 'I don't think you're going to get much of a choice unless you say so now. Here comes Wyatt.'

Joy dragged the wet sheet around her, seemingly unaware that it was semitransparent. As he approached, Wyatt peeled off his shirt. 'Joy. *Remerciez Dieu que vous etes vivantes. Come here, cher.*'

His voice was so tender, a knot rose in Flame's throat. She watched him bend down and hold the shirt out. 'I have my eyes closed, honey. Get rid of that wet sheet and put on my shirt. I brought an old pair of sweats as well.'

'I didn't even think of that, Wyatt,' Flame said. 'How thoughtful of you.' She took the soft sweatpants from Wyatt's hand since Joy seemed frozen in place.

Joy looked at Flame helplessly, afraid to move or speak. Flame pulled the wet sheet away from her bruised and battered body and replaced it with the warmth of Wyatt's shirt. 'Can you stand long enough to let me help you into these?'

'Just a moment,' Wyatt said. 'I'm going to lift you up, Joy. I'm just going to support you so you can step into the sweats.'

Joy was shaking so uncontrollably again Flame was afraid she'd shake apart, but Joy allowed Wyatt to hold her while she pulled up the sweatpants. He gathered her into his arms, cradling her to his chest. 'Your parents are going to meet us at the hospital. We're doing this all very quietly, Joy. We don' want to tip anyone off.'

Flame followed them, a little shocked at how heavy her legs felt. Raoul fell into step beside her, wrapping his arm around her waist. She leaned against his strength, grateful he was there. 'Remind me to tell Nonny she raised a couple of incredible men. He's so gentle with her.' She turned to look at him. 'The way you are with me.'

Gator brushed a kiss across her mud-smeared brow. 'I knew you were crazy about me. You look tired.'

She flashed a smile. 'Now you sound concerned. I'm just tired. I don't think wading through the water agrees with me. All I think about is when the next alligator is going to take a bite out of me.'

'You don' have to worry about that kind of gator takin' a bite, *cher*. This one is the hungry one.'

She rolled her eyes, her smile widening. 'Does your grandmother know you're such a goof?'

'At least you smiled for me.' Raoul tried to ignore the knots gathering in his belly and the alarm bells shrieking at him. She didn't just look tired, she looked beat. And pale. There were dark circles under her eyes. And more bruises. Fear came close to choking him, but he shoved it down where she couldn't see, opting for casual.

He glanced up at the sky. 'The sun is beginning to set and the storm's startin' to kick up a fuss. We've got a good doctor waitin' for Joy, one who knows how to keep his mouth shut. Kadan, Ian, and Tucker are calling Lily and asking for help on this one. We didn't notify the police and now we've got three civilians dead. It's going to be a nightmare and we'll need her political clout and military clearance to save the day.'

She raised her eyebrow. 'You never intended to arrest any of them.'

He shrugged his broad shoulders. 'I don' have the authority to arrest anybody. I rescued a friend. It's not my fault they forced us to defend ourselves.'

She took his hand to board the airboat, ignoring the pain throbbing not only in her arm, but her head. 'You're such a bad boy, Raoul Fontenot. It's all those curls. There's an old saying about curls and being bad.'

He groaned, bringing her hand to his mouth before settling into the driver's seat. '*Grand-mere* used to quote that to me. I don't have curls. I have waves. Wavy hair is much manlier.'

'I'll have to agree with that,' Wyatt said. He sat on the bench seat, cradling Joy to him. She had her face buried against his chest.

Flame put a thin blanket over Joy to help protect her from the rain. Her legs felt unsteady as she made her way back to Raoul's side. She leaned against the seat. 'This was a good thing. For once, the monsters didn't win.'

'No they didn't.' The boat flew over the water as fast as he could safely navigate. Darkness was falling and he needed to get Flame home and in bed. And he needed to think. To plan. Something had to be done soon or he was going to lose her. He didn't intend for that to happen. One way or the other, she was going in for treatment. Just the thought of her reaction made him swallow hard. Flame was a powder keg when either of the Whitneys was involved. And he'd need Lily Whitney to make certain Flame lived.

He wanted to talk with the other GhostWalkers and get their take on Lily. He couldn't quite make himself believe she was working with her adopted father, but if Peter Whitney was alive, he couldn't deliver Flame into her hands – and God help him, he was considering doing just that.

'You look upset, Raoul,' Flame said, rubbing his jaw with her palm. 'We've got Joy back. They probably would have gotten off if the case had gone to trial. People like that always do. They kill off the witnesses and buy off the jury or the prosecutor and tamper with the evidence. This is much better.'

'I had no idea you were such a pessimist.'

'I'm a realist.'

'Did Vicq put his hands on you?' His tone was low. Ugly. His jaw set.

She leaned closer and kissed the corner of his mouth. 'You're upset because I went into the cabin, aren't you? That silly macho part of you thinks you should have gone with me.'

'I'm upset over a lot of things, *cher.*'

'I can take care of myself in a fight, Raoul.'

He glanced at her, then back at the water. The rain was coming down harder, making it more difficult to see any dangers on the water's surface. He was forced to slow the airboat. All he could think about was that Flame had been in danger and he had allowed her to walk into it. He didn't care if it was macho of him to think that way or not. And the thought of another man touching her, hurting her, torturing her in the way Joy had been tortured, frankly made him ill. 'Damn it, Flame, just answer me. Did he touch you?'

Her breast still hurt and she knew she'd have bruises. She closed her eyes briefly. Why couldn't she just lie to him? 'Yes. And then I killed him.'

He slammed his fist against the box beside the seat, roaring out a string of Cajun curses. 'Where?'

Flame put her hand on his arm but remained silent.

'*Maudit!* Just answer me.'

She leaned against him, stroked his wavy hair, allowed her fingers to run down the side of his face in a soothing caress. 'My breast. It hurt like hell.'

He turned his head to catch the sheen of tears in her eyes. *'Fils de putain.'*

Her heart squeezed tight and the lump forming in her throat threatened to choke her. 'It got us Joy back so it was a very small price to pay.'

He circled her waist and dragged her against him. 'I feel so much pride in you, I don' have words to tell you.'

She laughed, relief sweeping through her. 'The swearing was good. That said it all. I knew you were praising me.'

Four hours later Gator was cussing up a blue streak again. He stood staring at Flame, his jaw dropping, mouth hanging open, unable to believe his eyes. 'Where the hell do you think you're going dressed like that?' he demanded. His breath squeezed out of his lungs in a burning rush. She wore fishnet stockings and long leather boots with thick high heels. The tops of her garters showed beneath the micro-miniskirt and her top might as well have been nonexistent. She'd slathered on makeup, something she didn't wear, and her hair was slicked back with some kind of shiny gel. 'You look ...' He trailed off, his heart pounding.

'Hopefully very slutty.' She examined her transparent top. Beneath it she wore a black push-up bra barely covering her nipples. 'What do you think?' She stuck out her hip and put her hand on it. 'Do you notice me, or the broken arm?'

'I didn't even see the arm. What the hell are you doing?' he repeated.

'I'm taking down Saunders. I found out where his men pick up women and I'm certain he's going to need solace tonight. He relaxes by beating and torturing his playmate of the night. I've seen them come out of his gatehouse almost nightly.'

'You think he was the one Joy was so afraid of.'

'I know he was. Joy told me. He'd sit in the corner and watch, sometimes direct the others to do things to her. He likes to see a woman in pain. I think my broken arm is going to be an asset in getting chosen for the dubious honor of having that man torture me.' She smiled brightly at him.

Gator sucked in his breath sharply. She was going to do this. He could tell by the determination on her face. He was going to have to endure the terror of losing her all over again. 'I wouldn't mind doing a little torturing myself, Flame. What are you thinking, going off by yourself for something that dangerous? Do you *want* to get killed?' He stepped closer aggressively, his fingers curling around her forearms like a vise. He gave her a little shake. 'Is that what this is all about? You have a death wish?'

'Actually no. I'm still here, aren't I? I was waiting for you.'

They stood eye to eye. Toe to toe. Gator slowly allowed his fingers to relax. 'Oh. Good. Well then. At least you're finally showin' good sense. And just where did this outfit come from? You haven't been out of my sight long enough to go on a shopping spree.'

She smirked. 'Your grandmother.'

Gator raked a hand through his hair, wanting to tug it out by the roots. 'Women were designed to drive good men crazy. Why the hell would my grandmother have a hooker outfit? All this time I've held out hope it was my brother who bought the toys for us. How the hell am I ever going to look her in the eye?'

Flame burst out laughing. 'Men have such double standards. It's perfectly okay for you to have good

341

healthy lust and want wild, uninhibited sex and you like a woman to look a little slutty for you once in a while, but women better not feel the same way.'

'I certainly don' want to picture my grandmother looking slutty.' He rubbed his hand over his face, covering his eyes as if that would drown out the picture.

She wanted to torture him a little more, but he looked so uncomfortable she took pity on him. 'These aren't your grandmother's clothes, you goof. I told her what I needed. There wasn't time to go shopping, so she called all her friends. They pooled resources and this is the result.'

Gator began to sweat. 'This is getting worse and worse. Are you telling me all of my grandmother's *friends* have clothes like that?' He covered his face with both hands, shaking his head. 'Don' say another word. I don' want to know anything. It's better to be ignorant.'

Flame found herself laughing at his horrified expression. She put her arms around him and leaned her body against his. It was impossible for her to resist Raoul when he turned into a confused male. 'It will be all right. You'll get over it.'

'I don' think so *cher*. This whole conversation just isn't right.'

'We don't have much time so you can seek sympathy while you're driving me to the corner where Saunders sends his men to pick up a woman. I intend to be that woman.'

'I'm asking the others to back us up,' he warned her. 'I don' like this at all, Flame. Saunders is a straight-up killer. He likes to hurt women and he's bound to be really confused about now. He doesn't have a clue what happened and doesn't know whether there's proof against him or not. He'll be looking to kill somebody.'

342

'Men like Saunders get away, Raoul. You know that.'

'He isn't Whitney,' he reminded gently. 'Even if you bring him down, *cher,* Whitney is still going to be shadowing you. Dead or alive, he'll always be there. You don' have to do this.'

She raised her chin. 'Yes I do. I won't be able to live with myself if he walks away unscathed after what he did to both Burrell and Joy. Maybe I do equate him with Whitney, but it doesn't make him less guilty.'

'He's surrounded by civilians and he has a small army,' he reminded.

'You don't have to come with me.'

His dark eyes glittered at her and Flame felt a shiver run down her spine. She turned away from him, refusing to be intimidated, refusing to back down. He caught her chin in his hand. 'I think we need to get something straight, *cher*. I love you. Straight out and I'm not afraid to say it. But you have this idea of me that isn't quite on the mark. I'm not always nice, Flame. I don' get pushed around, not even by the woman I love.'

She wasn't going to react to his declaration. It was a hell of a time for him to make it and she just plain wasn't going there, although she couldn't stop the way her heart and her treacherous body responded. She loved him goofy and she loved him when he went all alpha on her. God, she was pathetic. 'I wasn't trying to push you around, Raoul. This is important to me. I *have* to do this.'

She ducked her head, looked away from him so he couldn't read the real reason in her eyes. She was dying, and she wanted to leave something behind. She couldn't leave children, and if Raoul was telling the truth and he loved her, he was the only one. And he'd be the only person to remember her. She was going to rid the world of one more monster before she allowed the disease eating her up to take her.

'Let's go then,' Gator said. 'I'll send the others out to his house to back us up.'

They said little as he drove through the streets to find the Bourbon Street address she gave him. Most of the time he spoke on his cell, issuing instructions to the other GhostWalkers. The street corner was deserted with the storm battering the streets, filling them with water so fast the pumps couldn't keep up.

Flame leaned across the seat to give Raoul a kiss, her hand on the door. The slight brush of her mouth against his sent a small jolt of electricity through him. Angry or not, he couldn't resist her. He framed her face with his hands and held her still, kissing her the way he wanted, letting her taste his anger, the bite of his teeth, the dance of his tongue. He was wearing his damn heart on his sleeve and she gave him so little back. He was going to have to watch her walk away, stand on a cor- ner to entice a killer to pick her up.

'The car's shaking,' she said.

'Fuck the car.' He kissed her more. Long, drugging kisses. Hot, sizzling kisses. Dark, angry kisses. Every kind of kiss he could think of to hold her to him.

'I love you,' Flame whispered, her voice so low that even with his acute hearing, he barely heard. 'I've never loved anyone, Raoul and I'm not very good at it.' It was a confession, the best she could give him and she could only hope he understood what she was trying to tell him.

He rested his brow against hers. 'You're good enough at it,' he said. 'Don' get yourself shot or I'll be really pissed at you. I didn't throw the paddle away, you know.'

She laughed the way he knew she would, the sparkle

returning to her eyes. 'I threw it away. And I broke it in two first so you wouldn't get any more bright ideas.'

His hand dropped to her breast, her bruised, painful breast. He stroked her gently, lovingly, through the thin material. 'You like my ideas. I think you like the feel of my hands.'

The way he touched her was reverent, not at all playful like his words, so tender and loving she wanted to melt into him. 'I love the feel of your hands. Now go away before we get arrested.' She kissed him again and opened the door.

He caught her arm, preventing her from scooting out. 'Look me in the eye, Flame and tell me you aren't looking to die here.'

'I'd no more let Saunders kill me than I would Whitney.'

He held her a second longer, swallowed hard, and nodded.

She sauntered over to the corner, tucking back out of the rain, trying to look as if she were ready for a good time with the rain pouring down and the streets looking tawdry with the neon signs blinking through the gray haze. She didn't have any competition that she could see so, if she guessed right and Saunders needed to work off his frustrations, she'd be the logical choice. Surreptitiously she glanced at her watch. All the days of reconning Saunders had paid off. She had his schedule. Either they would come looking in the next few minutes, or tonight was a bust.

Headlights nearly blinded her as a car swept around the corner. She recognized the security vehicles Saunders used. *He bit all right. Let's see if I can reel him in.*

Don' go getting too confident, Flame.

She snuck a peek to see if she could spot him, but

there was no seeing Raoul when he was in hunting mode.

The window rolled down and a hand beckoned her to the car. The man handed her three hundred dollar bills without saying a word. Flame got in when the back door was opened. No one spoke as they drove her into the city to the Saunders's estate. They looked and smirked and she could tell they wanted to intimidate her. The one on the passenger side had a crooked nose and rubbed his crotch and grinned at her.

She looked right through him and thought about Raoul. She felt him close, knew if she whispered he would hear her. When Raoul looked at her she felt sexy. When these men looked at her she just felt dirty – and angry. As they swept through the back entrance straight to the gatehouse, the front passenger window shattered, safety glass exploding outward. The men reacted, drawing weapons and crouching low. Flame kept her smirk to herself. They were all nervous and the window shattering with no clear explanation added to the strain.

The gatehouse was neat and appealing on the outside, blending in with the beauty of the landscaping, but once inside, it was easy to see exactly what the place was used for. Saunders sat by the fake fireplace, drinking a glass of whiskey. He barely looked up when the men shoved her inside. The door closed with a solid thud.

Flame looked around her. Mirrors decorated the ceiling and three of the four walls. There was a rack holding all kinds of what looked like very painful instruments. 'So this is your little torture chamber. Very chic. I've heard about it.'

Saunders lifted his glass. 'My reputation precedes me?'

She smiled at him and wandered around the room

touching the various whips. They were all real, obviously made to produce as much pain as possible. 'It certainly does. I thought I'd come check it out for myself.' She leaned against the rack letting him get a good look at her figure. All the while she rubbed her hand back and forth on the spikes. 'You like to hurt women, don't you, Mr. Saunders?'

Her fingers mesmerized him. He watched the way she caressed the cold steel, almost as if it were a phallus symbol. Her voice was unbelievable, a sexy, sultry purr that made him as hard as a rock. Ordinarily he didn't allow the sluts to speak to him, but the sound of her voice vibrated through his body and played on his nerve endings like those stroking fingers.

'It turns you on and makes you feel big and powerful, doesn't it?'

He wanted to move toward her, but the room seemed to shift out from under him. He lurched unsteadily, wondering if there were earthquakes in Louisiana. He'd certainly never experienced one before.

The door burst open and Emanuel Parsons stumbled in. 'You son of a bitch. You killed my boy, didn't you?' He had his back to Flame, so intent on confronting Kurt Saunders that he hadn't checked the room for other occupants. 'The cabin is gone, burnt to the ground and they're all dead. Everyone is dead.'

'How the hell did you get in here?' Saunders set his glass carefully on the table, his hand remaining casually over the top of it.

'He was a good boy until you got him into your depraved way of life. You didn't want witnesses.' Emanuel tapped his cane on the floor. 'You didn't have to have him killed, Kurt.'

'I had nothing to do with the cabin burning. I have no idea what happened out there. I figure Vicq got

347

pissed and went crazy. He's always had a screw loose. As for your boy, he loved taking a woman and using her the way she was meant to be used. You always wanted to, but never had the guts. Get the hell out of here, Parsons. You make me sick. And don't think you can try to take me down. I've got enough on you and your son to bury you.'

'I won't have to take you down. The military was all over the area. Helicopters, forensic people, some pretty powerful people are shuffling through the debris and not anyone I knew. That tells me something, Kurt. They didn't trust the police. Why wouldn't they trust the police to investigate? Because *I* was under suspicion. And that means they know about you. I wouldn't have to do a damned thing to take you down, but you killed my boy.' Emanuel Parsons slowly brought his cane up. 'Burn in hell.'

The shot rang out, loud in the small room. Glass shattered behind Parsons and he stood swaying for a moment, staring at Saunders and the small gun in his hand. Saunders had swept the gun up from the small table where his glass still sat filled with whiskey. The cane dropped first, and then Parsons fell to his knees.

Saunders walked up to Parsons and pressed the muzzle of the gun between his eyes. 'You lose,' he said and pulled the trigger.

Flame stayed very still as Saunders turned the gun on her.

He shrugged. 'Sorry, honey. And I really wanted to play, but I'm afraid I don't have time.' He raised the gun, finger tightening on the trigger.

Simultaneously, a hole blossomed in the middle of his forehead, one in his heart, one in his throat and one through his mouth. Flame could barely separate the four shots they were so close together. She rubbed the

348

metal spike with the napkin sitting on the table beside Saunders's drink before using it to open the door.

'No, this time, you lose,' she said and shut the door.

There wasn't a single guard in sight. She caught the glimpse of a body lying prone on the lawn and another in the flower garden. She walked to the edge of the high fence and jumped, landing in a crouch, waiting there in the shadows.

The car pulled up, passenger door open and she slid in and leaned across the seat to kiss Raoul full on the mouth. 'Great timing. Thank you.'

'I've got my uses.'

Chapter Eighteen

The shower was hot and helped take some of the sting out of the bruises marring her body. Flame leaned against the shower stall and let the water pour over her. She'd never felt so exhausted in her life. She concentrated on the feeling she had when she witnessed Joy's reunion with her parents. It had been an uplifting, yet incredibly sad moment. For some reason, she had shifted her attention from Joy and her weeping parents to Wyatt. He looked broken. Utterly broken. So much so that she had wanted to cry for him.

She never, ever wanted to see that same expression on Raoul's face. She put her head back and closed her eyes, allowing the water to cascade over her. Even if she stayed with him, when she died, it was going to tear him up. What was she supposed to do? She'd actually tried to talk to his grandmother about it, but before she could confess the truth, they'd been interrupted. She had no one to discuss things with and more than anything, she didn't want to see Raoul hurt.

'Hey! Are you planning on living in there?' A loud thump on the door made her heart jump. She swept back her hair and turned off the water.

'Sorry. I didn't mean to use up all the hot water.' She

caught up a towel and wrapped it around her.

'I don' care about the hot water, *cher.*' He poked his head in the door. 'I just needed to know you were safe.' His sharp gaze roamed over her bare skin.

Her heart sank when he frowned. She knew she looked bad. There was no way to hide the bruises from him. They were everywhere, large black and blue patches that looked hideous. She ducked her head. 'It looks worse than it really is.'

Gator stepped into the room and skimmed his fingertips over the outline of the dark bruise riding the swell of her breast. His touch was light, barely there, but her womb clenched and her stomach muscles contracted in response.

'Does it hurt?'

His gaze roamed her face, his eyes dark with emotion. She stroked the hard edge of his jaw. 'I'm all right, Raoul. You can't look at me like that.'

He caught her hand, pressed her palm against his mouth. 'I don' know if my heart can take you getting hurt anymore, Flame.'

No one had ever looked at her like that and she didn't know if *her* heart could take it. Her chest actually ached. 'I'm not hurt,' she tried to reassure him. 'Even my arm is feeling better.' She managed a smile. 'I'm a tough chick.'

'You're something.' He drew her out of the bathroom.

The house smelled of the fresh baked bread, fried chicken, and pecan pie his grandmother had sent home with them. He hadn't bothered with the lights, but had scattered candles all over so that the room seemed to glow. The small rustic cabin suddenly seemed more than a trapper's cabin. It was intimate and comfortable and all too homey.

She rubbed her temples, pressing deep with her fingers. He was killing her, offering her things already out of her reach. She wanted to weep for both of them, but instead she let him seat her in the chair across from his. If she was what he really wanted, knowing she didn't have very long, she was going to accept the gift given to her and hang on tight to him with both hands.

'You're so lucky to have your grandmother, Raoul. She's incredible.' She picked up her fork as he dished the food onto her plate. 'She was so sweet to send a care package with us.'

'When she's nervous, or upset, *Grand-mere* cooks. When I was a boy I used to smell the food long before I ever reached our cabin. We always had plenty of food.' He gestured toward all the candles. 'I told her I wanted soft lights and a relaxing, soothing atmosphere for you and she gathered every candle she'd made with the right scent.'

'For me?' Flame looked around her, awed by the trouble he'd gone to. 'You did all this for me?'

He grinned at her. 'Well, you didn't think I normally lit candles all over the house, did you? I only do it for you. This is used mostly as a hunting cabin now. We fish and trap and drink a lot of beer in here, but this is the first time I've ever done this.'

'Your grandmother didn't happen to send another shopping bag filled with strange items, did she?' Flame asked suspiciously.

'No, *cher*. I was tempted to ask her, but if she wasn't the one to buy us those toys then I'd have to explain it all and I'm not talking to Nonny about vibrating eggs.'

Flame nearly choked on her food. The towel slipped and she had to reknot it to keep it in place. Her hands trembled. Just the thought of being alone with Raoul was enough to make her happy, and that was frightening. He made her laugh with his outrageous comments.

The old hunting cabin he used for fishing and trapping felt like a home with the candles and the food and Raoul sitting across from her. 'You just were very lucky growing up with Nonny as your grandmother. How old were you when you went to live with her?'

He shrugged. 'About seven I guess, although we stayed with her more often than not before that. Our family was very close so if we weren't at one house, we were at the other, or sometimes we all lived together.'

'You enjoyed your childhood, didn't you?'

He ducked his head, suddenly all too aware of the differences in their lives.

'You goof.' There was affection in her voice. 'I *like* hearing stories of your childhood or I wouldn't ask. I think your grandmother is one of the most awesome people I've ever met. She really cares, not only about you and your brothers, but her neighbors and friends. Did you see her face when Joy's parents saw Joy alive?' She smiled, her eyes lighting up. 'It was beautiful. She's genuine, Raoul. Completely genuine.'

He reached across the small table to take her hand. 'I don' know how you turned out to be so wonderful with your background, but you have.'

She laughed. 'I doubt there's a single other person who would think that. I'm not all that nice, Raoul, and you know I'm not. I have a very low tolerance for certain things.'

'You look so beautiful with the candlelight playing over your skin. I'm getting a little uncomfortable sitting in this chair.'

She put down her fork and raised her eyebrow. 'Uncomfortable?'

'Damned uncomfortable.'

'And just how are you uncomfortable?' Flame leaned her chin on the heel of her hand, looking into his eyes.

353

She loved the way his eyes went dark with need and desire. She loved the stark hunger on his face and the raw sexuality that he exuded. Mostly she loved the way he told her, straight out, honestly, that he wanted her.

'I'm so hard, *cher*, I might not be able to walk.'

Laughter rose up again. Happiness. She felt it burst through her, bright and powerful, driving out worries of a future and leaving her basking in the here and now. Her heart did some fluttering and her muscles clenched in the most delicious way, but most of all, she loved him. Really loved him. And that was a priceless gift.

'I'm not even wearing a knife,' she teased. 'I'm not wearing anything at all but this towel.'

He groaned. 'That wasn't nice, Flame. You know I've been sittin' here imagining all sorts of things and then you go and say a thing like that.'

'It's rather obvious.'

'Knowin' and sayin' it aloud are two different things.'

'I want to see.'

'See?' he echoed, his voice turning hoarse. 'You want to see me hard and ready for you?'

She nodded. 'If I'm going to put aside the chance at this great meal for something else, I think I should see what I'm getting.'

'I'm hearing a bit of a challenge in your voice, *femme*. You can't be thinkin' I'm not up for the task?'

Flame loved him for that, the playfulness in his voice, the teasing in his eyes. He stood up, shrugging out of his shirt and she drew her breath in sharply at the sight of his chest. His hands dropped to his waistband and the air left her lungs in a rush. His body was hard, muscular and compact, and she appreciated every inch of it. He slowly pushed the jeans over his narrow hips so that his thick erection sprang free.

'I'm definitely up for the task, *cher*.' His hand cir-

354

cled the broad length of him.

She moistened suddenly dry lips. There was something sexy about seeing his fist wrapped intimately around his erection. 'I'll need a closer inspection.' She moved around the table, nearly mesmerized by him. His broad shoulders and beautiful male body, the flash of his white teeth when he smiled, but most of all, by his eyes and the way he looked at her.

There was raw lust. She wouldn't deny that and in any case it simply added to her excitement. But more than that, there was love. And that was the most powerful aphrodisiac of all. Someone loved her. Not just anyone, but Raoul Fontenot. Her fingertips brushed over him, producing a visible shudder of pleasure.

He tugged at the knot and her towel fell to the floor. At once he bent his head to her bruised breast. His tongue slipped over the dark smudges with extraordinary gentleness. 'Does it hurt, Flame?'

'No.' He continued to look at her steadily. She shrugged. 'Well. Maybe a little. It doesn't hurt when you do that.' He'd been so careful of her. His tongue felt like velvet, his touch light and soothing.

'Good. I don' want anything to hurt you tonight. I just want you to feel good.' He reached for her, drew her body against his, needing to feel the softness of her skin and the lush curves that were such a temptation to him. 'I'm going to make you feel so good, *cher*,' he murmured, kissing her ear, his mouth wandering down her neck. 'No matter how angry you get with me, you're going to want to forgive me.'

Flame threw her head back to give him better access to her throat. 'Really? You're going to be so good in bed that every time we argue, I'm going to want to let you win? Or just forgive whatever macho, chauvinistic thing you do?'

He kissed his way up her chin to the corner of her mouth. 'I'm thinkin' I might be a little on the macho side for a woman with your stubborn streak of independence and I might just get on your bad side occasionally.'

'Occasionally?'

He grinned at her. 'So let's just say, I'm goin' to find other ways of pleasin' you to make up for it.'

His mouth settled on hers, taking her breath, heightening her passion with the sinfully wicked edge he always seemed to have to his kisses. She could kiss him forever, just melt into his body and let his hot mouth take her somewhere far away. He brought her body to life and made her feel totally alive.

'I know you're a macho idiot.' She whispered it into his open mouth, her fingers tangling in his hair. 'I don't get pushed around easily so we're pretty even.' She kissed him back, exploring his mouth, and kissing him more. 'Not that I mind at all if you want to find lots of ways to please me.'

She found herself in the bedroom and wasn't certain how he'd managed to walk her backward, kissing her every step of the way. She hadn't been aware of anything but his mouth and the electricity zinging through her body. He laid her across the bed and stood over her, looking down at her.

'You have to be one of the most beautiful women in the world.'

She should have felt embarrassed, but all she felt was happy – and turned on. She wanted him with every cell and nerve ending in her body. 'You make me feel beautiful, Raoul.' And that was it. He made her *feel* wanted, beautiful, loved even. He didn't see the flaws and the bruising wasn't a turn-off to him, he just kept looking at her as if he needed to devour her.

Raoul pushed her legs apart, his hand skimming over her mound. He dipped a finger into her and licked, his tongue savoring her taste. She lifted her hips in an effort to entice him, but he shook his head. 'This is the bayou, *cher*. We like things slow and easy in the bayou.'

'You weren't slow and easy last night.'

His hands went to the insides of her thighs, slowly caressing her with long smooth strokes. He wasn't touching her breasts, but her nipples tightened into two hard buds. A shiver went down her spine and warm liquid pooled in welcome for him.

'Tonight's different. Tonight's all about slow and easy.' Raoul poured warm oil into his hands and picked up her foot. His fingers began a deep massage that somehow was as sensuous as it was relaxing. 'Close your eyes, *cher*. Just enjoy for me.' He worked slowly up her calves to her thighs.

Flame lowered her lashes and concentrated on the feel of his hands on her body. He was careful to skim any bruise, but whatever oil he was using seemed to take the sting out of the bruises. He massaged her belly, her breasts, and then her shoulders and her one good arm, leaving her feeling like a puddle of melted flesh in the bed.

'Feel good?'

'You know it does.' Her body tingled everywhere.

He took her face in his hands and kissed her. Flame closed her eyes and just absorbed the feel of the sheer mastery of his mouth. She thought it sinful to have a mouth like his and a kiss like he delivered. So hot, so perfect, she wanted to drown in his kisses. His hands roamed over her body. She reveled in the possessive way he touched her, yet he was incredibly gentle, even tender, swirling a fingertip over her bruises, kissing and nibbling his way to her breasts.

She ran her hand over his back, tracing the line, his narrow hip, even as she arched into his mouth, a soft moan escaping as he laved her nipples. He didn't stop but continued the foray with his tongue, gliding lower to tease the flames riding her hip, to kiss her scar, flicking his tongue over her belly button and kissing his way lower still.

Gator shifted position, drawing her bottom to him and lifting her legs over his shoulders. Flame gripped the quilt beside her, shocked at the sudden convulsing of her tight muscles. He breathed and muscles contracted. 'I might not survive,' she whispered.

He ran his thumbs over her soft folds and she arched her back, unable to stop the response. Her fingers bunched the material of the quilt into her hand. She had to hang on to something. Raoul licked her. Long. Slow. Like an ice cream he was savoring. She writhed on the bed, every nerve ending shrieking with awareness. He spent time stroking caresses over her mound, around it, on her soft inner thighs and then he went back to those long slow licks, his tongue broad and flat and sweeping over the outside between her legs until she thought she might really die from sheer pleasure.

'You have to stop.'

'I'm just gettin' started, sugah. This is me loving you, Cajun-style.'

He stabbed deep with his tongue, and she screamed, her breath coming in wild gasps. His hands went to her breasts, his fingers wrapping gently around the lush flesh. Once more he began his slow movements, circling her clit with easy sweeps, driving her out of her mind. Her breathing went ragged, and she couldn't stop bucking with her hips or arching her breasts more fully into his hands.

Raoul began slow circles with the pads of his fingers on her aureoles, heightening her pleasure. And then he sucked, the tip of his tongue dancing wickedly, flicking her clit while humming softly. The vibration spread through her body with the strength and sensation of a vibrator. He tugged on her nipples, squeezing in time with the vibration of his humming. Her muscles went into overdrive, clamping hard in a long, convulsing spasm. The orgasm tore through her like a rocket, from her breasts to her belly, engulfing her womb and hot channel until she sobbed with the strength of her release.

Raoul kissed his way up her belly to her breasts, paused to flick her nipples with his tongue and rub his face between the soft mounds. She felt so soft, so hot, almost melting into his body. She moaned softly and he felt it vibrating through his cock. He was so hard, unbelievably so, but this was for her. This night. He had one night to show her he loved her with every fiber of his being.

He lifted her hips with one hand, pressing the head of his erection against her welcoming entrance. She was soaked with desire, and he thrust in, driving through her impossibly tight folds, the pleasure so intense it tore a groan from his throat. He caught her hips in his hands, pulled back and drove as deep as he could go.

She cried out, her body holding his in a hot fist so tight his balls ached with the need for release. All the while her muscles rippled and quaked, adding to the pleasure coursing through him. 'You're so ready, *ma belle femme*. So damn sexy I don' know if I'm going to be able to make this last.' He thrust again, a long hard stroke that pushed him to the edge. 'You come for me, Flame.'

'I already have.' She wasn't even sure how many times.

'Again. I want you to come apart in my arms. I want to hear you screaming, *cher*.' She was panting, her breasts rising and falling with her labored breath. Her hand went to his hip again, fingers digging in deep while he surged in and out of her slowly.

'Then give me more, Raoul. Give me all of you.'

He sank into her, felt the heat rushing through him with the speed of a fireball. He pulled her hips close, lifting her legs over his shoulders and began to ride her hard, long, deep strokes, faster and faster, over and over, burying himself so deep his balls slapped against her bottom. Sweat broke out on his body. The angle allowed him to penetrate her deeply while increasing the friction on her most sensitive spot. It felt like he was surrounded by hot velvet, living, breathing velvet wrapped so tightly around him it was squeezing and milking him.

The walls around him tightened, clamped down with ferocious intensity. Flame screamed and bucked wildly, sending him crashing over the edge right along with her. There was a roaring in his ears, little hammers tripping in his head and the rush started in his toes and consumed him completely. He emptied himself into her, caught somewhere between heaven and hell. It was the most explosive orgasm he'd ever experienced, the best sex, lust and love tightly intertwined.

He lay over the top of her, shifting enough to stay away from her injured arm, but burying his face in her neck. He closed his eyes, savoring the scent of her, the taste of her, the way her body held so tightly to his. Her hot channel had clamped down so hard on him, she'd ripped the climax out of him before he could stop, before he could make it last longer. And, *Dieu*, he wanted longer – he wanted forever.

'Marry me.' It came out of nowhere. He hadn't planned asking. Hadn't thought about asking. But there it was. Two words that might save them.

She went still, her breath catching in her throat with a little audible hitch. Her breasts heaved against his chest, nipples hard and tight against him. Her fingers dug into his shoulder. 'Raoul. Don't. You can't ask me something like that.'

'Why not? I'm never going to love another woman the way I love you. I want this, what we have right now for always. Don' you?' He propped himself up on one elbow to stare down into her eyes. He wanted to beg her to save them, but he could only do his best to convince her. 'Don' you want me, *cher*?'

She cupped the side of his face with her hand, her thumb sliding back and forth over his jaw in a small caress. 'I want you more than I've ever wanted anything in my life.' She rubbed the pad of her thumb over his lips. 'Marriage ceremonies leave paper trails. You know that as well as I do. I believe Peter Whitney is alive. If I were to marry you he'd come after both of us.'

'Lily married Rye and no one's bothered them.'

'Now that's a real shocker. You're just adding to my belief that Lily knows exactly what Whitney is up to.'

'So maybe that wasn't the best example. What about Nico and Dahlia? You can't think they're involved with Whitney.'

She shook her head. 'I can think a lot of things you don't, Raoul. You know Nico, I don't. For all I know he married Dahlia, and Whitney stays away because she's right where he wants her to be.'

He kissed her. He tasted his own desperation, his fading hope. He tasted bitterness. 'Just let's do this, Flame. We can go to a friend of mine, here in the bayou. *Grand-mere* and Wyatt can go with us. I won't even tell my friends if you'd rather I didn't. We'll be low-key.'

'I'm not going anywhere. I'll stay with you until you have to go back.'

Gator turned over onto his back, his fingertips pressed against his eyes. 'And then, what? It's over? You just walk away like nothing happened?'

'I have cancer, Raoul.' She was grateful for the candlelight. It made it so much easier to say the simple truth. She wouldn't be around all that long once it took hold.

'Whitney put it in remission twice. We'll go to a doctor.'

'And I'll be in the computer system for Whitney to find.' She sighed and reached for his hand. 'Whitney manufactured his own variety of cancer that last time. He told me he did. If just any oncologist could put it in remission, why would I ever go back to him?'

'Did you ever have it checked out to see if it was the truth?'

'I hacked into his records. At that time, he probably let me, so who knows how accurate they were?'

'Then let's give it a shot.'

She rolled onto her side. 'Raoul, I love you. I know that I do, but I'm not signing your death warrant. I believe Peter Whitney is out there and that he's looking for me. I will never, under any circumstances, go back there alive.'

'Then we'll go to Lily.'

'They're one and the same to me. It's all right.'

'It's not all right, damn it.' Raoul closed his eyes briefly and made himself breathe. There was no reason to argue; she'd made up her mind and he knew he couldn't change it.

'Let's just take this one day at a time. Who knows what will happen?' Flame suggested.

'Yeah. You're right.' His voice was husky, tears clogging his throat. She was giving him no choice.

'I'd marry you in a heartbeat if things were different.'

He forced a smile and sat up. 'I want you to sleep tonight, so I'm going to make you some hot chocolate.' He stood up quickly before she could stop him. He took care to mask the emotion in his voice.

'You don't have to do that. I doubt if I'll have any trouble sleeping.'

'*Grand-mere* makes this special blend and she gave me the recipe. I made it up for you already. It won't take any time.' He hurried into the small kitchen area and hastily poured the chocolate from the thermos he'd brought. It was still hot and steam rose from the mug. From the kitchen cupboard he pulled a small vial of clear liquid and stood for a moment staring at it.

'Are you having some too?'

'Yes.' He closed his eyes briefly and then dumped the liquid quickly into the chocolate, stirred, and added a bit of whipped cream before filling a second mug with chocolate.

'Here you go, *cher*. There's nothing like it before bed.'

Flame sat up and took the mug from him. The sheet slipped down exposing her breasts and he kept his eyes fixed on the bruises while she drank.

'This is good. An old family recipe?'

He nodded as he settled back on the bed beside her. 'She made it for us on special occasions.'

'What kind of special occasions?' She loved his childhood stories. She could so easily picture him as a little boy with tousled curls.

'If we managed to get a decent grade in school. Or if we didn't have a fistfight for an entire week with any of our friends – or enemies.'

'Did you have trouble getting good grades?' She tilted her head to look at him. 'I imagine you would have been very good in school.'

363

He shrugged his shoulders. 'I didn't always go. I was the oldest and someone had to do the fishing and trapping. I worked on a couple of shrimp boats two or three times a week. I lied to *Grand-mere* because she said an education was more important, but of course she knew when she found the money in her drawer every week.'

She looked at him over the cup of chocolate. 'Sometimes the things you say melt my heart.'

'It wasn't a bad thing, Flame. I loved workin' on the boats. It was simply our way of life. I preferred being out in the bayou to school any day of the week.' He leaned forward and licked a small dollop of whipped cream from the corner of her mouth before he could stop himself.

She made a face at him and leaned in to him for a kiss. He tasted of whipped cream and chocolate. Raoul took the drink from her hand and set it on the small table beside the bed. 'Go to sleep, *cher*. You're very tired, aren't you?'

She stretched out and then curled on her side, cautious with her broken arm. 'I am tired. It's been a long day, but Joy's reunion with her parents was worth it all.'

'You were good with her.'

'Wyatt was good with her. I feel so bad for him. If the expression on his face was anything to go by, he's a little in love with her. It will be a long time before she ever is able to trust a man enough to have a relationship with him.'

A lump formed in his throat and he ducked his head. Gator lay down beside her, drawing her into his arms and curling his body protectively around hers. He stroked back wisps of hair from her face.

She tangled her fingers with his. 'Tonight was the most beautiful night of my life, Raoul. Thank you.'

Her voice was drowsy, sensual, playing over his body

like fingers. His heart shifted in his chest and he felt a vise begin to grip, take hold, and squeeze until his chest felt as if it might explode. He pressed his free hand to his chest while he held her other one and watched the drug take her.

The clock ticked loudly on the wall as time passed. He sat watching the candlelight flicker over her face, the dancing shadows play over her body, and he bent down to brush a kiss across her eyes. She didn't move.

Gator dressed quickly. The syringe was in his drawer and this time he didn't hesitate. He couldn't take a chance that she might wake up. He gave her a shot in her thigh, injecting the full dose into her.

It's done.

We'll bring in the copter. We have a plane standing by to fly us out of here and Rye has the compound ready.

It was difficult to put a robe on her, but he managed. He didn't want her naked when they came for her. He snatched up her duffel bag and shoved her new clothes inside. His own bag was already packed and ready to go.

He sat listening to the sounds of the helicopter as it flew overhead and swung toward the clearing just south of his cabin. It wasn't long before he heard the men as they approached the house, bringing the stretcher with them. One by one he blew out the candles until the room was dark.

Chapter Nineteen

Flame awoke to the scent of lavender. She was lying in a bed, but it wasn't the same bed she'd gone to sleep in with Raoul's body wrapped closely around hers. Her heart slammed hard as she realized that there was a port directly into the vein under her collarbone. The last time she'd had something like that stuck in her body had been when Whitney gave her the cocktail of medicine needed to get rid of the cancer he had manufactured.

Oh God. Please God. Don't let this be happening to me. Anything but this. Anything at all. I can't do this. She sent the silent prayer over and over while she slid her hand up to feel the port, hoping she was having a nightmare. She felt the edges of the dressing and knew the port was stitched in place and the catheter was under her skin. She fought the urge to yank the foreign object out of her body.

Someone sat nearby in a chair. There was movement to her left. She feigned sleep, struggling to keep her heart under control when it insisted on accelerating, when adrenaline flooded her body, triggering every alarm in her system. Betrayal was a bitter taste in her mouth. She ached with it. Screamed silently with it.

Tears burned but she refused to give them license.

Raoul Fontenot had delivered her back into Whitney's hands.

The person to her left moved to the edge of the bed and bent over her. She smelled him. Knew his touch. She reached for rage, needed it to survive, but there was only pain. She gasped aloud, shocked at the intensity of her anguish. She'd never felt so raw, so ripped open and vulnerable.

'I know you're awake. I can hear your heart, your breathing. Open your eyes, Flame. It isn't what you think.' Raoul's voice was low, almost pleading.

'No?' She lifted her lashes, couldn't stop the tears from swimming where he could see them, but she didn't look at him. Couldn't look at him. 'You didn't seduce me? You didn't drug me and take me to the one place you knew I swore I'd never go back to? You warned me. I can't say that you didn't. You said you were supposed to bring me back, but I let you seduce me into forgetting.'

'Flame, you know better. Look at me. You know it wasn't like that.'

She was going to be sick. Her stomach churned and she could hear the silent screams in her head growing louder. There was so much pain. She hadn't expected it to be so bad, the utter humiliation of knowing he had slept with her to do his job.

Surprisingly she wasn't restrained. She struggled into a sitting position, batting away his hands when he tried to help her. 'Don't touch me. I never want you to touch me again.' She pressed a hand to her stomach. 'Where's the bathroom? I'm going to be sick.' It was already too late. He shoved a small tray into her hands and she was further humiliated by throwing up over and over again in front of him.

He left her side for a brief moment to return with a cool washcloth and towel. She took it without looking at him. She knew if she looked, if she saw his face and his lying eyes, the terrible storm inside of her would crash over her and she would break apart, shatter so completely that she wouldn't be Flame anymore.

Raoul took the small tray from her, dumped it and rinsed it out, returning it to the bed within reach of her hand. The sight of the tray triggered childhood memories. Ugly. Torturous. She felt dizzy and for a moment couldn't catch her breath.

Control. Discipline. Patience. She repeated the mantra silently. She knew what she had to do. She was prepared; she'd been prepared ever since the first moment of her escape. Death wasn't nearly as bad as living as a lab rat.

She let her breath out slowly. 'I guess you didn't believe me when I told you I'd destroy everything before I'd be put in a cage again. I'm willing to die here, Raoul, are you? Because you have about two minutes to get the hell out and take everyone else with you.'

'Why warn me, Flame? Why not just do it?'

'Get out, Raoul.' She was tired. Desperately tired and drained. The screams in her head had subsided, but now, somewhere deep inside she was silently weeping. Great terrible sobs that she couldn't control were shredding her heart. Her body shook with sobs, her chest ached and her throat was nearly closed with the tears clogging it, but no sound escaped. She refused to give that to him.

'I'm not leaving your side.'

'Look, you did your job. You can go tell all your buddies how great you are. You royally fucked me.'

'*Maudit!* That's not the way it was.'

'That's *exactly* the way it was. You knew you couldn't

force me back so you pretended to fall in love with me.'
She shook her head. 'I can't believe I fell for every word
you said. Be proud of yourself. Maybe Whitney will give
you a nice bonus. Just get the hell out of here. I can't stand
the sight of you.' She pressed the wet cloth over her face,
hoping it would cool her burning eyes.

'You would never have come in on your own, Flame.
Never.'

'Where am I? The room is soundproofed, but it's no
hospital.'

'I couldn't risk taking you to Lily's home. All of us
stay there on and off and Lily's pregnant. If you decided to retaliate, I had to find a way to contain the damage. You can kill me, Flame, but I'm not going to let
you take out the others. They only did what I asked
them to do because they wanted to help you.'

She looked at her broken arm, at the new cast,
unmarred by the rain and water of the bayou. 'I suppose you're going to tell me Lily did this.'

'She had to check to make certain there was no infection from the alligator bite. You're on strong antibiotics
and painkillers, but with the cast getting wet—'

'Where's Peter Whitney?' she demanded, cutting
him off.

'I have no idea. I've brought you to a facility where
Lily can treat the cancer and we can guard you from
Peter Whitney, if, in fact, he's still alive and is trying
to take you back. Peter Whitney has *nothing* to do with
this – or with me. I brought you here because it was
the only way to keep you alive.'

'That's not your decision to make.' She was holding
on by a thread, rocking back and forth to try to soothe
the pain. How could he have taken away her free will?

'It is my decision, Flame. It should have been. I love
you and . . .'

'Damn you to hell for even saying that.' She jerked the cloth from her face and for the first time forced herself to look at him. It was a terrible mistake. He didn't look like the devil. He looked like the man she loved with his dark wavy hair and his impossible eyes. His sinful mouth and perfect body. Instead of the anger and rage she so desperately needed, she broke down.

The storm inside her body took over and she heard a long wail of grief break free. It tore through her insides and escaped before she could contain it. Flame buried her face in the pillow in an attempt to muffle the sound of her sobbing. She'd given him something so precious. Not her body, or even her love, but she *trusted* him. She didn't want to see shadows in his eyes, or a face ravaged by worry. She wanted to hate him the way he deserved to be hated.

The bed shook with her sobs. The room shook. Gator stood against the wall listening to her crying as if he'd not just broken her heart, but ripped it out of her body. He'd destroyed her. There was no way to comfort her, nothing he could find to say that she would understand. He sank into the small armchair he'd set by the door and covered his face with his hands. He'd expected anger, rage, an emotion he could cope with, but she was killing him with her grief. And it was grief. Her grief was destroying him.

He felt her pain as if it were his own. He'd done the right thing, taken the *only* avenue available to him. His chest tightened and his throat ached. Tears burned in his eyes. He'd done this to her. He'd made the decision to save her life, knowing he'd probably lose her, but he hadn't considered the consequences beyond that. He thought he could bear losing her as long as he knew she was alive, but he couldn't bear being the one to cause her such pain.

Flame felt a hand on her shoulder. Her first reaction was to shrug it off, but the hand was soft and thin, the scent strong of lavender. The hand stroked back her hair and a soft voice murmured comforting words. 'There, there, *cher*. It will be all right. I'm here now. We'll make it all right.'

'Nonny?' Was she hallucinating? She turned her head to see the little old lady standing beside her bed, her eyes filled with concern. 'You can't be here.' She tried to get the words out between the tearing sobs. Her breathing was so ragged, her throat so sore, she could barely get the words out. Worse, she was going to be sick again.

Flame groped blindly for the tray, vomiting over and over until she had the dry heaves. Nonny took the tray from her and pushed the wet washcloth into her hand. Somewhere in the room, Raoul watched and that knowledge only added to her humiliation. How could he do this to her?

Nonny was back, slipping an arm around her and taking the cloth, replacing it with a glass of water. 'This will pass, Flame. Lily said you might be sick.'

Flame fought to control the wild weeping. She'd learned a long time ago it didn't do any good. It only gave her a headache and made her angry with herself for giving Whitney the satisfaction of getting to her. Now it was Raoul. Another sob escaped. *How could he have done it?*

I had no choice.

Flame closed her eyes, ashamed of her lack of control. The intensity of her emotions was so strong she was connecting with him. She made an effort to pull herself together. Control. Discipline. Patience. She repeated it over and over until she calmed the wild storm enough to sip the water and gain a semblance of control.

'How long have I been here?'

'Forty-six hours,' Raoul answered. He leaned back until his head rested against the wall. He'd had forty-six hours to prepare for this, yet he had never considered her heart – or his – would break.

'That can't be. Nonny, you have to get out of here, now. It's too dangerous for you to stay. Raoul, get her out of here.'

Nonny patted her hand. 'Now, now, child, don' be gettin' yourself riled up again. Raoul explained you were like him, some kind of government weapon, and that you could lose control and maybe bring the building down on top of us.'

'Not maybe, Nonny, I could. I don't know what he was thinking, bringing you with him.'

'He told me what he was goin' to do, and I knew you'd be plenty angry with him. It was wrong to take matters into his own hands, but he's always been like that. I knew you'd be upset and you'd need me. I don' care about the danger. Raoul loves you. You're family, girl. I take care of my family.'

Flame shook her head. 'This is crazy. You can't stay, Nonny. Bad things happen in these places. Raoul knows that. He should never have allowed you to risk your life.'

Nonny laughed. 'Honey, I'm on the backside of my life. I've lived full and long and had a good run. You're just beginning, same as Raoul. I was the one who told Raoul I was going to come with you. He tried to talk me out of it, but I told him you were goin' to need me.'

Flame closed her eyes. She couldn't risk Nonny's life. She just couldn't. She looked so innocent, so frail, so determined to help and yet she didn't have a clue how utterly dangerous staying really was. 'Listen to me. I swear to you, I won't use sound as a weapon. I'll do everything they tell me, but you can't stay here. If Raoul is telling the truth and he isn't working for Peter Whitney, then believe me, Whitney will send others to get me back and a whole lot of people are going to die here. You can't stay, Nonny.'

'You're a good girl, Flame. I'm here and I'm goin' to watch over you and see things done right. If someone is trying to take you from my boy, well you just trust him to keep you safe. He swore to me he and the others would stay with you every minute and I believe in him.'

Flame sank back onto the mattress. Of course Raoul's grandmother believed in him; he hadn't ripped her heart out of her chest and stomped on it. She closed her eyes and turned her face away, tears leaking onto the pillow. 'Are there cameras in here, Raoul?'

'No. You aren't restrained, but the door is locked and guarded. I'll be inside with you at all times. Kadan, Tucker and Ian are guarding the building around the clock. A couple of other members of my team, men I trust implicitly, will be joining us. Both Lily and Ryland are here as well. Nico and Sam are out on a mission but, Dahlia's en route. They should be here in a few hours. The general sent us some help as well. They aren't enhanced, but they're good soldiers and highly trained.'

Gator kept his tone informative and made no attempt to go near the bed. Flame was obviously hanging on by a thread and it was only his grandmother's presence that kept violence from erupting. There was always the possibility of suicide, but she would never do such a thing as long as she felt she had to protect Nonny.

Flame took a deep breath and let it out, forcing her mind away from betrayal and back toward logic. 'When do you think he'll try to hit us?'

So she was accepting the fact that he wasn't working for Peter Whitney. That was the first step. A small one, but he'd take it. 'If he's really looking to reacquire you, and the general consensus is that either he, or someone familiar with his program, is, then the logical action would be to come after you immediately, before we're set. We found tranquilizers, not bullets in the sniper's rifle.'

'He has to have an informer, or he wouldn't have known I was in the bayou.'

'It isn't Lily. And the computer probably tells him the same thing it tells Lily. If he wrote the program and feeds in personalities, the program will tell him what you're most likely to do next.'

'You need to get Nonny out of here. We don't have enough manpower to keep her safe.' She looked around her. 'Where are my clothes?'

'You aren't getting up.'

She turned her head to stare straight at him and there was fire in her eyes. 'Don't you tell me what I can or can't do.'

Whatever drugs they'd been giving her to keep her knocked out still lingered in her system. She felt slow, her mind a little hazy. And obviously Lily had started a chemotherapy treatment. Flame wasn't one of the lucky ones. Chemo treatments often made her violently ill. Her stomach was heaving again and she turned her face away from Raoul so he couldn't see her gagging. 'Nonny. Please cover your ears for me.'

'Are you going to blast my boy?'

'I should, but I'm not.'

Nonny covered her ears.

Flame glared at Raoul. 'When my hair falls out I'm going to shave your balls with a rusty knife.'

He flinched visibly. There wasn't much he could say

374

to that and the warning made his cock jerk with fear. The woman was more than capable of carrying out the threat. He studied her expression. Proud. Defiant. Hurt. *Scared*. His heart sank. *When her hair fell out*. Not if, but *when*. She'd been through this before, knew what was coming and she was going to lose that mass of beautiful red hair. He wanted to hold her, tell her it didn't matter, that her hair didn't define who she was, that it would be all right, but she held herself away from him and there was no way to bridge the gap. Still, he tried.

'Look, Flame, you told me you wouldn't allow Saunders to kill you any more than you would Whitney. If you die of cancer, you're letting Whitney kill you. You'd be letting him win.'

She ignored his logic. 'I'll need my weapons.'

'You think I'm going to arm you when you're so pissed off you want to shave my balls? You're a powder keg right now.'

'Give them to me.' Flame reached out and tapped Nonny's arm. 'You can put your hands down now, I'm not talking to him anymore.'

Nonny patted her hand again and leaned very close. 'When you get to feelin' better, I might have to wash out your mouth with soap.' It hadn't done much good to press her hands over her ears.

'That should be an experience,' Raoul muttered under his breath.

Flame flicked him a quick glance, meant to wither him on the spot, but her voice was gentle, compliant even, when she spoke to Nonny. 'I'll work on it.'

'Good girl. We can't have you talking that way in front of the babies.'

Flame's heart twisted in her chest. 'There won't be any babies, Nonny.'

'Sure there will. Raoul is one potent Cajun. All the Fontenot men are.'

'I'm sterile.'

'But Lily said . . .'

'Grand-mere!'

Raoul's harsh tone set Flame's teeth on edge. She slid out of bed, gripping the handrail to prevent falling. 'By all means, keep whatever Lily said a secret, Raoul. That will keep me from . . .' She turned her head and sent her voice directly to him. *Slitting your throat.*

The walls of the room expanded and contracted as if breathing. Oh, yeah. There was the rage she'd expected earlier. It swept over her like a tidal wave. She clenched her teeth and fought it back, afraid of hurting Nonny.

Damn you for that, for allowing your grandmother to place herself in danger.

You mean I should have taken charge and acted in her best interests?

She forced air through her lungs, watching the walls as they undulated, as they slowly became still. 'Just tell me what Lily said and cut the crap.'

'Lily found eggs and sperm stored from each of us. The eggs were frozen in a cryoprotectant, which is a special formula that protects the eggs from damage during freezing and thawing and then they were stored in the Whitney Trust Laboratory right here in this compound in liquid nitrogen tanks.'

'Why would Whitney do that?'

He cleared his throat. 'Lily said she feared Whitney is exploring a second-generation experiment.'

'Exploring a second-generation experiment?' Flame repeated. 'Is that how she put it to you? My God.' She pressed her fingertips to her throbbing temples. 'So very scientific of her to notice.'

'You're angry with me, not her,' he reminded quietly.

Her head snapped around. 'Don't think for one moment I don't know that.'

A chill went down Gator's spine. She wasn't going to forgive betrayal. She'd never see what he did as an act of love – of desperation. He had done to her exactly what Lily had done. He'd known all along he could lose her, but he had held out hope that she'd get better and realize it was the only way to save her life. That look told him differently. In that moment his world crumbled. Shaken, he lifted his hand to cover his face. He had become *the enemy*.

They're coming, Gator, and they're coming in force. We're going to need you on the outside. That was Kadan, calm and self-assured. Ready for battle.

We agreed I'd stay inside with Flame.

Too many of them out here. We need you now!

Gator shrugged off emotions and forced himself to think like the soldier he was. 'They're here. Get dressed, Flame. Your knives are in the top drawer of that bureau over there.' He indicated it with his hand. 'There's a semiautomatic and a small handgun with several clips of ammo in the closet. Get them and get ready. *Grand-mere*, do whatever Flame tells you. Do it fast and stay absolutely quiet.'

Flame didn't say a word but dropped her hospital gown to the floor and jerked open the drawers to find clothes. The fiberglass cast on her arm was light and smaller, leaving her arm much more mobile. She dragged a shirt over her head and struggled with her jeans. 'Where are you going to be?'

'They need me outside.' He wrapped his arms around Nonny. 'Don' be afraid, *Grand-mere*. Flame won't let anything happen to you.'

377

Nonny hugged him back. 'I'm not afraid. This is excitin' stuff at my age.'

Gator stood for a moment, wanting to say something to Flame, to tell her how much he loved her, but he couldn't find the words. He looked his fill and abruptly turned on his heel and walked out.

He heard Flame's soft whisper behind him as he closed the door.

'It was you that went shopping for our romantic night, wasn't it, Nonny? It wasn't Wyatt after all. I don't think you should be talking about washing my mouth out with soap.'

There was a hint of laughter in Flame's voice, maybe forced, but Nonny wouldn't hear that. She'd only hear how confident and natural Flame sounded. His heart clenched hard. He'd lost her. She'd never panic. She'd fight with her last breath to protect Nonny. She was everything in a woman he'd ever wanted, or imagined, and he'd thrown away his chance with her.

He locked the heavy door behind him and ran down the corridor leading to the outside. It wouldn't be easy to break in, but it wasn't impossible. For the first time he allowed himself to really think about Flame's childhood. He had never dared to examine her past before, knowing it was too dangerous. Now, they were coming for her, and if he felt rage toward them, if his control slipped, the consequences were on them.

Her childhood had been ruthlessly ripped away from her and she'd been used exactly like a laboratory rat. *Exactly.* Whitney hadn't liked her, couldn't control her, so she had been the perfect object for his experiments. He'd dehumanized her in his mind and simply used her.

Yeah, he felt rage all right, but it was cold and calculating and very scary. It welled up like a volcano, a meltdown of his careful control. He shook with anger,

378

with the need for action. *You're not going to get her, you son of a bitch.* He meant it. He'd kill everyone; flatten them all before they laid one hand on her. And God help Whitney if Gator ever found out where he was hiding, because there would be no mercy for him.

He stepped into the night, crouching low and remaining motionless to acclimate himself to the sounds outside. He heard the scurry of steps, men moving in standard two-by-two formations. Cover and move. It was a textbook play. He counted eight coming in from the north and four at the front and back of the building with another eight on the other side. Whitney wasn't playing games – he wanted Flame back.

Around the corner he found a downed soldier. He knelt to feel for a pulse. The kid didn't look older than twenty and he was already dead – dead because a madman thought himself above the law. Fury shook him.

Kadan. Clear our men away from the north wall. Have all the general's men drop back completely clear of the area. Send them away. I'm not having these kids die for a son of a bitch like Whitney.

There was a small silence. Kadan's voice was very calm. *Negative, Gator, stand down. That parking lot funnels directly into the street. It's a natural corridor for sound to travel.*

Then fuckin' do your job. You're shielder, throw up a shield at the far end of the lot because I'm taking them down. You have about ten seconds to get everyone clear.

Kadan didn't bother to argue, reading the tone and knowing it was useless. *Move them out of there, Tucker. You too, Ian. Send them to the far end of the compound and tell them to take cover. Signal when you're all clear. And Gator, I'll need more time to seal the place off. It's not that damned easy.*

Rage was boiling. Gator couldn't have stopped it if he tried. His body trembled, broke out in a sweat with the effort to contain it. His vision narrowed, tunneled, until every detail of the northern side of the building was etched into his mind in vivid imagery. He saw the men as shadowy targets, nothing more. They had come for one purpose. To take Flame back to a cage where Whitney could torture her, infect her with diseases. God only knew what he would do next. Impregnate her? Take her child from her? The man was capable of anything.

He snapped his teeth together, biting down hard as the sounds welled up, demanding release.

Maudit! What the hell is taking so long? I'm not going to be able to hold back.

Damn it, Gator. Have you even thought about what you're doing? You could be blowing your entire career.

I'm taking out his army. I can't get him, but I can hurt him, put him back several years. I don' care how much money the bastard has, it takes time to build up manpower.

The general isn't going to be happy about this. Kadan gave it one last try.

Where the fuck is the seal?

The soldiers are clear but the seal isn't finished on the street. A couple of innocents driving by. We can't take the chance. You have to hold. Kadan's tone said he expected it, didn't like it, but knew he couldn't stop the inevitable.

Ian's voice broke in. *I'm taking out the four in the front.*

Wait for backup, Ian, Kadan instructed. *Tucker's on his way to you.*

Gator's gut churned, knotted, the rage moving through him like a living entity. It was rising, much like lava needing to spew forth, impossible to contain. It was all there, swirling like a tornado inside of him. Flame believing he'd betrayed her. Whitney's atrocities. The terrible deeds done to Joy. The dead soldier.

You have a go.

The note burst out, a low-level wave of infrasound invisible to the human ear. It traveled the corridor along the north side, slamming into everything in its path. It traveled through a small structure, flattening it as the sonic wave struck. It hit living tissue, vibrating internal organs. The wave remained at seven cycles per second, corresponding with the median alpha-rhythm frequencies in the brain.

They're down. They're down. Back off.

Like hell. I'm going to the south side. Eight came in that way. Let me know if our soldiers are in the clear.

Gator took a breath and let it out, trying to calm the seething rage as he surveyed the downed targets. Infrasound waves stayed close to the ground. They traveled long distances through just about anything in their path and were considered unstoppable. As the GhostWalkers had discovered in earlier field tests, without Kadan's shields, the sound waves continued to travel, destroying everything in their path.

There were eight downed targets with eight more on the opposite side of the building. If the other GhostWalkers were able to take down this sizable force, it would be a significant blow to Whitney. Even paying for an army meant finding good men and if Whitney was enhancing some of them, that took time.

Gator began moving around to the other side of the building. *Moving through the front area. Don' mistake me for a target.* He crouched low, rifle in hand, and eased his way through the wide row of trimmed bushes.

Go in close to the building, Tucker advised.

Gator worked his way to the southern corner of the building where the other eight mercenaries were closing in. *I have a visual. I count eight. You have a shield up?*

It won't work on this side. The opening is too large and the sonic wave will break through. You have to narrow the corridor, Kadan answered.

Gator studied the layout of the buildings and fences. It looked like a maze and Kadan was right. He not only would flatten several buildings, killing anyone inside, but they would be unable to contain the infrasonic wave. It would travel through the streets smashing everything in its path with the force of a volcanic eruption. He pushed back the need to strike, to neutralize the threat against Flame instantly, and forced his mind to think logically.

The best bet is to push them toward the maintenance yard. We'll have to go in and take them out.

Gunfire erupted around the front of the building. It acted as a signal and immediately the eight men on the south side began spraying the area around them, moving in a much tighter and faster formation toward the building. Four gained the wall and flung what appeared to be grenades into the bank of windows Gator knew were offices. The explosion blasted the smoke into the air, obscuring vision.

Ian? Tucker? Check in, Kadan demanded.

Two down in the front. Two to go, Ian reported.

Tucker interrupted. *He's hit.*

I'm not hit – well, maybe a little hit, but no problem.

Gator swore under his breath. He'd been the one to pull the soldiers back. He had eight men swarming one side of the building with at least six more front and back. Ian was hit and there were men on the roof. For one brief moment insanity rode him hard and he contemplated wiping them all out. One long pulse would do it. Whitney's army would be gone and Flame would be safe, at least for the time that it would take Whitney to rebuild. In the meantime, the GhostWalkers could actively search out their enemy.

He brushed away the idea, refusing to give in to temptation. He couldn't hurt innocent people, not even to keep Flame out of the hands of a madman.

Tucker, stay on Ian, take out the other two and get around to the back. Gator and I will work our way to the southern side.

The four men at the windows, threatening to gain entrance to the building had to be removed. Gator moved like a silent wraith through the tall hedges, utilizing the cover to get close to the first of the two-man teams. One man dressed in black signaled his partner to come forward to use him as a human ladder to gain entrance into the building. Gator took them both, two shots, two kills. A bullet spit into the wall next to his head and he spun around, spraying covering fire as he dove toward the ground behind a two-foot wall of cement.

Coming up behind them, Kadan informed him.

Gator held his fire, afraid of hitting Kadan. He waited, eyes searching out the second two-man team nearest the building. They'd gone to ground at the first gunfire, but at least they hadn't gotten into the building.

Kadan moved like a phantom, so fast, so silent, he was a blur as he crossed Gator's line of vision. Gator blinked twice wondering if he'd really seen him.

You're clear. Two down.

Tucker reported in. *We've got two more down here and are going around to the back. Ian's bleeding like a stuck pig.*

It's a scratch.

Tie it off, superhero, Kadan ordered.

Gator crawled through the shrubbery, careful to keep from moving any of the foliage. He could just make out a boot and part of a leg. In the shadows it looked like a fallen log. The leg moved as the enemy propelled his body forward toward the building. Gator heard the whisper of an order on a radio. He only caught three disjointed words, but it was enough to have him rolling to his right. Bullets thudded into the ground right where he'd been. The shots came from above and the fire continued, pinning him down.

They've got a sniper on the roof of the laboratory. He warned the others. *He's using infrared.*

I've got him, Ian said confidently.

A single shot rang out and Gator saw the sniper fall. As the noise cleared away, he heard another sound and his heart nearly stopped. *Maudit, Kadan. I hear them going into the vent. Warn Flame. I'm going in after them.*

Flame. Kadan reached for her immediately. *Gator hears the enemy in the vents. Can you hear them?*

Yes. We'll take care of it.

Gator's coming in after them. Don't shoot him, no matter how angry you are with him.

I can handle this myself. She didn't want Raoul risking his life for her. She didn't want any of them to do that. Flame turned to Nonny. 'I want you to get into the bathroom and lock the door. Don't open it unless you hear either Gator or me tell you to, understand?'

'I can use a gun. I've been hunting all my life,' Nonny said. 'I don' want to be in a bathroom hiding when they come. I wouldn't know what was going on.'

Flame handed her the semiautomatic. 'Have you ever used one of these?'

'Gator showed me how. If it's a gun, I can shoot it.'

'Then you get into the bathroom and stay there. Leave the door open if you prefer, but stay undercover. It will be easier for me to consider everyone in the room an enemy. Don't fire unless you have to because you might hit me.'

'I'd rather stay out here with you and just gun them down as they come.'

'I'll have the advantage, Nonny. They don't want to kill me. That's why it was so easy for me in the swamp. Raoul told me the sniper had tranqs in his gun. If someone tranqs me, feel free to shoot them.'

Nonny took the gun. It looked too big and heavy for her but there was a no-nonsense air about her that gave Flame added confidence.

Flame rolled the blankets in the bed and jerked the top sheet over them to make it look as if a body were asleep in the bed. She waved Nonny to the bathroom as she plunged the room into darkness. She went to the wall with the ventilation opening and crouched down, listening. It always amazed her when sight was taken away how acute all other senses became. She faced the grate as she detected the sliding of clothes along the inside of the ducts.

She sent a single note through the grate, a low pulsing wave that raced through the ducts. She kept it non-lethal, not knowing who else might accidentally be in the way of the sound wave. Stepping back against the opposite wall, she waited, knife in hand. Gator had provided her with an array of throwing knives, and she was grateful. She was accurate with them and trusted them much more than she did a gun.

Nausea came in waves, cramping her stomach. She broke out in a sweat, weak and sick. Chemo had a very bad effect on her; it always had. It didn't make sense to go through it all again if the cancer was going to return. Maybe she'd have to talk to Lily and ask a few hard questions.

The sounds coming from the air duct were getting louder. Whoever was in there seemed pretty sick and disoriented, thrashing wildly at one point. She held the gun against her thigh with her broken arm and the throwing knife clear of her body with her good arm. Maybe she'd get lucky and not have to kill him, and they'd have a chance to find out where Whitney was hiding out.

The grate was pulled off from the inside and the muzzle of a gun appeared, a small red dot shining around the room, searching the corners, the door, dwelling on the bathroom door. Flame willed Nonny to stay very still. Finally the red dot went to the bed and the stranger slipped into the room, gun held steady.

For the first time, Flame was unsure of herself. She thought there were three men in the ducts, but she couldn't be certain. She was too sick to be able to concentrate properly. She was fighting the dry heaves and even her vision blurred. She felt behind her for the wall and the hilt of her knife scraped against it.

The man spun back, the red dot centered on her chest. 'Drop it.'

She swayed. She wasn't going to be able to do this. She couldn't bring up the gun or the knife. She didn't drop either weapon. Two men wiggled out of the duct behind the first one. They trained their weapons on her as well.

'Put it down,' the first man repeated. He held up one hand, softening his voice. 'No one wants to hurt you, ma'am. Just put down the weapons and come with us.'

The other men had spread out and were beginning to go through the room. One neared the bathroom. Flame shook her head and pointed the gun at the one closest to Nonny. 'I'll go with you, but I'm keeping my weapons.' She tried to push off the wall and the movement caused her stomach to cramp. There was no way to stop from getting sick. She turned away from them, resting her head on the wall, her finger on the trigger of her gun, hand up to her head.

Even in her misery, she heard the whisper of a body in the air duct followed by the impact of a knife hitting a target. She managed to turn her head to see Raoul, arm around one of the enemy's neck, holding the body in front of him like a shield, gun trained on the man near the bathroom. The body of the third man lay on the floor practically at her feet.

Instantly a red dot appeared over her heart. 'Put it down or I'll shoot her.' The stranger backed up toward the cover of the bathroom.

Nonny. Flame sent the warning to Raoul.

Hit the floor. Gator squeezed the trigger three times, rapid fire. One bullet in the head, two in the heart.

The stranger fired from reflex, but Flame had dropped down and the bullet went into the wall where she'd been standing.

The man Gator had in a headlock stabbed down with a knife, driving it into Gator's thigh. He fell backward, stumbling, tracking with his gun a heartbeat too late.

Flame threw the knife from a prone position and the sound of a single gunshot echoed through the room. The enemy went down, knife in his kidney, bullet in the back of his neck. She turned her head to see Nonny lowering the semiautomatic.

Flame crawled to Gator, shouting to Nonny to bring something to tie around the wound. She pressed hard with both hands, ignoring his orders to get the hell out of his way. Nonny returned with towels and her rifle. She put the gun in her grandson's hands and took over.

Flame slid back until her head was in Raoul's lap. She closed her eyes, feeling his hand in her hair and she gave in, allowing the blackness to take her.

Chapter Twenty

Two months later

Flame sat on the cold tiles of the bathroom floor, her knees drawn up, head down, resting before the next wave of nausea struck. She kept the overhead light off. Her eyes were too sensitive to bother.

'I had dreams the other night. Nightmares, really.' The woman sitting next to her shifted closer and rubbed Flame's back. 'I'm beginning to remember sitting on the floor of the bathroom with you. We did it a lot, didn't we?' Dahlia Trevane said.

Flame nodded without lifting her head. She never thought she'd see Dahlia again. Whitney had hated her almost as much as he had Flame. 'The one good thing about this is that I got to see you again,' Flame said. 'I thought you were dead when I read about the sanitarium in the bayou burning down. I knew it belonged to the Whitney Trust and I was pretty sure you were locked in.'

'It was my home for a lot of years.'

'I know it's hard for you to be around so many people, Dahlia. I really appreciate you coming, but you don't have to stay with me.'

'I want to be with you. I missed you. I missed all the

girls. I thought for the longest time you all were figments of my imagination. Lily said Whitney tried to erase our memories.'

'Do you believe Lily when she says she isn't working with her father?' Flame's stomach twisted and she knelt up to the toilet.

Dahlia waited until she finished and handed her a washcloth. 'What's all over the floor? I can't see but it feels like strings of silk . . .' She trailed off, suddenly comprehending.

'My hair.' There was a catch in Flame's voice.

Dahlia reached out and touched Flame's face, felt the tracks of tears. 'This isn't the first time for that either.' She knew better than to pull Flame into her arms and try to comfort her that way. 'It always grows back more beautiful than ever.'

'You didn't answer me.'

'About Lily?' Dahlia sighed. 'You always get upset when we talk about Lily. You have enough to worry about without thinking about that.'

'Tell me, Dahlia.'

'Lily is our sister and friend. She saved your life years ago when she told Peter Whitney you were planning to escape and she's saving your life now.'

'Maybe. We don't know that. Whitney only put the cancer in remission. It always came back.'

'She knows that. She worked on new meds to knock it out completely.'

Flame rubbed her aching head. She couldn't remember how it felt to be normal, not sick every day. Sick and weak and unable to take care of herself. She couldn't remember the other Flame. Confident, independent Flame. There was only the bathroom floor and the daily shots and the terrible weariness. Days went by. Weeks went by and every day it was the same.

'I hope you're right. I hope she isn't working with Whitney.' Because Flame couldn't do this again – never again. She was so strong in so many ways, but this was asking too much – even of her.

'Lily's suffered more emotionally than any of us, because we knew Peter Whitney was a monster. We knew he was a liar. She didn't. He kept her from knowing for whatever purpose. I've read his letters to her. I've talked to Arly and Rosa, two of the people who were there when she grew up in that house with him. He acted the part of her father. She believed she was his biological child. This is all terrifying to her. It's like she woke up one morning to discover her father was a madman and everything she believed in was a lie. At least we knew all along.'

'Nonny says the same thing about Lily,' Flame said after a long silence. 'The thing about Nonny is she's very good at reading people. She says Lily is suffering.' She pressed her fingertips to her aching head. 'Everyone is suffering thanks to Whitney.' Flame rinsed her mouth out several times.

'I'm not.'

Flame looked up. 'What?'

'I'm not suffering. I have a good life. It isn't perfect, but then whose life is? I'm not letting Whitney dictate my life to me. I draw energy to me and I can't be around people for very long. You and Lily are anchors so it's easier. Nico makes it much easier to get rid of the buildup, but I still have to be careful and that's all right with me.'

'Whitney isn't after you, Dahlia. He isn't shooting up the swamp and killing innocent people. I put lives in danger. Nonny. Raoul.' Just saying his name made her ache. He'd been so good, so patient with her, but she'd refused to talk to him. She hadn't wanted to hurt

391

like that ever again. He came every day while he recovered from his knife wound. He conversed as if she answered him. He'd been the one to tell her the press had issued a huge story on terrorists attacking the compound. He'd been the one to bring her books and music – especially blues. He had been the one to talk to her night after night when she couldn't sleep – and she hadn't answered him. She had refused to offer him forgiveness.

Flame pressed a hand to her mouth, choking back a sob. How pathetic could a woman get? Just because she'd lost her hair and she felt lousy, she didn't have to sit and cry about it. Just because she'd sent away the man of her dreams, the love of her life, the one person who mattered most to her. Now he was really gone – not home to be safe in the bayou, but on a covert mission somewhere halfway around the world. He'd left without a word of comfort or love from her and all she could think about was that he could be killed.

'You aren't putting those lives in danger,' Dahlia pointed out. 'If they're in danger, Peter Whitney is the one responsible. All any of us can do, Flame, is to try to live our lives the best way we can. That's what I'm doing. If I don't, he wins. To me it's that simple. I'm not letting him dictate my life or my happiness.'

'Why do you think he keeps coming after me?' Flame took another sip of water.

Dahlia shrugged. 'We've all tried to figure that out. We might never know the answer, but maybe when Lily succeeds in knocking out the cancer once and for all, you won't be so valuable to him. He's a madman. I'm sure there's some logic to his thinking, but it's all his own.'

Flame had to kneel at the toilet again for another long bout, which became mostly dry heaves. 'I'm getting to be an expert at this.' She took the washcloth Dahlia handed her. 'I think I've inspected that toilet a million times now.'

'Lily said you've been doing a lot of exercises. Running on the treadmill.'

Flame's response was somewhere between a snort of derision and strangled laughter. 'If you call that running. Nonny does better than I do and makes a point of telling me, I might add.' She wiped her face repeatedly. 'Sometimes I think this will never end.'

'You're just at the worst point and about to start the climb back up. You've been here before and this time will be the last.' Dahlia spoke confidently.

'You believe in her that much?'

'Yep. By the way, Gator's back.'

'He is?' Flame felt her heart leap. 'No one's told me anything. They're all so damned secretive. I don't know how you stand it when Nico goes out.'

'Nico told me they went in to try to get Jack Norton out.'

'Wait a minute. I thought Raoul mentioned Ken Norton was captured and a team was going in.'

'Nico was on that team. They pulled out Ken, but Jack went down giving them cover fire. He waved them out and they were under orders so they left him behind. No one knew if he was captured. Gator and Nico went back with some others to see if they could get him. They hit the enemy camp, but he wasn't there. They found evidence he'd been there, but he was either moved, or he escaped.'

'Or they killed him.'

'There's always that possibility.'

Flame hung her head. 'Is Raoul all right?'

'He doesn't look good, not at all like himself. He never smiles, never laughs. He's thinner, but he came back without any more scars, if that's what you mean. Are you ever going to forgive him for saving your life?' Dahlia asked bluntly.

There was a small silence. Flame could hear her heart beating hard. She swallowed a sudden lump. 'I have to forgive Lily if I forgive him.' She closed her eyes. 'I don't know if I can do that.' She stood up slowly, dragging herself up by using the wall. 'I think I can actually go sit in a chair now.'

Dahlia stayed behind her in case she was too weak after her bout of sickness to make it into her room without falling.

Flame was surprisingly steady once she got under way. 'Once my nightly bout of sickness is over, whether it lasts an hour or six hours, I feel fine again. I usually walk on the treadmill and try to get in a little exercise before the morning bout starts. I don't seem to be able to sleep much anymore.' She paused for a moment to survey her room. There were no lights on, just dozens of aromatic candles. 'Nonny's been here. She's so sweet to me.'

Dahlia waited until Flame curled up in a chair, drawing her feet up under her and taking another sip of water. 'One of your best and worst traits is your stubbornness, Flame. I think it's saved your life, that determination and courage you have, the ability to dig in and go for something no matter what, but it also keeps you from admitting that you can be wrong.'

A faint smile touched Flame's mouth. 'You think that's why? That I don't want to admit that I'm wrong? I wish it was that simple.' She sighed and leaned back, resting her head against the soft back of the chair, all too aware of her bald head. She was vain enough that she didn't want anyone seeing her that way, not even Dahlia. 'I don't trust Lily. She has that same mind. The

394

need for answers outweighs moral issues.'

Dahlia shook her head. 'You're wrong. She has that same brilliancy, yes. You have it too, but she knows where to draw the line. Why are you so determined to believe she's in league with Peter Whitney?'

'He has to have an informer.'

Dahlia snorted. 'That's idiotic and you, of all people, know it. You know *exactly* how he's getting his information.'

'The computers,' Flame conceded. 'They were all his. Every computer in his lab at home, here at the compound, and just about every company he owned. He had access to them all and wrote many of the programs. The notes and data Lily are using belonged to him. He has a back door in to all of it.'

'Of course he does. And he knows she needs the information to help us all. She can't get rid of him. Arly's searching, but even if he finds one worm, he'll never find them all. So why do you need to see her as in league with Peter Whitney?'

Flame shook her head, her mind slamming the door closed on her childhood memories. She couldn't, *wouldn't* face that recollection ever again. 'I can't tell you. I just can't, Dahlia.'

Dahlia looked up, her gaze sharp and penetrating. 'It's all right, hon, don't worry about it. I'm going to let you have a few minutes alone because we both know as soon as Gator is finished with debriefing, he'll come straight here.'

Flame looked alarmed. 'No! He can't see me like this. I won't let him see me like this.'

'There's nothing wrong with the way you look.'

Flame leapt up and rushed to yank open a drawer. 'Nonny brought me these caps just in case.' She grabbed a dark navy knitted cap and pulled it over her head, glancing in the mirror and then looking quickly away. 'Keep him out of here.'

'No one can keep Gator out of here, not even you, Flame. He's coming to see you whether you like it or not. Whether you talk to him or not.' Dahlia walked to the door. 'You're going to have to deal with him sooner or later.'

The moment the door closed behind Dahlia, Flame blew out three of the eight candles lighting the room. She couldn't stop her wayward heart from pounding with anticipation, or the adrenaline from rushing through her body. She did her best, washed her face, brushed her teeth, tried makeup and removed it just as fast. She stood staring at her image. There was nothing she could do to look like the woman he would be expecting.

She spun around when she heard the door open. Raoul entered, pushing a motorcycle. Not just any motorcycle, but *her* motorcycle. She wanted to look at her motorcycle, the very symbol of freedom to her, but all she could see was Raoul. If she could have, she would have thrown herself into his arms. As it was, she just stood staring at him, transfixed. He did look thinner, but his shoulders were wide, his chest muscular, and his hair persisted in falling in waves no matter what he did to tame it. He made her weak-kneed, just looking at him. She was so glad he was there, alive and well and all in one piece, but she didn't want him to see her like this.

Straightening her spine, Flame drew in a deep breath and tried to look utterly confident. She touched the knitted cap she wore to make certain it was in place before crossing the room to touch her motorcycle. 'Who did this?'

Raoul straightened slowly and drank in the sight of

her. It was the first time since the assault on the compound that she'd spoken to him and she was staring at the bike, not him. She looked pale. Ravaged. There were dark circles under her eyes and she wore a silly knitted cap that fit her head close. Her cast was gone and her arm had several noticeable scars from the alligator's teeth. She looked beautiful to him. He'd missed her so badly he ached.

'I did it myself. Didn't want anyone else touching something you love. It runs like a dream. I can't wait for you to try it out.'

Flame glanced at him and then away. He realized she didn't have eyebrows. His throat closed up. He'd been off gathering intelligence and she'd been here. Alone. Sick. He stepped closer to her. '*Mon Dieu*, baby. I should have stayed with you.' He reached out a hand to frame her face but she sidestepped his touch.

'You shouldn't be here.' She would *not* dissolve into tears in front of him. He looked so wonderful. She wanted to touch him, but that would mean he could touch her back and she was far from the woman he thought so sexy back in the bayou. And if her changed appearance didn't bother him, and he managed to get through her thin armor, she'd fall into his arms and it would start all over again. She'd be swept away, not thinking, and she couldn't go through another breakup.

'Where else would I be?' Raoul allowed his hand to drop to his side. 'There's nowhere else I want to be.'

She rubbed her hand over the bike's black leather seat. 'It looks beautiful. Brand-new. Thank you.'

'You're welcome. I know how much it means to you.'

It meant much more now that she knew he'd taken the time to fix it himself. She wasn't supposed to love anything or anyone so much that she couldn't give it up, but she was so very afraid she'd broken her number one rule. 'You look good. Tired, but good.'

'I am tired. It was a long flight and a longer debriefing.'

'You didn't write.' Flame slapped her hand over her mouth. She hadn't meant for that to come out. Already she could see his slow, cocky grin spreading. Her heart did a slow meltdown. 'Your grandmother was worried.'

He shook his head. 'I don' think so, *cher.* I think you were worried about me. You sent me off with no kiss good-bye. No words of love to keep me safe.'

'We broke up. You don't get kisses or words of love.'

'I never broke up. I wouldn't know how.' His tone was utterly serious. 'I can't live without you, *ma belle femme*, and that's a fact.'

Flame shook her head. 'Even if we could get past everything else; what about children? You were born to be a father.'

'You worry so much over things that may or may not happen. I don' live my life in the future, *cher.* Your eggs are stored. We can demand them back. Hell, we should anyway, but if it doesn't work out, we'll adopt. And if that doesn't work out, we'll love each other just fine without all the rest.' He gave her another grin. 'I'm lookin' forward to that part.'

Flame didn't know how to react. It was impossible not to love him even with all his sins. She sighed softly. 'You're so crazy.'

He caught her hand, gave a little tug so that she followed him across the room to the large armchair. 'I'm tired. Sit on my lap.' He sank into the chair.

Flame backed away from him. 'Oh, no. I'm not getting near you. I know better than that.'

He steepled his fingers together and regarded her through half-closed eyes. 'Let's get this over with, Flame. I miss you. I miss holding you and kissing you and having you next to me when I sleep at night.'

'We only slept together a couple of times,' she pointed out. 'You can't possibly miss me like that.'

'I wake up in the middle of the night reaching for you. I miss your laugh and that stubborn, mulish look you get on your face right before you do something that turns me on. I miss all of it, *cher*, and I want it back. How do I get it back?'

He looked up at her, his eyes midnight black and her heart lurched. How did he do that? Just take over her mind, fog it, and make her body hot and restless when he wasn't doing anything but sitting there? Flame wrapped her arms around her waist. 'I don't know,' she whispered. 'There's this huge gap between us and I can't cross it.'

'You stay where you are. I'll come to you.'

Flame held up her hand, panic written clearly on her face. 'Stay there.'

'Why, *cher.* I do believe you're afraid of being close to me. You've been missing me, haven't you?'

'Maybe a little,' she conceded.

'I think more than a little.' He crooked his finger at her. 'Come here where I can touch you. I don' believe you're wearing a bra under that shirt.'

She looked down and saw her nipples pushing at the thin material. 'Well stop looking.'

'I love to look at you.'

She took a deep breath. 'My hair fell out.' She put her hand defensively on the cap.

He reached out and tugged on her sweats until she was standing between his legs. His voice lowered until there was almost a seductive note in it. 'Take off the cap. Let me see.'

'I'm not going to let you see my bald head. Sheesh.'
His voice alone could send butterflies fluttering through

her stomach. He was just so – *bad*. He looked at her with his dark eyes and his sinful mouth and she couldn't help the wicked thoughts sizzling through her mind. 'Stop looking at me like that. I'm *not* taking off the cap. *Ever.*'

He tilted his head, his hand skimming the ribbon of bare skin between her top and sweats. 'Aw, *cher*. There's no need to be like that. I've been fantasizing for the last few weeks about you being all sexy with no hair.' His voice dropped another octave. 'When you lose all your hair, do you lose *all* of it? All over your body?' He dragged out the last word, making it sound erotic somehow.

She blushed. She never blushed, but he was looking at her as if he might eat her like an ice cream cone. His tongue actually licked his bottom lip as if in anticipation. Heat flooded her body. 'You're freakin' nuts, Raoul.'

His fingers caressed her skin, slid down her hip to her thigh to massage her leg. 'Are you bald *everywhere, sugah?*'

His whisper skimmed over her skin, featherlight, like warm breath. She could feel it deep inside her where need pooled. She swallowed a protest. His hand found its way around to her bottom, kneading through her cotton sweats. He shifted in the chair, calling attention to the huge bulge at the junction of his legs.

'You cannot be turned on, Raoul. You can't be.'

He took her hand and guided it to the front of his jeans. 'I beg to differ, this here is a hell of a hard-on, *cher*, if I do say so myself.'

She should have snatched her hand away, it was the only safe thing to do, but he was pressing it over the long thick bulge, and despite herself she let her palm rub back and forth. He closed his eyes and drew in his breath, pleasure smoothing away the lines etched so deep – lines that hadn't been there before he'd brought her to the compound.

She had to do something to break his spell, otherwise she was going to forget what she looked like and jump him. 'Before you get too comfortable there, Cajun man, I seem to recall telling you what I was going to do to you if my hair fell out.'

He brought her hand to his mouth before leaning down to remove his boots.

Flame stepped back, one hand to her throat as he peeled off his jeans without even a blush. He was hard and hot and very erect. He grinned at her, unashamed of his obvious need. 'I brought the knife, *cher*. It isn't rusty, but it'll do.' His hands went to his shirt buttons, slowly opening the shirt.

Flame shook her head. 'No way. I meant it, Raoul. No freakin' way.'

'Just let me see,' he coaxed. 'I had more than one fantasy about shavin' you all clean and soft so you feel every lick of my tongue.'

The way he said it, the way he looked, sent shivers down her spine. In spite of herself, she was getting hot. 'I've been sick for hours. I can't very well get crazy with you.' She backed up until she was against the small bedside table, the bed looming large in her vision.

He was closer. How did he get closer? She didn't even recall him moving, but there he was, his hand slipping under her shirt to cup her breast, fingers gently rolling her nipple. 'You don' have to do a thing, I promise. Just let me see.'

He could make her weak without touching her, but the moment his hands were on her skin she was afraid she was lost. Didn't he see her? She felt very vulnerable, almost afraid. She knew her sexuality wasn't tied

up in her hair, but how could she feel sexy and exciting when most of the time she was so sick all she could
do was hug the toilet? She had a port in her chest, and
not a single hair on her body. She was bald, *bald*, for
heaven's sake. He was looking at her, touching her and
responding to her just as if she were the most beautiful, sensual woman in the world. Was it possible to fake
that look in his eye? The dark sensuality, the intense
hunger and raw desire? Could that be faked?

Flame's body trembled and she looked so damned
fragile Raoul bent forward to brush a kiss against her
soft mouth, wanting to reassure her. Her eyes were dark
and filled with shadows. He kissed her again because
he had to. He'd dreamt of her mouth often, so soft, so
sexy. At night when he lay alone in his bed he thought
of her taste and texture. The memory wasn't nearly as
good as the real thing. He licked along her bottom lip,
sucked it into his mouth, teasing with his teeth until she
made that soft little whimpering sound he loved – her
first real sign of surrender.

Catching the edge of her shirt he gently pulled it over
her head. He could see the line Lily used to put the
medicine directly in her vein. It was up near her collarbone. He ran his finger lightly along her bone and
down to the swell of her breasts.

'Does it hurt?'

Flame shook her head. She couldn't look away,
trapped in the heat of his gaze. She could only stand
there trembling, watching his face closely, while he
tugged on her sweatpants. She was terrified that he'd
be as repulsed as she sometimes was by the sight of her
naked body. She wouldn't be able to take that. She did-
n't know if she could take it if he wasn't. She felt so
exposed, her body completely open to his inspection.

'*Mon Dieu, cher*, you're so damned beautiful I'm

going to embarrass myself.' His hand absently stroked the length of his erection. There was no shyness, no modesty, he hardly seemed aware of his actions.

Flame could see the glistening moisture on the smooth, broad head topping his thick shaft. He couldn't fake that. He wanted her with that same intensity, that same *need*, he'd had weeks earlier when she had hair tumbling around her face and she felt confident as a sensual woman.

Gator dropped to his knees, circling her hips with his arms, dragging her closer so that she had to steady herself with her hands on his shoulders. 'You're so sexy, *cher.*' His voice was hoarse, his hands sliding down her hips to part her thighs. He leaned forward to press his mouth against her bare, silky-smooth skin.

Flame nearly jumped out of her skin. 'I'm too sensitive.' She hadn't thought it would feel different, his tongue moving over bare flesh, but it did. Every nerve ending seemed more heightened, more aware. 'My legs are going to give out.'

He blew warm air against her, pressed another kiss against her bare lips. He felt her shiver. Her body responded with inviting moisture. 'Hold on to me for just another minute. I can't stop, baby, not this time. You're so beautiful and perfect and I need this.' His tongue dipped and stroked, small caresses designed to send her temperature soaring. She was so sweet, he could spend hours devouring her. Her hand clenched in his hair and her entire body trembled.

With a little sigh he stood up, lifted her, and seated her on the very edge of the bed. 'I've waited a long time for you. I don' think I have much in the way of self-control.'

'I don't have much in the way of stamina so I guess we'll be fine.' The raw desire etched on his face took her breath away.

He bent to kiss her again. His mouth was commanding, wild even, yet he was careful not to rub against the open port. He kissed his way down to the tips of her breasts, hands exploring every inch of her body, reclaiming her, possessive. 'You're so damned soft, *mon amour*. Soft and silky and so hot. I can't wait to be inside of you.'

He nuzzled her legs apart, pulling her bottom to the very edge of the bed so he could press his throbbing cock into her body. He took it slow, watching her body swallow his inch by slow inch. It was an erotic sight, her bare lips stretching around his thickness, feeling the hot slick muscles of her channel open reluctantly for him, gripping him like a tight fist, surrounding him with a fiery friction every time he moved.

Flame couldn't stop the small little moans from escaping. She'd forgotten how good he felt inside of her. She'd forgotten how it felt to be a woman, sexy and exciting and wanted. *Wanted*. Raoul wanted her any way he could have her. She could see his eyes lit with a combination of love and lust. She could see the harsh sensuality etched into his face as he drove deep, picking up the pace, thrusting into her, fingers digging into her hips, pulling her into him as if he couldn't wait to be buried to the hilt.

Each long stroke took her breath until her lungs burned and her body wound tighter and tighter. She felt the clench of her muscles biting down hard, clamping around him as he swelled impossibly thicker, stretching her even more. His heat drove out the cold lodged so deeply in her, replacing it with hot streaks of pleasure so intense she knew she was lost – didn't care if she were lost. He took her away from the cold and the sickness and made her whole again. She threw her head back as he surged into her, letting each fiery stroke take her closer and closer to the edge.

'I'm sorry, baby, I can't hang on any longer. You're so damn hot I'm going up in flames.' Gator could barely get the words out, his body tightening, the explosion rocketing through him as he emptied his seed deep inside of her. Her tight muscles clamped down so hard around him the pleasure spiraled out of control and he couldn't stop until she was screaming his name, her body convulsing around his.

She slumped against him, her head on his shoulder, her breathing ragged. She was exhausted, but sated. She could feel her muscles pulsing around him, the aftershocks nearly as strong as the tidal wave of pleasure. She fought for breath as she waited for the intensity to fade.

'Lie back. I'm getting in bed with you.'

'I don't think I can move.' She did though, falling sideways until she felt his body slip from hers and the pillow met her head. She would have pulled up a sheet to cover her nakedness, but her arm felt too heavy.

Gator sat on the edge of the bed and watched her. He couldn't stop staring at her, the way she looked all sexy and innocent at the same time. Drowsy and satisfied, almost purring, her fingers tangling with his. He bent down and pressed a kiss against her intriguing belly button. 'I want you to marry me. Don' say no, *cher*. I know you want me to apologize for what I did, but I'm not going to lie to you. I'd do it again. I need you alive in this world, even if I can't have you. I should be sorry, but you left me no choice.'

She opened her eyes and looked up at him. 'You could have been wrong. Lily might have been working with Whitney.'

'Then I would have killed them both.' His gaze held hers. 'Why can't you forgive Lily? Your anger at me is

405

tied up with your anger at her. We both love you and we both cared enough to put our relationship with you on the line in order to save your life. You're a logical person, Flame. You don't carry a grudge unless there's a reason.'

She tried to smile, but it wouldn't come. 'I never let myself think about that. I can't.' She lowered her voice. 'I've never told anyone.'

'I'm not anyone. I'm the man you love and no matter what it is, I'm going to be right here with you, working it out. Let's just get this over so we can live our lives.'

'What about Whitney? He'll regroup and come at us again.'

'Fuck Whitney. While he's regrouping, we're going to be hunting him. It won't be so easy the next time. Now stop stalling and tell me.'

She was going to tell him. He was so bossy and so insistent on his way. Wheedling, bossing, it was all the same. He knew what he wanted and one way or the other, he got it. Could she live with that? Could she live with his particular brand of protection? She tightened her fingers on his. She didn't want to live without him – that was the bottom line. When she was feeling better, she'd be able to hold her own against him, but for now, she let him take over, let him push her into the past.

The door in her head was cracking open, the memory spilling out no matter how hard she tried to push it away from her. Lily betraying her. The men dragging her back. Whitney had stood there, staring at her with cold fury through the glass, soundproofed shield. His gaze held cold fury and he just stood there as the men slapped her face, stripped her room of everything she had, and then marched her in front of the glass, holding her still by the thick swatch of hair.

She hadn't meant to do it, pulse that low note of sound that the two men throwing her things around couldn't even hear. The man holding her by the hair thought her helpless, thought she was cowed by the three stinging slaps to her face. She was crying and after all, she was a child.

The two behind her went down hard and lay still, but the one holding her burst open, his organs rupturing. She screamed and screamed, the river of blood pouring over her. All the while Whitney stood watching, a strange, secret smile on his face.

Flame covered her face. 'I didn't mean to hurt them. I didn't know it would happen. I killed them and he left them there for hours. I had to beg him to take the bodies away before he'd do it.'

Somehow sharing the horror of that moment with him, telling someone about her guilt and shame made the knot of blame she held on to against Lily begin to dissolve.

Gator wrapped her in his arms, holding her close, fighting his own rising rage. He held her, rocking her back and forth, keeping her close to him, letting her cry it out. He kissed her shoulder, nuzzled it with his chin. He didn't have a choice now, he had to tell her the truth of his own guilt. She needed to know, needed to hear it. God help him if it was the wrong choice, because he honestly didn't feel as if he could let her go.

'I did worse, baby,' he confessed. 'Much, much worse. I took out civilians. None of us knew the wave would carry and we were working with it, field testing. One of my friends died that day and four teenagers who were just playing around on the hillside. They were just kids, innocent kids.' There were tears in his voice. 'I have to live with that, Flame. I wake up in a cold sweat thinking about those kids and their families. I have no idea what the families were told, or even if they were given the bodies, but I know if it were my child, I'd never get over it.'

She held him tighter. He felt rigid, his muscles locked, a tremor running through his body. 'It never helps to say it wasn't your fault, you didn't know, but you didn't, any more than I did. We're weapons, Raoul. That's why we were created.'

'I don' think so, *cher*. I think you were created for me, predestined, long before either of us was born.' He tipped her face up so she had to look at him. 'None of this was Lily's fault any more than it was yours. I have to take some responsibility in that I allowed myself to be enhanced and I didn't look far enough into it to see the consequences.'

'Maybe you didn't, Raoul, but, honestly? You're the best man I know. I've never met anyone better, and I'm a tough judge. I watch you, the way you look out for everyone, the way you care so much.' She ducked her head. 'I should have told you that before you left.'

He pressed a kiss to her temple. 'Thank you for that. No matter what's gone before, we both deserve a life. I want it to be together.'

'What if Lily can't get rid of the cancer?'

He shrugged. 'She says she can, but what if she can't? What if I go out on a mission tomorrow and get shot in the head?'

'Don't say that.' She swallowed hard. 'When you left, I swear you took my heart and soul with you.'

'The work I do is every bit as real a danger as cancer is to you. It's every bit as real as the threat of Whitney is to you. Life gives us choices, Flame. You either grab on with both hands and just go for it, or you sit on the sidelines. I'm a go for it kind of man.'

'So you're really determined to marry me.'

'Damn straight. I'm kind of partial to your body.' His hand roved down her spine to cup her bottom.

'You'd better see the real me, then.' Flame pulled off her cap and sat facing him, her heart beating too hard in her chest. She forced herself to stare at his face, to read his expression. She wanted the truth from him.

His tongue did a slow lick of his lips and his eyes lit up. She actually felt the stirring of his shaft along her belly. 'Damn, woman, you're so sexy I don' think my heart can take it.' He bent toward her, his mouth trailing kisses over the top of her head. 'How do you get your skin so soft, *cher*?'

'I'm going to wear wigs so don't get all hot and bothered thinking about my bald head.'

'Wigs?' He grinned at her. 'I can think of a lot of fun we could have with wigs. Although, to be honest, I was thinking about other bald places just then.'

'My hair is going to grow back, you perv.'

'Aw, but in the meantime . . .'

Other titles in the thrilling GhostWalker series from Christine Feehan, available now from Piatkus:

SHADOW GAME

The classified experiment is the brainchild of renowned scientist Peter Whitney and his brilliant daughter, Lily. Created to enhance the psychic abilities of an elite squadron, it can transform their natural mental powers into a unique military weapon. But something goes wrong. In the isolated underground labs, the men have been dying – victims of bizarre accidents. Captain Ryland Miller knows he is next.

When Dr. Whitney himself is murdered, Ryland has only one person left to trust: the beautiful Lily. Possessed of an uncanny sixth sense herself, Lily shares Ryland's every new fear, every betrayal, every growing suspicion, and every passionate beat of the heart. Together, they will be drawn deeper into the labyrinth of her father's past and closer to a secret that someone would kill to keep hidden.

978-0-7499-3877-2

MIND GAME

Possessed of an extraordinary telekinetic gift, Dahlia Le Blanc has spent her life isolated from other people. And just when she thinks she's finally achieved some semblance of peace, her well-orchestrated world comes crashing down . . .

For a reason she cannot guess, she has become the target of deadly assassins. Suddenly no place is safe – not even the secret refuge she's established long ago. Now she must rely on Nicolas Trevane – a dangerous warrior sent to track her down and protect her. Together they generate a scorching heat Dahlia never imagined was possible. But can she trust this man with her secrets – especially when some people would kill to get their hands on them?

978-0-7499-3878-9

CONSPIRACY GAME

Jack Norton is a GhostWalker, a genetically enhanced
sniper with a merciless sense of justice, a phantom
welcomed by the anonymity of the night. But a mission to
rescue his brother in the jungle has left him vulnerable to
rebel forces. His only salvation is his power of telepathy.
Then he meets Briony, an unusual beauty on a mission of
her own. But they share more than the sweltering heat . . .

Briony shares the GhostWalker powers. Yet she's
different. She doesn't know what she is, or what she's
capable of. But her enemies do. And Jack and Briony's
flight will take them into frightening conspiracy of mind
and body – across the globe and into the heart of darkness,
where the shocking truth is something neither of them
could have foreseen – or can escape . . .

978-0-7499-3899-4

DEADLY GAME

It began as a mission to find a notorious politician whose plane went down in the Congo. But the risky operation took an unexpected turn when Mari, a physically enhanced member of the rescue team, was taken hostage by rebel forces. Now, imprisoned in an isolated compound, Mari has only one chance for survival – escape.

What she doesn't count on is Ken Norton, expert assassin and himself a GhostWalker warrior, fighting to get behind the prison walls on a mission of his own – one that reaches into Mari's own past and the mysterious fate of her twin sister . . . and that will bind Ken and Mari in an intoxicating passion that raises the stakes on the deadliest game of survival they've ever played.

978-0-7499-3884-0

PREDATORY GAME

Saber Winter was running from her past when she meets Jess Calhoun, an ex-officer with the US forces elite Navy Seals division who's now confined to a wheelchair. Jess had sensed that Saber was a lost soul, and he'd given her a job and a home, hoping that she'd be willing to stay and finally share her secrets with him. But Saber has been on the run a long time, and Jess may be in a wheelchair, but he's also a GhostWalker, and both of their pasts are about to collide in the present when secrets they're both hiding get uncovered, and both must deal with betrayal before they're free to find a future together.

978-0-7499-3916-8

Other titles in the thrilling 'Dark' Carpathian series from Christine Feehan, also available from Piatkus:

DARK CELEBRATION

'Carpathians are an immortal race of beings with animal instincts and the ability to shape shift. Every Carpathian male is drawn to a life mate: a woman – Carpathian or human – able to provide the light to his darkness. Without her, the beast within slowly consumes the man until turning into a vampire is the only option.'

Mikhail Dubrinsky, Prince of the Carpathians, fears he can't protect his people from the extinction of their species – a fate that has become the wicked prayer of his enemies, who plot to slaughter all Carpathian females. Mikhail's lifemate, Raven, and their daughter, Savannah, are both vulnerable to the encroaching evil, but all is not lost. In this desperate season, Carpathians from around the world are gathering to join their strengths, their souls and their powers.

But so too are their adversaries uniting – hunters, vampires, demons and betrayers – bringing untold dangers into the fold of the Carpathian people . . .

978-0-7499-3846-8

DARK POSSESSION

Dangerously close to becoming a vampire, Manolito De
La Cruz has been called back to his Carpathian
homeland – and has unexpectedly caught the scent
of his destined lifemate, MaryAnn Delaney.

MaryAnn is human and well aware of the aggressive
instincts of Carpathian males. A counsellor for battered
women, MaryAnn has no room in her life for someone like
Manolito. But when she goes to South America to offer
guidance to a young woman, she has no idea of the trap
awaiting her. For she's been lured there by Manolito, who
has seductive plans for the irresistible human female.

Once there, she'll be his. Once his, she'll never be released.
She is his dark possession.

978-0-7499-0867-6

DARK GUARDIAN

Haunted by a traumatic childhood, Jaxon Montgomery is
a policewoman with a fearsome reputation. Trained by
special forces, she meets her match when she is set up to be
murderd by an enemy. Hunted on all sides, she can only
turn to the mysterious stranger who seems more dangerous
than any other she has ever known.

Lucian Daratrazanoff is the Dark Guardian of his people,
a Carpathian who has spent years pretending to have
turned to the dark side and become a vampire. And after
centuries of bleak, soulless existence, he finds himself
drawn to Jaxon . . .

978-0-7499-3811-6

DARK DESIRE

Seven years ago, Dr Shea O'Halloran experienced an unexpected and horrendous pain unlike anything she had ever known. It felt as if she were being tortured. Eventually the pain disappeared, but Shea never forgot. She has since devoted her life to trying to understand the cause of the rare genetic blood disorder that is slowly killing her.

The answers to some of Shea's questions start to reveal themselves when she is approached by two men, who accuse her of being a vampire. Shea runs for her life and – following a feeling she can't explain – her desperate wanderings lead her to Romania.

The ancient one known as Jacques Dubrinsky can explain. Seven years ago, Jacques was captured, tortured and buried alive by several humans and a Carpathian betrayer. The years of extreme pain and lack of sustenance that followed have nearly driven Jacques insane. He has been using what is left of his powers to psychically draw Shea to the region. But is Shea to be his healer . . . or his prey?

978-0-7499-3748-5